Gift
4-2002

Praise for Diane Farr's novels

Once Upon a Chirstmas

"Engaging. . . . I've always found Diane Farr's Regencies delightful reads, and this fourth book is no exception."   —*Romance Reviews Today*

Falling for Chloe

"Delicious. . . . Ms. Farr captures all the wonder and joy of falling in love. . . . [A] truly delightful heroine."
—*Romantic Times*

"Delightful . . . fast-moving and entertaining."
—*The Romance Reader*

Fair Game

"One of the most charming and utterly lovable heroines I have met in a Regency."—*All About Romance*

"A definite keeper. Imagine *Gigi* transported to Regency England and done much better. . . . *Fair Game* has the emotional intensity of Mary Balogh at her best."   —*The Romance Reader*

"The author's feel for the era is excellent, as is her writing craft, and she caps it all with a wonderful note of humor."   —*Romance Communications*

continued . . .

More praise for Diane Farr's novels

The Nobody

"Ms. Farr beguiles us. . . . Put this writer's name on your list of authors to watch."

—*Romantic Times* (4 stars)

"A delightful debut."

—Mary Jo Putney

"An intelligent, well-written debut by Ms. Farr. She knows the Regency period to a T. . . . Her plotting and characterizations are top-notch." —*Rendezvous*

"The author of *The Nobody* is destined to be a Somebody. . . . As charming a debut book as any reader could hope for. Diane Farr strikes all the right romantic chords . . . delightful."

—*The Romance Reader*

"Delightful . . . a wonderful blend of romance and humor." —*All About Romance*

The
Fortune Hunter

Diane Farr

Robert A. Frost Memorial Library
42 Main Street
Limestone ME 04750

A SIGNET BOOK

SIGNET
Published by New American Library, a division of
Penguin Putnam Inc., 375 Hudson Street,
New York, New York 10014, U.S.A.
Penguin Books Ltd, 80 Strand,
London WC2R 0RL, England
Penguin Books Australia Ltd, Ringwood,
Victoria, Australia
Penguin Books Canada Ltd, 10 Alcorn Avenue,
Toronto, Ontario, Canada M4V 3B2
Penguin Books (N.Z.) Ltd, 182–190 Wairau Road,
Auckland 10, New Zealand

Penguin Books Ltd, Registered Offices:
Harmondsworth, Middlesex, England

First published by Signet, an imprint of New American Library,
a division of Penguin Putnam Inc.

First Printing, April 2002
10 9 8 7 6 5 4 3 2 1

Copyright © Diane Farr Golling, 2002
All rights reserved

 REGISTERED TRADEMARK—MARCA REGISTRADA

Printed in the United States of America

Without limiting the rights under copyright reserved above, no part of
this publication may be reproduced, stored in or introduced into a
retrieval system, or transmitted, in any form, or by any means (electronic,
mechanical, photocopying, recording, or otherwise), without the prior written
permission of both the copyright owner and the above publisher of this
book.

PUBLISHER'S NOTE
This is a work of fiction. Names, characters, places, and incidents either
are the product of the author's imagination or are used fictitiously,
and any resemblance to actual persons, living or dead, business
establishments, events, or locales is entirely coincidental.

BOOKS ARE AVAILABLE AT QUANTITY DISCOUNTS WHEN USED TO PROMOTE
PRODUCTS OR SERVICES. FOR INFORMATION PLEASE WRITE TO PREMIUM
MARKETING DIVISION, PENGUIN PUTNAM INC., 375 HUDSON STREET, NEW
YORK, NEW YORK 10014.

If you purchased this book without a cover you should be aware that this
book is stolen property. It was reported as "unsold and destroyed"
to the publisher and neither the author nor the publisher has received
any payment for this "stripped book."

To Risa

1

*B*loody hell. It hadn't worked.

George Carstairs, Baron Rival, crumpled the letter with one fierce, spasmodic movement of his fist. He was tempted to toss the politely worded packet of bad news in the fire. He restrained himself from that irrevocable act, however, and pitched it instead onto the battered desk half hidden in the corner of his London flat. He would reread it later. After he had had time to think.

He prowled from the fireplace to the window. From the window to the sofa. From the sofa to the desk. From the desk to the fireplace. The room was small and Lord Rival was not, so his pacing did little to vent his frustration. *What now? What now?* hammered in his brain like a tune he could not banish.

What now, indeed. Everything took money, and he had none. He could not hire a staff and reopen the house. He could offer no relief to his struggling tenants. He could institute no reforms, purchase no advice, repair nothing, build nothing. Rye Vale had been ruined—not by him, but the responsibility was his to mend matters if he could.

Well, he couldn't.

He had stayed in this damnably cramped flat long after the Season ended, trying to scramble together a loan. The rest of the aristocracy had deserted London and trotted down to Brighton or back to their own estates. He'd declined every invitation to accompany his friends and stayed on, sweltering in the summer heat, trying to accomplish what he dared not attempt while the gossiping *ton* was there to observe him.

He'd approached every rich, social-climbing cit in London. You'd think that one of them, at least, would be eager to put a nobleman under obligation. But he soon discovered that a rake's title is worthless to a social climber. His scandalous reputation had devalued the only real collateral he had to offer, since all unentailed portions of Rye Vale had been mortgaged long ago. His efforts, therefore, had borne no fruit whatsoever.

George dropped into a wing chair before his tiny fireplace and rubbed his forehead tiredly. He had racked his brain for months and could think of nothing that he hadn't already tried. So little, so little could be done without funds. Land management—faugh! The sweet, green grass of Sussex was tailor-made for sheep, but his father and grandfather had brought in too many sheep, too quickly. He supposed the tenants, turned out of their homes to make way for livestock, must have cursed his family. If so, the curse had certainly come home to roost. Rye Vale was a wasteland now, and Lord Rival a pauper.

George's hands clenched impotently on the arms of his chair. All that cash, all that lovely, lovely cash his greedy forefathers had raised—and for what? Just to squander at the gaming tables. Why, if he could have a tenth of it back, he would pour it into the land and change everything.

It was a mistake to care deeply about something over which one had no control. He had inherited the title at the carefree age of twenty-two, and had managed to live twelve years in London without giving Rye Vale a thought. For twelve blissful, shallow, completely unmemorable years, he had drifted and smiled and sinned, hardening his heart against the inevitable day when the thought of home would rear its head. Sure enough, once the unwelcome specter had intruded, it gave him no peace. He longed for home now, chafed at his helplessness, and brooded incessantly about restoring Rye Vale's prosperity. He had invented a dozen plans and improvements—any of which would work; none of which he could implement. What a joke.

A mirthless smile twisted his features. A conscience was an inconvenient thing to acquire at the ripe old age of four-and-thirty. He wished he didn't feel the weight of his responsibilities suddenly pressing on him. He wished he didn't care so bloody much. He wished he didn't care at all, as a matter of fact. It was a damned nuisance.

What was a man's conscience for? It did no good to recognize the path to perdition if you had to take the path regardless. What choice did he have? He had to have funds. There was no honorable way to acquire a fortune. He could draw the line at theft, embezzlement, and murder, but he was still left with the filthy path that lay before him: fraud.

Disgust propelled him from his chair and set him to his restless pacing again. The notion of tricking an heiress into marriage turned his stomach, although he'd be hard-pressed to explain why. After all, his London existence had been a sham since the day he took up residence.

He was the only man of his circle who had no servants. He polished his own boots and pressed his own linen, dusted his own furniture, made up his own fire every morning—on the days when he could afford coal. He despised his life, but anything was better than letting his friends suspect his shameful poverty.

He'd spent many an evening dancing and smiling in some glittering ballroom or other, praying that the music and conversation would cover the sound of his stomach growling. He had always maintained his languid air of indifference as everyone went in to supper, and managed to nibble rather than gulp the hostess's lobster patties and watercress sandwiches. So far as he knew, everyone believed that his jokes about a hand-to-mouth existence were no more serious than the jokes of every other man about town.

He'd been a fraud all along. Why cavil at the prospect of this final deception? It was time to swallow his pride and face the obvious. It would take a fortune to replenish his estate. He could neither borrow it nor earn it. Very well, he must marry it.

Lord Rival's pacing led him back to his desk. There he halted, gazing absently at his neat stacks of bills and correspondence. The letter he had just crumpled perched incongruously atop his pencil box, the only item out of place. George Carstairs was a methodical man. He reached for it and automatically smoothed it open, setting it with the rest of his correspondence. His brow creased in a bitter frown.

The path lay before him. He would harden his heart, bid farewell to regret, and start down it immediately. All he needed was a plan.

He sat and sharpened a pen. After thinking for a few moments, he dipped his pen in the inkwell, pulled a sheet of foolscap toward him, and began jotting down a list.

Lady Olivia Fairfax slipped silently into the bedchamber. She hesitated for a moment in the shadows, gravely regarding the limp figure huddled beneath the bedclothes.

Edith whimpered in her sleep. "Ah, poor thing," Olivia murmured, moving to the bed. She laid a cool hand on Edith's forehead. Hot, but not fevered. She gently smoothed the tangled curls back from Edith's battered face and spoke softly to her. "I'm a beast to disturb you, but I will be leaving soon and expect to be gone for some while. How are you feeling this morning?"

The girl stirred, her pale brows contracting as awareness of pain returned. She opened the only eye she could. "Better, I think," she croaked.

It was obviously a lie. Olivia smiled and instantly resolved to stop thinking uncharitable thoughts about poor little Edith. She had assumed her sister-in-law was an idiot. Any female willing to marry Ralph had to be a fool, but Edith had proved to be, at the very least, a fool with a backbone.

"Brave girl. I hope you shall feel better yet, once we force a little tea down you. Could you stomach some dry toast? Or perhaps a little gruel? I daresay it doesn't sound very appealing, but I think it would do you good."

"Is it morning?"

"Yes, I'm afraid so. Shall I draw the curtains?"

"If you like."

Edith's thin little whisper sounded unenthusiastic, so Olivia, crossing to the window, only pulled one of the heavy curtains back a little. Sunlight poured through the crack, returning color to the Aubusson carpet, the highly polished furniture, and the French silk wallpaper. It was a very pretty room, all done in blues and creams that might have been especially chosen to flatter blond Edith as she lay in the canopied bed. This was wasted on her at the moment, however. Edith, wincing, raised a wavering hand to shield her bruised eyes.

Olivia returned to the bedside. "Let me look at you," she said gently. She sat on the edge of the bed, pulled the coverlet back, and subjected Edith to a swift assessment, studying the injuries for the first time in the clear light of day. It had been difficult to assess the damage by candlelight. Now that she saw the extent of what Ralph had done, anger simmered within her. Her anger at Ralph was matched only by her astonishment that pretty little Edith, of all women, had had sufficient fortitude not only to run away with nothing but the clothes on her back, but to travel all the way to Chelsea in her condition.

Olivia shook her head in amazement. "I cannot believe you attempted the journey here. You might have been bleeding internally. Whatever possessed you to take such a risk?"

"Risk?" whispered Edith. "The risk was in staying, it seemed to me."

"Yes, but to come *here*—why? You and I barely know each other. What if you had misjudged me? What if I had refused to shelter you? For all you knew, I would side with my detestable brother against you."

Since Edith's lower lip was cut, the wan smile that flickered at its corners faded quickly. "I was quite certain you would not. All the world knows that you are a champion of the oppressed and downtrodden. You are famous for it."

Olivia chuckled. "There is that, of course," she agreed. "And he is only my half brother, after all. But they do say blood is thicker than water."

"I could not stop to think of that. I had nowhere else to go."

"But—your mother? Surely she resides somewhat closer than—"

Edith's fingers closed on Olivia's wrist in a painful grip. "Oh, pray! Pray do not tell Mama I am here! She will send me back." Her voice was sharp with rising panic.

Olivia stared at Edith in disbelief. "No mother could send her child back to a villain who—"

"She will! I know she will! She has told me as much. I appealed to her once before when—oh, pray! She must not discover where I am!"

Edith was shaking with fear at the very thought. This was more disturbing than all the rest. One expected brutality from Ralph, but it was difficult to comprehend that Edith's mother would join with him in victimizing her daughter.

"Calm yourself," Olivia said soothingly. "Have I not promised to keep you safe? I will do nothing to jeopardize your well-being. If your mother has told you she would send you back to your husband if you ran away, we must, by all means, keep her from discovering your whereabouts."

Edith sank back on the pillows again, seemingly reassured. "Thank you," she said, in the thread of a voice. Tears welled up. "You are so kind. I was right to come here."

Olivia smiled, straightening the coverlet and pulling it over Edith's shoulders. "You were right to come here," she agreed. "And here you will stay, until we decide what to do with you. But all that is for the future. For the present, your sole task is to get well."

"I feel wretched," Edith confessed. "Even worse today than yesterday."

"Do you? I'm afraid that's to be expected, after jolting about in a carriage for six hours or more. One doesn't feel the injuries while afraid for one's life—a strange phenomenon, but typical, I assure you. Now that you know you are safe, you have leisure to notice how miserable you are." Edith did not smile at this sally, but it was difficult to read the expression on such a swollen face. Olivia studied her for another moment. "Do you think you could sleep again, or shall I send up a tray for you?"

"A tray, please, if you think it will help me get stronger."

"Good girl. I do indeed." Olivia patted Edith's uninjured hand. "Today will probably be the worst of it. I think no permanent damage was done. The only bones broken were in your finger, and now we've taped that up it should heal perfectly straight. Your pulse is strong and steady. Your color has improved—

I think." She smiled. "It's hard to tell, of course, what the underlying color may be beneath those spectacular purples you are sporting."

Edith's head moved restlessly on the pillow. "I can never repay you for your kindness."

"There's no need. I know you would do the same for me."

The wan smile flickered briefly again. "But you would never need it."

"Well, no. Likely not." Olivia looked mischievous. "I have never been the sort of female to whom misadventures occur. Or adventures of any sort, for that matter."

"I wish I were like you." Edith sighed. "It must be wonderful to be you."

Olivia wrinkled her nose comically. "What, and wake up one day to find yourself a desiccated spinster? I suppose spinsterhood must sound rather appealing to you at the moment, but I promise you, it has its own set of drawbacks."

"But your life is so *useful*. And you are forever out in the world, doing things. Doing things that *matter*."

Olivia smiled at her earnestness. "I will admit that I enjoy my life. But it's not suitable for everyone. You might find it a dead bore. Pray remember that I spend my days—and many of my nights!—doing charity work."

"Yes, but it's your own charity," Edith pointed out. Envy tinged her voice. "It must be very like owning a business, or an estate, or something of that sort. Women do not generally have an opportunity to manage something of their very own. We are not allowed to hold property, or enter into contracts, or do anything that might be considered important."

"No. Did you not know that? On a woman's wedding day, everything that was formerly hers becomes her husband's property."

"I knew it, but I—I wasn't an heiress, so I hadn't

thought what it would *mean*. A married woman owns nothing. Not even—not even her own body." Edith's voice sank to a defeated whisper. "I will be blamed for what Ralph did to me. He will say I provoked him. That I deserved it."

One of Olivia's finely arched brows flew upward. "Let him say it. He will have to do so where you cannot hear him. I shall hide you for as long as you have need. And that, my dear, is a promise."

"But—are you not afraid?"

"Pooh! Afraid of Ralph? What can he do to me, pray? He is unlikely to guess that you have come here. And if he does, so much the better. I doubt that he would dare, but I would enjoy it if he came to my home, roaring and threatening and breathing fire."

Edith's trepidation was palpable. "*Enjoy* it?"

"Yes, indeed." A martial light sparkled in Olivia's eyes. "It would give me great pleasure to give that brute a piece of my mind, and then show him the door."

"But what if—what if he *strikes* you?"

"I shall have him locked up," said Olivia promptly. "So let us hope he tries it. Bad Lord Badesworth has no authority over me, and I am not a nobody in Chelsea. If he raises a hand to me—or to you, while you are my guest—he will soon learn his mistake."

"How brave you are!"

"Nonsense. I had to learn, long ago, to deal from strength when dealing with Ralph. There has never been any love lost between the two of us. Why do you think I am allowed to lead this peculiarly independent existence of mine? It is because the head of my family—Ralph—simply could not care less what becomes of me. As long as I do not ask him for money, he doesn't care where I live or what I do. And that suits me down to the ground."

"How I wish I were as free of him as you are," Edith murmured. But then she looked apprehensively at Olivia's sympathetic countenance. "I know it is wrong of me to say so."

"On the contrary, it is perfectly understandable. I am fortunate, and I know I am. Most women are controlled by some man or other. There is almost always a father, a husband, a brother, or an uncle to claim authority. I am the only female I know who answers to no one." Olivia's eyes lit with amusement. "It's a bit galling to think that many people *pity* me for my single state. Such impertinence! And so misplaced! I am, I believe, the happiest woman of my acquaintance. I am certainly the freest."

She rose, shaking out her skirts in a businesslike fashion. "I do have a busy morning ahead of me, however, and had best be off. I shall tell Cook to make up a tray for you, and ask Bessie to bring it up. You do like Bessie, don't you?"

"Miss Fairfax? Oh, yes! She reminds me of my old nurse."

Olivia had to stifle a smile. She hoped Edith would not voice that observation to Bessie. Bessie was the dearest creature on earth, and the best friend anyone could have—but she was a bit touchy about her resemblance to everyone's old nurse.

Now that Olivia was standing, Edith's gaze was traveling doubtfully over her faded dress and stout shoes. Olivia's eyes twinkled. "Don't you approve of my costume?"

"It's quite nice," said Edith politely.

"No, it isn't! It'll do well for what is in my dish this morning, however. I must spend it digging through crates, up to my elbows in sawdust and crushed paper." She made a little moue of distaste. "Not my favorite occupation, I'm afraid, but there it is. An old friend of my mother's has passed away and left the contents of his house to the school I named after her. They tell me it's a shocking mess, so I must be prepared to dig through a bit of dust to put it all in order.

I prefer to do this sort of thing myself, you know, when no inventory has been made. I'm told that the house is full of valuable trinkets—the sort of odds and ends that would be easy for a crew of dailies to slip into their apron pockets when no one is looking. So I dare not hire strangers to help me."

"But—an entire house? It sounds a bit much to tackle all alone."

Olivia smiled. "I won't be entirely alone. Bessie has promised to come as soon as she is able, and a group of volunteers is coming from the school to act as charwomen. But as I have the keys, I must be the first to arrive." She gave a last pat to Edith's shoulder, taking care to touch her gently. "I will be back to check on you this afternoon. In the meantime, rest—and do not worry. You are safe now."

She closed the door softly behind her and moved quickly through the house, giving various orders to see to Edith's comfort. Toast and tea would be sent up, together with a small basin of gruel. Fresh flowers would be brought to her room, and hot water for the washstand. Someone would check on her from time to time and brew willow bark tea if she became feverish. The bell rope would be moved to within reach so she need not rise or stretch her arm very far to ring for assistance. Her presence in the house would be kept utterly secret. And someone would purchase additional nightgowns this morning, since Olivia's were too long and Bessie's too wide for petite Edith.

By the time Olivia reached the hall mirror near the front door, Bessie was trotting at her heels like the squat bulldog she resembled, grumbling and scolding. "How long are we to keep her here?" demanded Bessie, arms akimbo. "Badesworth will have the law on you, and then where will we be?"

"He'll have to find her first, and I mean to prevent that for as long as I can." Olivia tucked her dark hair neatly into a mobcap as she spoke. "There's no earthly reason why he should think to look in my house for his runaway bride. He'll try her parents first, I should think, and then her aunts—and it may be months before he has run through all her old schoolmates and friends. By then, we will have thought of something."

Bessie looked skeptical. "I hope so. I'll say this for you, Ivy: You generally do think of something."

Olivia laughed. "That's my reputation," she agreed. "Pray be kind to her in the meantime. I promised her you would bring up her tray and chat with her for a bit."

Bessie nodded briskly. "I'll be happy to do that. Poor little chick. Men are beasts. And that brother of yours is the worst of the lot."

"Half brother," Olivia reminded her. "I wonder what accounts for that brutish streak of his? Perhaps his life was blighted when his mother died."

Bessie snorted. "I'm old enough to remember Aunt Blythe, and I promise you that no one's life was blighted when she died! She had something of a brutish streak herself. Ralph is Blythe's to the marrow."

Olivia looked skeptical. "Do you think so? I think I see a bit of Papa in him. All the Fairfax men are tyrants at heart. Only look at the way my inheritance was left to me! Of all the skimble-skamble arrangements—"

"Uncle Reuben was a bully, there's no denying it, but he never raised a hand to anyone, male or female. Wouldn't demean himself. Ralph might have turned out better if he had! I never met a boy who needed caning more than that lad."

"Ah, well. Too late now! You are coming to Mr. Beebe's house later this morning, are you not?"

"I am, and I'll bring the group from the school, directly after I finish with Edith." Her dark eyes, already small, narrowed as she scowled at Olivia's cap. "I hope you don't mean to wear a mobcap on the public street."

Olivia bestowed a saucy smile upon her cousin. "I

suppose that would disgrace the family? You'll be relieved to know that I am tying a bonnet over it. The ruffle will peep out around my face. Very fashionable!"

"Humph. Anything fashionable will be wasted with that charity-barrel frock."

"It won't, for I shall don a pelisse to cover the frock," Olivia retorted, suiting her actions to her words. "You see? The Fairfax name remains unsullied."

"I'm glad to hear it. Now if you will walk sedately, rather than take those great long strides of yours, perhaps no one will notice the shoes."

Olivia rolled her eyes. "Were you planning to wear formal attire to dig through Mr. Beebe's crates?"

"Oh, be off with you," said Bessie gruffly. "It doesn't matter what I wear. *I'm* not the beauty of the family."

"Edith is the beauty of the family," said Olivia firmly, tugging on her gloves. "So we'll hear no more nonsense about that, if you please."

Two hours later, Olivia emerged from the depths of yet another carton full of jumbled odds and ends and listened to the pounding going on upstairs. It was growing louder and more insistent with each repetition.

"For heaven's sake!" she uttered, exasperated. Was Grimsby never going to answer the door? It was bound to be Bessie and her team of charwomen from the school. If Grimsby continued to ignore the knocker, Olivia would be left alone with this houseful of dust and clutter.

"This," she announced to the empty basement, "is what comes of hiring a deaf butler." She struggled to her feet and marched through the storeroom door and up the narrow stairs, wiping her hands on the apron she had tied over her dress.

She reflected, with wry humor, that Mr. Beebe might not have been an *intentional* recluse. Perhaps Grimsby simply never answered the door. He was not only hard of hearing, he was all-too-obviously hostile to strangers—particularly females—and he seemed to be the only retainer left in the place. The only living creatures she had encountered here were Grimsby and an overfed cat, and both had whisked out of sight as soon as they were able.

Still, it was hard to believe that no one had heard the knocker, when she had heard it all the way in the basement. Perhaps Grimsby had peered out the window, seen a gaggle of women waiting on the steps, and gone muttering and cursing back to his sanctuary.

The knocker was still flailing away as she reached the dim and cluttered hall. "I'm coming!" she shouted inelegantly, which at least caused the irritating rapping to cease. Really, this was too much! *Where* was Grimsby?

Frowning crossly, she finally reached the door, snapped the bolt back, and yanked it open. Whatever she was about to say to Bessie died on her lips. It wasn't Bessie on the steps. It was a stranger, looking every bit as startled as she must.

Olivia froze. Before her stood the embodiment of all her secret fantasies, her favorite daydreams, to the life. Divinely tall, elegantly dressed, broad-shouldered and capable-looking . . . heavens! What an attractive man.

Olivia was as tall herself as many men, and secretly hated it. The novelty of encountering a man almost a head taller than herself somehow made her feel a bit breathless. The gentleman's dark hair and eyes were beautifully set off by spotless linen and a coat of blue superfine that hugged his athletic form indecently well. He had an air of command combined with a graceful, relaxed posture—as if he were so powerful that he need do nothing to prove it. His catlike grace, elegant clothing, tilted hat, and silver-headed walking stick might make a lesser man appear effeminate. Not this man. He was as beautiful and as dangerous as a panther. And so purely masculine, just looking at him made her feel weak in the knees.

This was the man of her dreams. She had never envisioned him in such detail, but now that she was looking into his eyes she recognized him at once.

He did not seem to recognize her, however. In fact, after staring into her eyes for perhaps three seconds, he snapped, "Who the devil are you?"

2

*E*very week, it seemed, Grimsby took longer to answer the confounded door. *One of these days,* thought George angrily, *I am going to pound hard enough to break the hinges, and that surly old reprobate is going to lose his situation.* But just as he raised his walking stick to amplify his efforts with the knocker, he thought he heard someone within give a shout. He paused his knocking to listen. The call was not repeated, but he heard the bolt on the other side of the door slide back with an emphatic bang, demonstrating an irritation equal to his own. What cheek!

His brows snapped together in a black scowl, and he took a breath to say something blistering—but the door opened to reveal, not Grimsby's sour visage, but a fresh-faced and fierce-looking housemaid.

The thing one noticed about her, apart from a general impression that she had been interrupted in the midst of a pretty dirty job, was her eyes. She was tall for a female, so he had the unusual privilege of looking into them at almost eye-level. They were the most extraordinary pair of eyes he had ever seen. In fact, they were breathtaking. He was so surprised by them that he completely lost his train of thought for several seconds while taking them in.

It wasn't their size, or their shape—although both

were very fine, even to a connoisseur of women like himself. It was the color. Her eyes were a clear, light gray. Or blue. Or green. Gray, he decided. A gray that was almost platinum, with a dark line like a halo ringing the irises for emphasis. Set in a smooth, pale skin and framed with stiff black lashes, they were utterly unique. Her lashes formed little points that made each eye look as if it were the center of a star. An oval star. A silver star. Good lord, his wits were babbling.

He knew a portrait-painter who would give his right arm for the chance to paint those eyes. George felt a fleeting regret that a girl of her station would never be immortalized in that way. But eyes or no eyes, blast it, what had taken her so long to come to the door?

He opened his mouth to chide her for her negligence. What came out instead was an idiotic, "Who the devil are you?"

It was just as if he had dashed cold water in her face. For one crazy moment, Olivia felt crushed.

Imbecile, she scolded herself, inwardly rallying. Naturally the gentleman sounds annoyed. He *is* annoyed. He has been standing on the step and pounding the knocker for a very long time.

On the other hand, annoyance is no excuse for using strong language in the presence of a gently born female. Olivia gathered her wits about her and looked down her nose at him. "I'll thank you to keep a civil tongue in your head," she snapped.

One of his brows flew up, and one corner of his mouth turned down. It was the most perfect expression of mockery she had ever seen. "I beg your pardon," he drawled. "I was expecting Grimsby. Tell me, is the knocker on this door inaudible in the servants' quarters?"

Well, how rude! Handsome is as handsome does, she reminded herself grimly. This man only resembled her ideal on the surface. How dare he take that tone with her? She glared, furious with him for shattering her fantasy—and with herself for indulging it.

"You'll have to ask Grimsby," she said shortly. She glanced behind the man, then down the street. "Where are my charwomen?"

The handsome stranger's brows climbed higher. "I've no idea. Where is Grimsby?"

"I've no idea," she replied, parroting his tone. A wicked inspiration struck, and she hooked her thumb toward the back of the house. "If you've come in search of him, the servants' entrance is that way," she said helpfully.

He looked properly stunned, she noted with satisfaction. He even glanced at the numbers painted beside the door to make sure he had the right house.

Olivia stepped back, her hand on the latch, and the gentleman immediately proved that his reflexes were as pantherlike as she had somehow known they would be. The walking stick that had been tucked negligently under his arm half a heartbeat ago was now firmly wedged across the threshold, preventing her from closing the door. His features had darkened in a frown.

"Now, look here, my good woman—"

Olivia smiled sweetly as she interrupted him. "I think it only fair to warn you, I've no objection to breaking that expensive-looking stick of yours."

He hastily removed it. She closed the door. The instant the door was shut, she had to cover her mouth with her hand to stifle a giggle. Really, the expression on the man's face had been priceless!

The knocker sounded again, so loud beside her ear that she jumped. A baritone voice on the other side of the door was raised in fury, and she heard the words clearly even through the stout oak.

"I shall report your conduct to Mr. Beebe, you impertinent chit, and you'll find yourself banished to the kitchen!''

Her jaw dropped. He thought she was a *servant*! She whirled round to stare at herself in the dusty hall mirror. She had completely forgotten about her appearance. Her reflection stared back at her, garbed in an ugly stuff gown covered with an apron, her hair tucked up under a mobcap, and—horrors!—a smut of black dirt on her cheek. She scrubbed hastily at her face with the corner of her apron, mortified. How embarrassing. It was a relief, under the circumstances, that he had *not* guessed her identity. Or her rank.

The man was still pounding on the door. "Let me in at once!" his muffled voice commanded. "Mr. Beebe is expecting me!"

Well, whatever the gentleman thought of her, she must, in good conscience, reply to that. Since he believed her to be a servant girl—and since she would rather die, she thought, than let him suspect the truth—she would play the role for him a moment longer.

Olivia opened the door a crack and peered solemnly at him. She hoped he was neither a friend nor a relative. The information she must impart would be a terrible shock to a loved one. Still, from what she had been told, Mr. Beebe had no loved ones, which was why his earthly possessions had been willed to her charity.

"Mr. Beebe is no longer among us," she told the stranger gently.

He appeared nonplussed, but hardly grief-stricken. "Where has he gone?"

"As to that, I'm sure I could not say," she responded pertly, "it not being my place to judge my betters." This was very much in the manner of a wench she had dismissed from her own service for insolence. She wished Bessie could hear her do it. She rather fancied she had copied the tone perfectly.

He stared at her as if she were a madwoman. Olivia, relenting, opened the door the rest of the way. "He's passed on, sir."

"Passed on?" The gentleman looked stunned. "D'you mean he's *dead*?"

"Yes, sir."

The stranger suddenly got a very queer look on his face. He took a deep breath. "Dead. Why was I not informed?"

Olivia narrowed her eyes at him. "Why should you be informed? Don't tell me Mr. Beebe owed you money, for I won't believe you."

"For God's sake, girl, do I look like a tradesman? I was a friend of his!"

"Nonsense. Mr. Beebe had no friends."

Really, it was wrong of her to have so much fun at someone else's expense, but she couldn't help herself; there was something positively *liberating* about her impersonation! She felt a stab of unholy delight when the stranger whipped out his card and rather savagely presented her with it. She pretended to study it, lips pursed with suspicion. What a pity she could not let him in on the joke. He looked the sort of man who would love a good joke.

And then the meaning of the writing on the card suddenly registered. Merciful heavens, she was confronting the infamous Lord Rival. In the flesh! Her brows involuntarily flew upward, and then she looked at him with renewed interest. No wonder she had found him attractive. The man made a business of attracting women—or so one heard.

The most notorious rake in London seemed an odd choice of companion for the reclusive Mr. Beebe. "You say you were a friend of his?" she asked doubtfully. This time, there was no need to feign her incredulity.

Lord Rival suddenly looked very dangerous indeed. He leaned toward her, placing one hand on the lintel, which seemed, to Olivia, to bring his body unnervingly close. Her eyes widened as she stared into his. "Do you know," he said pleasantly, the intimacy of his lowered voice making her heart seem to skip a beat, "I am not accustomed to having my word questioned."

She blinked helplessly at him. She could not seem to move away. She felt paralyzed, with her arms held stiffly at her sides and her face too close to his. "There's a first time for everything," she retorted faintly.

Startled laughter lit his eyes. He straightened, and the movement of his body away from hers broke the spell that had gripped her. Olivia felt she could breathe again.

"So there is. Perhaps you should ask Grimsby who I am," Lord Rival suggested. "Or is he dead, too?" Amusement still quivered in his voice.

Olivia's lips twitched, but she managed to look stern. "Grimsby is still among the living, sir."

"Good. Then he can tell you I play cribbage with Beebe every Thursday at this hour."

"Played," she reminded him. She looked him over skeptically. "You don't look like a cribbage player."

Some of his exasperation returned. "Well, you don't look like a Bedlamite, which you certainly must be! Let me speak to whoever is in charge here."

Olivia lifted her chin at him. "No one is in charge here, sir. Unless I am."

It was Lord Rival's turn to look suspicious. He leaned on his walking stick, studying her face. Olivia tried to remain impassive beneath his scrutiny. "Tell me," he said at last, "if Mr. Beebe has gone to his reward, why is the knocker not tied up with crape? Why is there no wreath on the door?"

She glanced in surprise at the door. He was right, of course; none of the advertisements of mourning were present. "The curtains are drawn," she offered.

"The curtains of this house are always drawn."

"Oh." Olivia did not know what else to say.

"You didn't know that, did you?"

"Well, I—"

"You just told me you were in charge here."

"So I did. So I am!"

"I don't believe it. You're new. I've never seen you before in my life."

She tossed her head. "You're very sure of that, of course!" she scoffed. "Do you remember every female who crosses your path?"

His teeth gleamed in a swift, jeering smile that seemed to acknowledge his own notoriety. The arch of his eyebrow mocked her for knowing his reputation—and himself for earning it. "Not every female," he said, his voice low and teasing. "But I would remember you."

Olivia felt a blush rising to her cheeks and tried in vain to suppress it. She knew it was foolish to feel so flattered. She knew Lord Rival did not suspect her rank, and believed himself to be flirting harmlessly with a housemaid. She knew he meant nothing, nothing whatsoever by his light words. But they came so close to describing what *she* was feeling, she could not prevent her reaction.

She could prevent him from perceiving it, however. She drew herself upright and glowered at him. "You are hoist with your own petard, sir," she said tartly. "For you *don't* remember me."

A speculative gleam lit his eyes. "Shakespeare," he observed. His gaze flicked over her, reassessing her. "Why, here's a mystery. An educated woman—and a damned fine-looking one—apparently employed as a maid of all work. And I haven't seen you before, whatever you may say. I repeat my earlier question: Who are you?"

Olivia nearly gasped aloud at his effrontery. She had never been spoken to so in her life. *Remember your role!* she reminded herself desperately. But she was so taken aback, all she could do for a moment was splutter helplessly. Finally she managed to snap, "Who I am, sir, is none of your affair!" It occurred to her that she had sounded more like an outraged spinster than a saucebox, so she added, more archly, "I cannot give my name away to every Tom, Dick, and Harry."

"But I'm George," he told her, smiling in a way that only increased her confusion. "And I think you should let me in."

He had somehow invested his words with a double meaning. Olivia was so rattled by what he *seemed* to mean that she merely stared at him, slack-jawed. Lord Rival took shameless advantage of her loosened grip on the door and pushed smoothly past her and into the house. He stood very much at his ease, stripping off his gloves and looking about. Olivia realized she looked silly, holding the door open behind a man who had already entered, so she closed it, fuming.

"I'll try to find Grimsby for you," she said stiffly. "Pray wait in the—" she waved her hand vaguely. There was a sort of parlor-cum-library near the hall, but she had no idea what the household called it.

"The bookroom?" he supplied helpfully.

"Yes. The bookroom."

"I think I had better go with you."

Olivia stared. "Go *with* me?"

"Yes. To find Grimsby."

"Why, I . . . I never heard of such a thing! Why not wait in the bookroom, like a civilized man?"

The laughter lit his eyes again. "I'm not a civilized man. And I feel quite sure that if I let you out of my sight, you will leave me to kick my heels in the bookroom for at least the next quarter of an hour."

He was right, of course. In the first place, she had no idea where Grimsby might be. And in the second, she had already decided it would teach Lord Rival a lesson to be kept waiting. Now, how had he guessed that?

Olivia pursed her lips and tried to stare him down. She failed. The amusement in his eyes, and his falsely meek expression, were irresistible. She felt her lips begin to twitch despite herself, and had to look away to keep from laughing.

"You're an impudent devil," she told him severely. "I don't know what you deserve."

"Ah, but seldom on this earth do the wicked receive what they deserve," he observed piously.

"Very true. In the next life, my lord, you will spend many hours kicking your heels in a bookroom. I feel sure of it."

"Then you need not inflict it on me today. In fact, you need not inflict Grimsby on me today."

"I thought you wanted to see him?"

"I have changed my mind. I would rather see you."

Olivia's foolish heart skipped another beat, but she was becoming used to that after spending several whole minutes in Lord Rival's company. This time she neither blushed nor stammered. She gave him the look her old governess used to give her when she misbehaved. She must have done a good job of it, too, for Lord Rival burst out laughing.

His laughter was infectious, but Olivia resisted it, although she felt her eyes twinkle. "I have a great deal of work to do this morning," she scolded him. "I can't be bothered with a harum-scarum boy trotting at my heels."

He placed one hand against his heart as if pained. "A *boy*? Madam, you wound me! I haven't been a boy these twenty years."

"You, sir, are a boy to this day, and likely to remain one," she informed him loftily. "I'll thank you to go about your business and leave off plaguing me."

"That's better," he said, his voice warm with congratulation. "You sounded very like a housemaid that time."

Olivia gave a tiny gasp, then rallied. "Perhaps you could tell me, my lord, what it was that you wanted to ask Grimsby. If I can answer your questions, I will do so—and then you may go."

"Certainly. I have two questions. First, I want to know what became of poor old Beebe, since he seemed hale and hearty the last time I saw him. And second, I want the identity of the charming girl who just answered the door."

Olivia lifted her chin at him. "I am no more a *girl,* my lord, than you are a boy."

"Ah, that rankled, did it?" he asked sympathetically.

Olivia gave up. "Very well," she said, resigned. "Mr. Beebe died peacefully in his sleep four nights ago. It was entirely unexpected, as you so sapiently observed. A private service was held yesterday." Her voice softened. "And if you were truly a friend of his, my lord, it was a sad oversight that you were not invited to the service, and I'm sorry for it."

Lord Rival inclined his head in acknowledgment and frowned at the tip of his walking stick. "I've been acquainted with Beebe for years, but our friendship is of fairly recent date," he said shortly. "I'm sorry to hear of his passing, and would have paid my respects had I known. But I'll not mourn him, precisely."

Olivia nodded sadly. "No one seems to be mourning him, precisely. The few people who knew him held him in affection and esteem, but apparently he had no intimate friends. It seems a great pity."

Lord Rival's brow quirked, and he glanced keenly at Olivia. She suddenly realized that she had slipped into conversation with him as if they were social equals. Her last remarks were completely unlike those a servant ought to make, particularly about her employer. She bit her lip, chagrined, and braced herself for another round of questions about her identity. However, Lord Rival made no comment. He walked thoughtfully to the hall table and deposited his hat, his gloves, and his walking stick upon its surface. Without turning to look at her, he asked, "Can you tell me if Lady Olivia Fairfax has been apprised of Mr. Beebe's death?"

His voice sounded perfectly neutral, but Olivia felt her heart leap into her throat. She swallowed painfully, and tried to match the neutrality of his tone. "Oh, yes, my lord. Certainly she has."

He turned to look at her, but the moment he had given her while his back was turned had been sufficient time for her to paste an innocent look upon her face. And a good thing, too, for his gaze was searching. "Are you acquainted with Lady Olivia?"

"Yes, my lord. Quite well." *Which is more than you are,* she thought indignantly. But, to her surprise, he did not claim acquaintance with Lady Olivia. Instead, his gaze sharpened with interest.

"How do you know her?"

"How?" She blinked, stalling for time. How would a servant in Aloysius Beebe's house know Lady Olivia Fairfax? The answer was, she wouldn't. Olivia had never been here prior to this morning. Lord Rival would not know that, however. She plucked up her courage and answered confidently. "Mr. Beebe was a great friend of Lady Olivia's mother, once upon a time. The late Countess of Badesworth, you know."

"Yes, I know." He looked amused. "So you met Lady Olivia during the course of her visits to Mr. Beebe."

Olivia felt herself to be on dangerous ground. "Yes, my lord," she said woodenly. "Now, if you'll excuse me, I must return to my work."

"Well, you know, I don't think I *will* excuse you," he said apologetically. "In fact, I think I had better accompany you."

Her jaw dropped again. "Certainly not! Why would you?"

"There's something dashed havey-cavey about you, that's why. If you'll forgive my saying so, of course."

"Forgive you? I don't even know what you mean."

"What, by havey-cavey? I mean smoky. Brummish. Fishy." When she still stared uncomprehendingly at him, he chuckled. "Suspicious, questionable, and downright suspect, my good girl."

Olivia's eyes sparkled dangerously. "If *that* is what you mean, then no, I do not forgive your saying it! How dare you question my motives—or my presence in this house? What business is it of yours, I should like to know?"

"It is the business of every good citizen to foil thievery."

Olivia stamped her foot and pointed furiously at the door. "Out!" she cried. "Get out of this house! Leave this instant, you—you—"

But the impossible man was laughing now, moving toward her, actually touching her, to take her arm back down to her side. "Why, here's a heat! I beg your pardon. Pray do not summon the Watch; I'll try to behave myself in future. I don't promise to succeed, mind you—but I shall try."

Saints in heaven, she was actually in Rake Rival's arms. Or very nearly. It was difficult to stay angry in the midst of the most exciting thing that had ever happened to her. The most dangerous man in London was lightly gripping her shoulders, and his bold eyes were laughing down at her.

Confused and shaken, Olivia pulled out of his hold and tried to remember what had just transpired. Oh, yes. He had been joking—or at least half-joking—and she had responded by raising her voice and shouting at him like a fishwife. Her cheeks burned with shame, both for her display of temper and her ridiculous reaction to his nearness. She scarcely recognized herself this morning; what was the matter with her?

"I have as much right to feel suspicious of you as you have to feel suspicious of me," she informed him icily, willing her voice to not shake. "More right, actually."

"Really? Then you would do well to keep me under your nose."

She regarded him for a moment, arms crossed while she regained her poise. He was right. She could hardly go back to work and leave him here unsupervised. She had no clear idea where Grimsby was. She could obviously not force Lord Rival to leave. It was really an impossible situation; she was at a loss as to what she should do.

"Your point is well taken, sir. Follow me," she said crisply, and headed for the basement stairs. Ten minutes in Mr. Beebe's dusty basement, she thought, should cure Lord Rival of his odd determination to accompany her.

3

*H*e grinned at her departing form, ramrod-straight with outraged sensibility, and willingly trailed in her wake. He no longer believed that this intriguing young woman was a housemaid, so he was surprised when she pulled open a door at the back of the hall and descended unhesitatingly to the basement. He followed, feeling more curious every moment.

The area at the bottom of the stairs was dark and cramped. It seemed to be a sort of wine cellar, but Grimsby had evidently wasted no time in depleting his deceased master's stock. The wine racks were mostly empty now. The woman, without a word or a backward glance, opened a door at the opposite end of the wine cellar and walked through it. He followed her into a large, and obviously long-neglected, lumber room. Windows near the low ceiling let in daylight, filtered through dusty panes of glass. The place looked like a madman's notion of a museum.

Items too large to fit into crates were scattered throughout the room, as if they had been carted in and dumped anyhow. Some of these objects were obviously of value. Many, however, were simply household castoffs and other discarded junk, tossed in with the valuables willy-nilly. There were several pieces of Egyptian origin. A large mummy case dominated the room, its impassive face turned to view a tangle of broken furniture. A dented coal scuttle held pieces of broken crockery, saved for what purpose he could not imagine. A magnificent cabinet clock stood, aptly enough, upon a stack of tombstones.

In addition to the assortment of freestanding articles, the room was stacked, floor to ceiling, with an intimidating jumble of boxes and crates. Several of these had been pried open with a crowbar. Sawdust and screwed-up papers, presumably unearthed within the opened boxes, littered the floor. The crowbar was resting atop the crate that must be next in line for exploration, together with a pencil and a notebook. Lines of neat and numbered text were visible on the top page of the notebook, and various oddities, smaller than the pieces that stood unboxed, had been set in orderly fashion to one side. George had apparently interrupted the young woman while she was making an inventory.

"Good God," he murmured, appalled. "Are you cataloguing all this rubbish? The labors of Hercules pale in comparison."

She actually chuckled. It was a charming chuckle, low-pitched and throaty. "Now you understand my dismay when I opened the door to you. I was hoping to find a team of charwomen on the step."

"A crushing disappointment! I forgive you all your incivility."

She bit her lip. "I was uncivil, wasn't I? I beg your pardon."

"Not at all. Perfectly understandable." He looked round the room with distaste. "My advice to you is to go back upstairs and wait for the charwomen to arrive."

"Oh, pooh." She plopped cheerfully down beside the open box, heedless of the dirty floor. "I had as lief be useful while I wait. The main difficulty is that no order has been imposed; everything has been packed higgledy-piggledy."

She was on her knees now, burying herself head-first in the open crate. He lifted the notebook and quirked an eyebrow at her. "You seem to believe you can rectify the situation."

"Certainly I can." She glanced up at him from the depths of the crate, eyes twinkling with mischief. "I'm quite good at bringing order out of chaos, actually."

I'll bet you are, he thought, amused. "One person cannot possibly catalogue this jumble."

The mischief in her eyes increased. "Two persons."

George immediately dropped the notebook and flung up his hands in mock horror. "My dear girl, you can't expect me to crawl about on the floor and dig through sawdust!"

He read condemnation in her eyes, but then she noticed his clothing and seemed to relent. "I suppose not. You are dressed for—what was it?" Her lips twitched. "Cribbage."

"Quite right," he said firmly. "Cribbage. And even if I weren't dressed for cribbage, anyone can see that I'm a foppish fellow, wholly unsuited to manual labor."

The low chuckle shook her again, and he saw her gaze travel lightly down his body—with some appreciation, it seemed to him. Vigorous pursuit of various sports had had its inevitable effect upon a frame already predisposed to powerful muscles. He looked, in fact, like a man who would have a positive *talent* for manual labor. He watched in wicked amusement as she opened her mouth to comment on this—and then thought better of the impulse. Her pretty mouth closed with an almost audible snap and she dove back into the crate, pink-cheeked.

This lady, whoever she was, had all the earmarks of a sheltered virgin. She was too young to be a house-keeper, had too much authority for a maid, and had, besides, an unmistakable air of gentility that disqualified her for either position. He would have taken her for a governess—but what would a governess be doing in Beebe's childless household? Who the devil was she?

He knew who he *hoped* she was. It seemed just barely possible . . . improbable, but possible. He leaned against a stack of crates and watched her for a moment, studying the graceful way she moved and the unconscious assurance that pervaded everything she did. It was an attractive quality. She wore her poise like an invisible mantle of confidence. One felt instinctively that she was capable of dashed well anything, the very person to have at one's side in a crisis. Or at the helm, for that matter.

"May I ask you a question?"

She tensed, almost imperceptibly, and looked up warily from her work. "What sort of question?"

"Oh, it's nothing personal," he assured her. "It's not about you."

Her shoulders visibly relaxed. "Very well. What is it?"

He bent his most ingratiating smile upon her. "Tell me something about Lady Olivia Fairfax. I've never met her, you know."

Was that alarm that flickered in the back of those wide, gray eyes? Or merely surprise? Before he could decipher her expression, she disappeared back into the crate, hiding her face from him. "I can't imagine what you would want to know," she announced to the depths of the crate. "Nor why you would want to know it."

"Well, she's something of a mystery," he said equably. "I'm as curious as the next man. One hears that she's fabulously wealthy, but she never goes about in society. Rumors always fly about that sort of person. The *beau monde* is very unforgiving when it feels it's been slighted."

"Slighted? How so?"

He grinned. "The well-heeled daughter of an earl is expected to spend a Season or two in London and give all the fortune hunters a crack at her. Lady Olivia never did, so the *ton* has decided she is hopelessly eccentric. Is she?"

The girl shrugged evasively. "Oh, I don't know. I hear she has a temper. And, of course, she's a very *managing* female. So perhaps it's just as well she kept herself off the Marriage Mart."

George pricked up his ears. This was already more information than he had been able to glean in weeks of carefully pumping Aloysius Beebe. He hid his intense interest behind another bland smile. "She must be something of a hermit. Apart from Beebe, you're the only person I've ever met who claims acquaintance with her." He paused, then smiled again. "I don't even know what she looks like."

"Oh!" said the lady brightly. "Well, I can tell you that much." She emerged from the crate, a smudge of dust adorning her jawbone. A tiny, almost secretive, smile lifted the corners of her mouth. "Are you acquainted with Lord Badesworth?"

"Her half brother? A little."

"She looks very like him."

"In what way?" he asked cautiously. Badesworth was a singularly ugly man with a habitual scowl. It was impossible to imagine a feminine version of those coarse and twisted features.

She tilted her head and looked at the ceiling for a moment, as if considering. "I think it's the nose," she said at last. "She has his nose. And his complexion, of course."

George was startled into exclaiming, "The devil you say! I thought the red face was due to drink."

She shook her head emphatically. "Oh, no. It runs in their family." She paused for a moment, then added, "I daresay by the time she's his age, she'll have

the bumps as well. She already has a few *warts,* you
know—but they're barely noticeable. For the most
part."

"Good God!"

"One always notices the warts that sprout hairs, but
very few of hers do." She frowned a little. "Except
for the one on her chin—the big one. But I think she
plucks the hair from time to time, because I've seen
it with the hair, and I've seen it without." ·

"But—devil take it, she's only twenty-six years old!"

The girl opened her eyes very wide indeed. "No.
You don't say! I had thought her forty, at the least."
She looked thoughtful. "I suppose it's the baldness
makes her look so old."

George's eyes suddenly narrowed. "You're doing it
much too brown, my girl! Warty, big-nosed, red-faced,
and *bald*? I don't believe it."

A silvery laugh escaped her. "Oh, she's not *completely* bald," the lady assured him. "She has quite a
bit of hair left." She paused again. "Here and there."

"On her chin, I suppose you'll tell me next!"

"No, no! Only on that one wart. At least, that's the
only hair I've *noticed* on her chin. She has hair on her
head." The lady's tone indicated a belief that Lady
Olivia was to be congratulated for this. "It's thin, but
there are quite a few tufts. She'll never be a beauty—"

"I should think not!"

"—but I always rather liked her. Despite the stories
one hears." She lifted a clay object from the crate and
held it up to the light, her expression serene. "Now,
what would you call this bit of pottery? It looks very
like a pipe rack, but that can't be right."

"I've no idea," he said shortly. "What 'stories' have
you heard about Lady Olivia?"

The girl looked prim and shook her head. "I'll not
tell tales out of school," she said demurely, and
reached for her notebook.

It occurred to George in a flash that she might mean that literally. He had learned, in the course of his investigation, that Lady Olivia Fairfax ran a charity school for orphaned girls. Was this young woman connected with the school? Had she heard unflattering stories about Lady Olivia there?

While she was busy jotting in her notebook, he studied the clothing she wore. It didn't tell him much. The frock was old, but seemed to have been made of quality material—the very sort of frock, he thought, that a rich lady might donate to charity once it had become too worn. It was modest and serviceable, high-necked, long-sleeved. This woman might very well have been educated at the charity school. She might have obtained this gown there. In fact, his early impression that she was a governess-type might have been near the mark. She might be a teacher at the charity school! If she were, she would, in fact, be acquainted with the elusive heiress.

George felt a stab of dismay. Could any of the wild things he had just been told be *true?* If Lady Olivia were ugly, hot-tempered, and bossy, that would certainly explain how a woman with her lineage and fortune had managed to stay single. And, besides that, why would this odd, intriguing female want to play a Canterbury trick on him? There must be some truth in the portrait she was painting.

Unless . . . no; he would reserve judgment for now, and take what she was telling him with a grain of salt. A very large grain of salt. She might have any number of reasons for misleading him. Perhaps everyone at the charity school was under strict orders to protect Lady Olivia's privacy. That was, actually, more probable than not. And he still clung to a glimmer of hope that this young woman might, herself, be . . .

And whoever she was, what the deuce was she doing here? He frowned and straightened from his pose against the crates. "Let us turn to another subject," he said. "Why are you cataloguing Beebe's possessions?"

"Because it must be done, of course. For the probate of his will." She rose from her knees and briskly shook out her apron.

"Yes, but why must *you* do it? Who are you?"

She picked up her notebook and pencil. "I think it very ill-bred of you to lounge about, asking impertinent questions, while I do all the work," she said severely. "Kindly pry open the next box for me."

"With a good will, ma'am," he replied, picking up the crowbar. "As soon as you tell me your name."

Her eyes snapped dangerously. "And if I will not?"

She looked capable of snatching the crowbar out of his hands. George decided to change tactics. He held the crowbar out of her reach and smiled disarmingly at her. "Come, now, it's not an unreasonable request. What am I to call you? I cannot continue to address you as 'my good woman' or 'dear girl.' "

"You may address me as 'ma'am,' just as you did a moment ago."

He chuckled wickedly. "Oh, that was a slip of the tongue. You can't expect me to call you 'ma'am.' What are you—some sort of chambermaid?"

Aha. She looked completely flummoxed. She had forgotten she was a servant, begad! Well, before she confessed her identity, he'd better seize the moment. Once she told him who she was, the chance would be gone. He set the crowbar down and swiftly reached for her.

He heard the startled intake of her breath as his hands closed on her upper arms, pulling her toward him. He had meant to kiss her quickly, roughly, the way an arrogant lord of the manor might handle a lowly chambermaid—*that* would shock the truth out of her!—but something stopped him.

What a pleasant surprise. She was beautiful. Why

had he not seen it until now? He must not have looked properly at her.

He paused for the merest fraction of time, savoring those impossible eyes so close to his. They were wide with astonishment, silver in the half-light. Lovely. His nostrils caught a faint fragrance from her, a whiff of something sweet and nostalgic. Roses and . . . apricots. She smelled of summer, mellow and warm and sunlit. It suited her perfectly.

In the heartbeat of time while George took all this in, the front door opened upstairs. Some quirk of the house's construction immediately sucked the storeroom door shut with a *whoof*. Still he stood, drunkenly staring into the nameless girl's eyes. It was she who suddenly broke away and, with a cry, rushed over to tug futilely at the closed door.

"Minding the proprieties? It's a bit late for that," remarked George, strolling over to help her. "Allow me."

"Oh, do you think you can open it?" she asked eagerly, stepping aside. "Grimsby told me that it locked when it closed."

This sounded ominous. He rattled the doorknob, but it refused to turn. He tugged with all his strength, but the door remained securely in its track.

"What idiot would design a basement door to automatically lock from the wrong side?" he asked, exasperated. She must have known his question was rhetorical, for a sympathetic look was her only reply. "Stand back," he ordered. She did so.

He put his shoulder to the door and shoved mightily, grunting with the effort. The thick wedge of English oak did not budge. Panting, he stood back and regarded it for a moment. "Hand me the crowbar."

"Oh, dear," she said faintly. "Do you really think we ought to take the door apart?"

"I only *hope* we can take the blasted door apart! It's more likely to bend the crowbar."

He thought he was joking. Five minutes later, however, they were staring incredulously down at a bent and ruined crowbar. George flung it on the floor in disgust. The door was barely scratched—and still securely locked.

"I wish I knew what Beebe paid for that crowbar," he said sourly. "What's it made of? Tissue?"

"It opened the crates," the girl offered.

George snorted, then looked speculatively around the room. "I wonder if there's a cannon among all this trash."

He heard a choke and glanced down in surprise. The lady at his side, despite the dire straits she was in, was stifling a laugh with one hand. "I'm afraid not," she said apologetically, laughter still quivering in her voice. "This appears to be the Egyptian Room. More or less."

A grin tugged at his mouth. "Well, where's the medieval collection? I'll settle for a battering ram."

They both dissolved into helpless laughter. "Oh, my!" she gasped at last. "Truly, truly, it's not funny in the least. What will we do?"

"Give up, I think, and climb into that sarcophagus to begin our final rest."

"I am not so poor spirited." She rose determinedly from the box where she had been seated, and looked purposefully about her. "Perhaps there is another exit."

George ambled over to the sarcophagus and sat irreverently upon its lid. He stretched his long legs out before him, crossed his arms, and watched in amusement as his companion prowled through the room, poking into this corner and that. "For myself, I am perfectly content to remain in the basement with you," he said teasingly.

Her head popped round the corner of the mummy case to bestow a minatory frown upon him. "Well, I have no intention of remaining in a basement with you," she scolded him. "Nor anywhere else, for that matter. The idea!"

She disappeared behind the case again. George grinned. "You had better tell me who you are, you know," he called after her. "You're no more a housemaid than I am. Are you one of Mr. Beebe's relatives?"

Her voice floated back to him, muffled by the surrounding crates. "If you think I am going to sit in this excessively dusty basement with you and play Twenty Questions, you are sadly mistaken."

"You needn't sit," he promised. "Although if you were to join me, that would be sporting of you."

She appeared from behind a bookcase and glared at him, arms akimbo. He patted the sarcophagus invitingly. Was that laughter he saw in her eyes? He hoped so, but before he had a chance to find out, faint sounds emanated from beyond the locked door. Footsteps. Someone was coming down the stairs in the next room.

The relief George felt was tempered with disappointment; he wished their rescuer could have delayed for another five minutes. Or ten.

The girl's eyes, however, lit with unqualified relief. She made an instant dash for the door—and, on her first step, tripped over the coal scuttle full of crockery. Scuttle, crockery, and lady went flying. George leaped to her aid and both of them went down in the dust with a crash.

"Ivy?" From somewhere beyond the door, a feminine voice was raised in bewilderment and alarm. Whoever it was, she sounded fairly distant. "Ivy? Is that you? Where are you?"

"Here!" gasped the girl in his arms. "I'm here, Bessie!" She was choking on dust and breathless from her fall, but struggled to her feet and ran, stumbling and coughing, toward the door.

The distant voice sounded relieved. "Oh, lord-a-mercy, it's only a cat! You nearly frightened the life out of me, puss-puss." The rest of her words were unintelligible as the woman—Bessie, was it?—walked farther away. The faint sound of the door closing at the top of the stairs seemed to seal their doom. The rattle of pails and thump of feet overhead signaled that the charwomen had arrived with Bessie, and had immediately plunged into work. Shouts and poundings in the basement would definitely not be heard now.

The girl sagged against the door in defeat, bleary-eyed and still coughing a little. "Oh, this is terrible," she moaned. "Drat the cat! Could our luck be any worse?"

George rose from the dust, a slow smile spreading across his features. "Speak for yourself, my dear," he said pleasantly. "My luck just took a turn for the better."

She shrank back against the door as she watched him approach, apprehension stealing across her features. "It—it did?" she asked faintly.

"Yes, indeed," he told her. He was feeling an enjoyment that was almost exultation. What an exquisite situation! Locked in a basement with a pretty servant girl. If he had planned it, it could not be better. And to add a little spice, this particular girl was acquainted with the prey he had been delicately stalking for weeks. He banished the tug of chagrin he had felt at learning her name. Too bad it wasn't "Olivia," but he would not repine. "Ivy" was a plebeian name, resolving the lingering doubts he had had about her class. No gently born maiden would be christened "Ivy."

He placed his hands against the door on either side of her, caging her between his arms. "Well, *Ivy,* shall we take off our masks?" he suggested softly. "Since I now know who you are."

4

*F*or one terrified moment Olivia thought he had somehow guessed her identity. But then he chuckled and said, "I have a confession to make, Ivy. I was half hoping you were Lady Olivia Fairfax."

"Gracious!" she squeaked, then cleared her throat, hoping he would think her startled chirp was attributable to dust. "What made you think such a mad thing?"

His eyes are so dark, she thought, a frisson of mingled fear and delight coursing through her. She was very thankful he did not, in fact, know who she was. She was almost sure that what she was feeling at this moment was improper. It was difficult to keep her equilibrium when he called her by her nickname! No one but her family had ever called her Ivy.

He smiled, and his smile shot pleasure clear through her. "Well, everyone knows her to be an eccentric," he said, still smiling that devastating smile. "You must own, a woman of rank and fortune who dressed like a junior housemaid—and worked like one, as well— would have to be very eccentric indeed."

"Oh. I see." She tried to laugh, but failed. Fearing that he would somehow read the truth in her eyes, she ducked out from under his arms. He made no attempt to stop her.

"Not that I'm displeased with my present company.

Quite the contrary," he drawled, laughter lurking in his voice. "But you can't blame me for indulging a foolish fancy when you wouldn't tell me your name."

Olivia wasn't sure whether it was dust or alarm that was choking her at this point. She wandered over and pretended to study the narrow windows high on the wall, in an attempt to hide her face from him. Maddeningly, he followed and stood uncomfortably close behind her.

"Tell me, Ivy," he murmured teasingly, almost in her ear. "Is Lady Olivia really haggish? She can't be as bad as you said she was."

"Worse," said Olivia firmly. She gathered her courage and faced him, determined to end this particular discussion once and for all.

He looked searchingly at her, and seemed to conclude she was in earnest. He raked a hand through his hair, suddenly perplexed. "Damnation! What the deuce did Beebe mean, then, by telling me he thought we'd be well-suited?"

Olivia's jaw dropped. "He said that?"

"He certainly did!"

"Well!" she exclaimed, shaking her head in amazement. "What an extraordinary idea. One hates to speak ill of the dead, but it's my belief Mr. Beebe was queer in his attic."

Lord Rival grinned. "Having seen his basement, I feel sure you are right."

He strolled away from her and began pacing, frowning, plunged in thought. He seemed to be turning a memory over in his mind, trying to make sure his recollection was correct. Olivia watched him a bit wistfully, unable to escape noticing again how handsome he was—even covered with dust. And, wonder of wonders, Mr. Beebe, who had known them both, had believed that she and Lord Rival would be well-suited. One couldn't help longing to find out if it were true.

She sternly repressed the traitorous thought. Well-suited, indeed! No respectable woman could be *well-suited* to rakish Lord Rival! The idea was ludicrous. She realized with dismay that she had better set a guard on her emotions. She was far too attracted to him. *This man has ruined many a virtuous lady,* she reminded herself. Surely she had too much self-respect to join that sorry lot.

Lord Rival halted midstride, a slow smile dawning. "Well, I'll be damned," he muttered, seemingly to himself. Then, to her surprise, he threw back his head and uttered a crack of laughter. "That's it, begad! He was pulling my leg, the cagey old codger! Here I thought *I* was the one cutting a wheedle, and Beebe was up to every rig and row! I never guessed it. Would have fallen right into the trap, had he sprung it." He shook his head in rueful amusement. "What an excellent joke it would have been, too. A pity he never had the chance to play it."

Olivia felt a chill of foreboding. "What was the joke?" she asked, trying to smile. She was very much afraid that she did not want to hear the answer.

He dropped himself down on a wooden crate, his face alight with mirth. "The joke is, I was cultivating Beebe's friendship because he was the only man of my acquaintance whom I knew to be a friend of the Fairfax family. The old wheezer cozened me into playing cribbage with him every Thursday—*cribbage*! And I even let him win!" Lord Rival's shoulders shook with laughter. "All the while, I was working my way round to coax an introduction to Lady Olivia out of him. And he knew it! He must have guessed that I wanted to meet her—and he must have guessed why! He wouldn't tell me a blasted thing about her; just that he thought we'd be an excellent match. He tolled me along like a right one! He must have been enjoying it, picturing the look on my face when I finally met the witch."

Olivia was unable to join in his laughter, but he was

enjoying himself too much to notice. He was still shaking his head in amused appreciation. "I daresay old Beebe thought he would teach me a lesson." His teeth flashed in a wolfish grin. "He wouldn't have, of course, but I can't blame him for trying. He seemed fond of Lady Olivia, whatever her shortcomings."

Olivia felt her throat constrict. "Yes, I believe he was." Poor old Mr. Beebe. She had been fond of him, too.

"Well, heigh-ho! On to the next name on my list." He smiled and stretched, putting her irresistibly in mind of a panther again.

This was what she had feared, she thought miserably, but forced herself to ask. It was better to know. "What sort of list? Surely you don't *plan* your—your conquests?"

He seemed a bit startled, then winked. "So! My reputation precedes me." She must have looked appalled, for he suddenly grinned. "I'm a villain, but not as bad as that. How lowering to discover that one's unsavory exploits have trickled down to the servant class! I must be infamous indeed."

"Yes, you are." She sniffed. "You should be ashamed of yourself."

"Oh, no doubt I should," he said easily. He looked perfectly unperturbed, however. "I've enjoyed the company of far too many women. But I never did anything so crude as to make up a list of . . . er . . . targets. The thing is, I now have marriage on my mind, not pleasure. Ergo, I made a list."

"I see. A list of marital prospects," she said numbly.

"That's it. It's a short list." His grin looked a little bitter, as if he were mocking himself. "I cannot afford to marry just anyone."

Her heart felt as if it were sinking into her shoes. "I suppose you need an heiress?"

"Indeed I do," he said cordially. "Just as Beebe guessed. And you'd be amazed at the dearth of heiresses on the Marriage Mart these days! All the rich women I know are either married or hideous. Or boring."

Olivia assumed an expression of polite puzzlement. "But everyone knows that Lady Olivia is not interested in marriage. She's a confirmed spinster."

One of his brows flew up. One corner of his mouth turned down. Mocking devils danced in his eyes. "She may be. But I have a talent for persuasion."

Good heavens, the man was dangerous. More than dangerous. What a lucky escape she was having, Olivia thought feverishly. What if she hadn't known all this, and this gorgeous, teasing man had suddenly entered her life, introduced by a trusted family friend? She might have fallen—hard. It made her feel faint to think of it.

But he was leaning back, very much at his ease, seeming to enjoy explaining himself to a friendly ear. "Confirmed spinsters are often lonely souls. And innocent. They can be easy prey for a man of . . . persuasive talents. Just as confirmed bachelors often lose their hearts to clever little mantraps."

She forced a smile. "I suppose you are right."

"Lady Olivia's name was at the top of my list. She intrigued me. She's an unknown, and it's been devilish difficult to find out anything about her. I knew her age, her lineage, where she lived, the fact that she ran a charity dedicated to her mother's memory. And nothing else—not her personal history, nor what she looked like, nor anything about her. The more mysterious she was, the more interested I became. The thrill of the chase, I suppose."

Anger licked through her. She struggled to maintain her sympathetic expression. "I see. What a blow to discover she's as unappealing as the other rich women on your list."

His mask of urbane amusement slipped for a moment, and she saw the bleakness beneath it. "Ah, well.

I hadn't expected to enjoy this." He recovered his aplomb immediately, however, and his eyes twinkled appreciatively as he glanced over at her. "But I should count my blessings. Spending time with you has been quite illuminating. And far more amusing than cribbage with Beebe would have been."

"Amusing!" She choked. "We are locked in a basement, sir! This is not amusing in the least."

He rose and lazily approached. "You don't think so? Perhaps we haven't made the best use of our time."

Before she knew what he intended, he pinned her lightly against the wall, placing his forearms against the stones on either side of her head. She froze, her eyes widening with surprise and alarm. He was actually *leaning* against her. Even through her thick skirts she was aware of his lower body pressing intimately against hers.

Her mind raced, trying to think what to do, but came up blank. What would a saucy housemaid do, cornered by a rake? She had no notion. She knew, of course, what the well-bred and chaste Lady Olivia Fairfax would do. Should do. But she felt a strange reluctance to do it.

His gaze was traveling languidly across her face, studying her features. There was a hot, slow pleasure in the way he looked at her, like a gourmet savoring the aroma of a perfectly prepared meal before taking the first bite. He was almost certainly going to kiss her, she realized, terrified—and thrilled.

Would she let him?

Of course she would not! What a mad idea!

But, after all, he wouldn't know who it was he was kissing. Her reputation would be completely safe. Her eyes were wide open; she knew he was nothing but a heartless fortune hunter. She was in no danger of losing her head, nor of reading anything serious into his attentions.

And what an adventure it would be!

Olivia had always longed for adventure. Well, here it was. She was about to be kissed by the worst rake in England. How delicious! How utterly forbidden! She was about to sample the delights she had deliberately denied herself by forgoing marriage. Such a chance would doubtless never come again in the course of her staid and virtuous life. *Carpe diem!* she thought recklessly.

Inch by inch, he relaxed his body against hers, and Olivia made no move to stop him. Their eyes were locked the entire time. She might have said "no" at any point, but she did not. Giddy with excitement, she boldly answered his unspoken question with consent. She felt the alien pressure of a male torso against her breasts, which seemed to be straining against her stays in a most peculiar way. The wall stood firmly against her back, reassuring her that however dizzy the man made her, she could not fall.

She braced herself, tingling with anticipation, but he did not kiss her. Saints in heaven, why didn't he get it over with? The suspense was killing her. She was expecting a sudden grab, followed by a kiss of ruthless force. A rake's kiss. She was expecting an ambush, not—not *this*. He approached her lingeringly, softly, in a way that would have robbed her of resistance—had she been resisting.

"Ivy," he whispered, almost like a prayer, and bent his head to hers. His face came slowly closer, filling her world. She lifted her mouth to meet his kiss, but still it did not occur. Bewildered, she felt a whisper of warm breath against her lips, tantalizingly brief. Then his mouth moved past without touching hers.

A shock of desire went through her, frightening in its suddenness. She wanted his kiss now. She wanted it badly. The longer he withheld it, the more she wanted it. Did he know this? Was this why he was torturing her?

His lips lightly touched her forehead, then grazed her cheekbone. The sensation was magical. He was bewitching her, letting his mouth barely touch her skin, as if he had all the time in the world and was in no particular hurry to ravish her. Olivia was trembling; she could not help herself. Softly, so softly, his lips trailed across her cheek. She felt her eyes drift shut. He kissed her jawbone, so lightly she might have imagined the contact, and then she felt his breath stirring deliciously against her ear. "Tell me, Ivy, how well do you know Lady Olivia?" he whispered.

She opened her eyes, blinking dazedly. "Wh-what?"

His cheek touched hers. "Lady Olivia," he repeated softly. The sound of his voice unwittingly breathing her name was thrilling. "Do you really know her?"

He was murmuring the words so seductively, they might have been words of love. "Yes," she said faintly, closing her eyes. She was hardly aware of what she was saying. She probably would have said yes to anything he asked at this moment.

His mouth traveled back down her jawbone and stopped just below the corner of her mouth. Against her skin, he murmured, "You wouldn't be playing a May game with me, would you, Ivy? You wouldn't be pulling my leg?"

She couldn't speak. She couldn't think. She could barely breathe. Her entire being was concentrated in that one corner of her mouth where Lord Rival's lips were moving against her skin.

She couldn't stand it another second. Unable to stop herself, she turned her head a fraction and deliberately slid her mouth under his.

Oh, this was what she had dreamed of. For once in her life, she had done something wanton, and Lord Rival's reaction was even more exciting than she had thought it would be. She had surprised him! All trace of that maddening languor vanished, and he kissed her with all the heat and thoroughness she could desire. Thrilled by her own daring, she clung to him, determined to experience every nuance of his kiss.

All too soon, however, she had to pull her face away, fighting for air. For sanity. "Stop! Stop," she gasped, pushing feebly against his shoulders.

He relaxed his grip and touched his forehead to the top of her head for a moment. They were both breathing raggedly. "More than you bargained for, eh, my dear?" he said mockingly. But his voice sounded strained.

He fell back a pace and looked at her, his eyes dark with strange emotions. Desire, she recognized at once—and, oddly, confusion. "More than I bargained for, as well," he said hoarsely. He then jammed his hands into his pockets as if startled by his own confession, and walked away from her.

Well, she had done it. She had kissed Rake Rival. Olivia raised a shaking hand to straighten her cap and tried to compose herself. He was right, she thought miserably; it had been more than she bargained for. All she had wanted was an exciting adventure to remember in her old age. Not something that would haunt her dreams every night of her life.

The air seemed to hum with tension. Olivia cleared her throat. "Well, sir," she said, with a fair assumption of crispness. "I think you would be better employed in boosting me up to the window."

This surprised a snort of laughter out of him. "Well, there's an abrupt change of topic. Should I feel insulted?"

His eyes were smiling. Some of the tension had left the room. Relieved, Olivia smiled back. "If I cannot fit through the window, you will have an opportunity for revenge."

"Thank you, that will be balm to my wounds. While I am boosting you, I shall try to think of a cutting remark." He strolled over to her, his urbanity restored. "I suppose the gentlemanly thing to do is to offer to go through the window myself."

"Never mind," said Olivia kindly. "The leopard cannot change his spots."

He paused, his eyes glinting at her. "Spitfire."

She chuckled. "I could not resist! But in all honesty, sir, the window is quite small. You would never fit those shoulders through it."

His gaze flicked briefly down her body and his grin widened. "I shall refrain from making the obvious comment, and merely agree with you."

Olivia blushed. Impudent man! But since she had mentioned his shoulders, something a lady should never notice, she could scarcely upbraid him for his indelicacy.

She did fit through the window, but not easily. They tried it head first, then feet first, then head first again. On the third try, feeling desperate, Olivia pushed herself past the point where she had stopped the first time. After a few frightening seconds when she was quite certain she was stuck fast and they would have to tear the house apart to free her, she popped through and was able to crawl out. The window was only a few inches above street level. Not a soul was in sight, for which she was profoundly grateful. She scrambled to her feet and raced to the front door, let herself in with her key, and hastened downstairs to free Lord Rival.

When she opened the lumber room door he was there, leaning against the doorjamb and grinning wickedly at her. "Let's do it again," he suggested. "I especially liked the part where—"

"Oh, hurry, sir, for pity's sake!" exclaimed Olivia, tugging frantically on his sleeve. "You must leave at once."

"Leave? But I am having such a charming morning."

She hardly knew whether to laugh or scream. "Sir, I beg you to make haste! The house is full of people now. They will discover us at any instant."

"Where's the harm in that?" he protested, as she dragged him toward the stairs. "You need only say that I came to make an offer on the house. You were very properly showing me the wine cellar—"

"Very *im*properly, as anyone who sees us together will immediately perceive! What a sight we must be!"

"Oh. Am I as filthy as you are?"

"Yes, my lord, I'm afraid you are."

"How distressing. Still, you know, no one will guess that we have been rolling about in the basement. After all, why would we? It sounds absurd."

"They may not guess we were in the basement—but the *rolling about* they will surely guess! Will you kindly go?" Since her tugging was having little effect, she ran behind him and began pushing.

Still laughing and protesting, he allowed her to push him halfway up the stairs, then stopped and rounded on her. He gripped the rickety banisters with both hands, effectively blocking her on the step below him. "I will go, on one condition."

"Anything, if you will go at once!"

"I will," he promised. "When you tell me I may see you again."

Nonplussed, she stared at him. He certainly knew how to take the wind out of her sails. It was impossible to give him the answer he sought.

Olivia dropped her eyes to cover her confusion. "My, you are a chap of one idea!" she complained. "What became of your courtship of Lady Olivia?"

"Oh, any heiress will do," he said lightly. "It's my hope that you are Beebe's long-lost granddaughter and he has left all his fortune to you."

"Well, you're out, there," she informed him, with spirit. "He's left most of it to charity."

"May I see you again?"

She tried to look coldly at him. "Oblige me, please, by leaving this house."

He placed his hand on his heart and winked at her. "Obliging you, Ivy, is all I live for."

To her relief, he then turned and climbed the stairs without pestering her further. Her relief was short-lived, however. He took his things from the hall table, solemnly placed his gleaming hat upon his disordered and dusty hair, and allowed her to open the door for him. But he stopped in the doorway and caught her wrist.

"Let me go!"

His eyes bored into hers, teasing but insistent. "I want your promise first. May I see you again?"

"Oh, very well!" she said, exasperated. "You may."

"Excellent." He instantly let her go and stepped through the door, a broad smile wreathing his features.

"Then again," she added pertly, "you may not." And she closed the door with a snap.

All afternoon, as she scrubbed the dust from her face and hands, as she worked with Bessie and the charwomen, as she walked home, as she looked in on Edith, as she did a hundred little chores—whatever she was doing, she caught herself smiling for no reason and chuckling at odd moments. Lord Rival's face would pop into her mind, or the remembrance of something he had said, and she would feel strangely exhilarated. On the whole, she did not regret her encounter with a rake, she told herself. Really, he had been quite good company. For the most part. A very stimulating . . . conversationalist.

She dared not think too much about the kiss.

5

*T*he next day, George bearded Grimsby in his lair and peppered him with questions. His detailed description of Ivy, however, was met with a blank and surly stare. Grimsby declared that females were plaguey creatures and professed not to know one from another. Yes, an army of women had descended upon the house yesterday, swarming about and kicking up a riot, but he hadn't noticed any one in particular and couldn't say which of the horde was the first to arrive. The only information George was able to obtain was confirmation that the invaders had come from a "school for orphings."

George did not need to be told which school. He returned to his flat disappointed. Ivy was the most entertaining, intriguing woman he had met in years—or, perhaps, ever. But she appeared to be connected to the Helen Fairfax School for Girls in some capacity, just as he had suspected. This meant that she was—again as he had suspected—a respectable and educated woman. George knew the rules. Such women were not, alas, fair game. A pity, but there it was.

He toyed with the idea of tracking her down at the school, then reluctantly decided against it. However tempting the notion was, nothing good could come of seeing Ivy again. His intentions were strictly dishonorable, he reminded himself bleakly. They had to be.

So, as a mark of respect to a woman he genuinely liked, he determined to stay away from her.

It cost him a pang of real regret. And the regret continued to pop into his mind at odd intervals. It was made worse by knowing exactly where he could find her. Over the next day or two, he had to exercise a disconcerting amount of self-control to keep his footsteps from straying in the direction of the Fairfax School. He was fighting an absurd urge to take a hackney to Chelsea and hang about in the hope that she would step out the door.

And then what, moonling? he asked himself, disgusted. *Will you seduce and abandon her? Aye, there's a gentlemanly hobby to while away the autumn months! Or, now that Beebe's gone, will you use poor Ivy to secure an introduction to the elusive Lady Olivia?* What a nightmare that would be! He pictured himself paying court to an ugly woman for the first time in his life, with Ivy, of all women, watching from the sidelines. It fairly made his hair stand on end.

He had decided that he would, despite Ivy's description, meet Lady Olivia before striking her name from his list. After all, she was the only woman on it whom he had not already met, and he had spent a considerable amount of time and effort pursuing her. He hated to give up the chase without so much as *seeing* her. Any man could tell that Ivy had a bit of mischief in her; perhaps she had been pulling his leg for some reason. He had been attempting to tease the truth out of her when—

But he wouldn't think of that. Remembering that kiss undermined his determination to keep his distance from her.

He was still considering and discarding various unsatisfactory plans to encounter Lady Olivia Fairfax when a miracle occurred. He received an invitation to the reading of Aloysius Beebe's will.

What luck. Lady Olivia would surely be present. He

would meet her at last, with no contrivance on his part whatsoever. But that was not the thought that held him for a full minute, staring at the sheet of pressed paper upon which two brief, polite sentences were printed. The letter from Beebe's solicitor could mean only one thing: George was a beneficiary. He was named in Beebe's will.

This was one of the long-shot hopes George had indulged when befriending Beebe—a wealthy old man with no family and no known intimates. But he had never seriously believed that this horse would come first past the post! And Beebe had never mentioned writing George into his will.

He struggled to quell the wild hope surging through him. After all, Ivy had said that the bulk of Beebe's fortune was left to charity. The presence of a group of women from the Fairfax School, tidying and inventorying Beebe's house, confirmed that. But who knew how vast Beebe's fortune might prove to be? George must have been left *something*. Perhaps the sum was substantial. It was impossible not to dream, however briefly, of restoring Rye Vale . . . without the need to marry an heiress.

It was a sweet dream. What surprised him was that Ivy appeared in it. If he need not marry money, why, anything was possible. He could marry for love.

The thought brought him back to earth with an almost audible thump, and he chuckled at his own foolishness. How absurd, to think for even a moment of courting a penniless schoolteacher. Besides, he knew nothing about her. Of course, the fact that he knew nothing about her was probably the reason why she had retained such a powerful grip on his imagination. Women were always more interesting before one got to know them, he thought cynically.

On the day named in the solicitor's letter, George dressed with more than his usual care. Mourning attire would be too much, but it was important to strike just

the right note of sobriety. He wished to look his best,
naturally, when meeting Lady Olivia Fairfax. But
there was a certain impression he wished to convey,
and it took him some time to feel satisfied that he had
accomplished it. At last he stood before the glass in
his bedroom, a wicked smile playing across his features. He had done it.

He was dressed very correctly, even handsomely, in
a charcoal-colored morning coat and spotless white
linen. His waistcoat was a lighter gray, with just a hint
of a stripe to offset the impression of mourning. A
man with a valet could not have done better. "Why,
George, you old trickster," he murmured to his reflection. "You look pious, respectable and rich—three
things you most assuredly are not."

He carefully added a modest pearl stickpin to his
ensemble. The pearl was imitation, of course, but only
a jeweler would know that. *Just right,* he thought, with
another grim smile. Nothing flashy, none of the ex-
tremes of fashion, but a general impression of good
taste and wealth.

The solicitor's office proved to be a large, slightly
shabby, apartment predictably stuffed with books. A
massive desk took up most of the space at one side
of the room, but straight-backed chairs had been ar-
ranged around the walls and in rows opposite the
desk. The curtains were drawn back from the windows
to let in light, and a small fire crackled in the grate.
The solicitor was nowhere in sight, but George was
not the first to arrive. Grimsby sat at the back of the
room, holding a rusty black hat in his lap and looking
ill at ease. Three dour-looking women in black bombazine perched on chairs against the wall, like crows
hunched atop a fence. At the sight of them, George
had a sinking feeling. These women had "charity
worker" stamped all over them. Which of these harri-
dans was Lady Olivia? He suppressed a shudder and
pasted a pleasant expression on his face.

Standing by the desk with her back to him was a tall, slender female in an expensive redingote and a very modish hat. She was talking to a thin, elderly man who looked like some sort of banker, and a short, fierce-browed woman who reminded George irresistibly of his old nurse.

His swift assessment ruled out the nursey woman— thank God—and at least one of the three crows as too old to be the lady he sought. The other two women had the ageless severity of females who spend their lives in thankless toil. They might be any age between twenty-five and forty, he supposed. One of them, then, was almost certainly Lady Olivia Fairfax.

He turned his eyes away from the group by the desk and surreptitiously studied his two possibilities, looking for any resemblance to Lord Badesworth. One of them was hugely fat—something Ivy had not mentioned—but the other had a complexion pitted by the ravages of smallpox, and she hadn't mentioned that, either. Both women were plain to the point of ugliness, but neither suffered from warts, he noted indignantly, nor big noses, nor baldness, as far as he could tell. Just as he had thought! Ivy had been pulling his leg. If he ever saw that minx again, why, he'd—

A low chuckle sounded from the other side of the room. George's head snapped round to stare once more at the group by the desk. The tall woman was laughing at something being said by the short woman. Her hat still obscured most of her face, but there was something about her profile, something about her laugh—

And then she swung gracefully round to face him. George suffered a severe shock. "Ivy!" he gasped, his mind reeling.

Ivy's finely drawn brows arched upward. "Sir?" she said frostily. "You are in error. We have not met."

He stared. Where was the mischievous saucebox who had spiced his daydreams for the past week? This woman bore Ivy's face and form, but she was the picture of genteel hauteur, looking down her nose at him as if he were just *anyone,* an insolent male offering an affront to a lady of quality.

For one paralyzed instant his thoughts raced with crazy possibilities. Among the most likely was that he was dreaming. Or mad. Twins separated at birth occurred to him. He also wondered for half a heartbeat if Ivy was, after all, Beebe's long-lost granddaughter. Anything, everything, was possible—but, please God, *not* that she was—

"Lady Olivia Fairfax," she said, extending her hand with a nice mixture of reserve and graciousness. To everyone else in the room it must appear that she was relenting, in Christian charity, and providing a stranger with her name to keep matters on a friendly footing. "Since there is no one here at the moment to perform introductions, I suppose we must take it upon ourselves."

He stared numbly into those impossible eyes of hers and shook her gloved hand. "Lord Rival," he croaked, bowing perfunctorily. He knew he ought to say something more, but could not, for the life of him, manage another word.

"Bessie, may I present Lord Rival to you? Lord Rival, this is my cousin, Miss Fairfax."

White-lipped, he turned to bow to the short, dark-haired woman. Her expression reminded him once again of his childhood nurse. She was glaring at him, her brows beetling with suspicion. "How do you do?" she said gruffly.

Bessie. So this was Bessie. Good God, what a sap-skull he had been. His investigations had told him that Lady Olivia lived with her cousin Elizabeth, but he had never made the connection when he heard Ivy calling to "Bessie."

But then, why should he? *Ivy?* Why the deuce had Miss Fairfax shouted for *Ivy?* Why not Ollie, or Livvy, or—dazed, he realized that Lady Olivia was introducing him to the three crows. He bowed and smiled, but caught none of their names. His brain was awhirl with painful conjecture.

His morning did not improve. The more time he was allowed to think, the more tortured his thoughts became. Beebe's solicitor arrived and the reading began. George found it impossible to concentrate as the solicitor's voice droned on, reading paragraph after paragraph of legal gibberish. His mind was fully occupied by his own inward writhing. Wave after wave of chagrin and horror washed through him as he realized the implications of this morning's revelation.

He should have trusted his intuition. Damn it all! Why had he not? His instincts, finely tuned through years of living by his wits, seldom led him astray. He had guessed at the outset that Ivy was Lady Olivia Fairfax. Unlikely as it seemed, he had *suspected* it, and he had been right. If only she hadn't answered to that common-sounding name—a servant's name, by the rood!—a name which bore no conceivable relationship to her Christian name!

Well, there was no use belaboring the point. She had answered to it, whatever the reason, and his goose was well and thoroughly cooked.

He mentally reviewed the morning he had spent with "Ivy," and felt himself turning pale. He had told her with his own lips that he was hunting Lady Olivia for her fortune. What the devil had made him confide such a thing? To anyone, let alone a wench he had barely met! It was completely unlike him to blurt out his business so carelessly. He had to grit his teeth to keep from groaning aloud as he marveled at his own colossal stupidity.

When he thought of the sheer waste of time—precious weeks spent in carefully courting Aloysius Beebe, of all people—playing cribbage, a game he loathed, while fawning and smiling and angling for an introduction to Lady Olivia—faugh! It was sickening! To have come this close to success and then lose all, with no one to blame but himself—incredible! He deserved to lose. For once in his life, he had played his hand with spectacular clumsiness. *And wouldn't you know it,* he thought bitterly, *that the one time I make a misstep,* everything *would be riding on the outcome.*

He glanced across the room to where she sat, providing him an excellent view of her elegant profile. She was pretending to listen to the solicitor's reading, but George was not deceived by her air of feigned interest. She was every bit as aware of him as he was of her. Damn, damn, damn. He had finally met an heiress who was interesting *and* attractive, and had promptly annihilated whatever chance he might have had to win her.

He forced himself to appear calm, to show not a glimmer of his fury and humiliation. He knew he must bid farewell to his pursuit of Lady Olivia—and to his secret dreams of Ivy—but something good might yet come of this disaster. Had he not been hunting this particular prey, he never would have befriended Beebe. And, he reminded himself, befriending Beebe had put him in the will.

By the time George bent his attention to the actual words of the will, the bulk of the provisions had been read. The long list of bequests to the Fairfax School, with the elaborate and precise numeration of various articles, funds, and holdings, was nearly at an end. Next was a small pension for Grimsby, with instructions for how it was to be paid—quarterly—and from what fund. And then, at last, George heard his own name.

"To George Carstairs, Baron Rival." The solicitor coughed and looked up, meeting George's eyes with an apprehensive, almost apologetic expression before continuing. "My beloved pet, Tom, a black-and-white feline, together with his effects, to wit: one pillow cushion, red; one covered basket with handles, yellow straw; porcelain bowl with painted flowers . . ."

A cat. That was the reason he had been summoned here to endure this mortification: He had inherited a bloody *cat*. He hated cats.

George was sure, now, that he had strayed into the realm of nightmare. He did not need the will's final paragraphs to confirm it, but confirm it they did. Incredibly, his morning deteriorated still further.

The solicitor cast a nervous glance first at Lord Rival and then at Lady Olivia, settled his spectacles more firmly on his nose, took a deep breath, and hurriedly read through a set of provisions so fantastical, so outrageous, it was difficult to believe they were still listening to Mr. Beebe's prosaic will. George had been left an annuity after all—a generous, almost staggering annuity of eight hundred pounds per annum—but there were strings attached. He would receive these funds at the sole discretion of Lady Olivia Fairfax, contingent upon his satisfactorily performing, in whatever capacity she deemed appropriate, some function or functions useful or necessary to the Helen Fairfax School for Girls.

George discovered that, at some point during the reading of these fearsome paragraphs, he had risen to his feet. By the end of them he was certainly standing, and so was Lady Olivia. She was clutching the back of the chair ahead of her and leaning forward in a sort of frenzy of disbelief.

"This cannot be!" she exclaimed. "It is—it must be!—some sort of joke."

The solicitor clutched the papers more firmly, as if afraid she would tear them from his hands. She did, in fact, look as if she were about to do just that. "I beg your pardon, madam," he said hastily, "but Mr. Beebe was quite adamant upon this point. Quite taken with the idea, in fact. I could not dissuade him, or convince him that you ought to be consulted before he placed you in such a comprom—that is, before he forced you into close association with a—" he rolled his eyes nervously in the direction of Lord Rival. The expression on George's face must have been terrifying to behold, for the solicitor blanched and removed his spectacles. "Regrettable, most regrettable! But perfectly legal, I'm afraid. I daresay the bequest seems a bit whimsical—"

George uttered a crack of mirthless laughter. The solicitor flinched, but went bravely on. "—so perhaps I should explain that Mr. Beebe was in the habit of frequently altering his will. One might almost say he altered it *regularly*. And always to reflect some fanciful notion that he later would revise or discard. Bless my soul! I never dreamed that this particular document would prove to be final. Had I any inkling that so little time remained to my client, I might have tried more vigorously to—well! That is all water under the bridge."

"Let me be sure I understand you," said George pleasantly. "My friend Beebe has left me a tidy little income, but my actual receipt of it is wholly dependent upon the whim of Lady Olivia Fairfax. Absent her goodwill, I shall receive none of it."

The pleasant tone apparently did not deceive the solicitor. He looked frightened, and began furiously polishing his spectacles with his handkerchief to avoid meeting George's eyes. "Well, yes, I suppose one could put it that way. Lady Olivia is, naturally, a reasonable person, and so long as everyone acts in good faith I do not foresee any difficulty about—of course, should some dispute arise regarding the bequest, I would be happy to—"

"May I decline it?"

The solicitor looked startled. "Decline it? Gracious. I—I don't know quite what would happen if—" He returned his spectacles to his nose and began hurriedly shuffling through his papers. "Let me see. I don't believe that contingency was provided for, per se. One tries to anticipate—one attempts to cover every possible—hum! It did not occur to us, actually, that you might not wish to receive—"

"Let me put it this way. What will happen to my annuity if Lady Olivia, in her infinite wisdom, decrees that I have *not* proved sufficiently useful to the Fairfax School?"

"The monies would stay in the fund if they were not disbursed to you. So the Fairfax School would have the use of them, I suppose."

George could no longer keep the angry edge from his voice. "In that case, clearly the most useful thing I can do for the school is repudiate the bequest and decline the annuity. And I do so. Here and now."

He was suddenly aware that they had an audience. The three crowlike women from the school were hanging on his every word with breathless avidity, and even Grimsby—scowling with resentment that George's phantom annuity was larger than the pension Beebe had left him—was leaning forward with one hand cupped to his ear. This unexpected bit of drama had added a bit of excitement to the otherwise dull morning.

George's mouth twisted in sardonic amusement. It was always good to have an audience when making a grand gesture. And that was all he was doing—making a grand, but meaningless, gesture. So long as a woman he had insulted held the reins, he would never see a penny of Beebe's money. He might as well pretend he didn't want it and keep what remained of his dignity.

The solicitor looked perplexed. "Well, milord, I am not entirely sure you can do this. Really, it is most irregular."

George attempted an austere expression. "If Aloysius intended to leave his money to charity, let him do so. I'm sure the Fairfax School is a worthier cause than I." He drew himself upright and folded his arms nobly across his chest.

A clear alto voice broke into this theatrical moment. "Very affecting," said Lady Olivia, in a no-nonsense tone that demonstrated how little she had been affected. "But you are being a trifle hasty, Lord Rival, are you not? We must not let our emotions get the better of our judgment."

He rounded on her, but controlled his angry impulse when he saw that she was not sneering at him. She was a little pale, but had mastered her initial reaction to the news. Her gaze met his levelly, and she looked perfectly serious. "I suggest we do nothing today, but wait until we have thoroughly studied the language these paragraphs contain. This arrangement is no more welcome to me than it is to you, Lord Rival, but it may be that some alternative will present itself. A loophole may appear."

The solicitor puffed his cheeks with annoyance. "The language is clear and concise, I assure you," he said testily. "The bequest is airtight, madam, and not open to interpretation."

"I beg your pardon." Her quick smile smoothed the solicitor's ruffled feathers. "I am sure you drafted it most skillfully. It would oblige me very much, however, if you would allow my personal solicitor to view it. Mr. Culpepper?" She turned to the elderly man whom George had taken for a banker. "Would you be so good?"

Culpepper bowed and approached the desk. Beebe's solicitor rather grudgingly made room for him, and the two men bent their heads over the document. Lady Olivia then turned to the room's other occupants. "I believe we have completed this morning's business," she announced, calmly usurping whatever authority Mr. Beebe's solicitor had to dismiss the gathering. "Thank you all for coming." Her natural air of command was so impressive that George was not surprised when the three charity women obediently rose and departed, Grimsby grumbling in their wake.

Bessie Fairfax remained, glaring ferociously at George. She had clearly taken a disliking to him. But his attention was caught by Lady Olivia, who was approaching him, hesitant but resolute. As he looked into her eyes the rest of the room receded. The murmuring of the two solicitors dwindled to less than the droning of a fly, and Miss Fairfax's disapproving gaze seemed miles away. An instant intimacy seemed to surround George and Olivia, as if the meeting of their eyes closed off the rest of the world. All they had done was look at each other, but it felt eerily as if they had sneaked out of the room together. She seemed to feel it, too. Her cheeks turned faintly pink, as if she were doing something wrong.

She stopped while still at a discreet distance from him, but an invisible pull seemed to emanate from her slender form. He was acutely aware of her nearness. God in Heaven, had he ever felt so drawn to a woman before? Not even Clarissa, back in his salad days, had had this effect on his senses.

She spoke softly, but he heard every word. "This is a judgment on us, I suppose." She was definitely blushing now. She dropped her eyes and clasped her hands nervously before her, like a schoolgirl ill-prepared to recite her lesson. "For my part, sir, I am sorry for the . . . the misunderstanding that arose between us when . . . when first we met."

Not as sorry as I am, thought George bitterly. It was difficult to contain the agonized rage sweeping through him; Lady Olivia was all that he had hoped she would be—and more—but his own blundering had placed the prize out of reach. Worse, Aloysius Beebe had presented him with the perfect scenario for a successful wooing. Had he kept his mouth shut, he would even now be on the road to a cozy partnership with her, working together on her favorite hobbyhorse, the Fairfax School. It made him sick to think of it; a golden opportunity shattered by his own stupendous folly.

She paused, probably expecting him to chime in with his own apology. He was too occupied in gritting his teeth to speak. When he said nothing, she glanced uncertainly at his face, then looked back down at the carpet, her blush intensifying.

"I feel I owe you an explanation. You see, when you took me for a housemaid I was so mortified that I . . . well, I felt I would rather die than reveal to you that I *wasn't* a housemaid. I had thought to turn you away at the door, you know. But then you came in the house and . . . and I had to continue the impersonation rather longer than I had planned." Her cheeks were scarlet. "And even then, I believed no harm had been done because . . . I thought I would never see you again. When I learned you would be present at the reading today, you cannot imagine how I felt. I . . ."

Her voice trailed off. She paused again, obviously deeply embarrassed, and still silently begging him to say something. It was downright painful.

He smiled at her, masking his chagrin with flipness. "Is it my turn to apologize? Is that what you are waiting for? You'll have a long wait, my girl. I never bother with remorse." His shoulders shook with warped amusement. "I'll accept your apology, however."

She lifted startled eyes to his, her blush fading in affronted surprise. "Oh, you will, will you? How excessively kind!"

"Yes. I'm a forgiving chap." He felt his forced smile relaxing into a genuine grin as she transformed before his eyes into the tart-tongued lass he remembered. "What's the matter? Would you rather I *not* accept your apology?"

She delighted him by ruffling up immediately. "That's nothing but cheek, my lord, since you have far more to apologize for than I!"

"Well, I'll tell you a secret. If I apologized for each of my transgressions, I would spend so much time groveling that I'd have no time left for sinning. Can't have that." He winked. "I enjoy the sinning too much."

"I don't doubt it," she said crossly.

He leaned toward her, bringing his face as close as he dared in such a public place. "I'll tell you another secret," he said softly. "You'd enjoy the sinning, too."

Her lips parted in shock. His gaze flicked down to her mouth. He wished he could kiss her again, just once, before she walked out of his life. With an effort, he returned his gaze to her eyes and saw, God help him, that she not only knew what he was thinking— she was thinking it, too. That was desire he read in those extraordinary eyes of hers. Seeing it kindled the hottest rush of pure lust he had felt in years. If they were alone, by heaven, he'd . . . but they weren't. They weren't alone. It was foolish to torture himself by picturing things that could not be.

Did she know how transparent she was? Probably not. She looked confused and frightened. And angry. He burned with wanting her, but knew that whatever she felt, she would force herself to withdraw. Sure enough, she took a step backward, stiffening in denial—denial of him, of his desire and of her own.

"You are insolent," she said, but her voice sounded choked and faint. "I will not bandy words with you, my lord—"

"Too late."

"—I will only say that if you feel *you* need not apologize, I most assuredly feel that *I* need not!"

"Oh, I didn't say I *shouldn't* apologize," he explained. "I merely said I wouldn't."

"Then neither will I, for at least I meant well," she

declared indignantly, recovering her aplomb. "Whereas *you,* my lord, intended nothing but mischief from the start! Hoaxing poor Mr. Beebe into thinking you were his friend—scheming to seduce an innocent woman and take her money—why, the whole purpose of your visit was wickedness, pure and simple!"

"Wickedness is never pure. And, come to think of it, it's rarely simple."

"Really? How interesting." Her eyes flashed. "I shall take your word for it, my lord—since wickedness is your area of expertise."

He chuckled. "Very wise. A novice should always defer to an expert. Now, let me see . . . how shall I put my expertise to work for the Fairfax School? I daresay you have a crying need for an infusion of wickedness. Well, I am just the man to provide it. Eight hundred pounds per annum ought to buy you quite a healthy supply."

She tapped her foot, fuming. "You jest, sir, but we find ourselves in a most unpalatable situation."

He pretended to misunderstand. "What, the school?"

"No! You and I. This is perfectly dreadful." She suddenly looked despairing. "I had hoped never to see you again, and now—now I must."

He knew she would feel that way, of course. He jammed his hands into his pockets, furious with himself for feeling a pang at her rejection. "You forget," he said tightly. "I have declined the bequest. All joking aside, I will have naught to do with your precious school. Your sufferings will soon be over, madam. We are having our last conversation."

She looked up at that, her brows knitting. "But why? Why decline it? Your need for funds must be desperate, or you would not be seeking to marry money."

He almost winced at her bluntness. "I will never be desperate enough to place myself under *your* pretty thumb," he snapped, goaded. "Do not pretend that you would actually let me have the annuity! Only a saint could resist such a perfect chance to punish me." His teeth flashed in a sardonic grin. "And you, madam, are no saint."

An angry flush heated her cheeks. "How dare you? Sainthood has nothing to do with it. I would let you have the annuity if you earned it. Why wouldn't I?"

He sketched an ironic bow. "Oh, excellent! I applaud you. You would let me have the annuity *if I earned it.* And what task would you set me, my lady? How might I earn my eight hundred pounds? Heaving coal? Emptying slop buckets? Put your mind to it, madam—I must perform at your command! And then, after all, no matter what I do, you will be within your rights to say that it is not enough and deny me the funds."

Her expression had changed from bewilderment to scorn. "I see," she said at last. "You are not trying to be noble. You are declining the bequest only because you believe you will not receive it in any event."

"Precisely." His teeth flashed in another sardonic grin. "I am devastated, of course, that you have discerned my ignoble motive, but you are quite right. I seek not to bestow an additional gift upon your worthy charity, but to save my sorry hide from further humiliation. I have suffered the sting of mortification for several hours now. I find I have no stomach for a year's worth."

The bewilderment had returned to her face. "But I have no wish to humiliate you, or unfairly withhold your money. That would be shabby treatment, would it not?"

"Indeed it would," he said promptly. "But, being only human, you doubtless feel that shabby treatment is exactly what I deserve. You may be right, my dear, but I feel disinclined to stay and receive it."

Her brows snapped together. "I understand you now!" she exclaimed hotly. "You think I want revenge. How dare you ascribe such pettiness to me? Really, I don't know whether to laugh at you or—or box your ears!"

She seemed genuinely perturbed. He stared at her, startled. Had he blundered again? Was it possible he had misjudged her? Surely no woman could resist this heaven-sent opportunity to grind her slipper in the face of a man who had cold-bloodedly plotted to enrich himself at her expense. It was preposterous. No one could be that charitable.

Charitable. Good God. If any one word described Lady Olivia Fairfax, surely *charitable* was it.

He took a deep breath, feeling oddly shaken. "My dear girl—"

"I am not a girl!"

"Stow it!" he ordered, taking her sternly by the shoulders. His eyes searched hers keenly, and saw no guile in their depths. Only righteous indignation. "You must be angry with me, whether you admit it or no. Would you really have no objection to my presence at the Fairfax School?"

Caution flicked across her features. "Oh, well, I—I don't know—I daresay some of the older girls may be a bit impressionable—"

"I've no interest in schoolgirls!" he interrupted her. "I am asking if *you* would object to my presence. Surely you would! You're an intelligent woman."

Her cheeks were turning pink again. She dropped her eyes. "Mr. Beebe clearly meant for you to help us in some way. After everything he has done for the school, I shouldn't care to thwart his last wishes."

"Rubbish."

"No, it's not," she insisted, but she still did not meet his eyes. "It's simply a matter of finding an appropriate position for you to occupy. If we put our minds to it—"

"That's not my question," he said roughly, his hands tightening on her arms. "Any connection to the Fairfax School will let me in your life. How can you agree to that? How can you allow me anywhere near you? I think the answer is obvious. You can't."

He saw Miss Fairfax rise from her chair and almost fancied he could hear a low growl coming from her throat, like a pug who sees its favorite bone being sniffed by a stranger. He dropped his hands from Lady Olivia's shoulders, inwardly cursing. "We are in too public a place for this conversation," he said shortly.

She turned and caught Miss Fairfax's eye, giving her a tiny signal with her hand. Miss Fairfax, still rigid with disapproval, retreated. Olivia turned back to him then, her face troubled.

"What you are saying is true," she said in a low tone. "My reputation is valuable to me. I would greatly dislike it if my association with you were to . . . tarnish it."

She still did not understand! It was maddening. Did he have to say it out loud?

"Hang your reputation!" he exclaimed impatiently. "Don't you remember what I told you? I am a fortune hunter, Lady Olivia—the lowest form of life." He leaned closer, lowering his voice to an urgent undertone. "If you had not tricked the truth out of me, I promise you you never would have guessed it. I would have done everything I could to steal your affections. I would have driven you into such a state that you would ignore all the warnings and pleadings of your family and friends. You would have given your heart to me, believing that I loved you. And I would have dragged you to the altar—to marry not you, but your bank accounts. How can you not want revenge for that?"

Her eyes met his. She looked perfectly serene. "It is very bad," she agreed placidly. "But I am not a vengeful person."

He raked his hand through his hair, exasperated. Hang the chit! Why was he explaining it to her? Nothing worse than an honest rogue! But he *liked* her. That was the difficulty. He liked her too well to prevaricate.

He sighed. "So if I accept this ridiculous bequest, you will let me have it?"

"Certainly."

"Even though you know I am a villain?"

He suddenly recognized sadness in the depths of those serene gray eyes. The corners of her mouth lifted in a tiny, worldly wise smile.

"My dear Lord Rival," she said, gentle amusement lurking in her voice, "if I shunned everyone who found my money interesting, I would have no friends at all."

6

"*Twenty minutes* you spent off in that corner with him. Twenty minutes, by the clock."

Olivia bit her lip, but could not keep the twinkle from her eyes. "Pray do not scold me, Bessie," she coaxed. "I'm sorry if I worried you yesterday. But, really, what harm could he do in a solicitor's office? Forgive me, but this fretting strikes me as absurd."

"I know you, Ivy," said Bessie grimly. She pointed an accusing finger at her cousin, who was turning her head this way and that, smiling dreamily at her reflection in her dressing table mirror. "You're brewing mischief, and that's a fact. You flew into high fidgets when Culpepper told you Lord Rival would be present at the reading, but I thought nothing of it at the time. Any respectable female might be apprehensive about finding herself in the company of that—that *libertine*. But I knew something was up when you rushed out to buy a new hat for the occasion! When did you ever care for fashion?"

"Pooh! I thought you would be pleased. You have lectured me for years about dwindling into a dowd. What say you to this?" Olivia turned to show Bessie the effect of twisting her dark locks into a shining coil at the top of her head. "Do you think it becomes me?"

"Everything becomes you," said Bessie gruffly. Her

sharp eyes were full of worry. "Ivy, pray be careful! You know little of men and their wiles."

Olivia laughed out loud. "And you know more, I suppose?" She shook her head, her eyes dancing with mischief. "I mean to enjoy myself, and flirt with a handsome man before I grow too old. And that is all."

"What you mean to do and what *he* means to do may be two different things! You are too inexperienced and too innocent to prevail against that devil."

Olivia waved an airy hand. "You are not a judge of such matters, Bessie. You have always disliked and mistrusted men. The Fairfax influence! We have some nasty specimens in our family, but most men are decent enough." She chuckled. "Not Lord Rival, of course. You're right that he's a devil, but he's an entertaining devil." She lifted a strand of pearls from her jewel box and held them up to her throat, still considering her reflection. "These are very fine. Have I ever worn them? I think not. What a waste."

"You're frightening me," Bessie declared, watching worriedly as Olivia, humming a tune, set the pearls to one side and began rummaging through her jewel box for more baubles. "You've never expressed the slightest interest in flirting with a man, handsome or otherwise! What's come over you?"

"Why, nothing in the world. It seems to me that something odd has come over *you*, for I never saw you made uneasy by so trifling a cause. Surely I am past the age where I must be chaperoned every time I speak to a man! We conversed for a few minutes only, and never left your sight. Where's the harm in that?"

"He touched you!" exclaimed Bessie, as if suddenly remembering the root of her suspicions. "And when he first saw you, he called you *Ivy*. I heard him! Where did he learn that?"

Olivia felt a telltale blush creeping up her neck. She

hastily dropped her jewels back in the box and bent to retie her slipper, hoping to hide her pink cheeks from Bessie's sharp eyes. "Who knows?" she said, with a rather unconvincing laugh. "He must have heard you use it. You do call me Ivy in public from time to time." She sat up, inwardly congratulating herself for passing this off so well. But then she saw Bessie's troubled face in the mirror and immediately felt guilty.

Bessie's face seemed to crumple. "Olivia, for pity's sake! Guard your heart, I beseech you."

Olivia was astonished to see that tears were actually welling in her cousin's eyes. With an exclamation of remorse, she rose and went to embrace her loyal companion. "Oh, Bessie, I am sorry," she said ruefully. "I don't want to keep secrets from you. I just wish you trusted my judgment a little more. I am not completely hen-witted, you know, and I am no longer a green girl."

"Yes, you are," said Bessie fiercely. She gave a defiant sniff and pulled away from Olivia, hunting in her pocket for a handkerchief. "You are entirely too trusting. You believe everyone is good at heart and all's right with the world. But not everyone *is* good at heart, Olivia, and there is much that is wrong with the world." She dabbed at her eyes and sniffed again.

"I know it," said Olivia quietly. "Believe me, Bessie, I have no illusions about Lord Rival. Do you remember Captain Hatfield, the summer I turned eighteen?"

"Who could forget?" exclaimed Bessie. "I thought you would never recover."

"Yes, but I did," said Olivia firmly. "It was the hardest lesson I have ever learned, but I learned it well. Lord Rival is just such another: all charm and no principles! I won't give my heart to a fortune hunter again. Once is enough for that mistake."

"A fortune hunter." Bessie's eyes went round with horror. "Well! I've heard any number of scandalous tales about the man, but I never heard *that*."

Olivia instantly regretted her remark. "I may be mistaken on that point," she said lightly, crossing to the wardrobe to survey her gowns. "But those who do not learn from history are doomed to repeat it, you know! I have formed a habit of assuming that any man who shows an interest in me is dazzled by my purse." She pulled out a modest morning dress of jaconet muslin and inspected it, frowning. "Is this the best I have? Why, in heaven's name, don't I own anything *pretty*? I can't bear it. I'm going to London this very afternoon. Do you care to come with me?"

"You should take Edith. She's pining for an outing."

"Very well. She'll have to be veiled, of course, for one never knows—it would be dreadful if she were recognized on Bond Street, and in my company! We'd have Ralph on us within the week." She sighed, and held up the muslin again. "In the meantime, I shall have to make do with this." She tossed Bessie a mischievous smile. "Lord Rival may arrive at any moment."

She was hiding a pleasant bubble of anticipation when she walked placidly down the stairs and into her parlor. It wouldn't do to show it, of course, but really, Lord Rival's presence in her house would be quite exciting. Something about the man made her feel so . . . *alive*. She would meet with Culpepper first, but Rival would soon join them to discuss the terms of Mr. Beebe's bequest. It would be difficult to listen to dear old Culpepper while expecting Lord Rival to walk in, she thought, smiling a little.

As she entered the parlor, however, she checked on the threshold. Culpepper was nowhere to be seen, but to her consternation, Lord Rival was already present.

He rose and bowed, an appreciative gleam in his eyes as his gaze traveled lazily over her.

Olivia was acutely aware that they were alone together. Merciful heavens, the man was handsome! He seemed to fill the tiny room, towering over her in a way that made her feel . . . peculiar.

"Where is Mr. Culpepper?" she asked faintly.

He grinned. "Every time we see each other, one or the other of us is expecting someone else. I haven't seen Mr. Culpepper. Was I not announced?"

"No." She felt herself blushing. "I came down because I thought Culpepper was waiting for me; he is almost always early for our appointments. Oh, I beg your pardon! How do you do? May I send for some . . . tea, perhaps?" She took one step over the threshold, but halted again, as nervous as if the room contained a wasp.

"I am not usually a tea drinker, but I think I would be glad of it this morning." His expression darkened. "I am by no means reconciled to this infamous annuity. By the end of the morning I may be ready to hand *both* my bequests over to the Fairfax School."

She had to think for a moment before she understood him. "Surely you don't wish to give us your cat, do you? My dear sir, it would be cruel! Tom is accustomed to a bachelor household."

"That animal's convenience has already been too much considered, in my estimation," he said tartly. "Friend Beebe has much to answer for! I hope, wherever he is, he is paying dearly for the tribulations he has inflicted on me. I barely slept a wink last night."

"Oh, dear." She ventured a few more steps into the room and tugged on the bellrope. "Did poor Tom keep you awake?"

"Poor Tom? Poor George, you should say! The infernal creature refused to leave my side. First I had to carry the brute through the streets of Mayfair in a covered basket, a journey that he enlivened by setting up such a din as I hope never to hear again this side of hell. We entertained half of London en route from Beebe's home to my own. Had I been able to sell tickets, I might have made my fortune then and there. Thank God the majority of my acquaintance is out of town! I would have never lived it down, had any of them witnessed the spectacle."

She looked reproachfully at him. "What was uncomfortable for you, my lord, must have been painful indeed for the cat. Only think how frightening, to be removed from one's home and shut in a basket! I sincerely pity him."

"Tom's sufferings were as nothing, compared to my own," Lord Rival informed her with asperity. "The instant I let him out of the basket, he ceased howling and attached himself to my person—with every indication of satisfaction, I might add. Made himself completely at home in the twinkling of a bedpost. You'd never know he had lived anywhere else."

"But this is wonderful! He must have an affectionate disposition."

Lord Rival looked disgusted. "Oppressively affectionate! I attempted to eject him from my bedchamber last night, and he pounded his furry feet against the door until I opened it. I put him out the window, and he wept uncontrollably. Since I value my neighbors' goodwill, I was forced to allow him back in. He lay on the foot of my bed until morning—and deuced crowded I found it! A nasty, sneaking *cat*! Every time I fell asleep, he purred at the top of his lungs and pummeled me with his paws."

"Do you dislike cats?" asked Olivia, dismayed.

"Excessively! They are sly, promiscuous creatures with not a loyal bone in their bodies. No morals whatsoever. You should see the way this Tom toad-eats me! Utterly shameless. He falls at my feet and looks at me with these great, cow eyes—flirting with me! Ha! He knows I hold the creampot."

Olivia lifted an eyebrow. "He sounds an excellent choice of pet for you," she said demurely. "You have so much in common."

The tea arrived at this propitious moment, so Olivia escaped what would doubtless have been a wrathful reply to this sally. Culpepper hurried into the room directly behind the tea tray, apologizing profusely for his tardiness. They all drank tea and Culpepper delivered his report on the pertinent provisions of Mr. Beebe's will.

Neither Olivia nor Lord Rival were able to finish their tea. Both cups were soon set down, forgotten, as they listened in growing vexation to what their supposed friend had inflicted upon them. Culpepper, in his dry, fussy way, outlined the basic terms of the bequest and regretfully informed them that, in his educated opinion, the paragraphs had been very well drawn and there was no easily identifiable escape from their requirements. Lord Rival must perform some useful function, either on the premises of the Fairfax School or elsewhere on the school's behalf, and his actions must directly benefit the school. So long as he did so, the annuity was his, paid quarterly. But it was Lady Olivia's responsibility to decree what task or function he must perform, to oversee the performance, and to pass judgment upon whether or not he had performed satisfactorily. Worse, this responsibility was ongoing, because the funds would not be released on any quarter day wherein she did not deem he had fulfilled his part of the bargain. Absent her express approval, the funds would revert to the school.

By the end of his report, Olivia was tapping her foot in irritation and Lord Rival looked black as a thundercloud. She had completely forgotten her earlier nervousness and her fear that it would be difficult to concentrate on Culpepper's words with Lord Rival in the room. It was impossible *not* to concentrate on a problem of this magnitude.

"But this is intolerable!" Olivia exclaimed at last.

"Am I to *supervise* Lord Rival? I haven't time for such nonsense!"

"I am sorry, my lady, but those are the terms."

A muscle was jumping in Lord Rival's jaw. "She hasn't the time, and I haven't the temperament. Tell me, would I be an *employee* of the Fairfax School?" His voice was filled with repugnance.

"Well, no, not an employee," said Culpepper, placing his fingertips together very precisely. "You would not even be an employee of Lady Olivia. Not in a legal sense. Although it appears the relationship would be quite similar."

Lord Rival spoke through his teeth. "I would dislike that. Extremely."

"So would I!" said Olivia swiftly. "But there must be a solution. There *must* be." She rose and took a hasty turn about the room, then halted, snapping her fingers. "I have it. We shall simply draw up an agreement—a statement for me to sign, perhaps—guaranteeing Lord Rival his annuity. I shall give my approval for the disbursements in advance, and in perpetuity."

Culpepper looked very severe. "No. You cannot. Such an arrangement would violate the clear intent of the will."

"Very well, let's try another." Her chin jutted with determination. "May I delegate my authority to some proxy?"

"Perhaps," said Culpepper cautiously. "Under certain circumstances."

"Excellent," she said triumphantly. "I shall delegate the authority to Lord Rival. Let *him* decide whether or not he has earned his ridiculous annuity!"

Culpepper clucked his tongue with disapproval. "No, no, no! Utterly unacceptable. My dear Lady Olivia, I beg you to take this matter a trifle more seriously. These wild ideas of yours are serving no useful purpose. Pray be seated, and let us contrive a little."

She flung herself crossly back into her chair. "I say we let the annuity stand untouched. If I cannot decree that he has earned it in perpetuity, let me decree that he has never earned it, and never can. Let the funds revert back to the school. No, pray, hear me out! In their place, we could draw up an agreement here, this morning, for the school to simply pay Lord Rival eight hundred pounds per annum on the same terms *as if* he were earning it."

Lord Rival looked incredulous. "What, pay me for nothing? Why would you do such a harebrained thing?"

Olivia rolled her eyes, exasperated. "Well, for heaven's sake, it's only eight hundred pounds! Let me take it out of my own purse, Culpepper. The time I would spend in supervising all this folderol is worth more to me than that."

Culpepper looked pained. A rather ugly expression descended upon Lord Rival's face. "I congratulate you, my lady," he drawled. "Eight hundred pounds is not mere pocket change to most mortals."

She flushed, realizing she had been far too frank. It had almost sounded as if she were bragging about her wealth. "I beg your pardon," she said stiffly. "I did not mean to say anything so—vulgar."

Lord Rival's eyes gleamed. "Never mind. The provocation was extreme. I'm ready to say something vulgar myself."

Culpepper folded his lips primly. "Pray let us return to the subject at hand," he said austerely. "Before we begin, I believe it would be useful to determine what sort of occupation, or function, might best suit his lordship." He picked up a quill and looked expectantly at Lord Rival.

Lord Rival's brows shot up. "Are you asking me?"

he inquired politely. "I thought my occupation was to be left entirely to Lady Olivia's discretion."

Olivia frowned. "Don't be absurd. I barely know you. How am I to guess where your talents lie?"

His teeth flashed in a wolfish smile. "All the world knows where my talents lie."

Culpepper looked puzzled, but hopeful. "Then you do excel at something, my lord?"

"Oh, yes."

"What is it?"

Lord Rival's eyes flicked toward Olivia. She gave a tiny gasp and closed her eyes, praying that he would not say—

"Piquet."

Olivia opened her eyes and breathed a little easier. Still, it was an outrageous answer. Culpepper looked completely taken aback.

"Did you say *piquet,* my lord?"

"I did."

"Well. Well, well, well. Piquet." Culpepper scratched his ear distractedly. "Really, my lord, I don't think the young ladies need to be taught piquet. Have you any other skills?"

"Well, I am generally held to be an excellent shot. And I have a certain reputation in the boxing ring."

Olivia had to bite her lip to keep her countenance. Culpepper looked visibly dismayed. "Pistols, my lord? And *fisticuffs*?"

"Perhaps he could patrol the grounds at night," she suggested, her voice quivering.

Lord Rival shot her an amused glance. "Most evenings, I am otherwise engaged," he said apologetically.

She choked. "Playing piquet."

"Exactly."

"Come now, come now," said Culpepper testily. "There must something else you can do."

Lord Rival assumed a modest demeanor. "There are those who admire my dancing," he offered.

Culpepper brightened. "Ah. Dancing." The quill sputtered across the page.

Olivia shook her head. "Worthless. These are orphans, not debutantes."

Lord Rival's face fell ludicrously. "May I not teach the girls to dance?" he asked plaintively. "I'm told my waltzing is divine."

Olivia lifted one eyebrow at him. "Really? I've heard it's not as good as your piquet."

"Yes, but my piquet game is truly extraordinary," he told her earnestly. Olivia had to stifle a laugh behind her hand.

Culpepper tapped the edge of the quill against his chin. "Hm. I suppose there would be very little dancing required of these girls. Most of them will be apprenticed in some trade or other. They will become milliners and pastry cooks and things of that nature."

Lord Rival looked regretful. "Alas, I am a poor hand at trimming hats. Or rolling dough, for that matter."

"I daresay you haven't practiced sufficiently," Olivia suggested brightly. "Who knows, my lord? Untapped genius may lie beneath your useless exterior."

He looked perfectly grave, but she saw that his eyes were laughing. "Nevertheless, I think it would save time if we focused on my *tapped* genius."

"What's the point of that? You seem to have developed a set of skills that are of no earthly use to anyone."

One of his brows shot up. One corner of his mouth twisted slyly down. For an instant, he looked pointedly at her mouth. By the time his gaze flicked back to meet hers, she could feel a blush creeping up her neck.

"Would you say that *all* my skills are useless?" he asked blandly. "How disappointing."

Olivia's pertness deserted her. She dropped her eyes in confusion and stammered, "Certainly the—the skills you have enumerated this morning are somewhat— somewhat frivolous, my lord."

"I see. Well, I haven't listed *all* my skills." He crossed one leg negligently over the other. "I wonder what gifts I possess that a set of young ladies might find valuable," he mused, evidently pondering the question.

Olivia gasped. Her frightened eyes darted to Culpepper, but the solicitor looked merely attentive. She tried very hard to catch Lord Rival's eye, but he was now gazing soulfully at the ceiling.

"I've never been especially good with children," he began, "but once a girl reaches a certain age—"

"My lord!" she interrupted desperately.

He glanced back at her, cocking his head inquiringly and waiting with apparent politeness for her to finish her sentence. She had only spoken in an attempt to stop him from saying something outrageous, however, and couldn't think of another word to follow her outburst.

Fortunately Culpepper intervened, saying genially, "I, myself, never know what to say to a very young child. Ahem! I am sure Lady Olivia does not mean to denigrate your talents, my lord. But I must agree with her that the pursuits of a man of fashion are neither suitable, nor practical, for young females of the lower social orders."

"Most of them are unsuitable for females of any order, young or otherwise," Olivia agreed, recovering her tongue. "After listening to his catalogue of skills, I am ready to pay Lord Rival to *stay away* from the Fairfax School."

"Now, now," said Culpepper indulgently. "We have already agreed that such a course is not possible." He began leafing through his pages of notes. "Although, I must say—with infinite regret—that it appears educating orphaned females is not really your milieu, my lord."

Under cover of Culpepper's paper shuffling, Olivia relieved some of her feelings by directing a glare at Lord Rival. He leaned in to her, his eyes alight with laughter.

"He's mistaken, you know," he told her, sotto voce. "I've educated many an orphaned female." His teeth flashed in another of his impudent grins. "Your own parents are deceased, are they not? I would be delighted to offer you my tutelage. Who knows? You could become my star pupil."

"Shameless!" she choked. "Will you *please* behave? There is nothing you can teach me—that is, there is nothing more I wish to learn! I mean—"

"Careful, Ivy," he murmured provocatively. "Don't throw away the chance of a lifetime. Your education seems, to me, to be lacking in certain areas. And here you have one of England's foremost authorities, more than willing to share his knowledge with you."

She shot Lord Rival a darkling glance, blushing hotly, and saw that his shoulders were shaking with laughter.

Culpepper looked up. "Did you say something, my lord?"

Lord Rival smiled. "Lady Olivia and I have merely reopened our discussion of—untapped genius. Especially as it relates to female education."

"Ah."

He leaned lazily back in his chair. "Females are often resistant to learning new skills, are they not? And yet I daresay it's the same for a woman as it is for a man; an activity that may not have appealed to her at all can become quite an obsession, once a lady discovers that she has a . . ." His smile widened. "A natural aptitude."

Olivia spluttered wordlessly, but Culpepper gave his lordship an approving nod. "That may be true, my lord. Within the limitations of her female nature, of course."

"Of course." Lord Rival shot Olivia another glance filled with suppressed laughter. "I was about to describe for Lady Olivia the benefits of diligent instruction, with frequent repetition, to truly hone a skill."

Culpepper beamed. "Yes, milord. Practice makes perfect."

Lord Rival inclined his head in courteous acknowledgment of this platitude. "Precisely. Especially, I believe, when the novice receives expert guidance. A skillful and gifted teacher can inspire true enthusiasm in the pupil, and it is enthusiasm which brings out the student's full potential."

His gaze, still brimming with devilment, briefly locked with Olivia's and heat shocked through her like a lightning strike. She was forced to acknowledge that diligent instruction from Lord Rival would definitely awaken a certain . . . enthusiasm . . . in this particular student.

Culpepper appeared impressed. "I did not know you were an educator, my lord."

Lord Rival shrugged modestly. "I have been known to dabble. Like any man, I daresay, I have a few, ah, pet theories."

7

*I*t was inevitable, he supposed, that the morning would end with a suggestion that Lord Rival tour the Fairfax School. A month ago he would have declined such an invitation with alacrity. Even vehemence. Odd, the twistings of fate!

He still had no interest whatsoever in Lady Olivia's charity, but he had a keen and growing interest in Lady Olivia. It was child's play to maneuver her into giving him a private tour. When Culpepper declared that he was at Lord Rival's disposal on any morning save tomorrow, all George had to do was regretfully (and mendaciously) claim that tomorrow was the only morning on which he could do it. Lady Olivia, bless her innocence, immediately rose to the bait and offered to escort him herself.

He called for her at the stroke of ten the next morning, suspecting that she was the sort of female who appreciated punctuality. Sure enough, she was ready and waiting when he arrived. She even expressed artless gratitude for his timeliness.

"You would not credit, I daresay, how many people think nothing of arriving a quarter of an hour past their time, or even more!" she observed, warmly shaking his hand.

"The world is full of laggards," he agreed. "I am

generally among them. But today, of course, I am striving to impress you."

She laughed. "You have chosen an excellent way to go about it."

She had chosen an excellent way to impress him, too—if that was her object. He glanced appreciatively at the pretty picture she made in an expensive-looking morning dress of sprigged muslin, belted beneath her breasts with a band of narrow kid dyed to match her gloves. It was the latest fashion, and she looked undeniably fetching in it. He raised his eyebrows in feigned surprise. "What! No mobcap? No apron?"

"Pray do not remind me of our first meeting," she begged. "I am covered with shame whenever I think of it."

"No need," he told her kindly. "Remember, I accepted your apology."

"Yes, you did, and very annoying I found it," she said tartly. "I am still waiting for yours." She looked pointedly at him, as if inviting him to speak. He gave her his blandest smile and bowed, indicating the door. She bit back a laugh and gave an indignant sniff, then led the way to where her footman was holding the door for them.

They stepped out into the wind. Lady Olivia stopped in her tracks. A hackney coach stood before her house. As her footman closed the door and disappeared behind them, the jarvey jumped down from his high perch and opened the hackney door, letting down the steps. Lady Olivia still stood, apparently frozen in place.

"What's amiss?" asked George innocently.

"I hope this hackney isn't yours!"

"Certainly not. I hired it."

"You know perfectly well what I mean." With one hand on her windblown bonnet, she tilted her head to glare up at him. "You're mad. You can't put me into a hackney."

"My, we are proud!" marveled George, deliberately misunderstanding her. "What's wrong with it? I can vouch for its cleanliness and safety, my lady. I rode in it all the way from London."

"A hackney with you in it is not safe for *me*," she retorted. "Are you so accustomed to the company of—of *fast* women that you have forgotten the rules? A lady cannot ride in a closed carriage with a gentleman." She held up a warning finger. "And if you are about to say that you are no gentleman, you may save your breath."

"Thank you," said George appreciatively. "I may not be a gentleman, but I can assume the role for however long it takes us to travel to the Fairfax School. If you insist."

"If? *If* I—oh!" she spluttered, blushing. "You are absurd! But the point, as you well know, is not whether you would behave properly. It is the *appearance* of misbehavior that is unavoidable. Once the doors are closed, it won't make a particle of difference what we do."

"Well, that's good news, at any rate."

She choked, but rallied. "It is nothing of the kind! Why, oh why, did you not hire a gig or a curricle?"

"An open carriage?" he asked incredulously. "It looks like rain."

"Pooh! A bit of wind and a cloud or two." She shook her head in despair. "Well, there's no use repining. We shall have to walk."

"My dear Lady Olivia! I am wearing new boots." He tried to look pathetic.

She was clearly not deceived, but at least she was primming her mouth as if holding back a laugh. "You really are the most *audacious* man!" she exclaimed. She studied him for a moment, tapping her foot against the pavement. He tried to look meek and harmless. This coaxed an unwilling laugh from her. "If you insist on riding with me in a closed carriage, my lord," she said at last, "my cousin must accompany us for propriety's sake."

The jarvey was still standing by, pretending not to hear. George drew Lady Olivia a little to one side. The muscles in her arm were rigid beneath his fingers, but she did not pull away.

"What are you afraid of?" he asked her teasingly. "Is your reputation so fragile? I think your good name will survive a ten minute hackney ride, even with me. Come on." He winked. "It'll be fun."

Her mouth opened in a little *O* of shock. "I have earned my good name, sir, by eschewing such—such dubious treats," she stammered.

"Well, what's the point of earning a good name if you can't trade upon it a little?" he asked flippantly. "High time you tested it a bit. Dare them all to gossip about you! You are not a child fresh out of the schoolroom. Who will chastise you? Who would dare? A woman of your stainless reputation cannot be condemned for merely riding in a hackney. And in broad daylight! It's absurd."

Uncertainty flickered in the back of her eyes. He pressed his point. "Tell me. Would you pass judgment upon any woman of your acquaintance for such a tiny transgression?"

She looked thoughtful. "Not without knowing the circumstances. There might be any number of reasons why a lady would do such a thing."

He spread his hands deprecatingly. "Well, there you have it."

Humor suddenly lit her features. "But I have no excuse, my lord. There are no extenuating circumstances whatsoever." Her gray eyes, wide and luminous, met his with disarming candor. "I would be riding in that hackney alone with you only because . . . I want to."

He felt his jaw slacken. God save the mark! She had surprised him again. He had a definite weakness for plainspoken women. He felt his pulse begin to pound, and sternly quashed his unruly libido. The situation called for delicacy. If he frightened her off, she'd inflict her cousin on him and ruin the entire day.

He took a deep breath. "Well, if you *want* to, that changes everything. Let's take the hackney back to London," he suggested. "Or, better yet, Dover."

His joking did the trick; she chuckled. "I will ride with you as far as the Fairfax School, and no farther," she said firmly. "Even a reputation as sterling as mine cannot withstand more than ten minutes behind closed doors with such a rakehell."

Victory. He could scarcely believe his good fortune; he had expected far more resistance. Outwardly composed but inwardly rejoicing, he assisted Lady Olivia into the dim, cramped quarters of the hackney coach. There was only room for two persons—a factor which had determined his hire of this particular hackney, since he meant to avoid Bessie Fairfax at all costs. Lady Olivia did not comment on this, and she did not object to his sitting beside her, but when the jarvey closed the door and clambered back up onto the box, he felt her tense and knew she was having second thoughts.

"I have never done such a thing in my life," she reminded him nervously. "I hope you will do nothing to make me regret my decision."

"I hope not, indeed," he assured her softly. "For I plan to coax you into doing far more scandalous things than this."

She almost jumped. "Why, this is—this is very frank!" she stammered. "What can it profit you, sir, to ruin my reputation?"

"I do not intend to ruin your reputation. I merely intend to be private with you whenever I get the chance." He smiled. "Having had a taste of your delightful company, I cannot bear to return to formality. It seems very flat to only see you with other people milling about. I found even poor Culpepper very much in the way."

"Oh, I know exactly what you mean!" she said unexpectedly. "It is great fun to speak privately with you, although I daresay it is shocking of me to admit it. Do tell me, sir, for you must know I have very little experience of such things—are all rakes as charming as you are?"

Taken aback, he stared quizzically down at her. She seemed to be quite serious. "Charm is a necessary accouterment for a rake," he admitted, laughter quivering in his voice. "Although, as you have probably guessed, few are as charming as I am."

She laughed outright. "Then I daresay the others fail to match your success rate."

"I wouldn't know about that, of course," he said modestly. "Discretion being another necessary accouterment for a rake."

"What an interesting life you must lead," she remarked, folding her hands placidly in her lap. "Pray tell me a few of your adventures."

"Not for worlds! It is your turn to tell me something."

"Oh, are we taking turns? Pray ask me something I can answer quickly, for I had much rather talk about you," she said mischievously.

He grinned. "Very well. A certain question has been tormenting me for the past forty-eight hours. Why does your cousin call you Ivy?"

"Oh, dear." She bit her lip. "It is—it is a family nickname. I have had it since I was a child."

"But why Ivy? It's not commonly used as a diminutive of Olivia."

"No. It's not meant to be. It has nothing to do with my Christian name."

She was studiously looking away from him. Incredulous, he took her chin between his thumb and forefinger and turned her face back to his. "Good God, are you *blushing*?"

Her eyes met his defiantly. "And what if I am?" she demanded. "This is a very personal question, sir. I am not entirely sure I should answer it."

"You made me discuss how charming I am," he reminded her, suppressing a laugh. "Whatever you are about to disclose couldn't possibly be worse than that. Come, now! Why does your family call you Ivy?"

She swatted his fingers crossly away from her chin and squared her shoulders. "Oh, very well," she said grudgingly. "If you *must* know, they call me Ivy because—" She took a deep breath, then sighed. "Because everything I touch, I take over."

He burst out laughing. She looked chagrined, but her eyes were twinkling. "I daresay it seems very funny to you, my lord—"

"Oh, yes! It does."

"—but my nickname was something of a trial to me, I assure you. Until I became used to it."

"It seems very apt."

She looked dismayed. "Heavens! Can you tell already? You hardly know me!"

"My dear girl, from the instant I encountered you I have watched you dominate everything and everyone around you. Only witness the ruthless methods you employed to keep me out of poor Beebe's house! Why, you stopped at nothing."

"No! How can you say so? I did not even succeed!"

His eyes gleamed. "No. Because that was the day you met your match."

She faced him in the half-light, indignant but laughing. "As to that, sir, only time will tell. If it's a contest between us as to which is more overbearing than the other, I would not hazard a groat on the outcome."

"No, nor would I," he said promptly. "And I'm a betting man."

There was something about shared mirth that invited intimacy. George was very aware of how close her face was, upturned to his, and how the rocking of the coach brought their bodies into repeated contact. He found it thoroughly enjoyable.

Her head tilted a little as she studied him, a smile still playing across her face. "I suppose it would be a mistake to underestimate you," she remarked. "I am very used to having my own way, as you have so unkindly observed! But when I think how you have managed to thwart and bully me—and on such short acquaintance!—I realize I really *must* be on my guard with you."

He neatly slipped his arm behind her. Her gray eyes widened but he ignored her alarm and smiled down at her. "Did I browbeat you into stepping into this hackney?" he murmured. "I think not."

"No, indeed!" she said cordially. "How silly of me to think so! It was all *my* idea. This is the very thing to give my morning its perfect start: ten minutes of peril."

She was laughing, but he could feel tension thrumming through her as if she were a tightly strung harp. She was very near repenting the impulse that led her to share the hackney with him. One false move and she would slip away. His instincts told him that a strategic retreat would reap benefits later in the game, but it was damnably difficult to let her go. He was once again conscious of the electricity that seemed to spark and sizzle between them. It was delicious to sit so close to her, in the intimacy of the rocking coach. It was delicious to have one arm around her, even so lightly. He hated to remove it.

He carefully lifted his arm, letting her see that it cost him something to do so. "Far be it from me," he told her regretfully, "to imperil you."

Her expression immediately sobered. She almost looked regretful herself, which was exactly the outcome he'd been hoping for. But just as he was congratulating himself on the success of his stratagem and filing it away for future use, she asked a question that rocked him back on his heels. She asked him softly, but with disconcerting directness, "Are you my enemy?"

It was a ridiculous question, almost theatrical in its exaggeration. He started to laugh, but as he gazed into the preternaturally clear eyes so close to his, the impulse died.

Pinned by those silver eyes of hers, it struck him in a flash that the rock-bottom truth was, he *was* her enemy. He meant to harm her. He liked her, he respected her, and he felt strongly attracted to her—but he would steal from her if he could. First her heart, and then her fortune. He had not thought of it in such bald terms until this very moment.

He wanted to make a flip remark, but could not. He felt his habitual suavity slip a little. It was not a comfortable sensation. Whatever she was reading in his face, it was causing her expression to become more and more grave. "You hesitate," she said quietly. "I see."

Good God. How could he recover from this moment? It was obviously too late to try the flip remark. He took one of her hands in a strong clasp, frowning.

"I hesitate because you seem to be in earnest. An easy answer would make light of your question." He looked quizzically at her. "You do not pull away when I touch you," he murmured. "There's no need to look embarrassed! I merely point it out to illustrate my predicament."

He lifted his other hand and ran a finger along the side of her face, thoughtfully tucking a strand of her dark hair back into her bonnet. A woman of her stamp would respond to directness more surely than to flattery or soothing words. He would abandon raillery and try honesty, at least as far as he could.

"I do not know whether we are at cross-purposes until I know what your purpose is," he said quietly. "I confess, I do not understand what you are about. If I were you, Lady Olivia, I would have nothing to do with me. I did not expect you to forgive my conduct at Beebe's house, let alone the remarks I made that day. Frankly, you should have acquired an unalterable disgust of me. Yet—here we are. Why?"

She pulled her hand out of his and looked away. "I owe Mr. Beebe a great deal—" she began.

"Faugh! Do not tell me you are only attempting to comply with the terms of his will. That won't fadge. You could have achieved that by fobbing me off onto Culpepper, and spared yourself the trouble and annoyance of dealing with me directly. Had you wished to avoid me, that is what you would have done."

Humor returned to her countenance. "Well, then, what's the mystery?" she said bracingly. "Obviously I don't wish to avoid you."

He must have looked as nonplussed as he felt, for she laughed at him a little. "You clearly know nothing about the life of a respectable spinster."

"No, that I don't! If I did, would I find your behavior less baffling?"

"Oh, I think so." Her smile was serene. "Do not misunderstand me, my lord. I love my life and would not trade it for another. But it . . . lacks spice."

"Aha." This was interesting. He raised an eyebrow, amused. "So you pine for adventure. Ten minutes of peril actually *is* the way you'd like to start your mornings. I never would have guessed it." His shoulders shook. "Although, in hindsight, I should have! You did provide a number of clues. Oh, do not blush! You were charming." He leaned back against the squabs, letting his gaze travel over the slender form perched primly beside him. He was acutely aware of her knee touching his thigh in the close quarters of the hackney. A slow smile spread across his features. "So. Your life lacks spice. You have chosen your man well, Lady Olivia. I will gladly spice up your bland existence."

She looked askance at him. "Mind you, I don't want it *too* spicy," she said anxiously. "It's just that—well, it's as if I were trying to live on oat porridge. I've really nothing to complain about. But even the best porridge grows tiresome if one must eat it every day."

"I understand you perfectly," he assured her. "Only a baby can live on pap. You are a woman. You crave something different—something savory. Something you can really sink your teeth into."

"Oh, dear." She pulled a face. "I think we have chosen a poor analogy."

"Not at all." He chuckled. "Your predilection for my company, which had puzzled me very much, now strikes me as completely logical."

"It is *your* behavior that is inexplicable," she informed him, her eyes suddenly dancing with mischief. "For a rake and a libertine, you certainly spend a vast amount of time moralizing. Pray tell me, Lord Rival, why you lured me into this coach if you did not intend to press your advantage? I put myself wholly at your mercy—but instead of seizing your opportunity, you have wasted valuable time preaching to me about what a ruthless villain you are and why I ought to have nothing to do with you. Your conduct has been more like a vicar's than a rake's."

"Why, you little minx!" George exclaimed wrathfully, seizing her in his arms. "I thought I was doing you a favor! If you only knew what it cost me to keep my hands off you—"

But she was laughing at him, pushing her hands against his chest to hold him off. "We have arrived," she told him, by way of explanation.

He had not been aware of the coach slowing. He cursed under his breath now, feeling the wheels stop. The woman had used her knowledge of the school's location to provoke him into action at the very moment when she knew she would be safe! He shot her a look that threatened revenge as the door opened, and she actually stuck out her tongue like a child, her eyes brimming with laughter. He could not suppress a grin.

All in all, he reflected, impassively handing the jarvey almost a fortnight's winnings from his slender purse, the trip had not been wasted. It was worth a great deal to learn that Lady Olivia was ready and willing to play with fire. Lighting the actual blaze could wait for a bit.

8

$\mathcal{A}$s the hackney drove off, George glanced upward at the forbidding exterior of the Helen Fairfax School for Girls. It was a massive and dreary structure of brick and stone, and it loomed hideously over the narrow street. It looked exactly what it was: a place where the desperate might find refuge. One would have to be desperate indeed, he thought with an inward shudder, to seek asylum in such a place.

His initial impression of overwhelming bleakness was belied, however, by the school's interior. The furnishings in the wide entrance hall were sturdy rather than pretty, but the place was well-lit, warm, and clean. The scarred wooden wainscoting had been polished until it gleamed, and the rag carpets placed with neat precision against the glossy floor were spotless, if a trifle threadbare. There was a homelike quality to the place. Once again, Lady Olivia had surprised him.

Within moments of their walking through the door his companion was surrounded by a flurry of people who seemed to appear out of nowhere, greeting her with relief and eagerness, clamoring for her advice on this problem or that, for a decision on one thing or another, or for news regarding the progress of outstanding projects. He hung back and watched, feeling decidedly like a fish out of water. She seemed to hear everyone's concerns with equal attention and courtesy, turning from one to another and making sense of the babble with perfect ease.

"Lady Olivia, that dratted goat got into the garden again and ruined the turnips. Two or three of the girls are determined to make a pet of him. What shall we do?"

"My lady, we have received no word from the Brixton Road workhouse."

"Lady Olivia, the attic roof is leaking."

"Lady Olivia, I beg your pardon, but—"

"Lady Olivia, forgive the intrusion, but—"

When her ladyship spoke, the other voices instantly hushed. "The children cannot make a pet of someone else's goat," she said calmly. "Maria, pray speak to Farmer Tipton. If he will not agree to confine his livestock, I shall ask Culpepper to intervene. Miss Stivers must write a third time to the Brixton Road workhouse, and this time we shall send Peter with our message rather than entrust it to the post. Is the attic leaking in the same place it leaked before?"

"Yes, ma'am."

"I will personally speak to Mr. Jessop. Lord Rival, may I introduce a few of my staff? Ladies, this is Lord Rival. He will be assisting us in future."

She turned to include him in the group and segued smoothly into the round of introductions, precluding any inquiry as to the exact nature of Lord Rival's assistance. He shot her an amused glance before bowing and smiling at the various females curtsying to him. A few looked awestruck as they beheld his elegant person. A few looked puzzled. One, at least, appeared both troubled and skeptical. He favored her with his coldest smile and a raised eyebrow. She blushed and dropped her eyes, appropriately cowed. He hoped.

And then Lady Olivia took him on a brisk tour of the facility. He found this glimpse of her life, and the school itself, much more interesting than he had expected—if a bit unsettling. It was odd to be shown a world so different from the one he inhabited, and to know that Lady Olivia moved easily from one sphere to the other. One could not help seeing her in a new light.

In every wing that they entered, she was hailed with what seemed to be universal admiration and affection. He was impressed despite himself, both with the well-run efficiency of the school and with the obvious esteem in which Lady Olivia was held. Had he been a lesser man, he reflected grimly, he might have found it daunting. The woman obviously led a life filled with joy and high purpose. It would not be easy to wean her from it.

The only men they encountered on the premises were a pair of laborers in gaiters and an elderly parson, whose function at the school had to do with religious instruction—and, Lady Olivia admitted, providing something of an object lesson.

She explained this to him as they were traversing an area where buzzing voices echoed eerily behind closed doors, attesting to classrooms full of pupils. "Many of our girls never encounter a respectable man until they come to us," she said, her voice lowered to avoid interrupting the classes. "They associate the male sex with drunkenness, brutality, and abandonment. Dr. Barker's shining example of simple human kindness is helpful in incalculable ways."

"Is it?" asked George cynically. "Take care, Olivia! If you teach young girls to trust men, you may be doing them a disservice."

She shook her head in swift denial, so intent on what was clearly a favorite subject that she did not even notice his use of her Christian name. "On the contrary," she assured him earnestly. "If a girl encounters only brutal men, she grows up expecting men to be brutes. It is this expectation that deceives her into accepting a life that is much more wretched than it need be." She selected a key from the ring at her belt and wiggled it in the lock of a large door at the end of the passage. "Dr. Barker lets the girls see how agreeable it is to meet with courtesy and respect rather than insults and blows. It's important to teach them that there are other sorts of men. Decent men." Busy with the lock, she glanced worriedly up at George. "I have not decided whether acquaintance with you would further this goal or not."

He choked, earning one of her quick smiles. "I beg your pardon, that sounded very bad! I only meant that—well, the children are insulated here from nearly all contact with the outside world. This heightens the importance and influence of the few men they do meet. You're a bit . . . dazzling. It won't do, you know, to give my girls a taste for elegance."

"Merci du compliment," said George. "Perhaps the gardener can loan me a leather apron to dim the brilliance of my beauty." He reached over and placed his hand upon the key that was giving her so much trouble. "Allow me," he said politely.

Since her hand was on the key, and the key was attached to a ring, and the ring was on a chain hooked to her belt, she could not retreat. His arm pressed intimately against her waist and his hand covered hers. He caught her fragrance again, like the golden warmth of summer teasing his senses.

Her fingers stilled beneath his. Amazingly, she did not pull her hand away. It occurred to him that she had never yet refused his touch. The thought sent a rush of heat through him. They were alone in the passage. He wondered what she would do if he buried his lips in her hair, or kissed the nape of her neck— it was so close to his mouth, all he need do was lean forward the slightest bit—

Instead, he tightened his fingers on hers and turned the key in the lock. He felt the tumblers turn and heard the *snick* of success.

"Thank you," she said. Her voice sounded a little breathless.

He willed her to look up, silently daring her to meet his eyes. *Look at me.* He still grasped the key, and her hand upon it. Neither of them moved for a moment. She stared, seemingly transfixed, at their joined hands—but she did not look up.

His mouth was only an inch or two from her ear. "You're welcome," he whispered. A tiny strand of her hair trembled and danced in the current of his breath. She shivered then, and stepped away, her eyes downcast and her cheeks tinged with color.

Before he could move to pull the heavy door open for her, she had done so, and moved aside to let him pass. The prosaic odor of cabbage cooking assaulted their nostrils, breaking the spell he had tried to cast. Resigned, he followed her into a high-ceilinged room where rows of clean-scrubbed tables awaited the serving of a meal.

He looked around the room in surprise. "You feed the children as well as educate them?" he asked.

Her brows flew up. "They live here. You did not know? The school is really an orphanage, but since we try to emphasize the education we provide—and since there are so many unpleasant connotations to the word *orphanage*—we thought it best to call it a school."

The vastness of Lady Olivia's undertaking struck him anew. He stared down at her in amazement, guessing for the first time how much her efforts must mean, and to how many people. "Good God, ma'am, it is a monstrous task. No wonder poor Beebe thought you needed assistance! How many children do you house, feed, and educate?"

"We have beds for ninety-seven girls between eight and sixteen years of age. I only wish we could do more. The need is terrible, and we rarely have vacancies."

"And where do the girls come from?"

"London, for the most part, but parishes throughout the south of England send us children. We have several workhouses on the lookout, you see, for suitable candidates."

"Fascinating." He studied her face, ruefully remembering how long it had taken him to notice she was beautiful. Men of his stripe were not used, he thought, to seeing beauty in a strong and self-sufficient female. He saw it now, God help him. She seemed to grow more beautiful every moment.

"What makes a child a suitable candidate?" he felt impelled to ask. "The direst need, I suppose."

Sadness crossed her features. "No." She sighed. "There are so many whose need is urgent! And we can save only a few. We ask the workhouses to recommend the children they judge to be most . . . salvageable. It is a dreadful thing to say, but there are girls who are beyond our help before their eighth birthdays."

He frowned. "So soon? How can that be?"

"Well, we cannot take anyone with a contagious disease, of course, which eliminates a woefully large number from consideration. And often a child's character is warped by poverty. Poverty always entails a certain degree of starvation, and exposure to crime and filth. Some of them are like wild animals. Some lose their minds. And some become hardened felons at a very early age."

She changed to a more cheerful subject then, as if afraid that a truly serious discussion would put him off. He was not sure whether to feel amused or annoyed by this, since it seemed to indicate how shallow she thought him, but he made no comment as she led him through the room and explained how the meals were organized. Everything was prepared under the supervision of the staff, with the girls helping on a rotating basis so that each learned some basic cookery as part of her curriculum. "And those who excel, of course, are encouraged to learn more."

"By Jove," George remarked, lifting one eyebrow. "I see that I missed a crucial area of intellectual development by receiving my education at home. I was never taught to cook."

Olivia wrinkled her nose appreciatively. "I daresay your education had a slightly different emphasis! I don't know why Culpepper seemed to think we might utilize your skills, whatever they are; the notion is absurd."

"I'm a dab hand at Latin and Greek," he offered.

She laughed. "There is no more point in teaching these children Latin and Greek than there is in teaching them dancing and cards! Cookery, on the other hand, may prove useful to anyone. We are always on the lookout for natural aptitude, which we then try to foster. We teach all the girls basic housekeeping skills—I hope you have noticed the spotless condition of the school? Good!—in addition to reading, writing, and simple arithmetic. We then expose them to weaving, sewing, laundering, bread making—"

He flung up a hand. "Enough! It sounds exhausting. And do you oversee the entire operation?"

She smiled. "I would say, rather, that I provide the funds and the vision. I have a wonderful and tireless staff who do most of the actual work."

"Speaking of doing the work, my esteemed colleague, isn't it time you showed me exactly what you have in store for me? I am trying to keep an open mind, but I must tell you—regretfully, of course!—that I draw the line at scaling fish and chopping onions."

She treated him once more to her delightful chuckle. "What a pity! But I do have something in mind that I hope will suit you, as I'm sure you have guessed. Let us go somewhere where we can discuss the matter privately."

His ears pricked up at this. Secluding himself with Lady Olivia was just what he was angling for. Of course, he supposed it was too much to hope that she would take him to a garden or a library, or anywhere where they might actually be comfortable. He was right. She led him to the school's office.

The office was a large, gloomy bookroom lined with shelf after shelf of ledgers on three walls, and textbooks and primers on the fourth. The floor was scarred from the furniture being repeatedly dragged about. The room held two desks, several tables of varying size, a Franklin stove, and a smattering of mismatched chairs. It also contained the fat woman he had seen in black bombazine at the solicitor's office, today wearing a cheerier hue and a look of welcome. Lady Olivia removed the keys from her waistband as she moved forward to greet the woman. It seemed the keys actually belonged to the plump chatelaine. He still did not catch her name, but it hardly mattered. Lady Olivia bestowed a reassuring smile on her and said calmly, "I think you may go, Jane. Pray leave the door open behind you."

"As you wish, my lady." The woman bobbed a placid curtsy and left them, neither her face nor her manner expressing disapproval or suspicion.

George was amused by her unhesitating departure. "Well! What a lackadaisical attitude," he commented, as if aggrieved. "The woman must not know who I am."

Olivia's eyes twinkled. "Her attitude derives, my lord, from knowing well who *I* am."

"Ah. How lowering. That reminds me, by the way— I wish you would stop calling me 'my lord.' It unnerves me."

"What am I to call you, pray?"

He flashed his most disarming smile. "You may call me George. We are friends, are we not?"

"Are we?" She remained at a distance and considered him gravely. "I thought we were still weighing the question of whether or not we are enemies."

He gave an easy shrug of his shoulders. "We are partners, Olivia, not enemies." Her swift frown told him that she had noticed the use of her Christian name this time, so he smoothly continued before she could object. "You are eager for adventure; I am equally eager to receive Beebe's annuity. Surely we will be able to reach some arrangement whereby we both receive what we want. What is it that you have in mind for me?"

She sank stiffly onto a high-backed wooden chair and indicated the wing chair roughly opposite to it. "Pray be seated," she said, in the manner of one girding herself for battle. "We have a few things to clarify first, I think. You have expressed, more than once, a lack of interest in receiving the annuity."

"Oh, never that." He seated himself in the chair she had indicated, casually crossing one leg over the other. "I am extremely interested in receiving the annuity. It's finding myself subordinate to *you* that I find objectionable."

She frowned, but it seemed an expression of puzzlement rather than anger. "Yes, I have gathered that. But why? It seems inconsistent. I have been agreeably surprised this morning by your attitude toward the school."

"What attitude? It is an impressive undertaking. I commend you on your obvious achievements. On your heroism. On anything you like. That does not mean that I envision a place for myself upon your staff."

"You don't understand." A smile glimmered at the corners of her mouth. "It is an interesting mark of your character, sir, that you do not even realize how unusual your attitude is. Most Englishmen disapprove of education for women."

George's eyebrows climbed. "Nonsense. That is no longer the opinion of the majority. A few benighted souls, perhaps—"

"Perhaps? Pray remember, I am educating *poor* women! Many people say I am giving my charges ideas that are above their station in life."

"By teaching them cooking and housekeeping? Ridiculous."

Olivia's smile was warm with relief. "Thank you," she said, with real gratitude. "I must tell you that I have met with a great deal of resistance—indeed, it is no exaggeration to say that I have met with strenuous opposition!—to my efforts here, from other members of your sex. Even the clergy." A shadow crossed her face. "I regret to say, *especially* the clergy. I have been chastised roundly and regularly, to the point where I am, frankly, quite sick of hearing it."

There was no need to feign his astonishment. "The impertinence!" he exclaimed. "Who dares to criticize you? On what grounds?"

"Oh, always on the same grounds. You see, I founded the institution myself, and quite alone." Her voice became hesitant, almost apologetic. "I used the money I inherited from my mother. Her entire legacy to me is bound up in the charity I named for her. The school is funded, staffed, and overseen entirely by women. I even—" She bit her lip and looked anxious, as if bracing herself for his censure. "I even do the banking."

Light began to dawn. "I see," said George slowly. "There is no man holding the reins."

"Yes." She stared woodenly down at her hands, folded tensely in her lap. "I am, therefore, criticized. There is nothing unusual about women working within a charity—indeed, they nearly always form the backbone of a charitable organization. But for a woman to actually *run* one is deemed unnatural. Unfeminine."

George frowned thoughtfully. "Do you need a figurehead? A puppet who will put his name at the top of your stationery, sign whatever documents you need signed, do your banking for you, et cetera, and silence your critics?"

She lifted her chin, her eyes flashing. "No, sir, I do not!"

"Well, don't fly out at me." He folded his arms across his chest and grinned sardonically at her. "I thought for a moment I had finally divined a way I could be useful to the school. I *do* know how to sign my name."

"Oh, no, you are missing my point. I do not need your assistance—at least, not quite in that way! I am merely commenting upon how odd it seems, to me, that you do not object to the education of these girls, nor to the institution being run by women. You only object to becoming a part of it."

"For an intelligent female you can be remarkably dense," said George, amusement coloring his exasperation. "A short while ago, you pointed out that I know nothing of a spinster's life. Allow me to tell you, madam, that *you* know nothing of men."

"I never claimed to," she said stiffly. "What of it?"

He leaned forward, resting his elbows on his knees, and assumed an expression of exaggerated patience. "Men, my dear, generally dislike being ruled by women," he informed her, his silky tone barely masking his irritation. "And our dislike increases in direct proportion to the personal stake we have in the woman."

Her eyes widened. "But you have no personal stake in me!" she exclaimed.

Something in his expression must have alarmed her. She shrank back a little in her chair. "Surely you have given up on—on that ridiculous notion you once had of *courting* me? We know one another now! We are—we are friends."

He bared his teeth in a wolfish smile. "Unless, of course, we are enemies," he reminded her.

Her brows snapped together. "Why, it was you who told me we were partners! After all, we will be working together."

"That is by no means certain," he said shortly. "We have yet to determine a function I can perform here, and I have strong personal objections to accepting your authority—whatever you may say." He leaned back in his chair and regarded her, his eyes hooded.

Olivia appeared rattled. "Well, how are we to get around it?" she demanded. "I hope you do not expect me to relinquish my post and allow *you* to run things, merely as a sop to your vanity!"

"I have neither the skills nor the ambition to operate a school for girls, thank you," he snapped. "I am merely telling you that I do not run well in harness. Even as a boy I was exceedingly difficult to rule, and I am no longer a boy! I feel reasonably certain that any attempt to adapt myself to a subordinate role will end in failure. Particularly, as I have said, if it is *you* before whom I must abase myself. You will find such unreasoning rebellion difficult to understand, I daresay—"

"No. Not at all." She gave a queer little laugh, then surprised him by reaching out her hand and touching it briefly, impulsively, to his sleeve. "You have at last said something I understand very well."

His brows shot up. "Have I?"

"Oh, yes! I have struggled with—with *unreasoning rebellion* all my life. It is my besetting sin, in fact— and very uncomfortable it has made me! Now, I wonder . . ." She leaned against her elbow, studying him with great seriousness. "I wonder if we could work together as equals?" she said slowly. "Neither of us commanding the other. Or each leading in a different area of endeavor."

"Ha! Interesting." He looked thoughtfully at her, then grinned. "Forgive me if I seem to have more interest in leading than in following. I am generally a stubborn fellow, and compromise has never been my strong suit. But since there is a tidy sum at stake, I am feeling unusually pliant this morning." He waved a languid hand. "Lead away, my dear. What can I do for you? Er, what can I do for the school, I *should* say."

She clasped her hands tightly in her lap. "I'm afraid I—I must begin by asking you a—a personal question, my lord."

His eyes gleamed at her. "You cannot ask a personal question of anyone you address as 'my lord.' "

She colored up at once. "Very well," she said, in the defiant manner of one throwing caution to the winds. "I have a personal question I must ask you—George."

One barrier down. He bowed gravely, careful not to let his triumph show. "Thank you. Ask away."

Her cheeks were pink, but her eyes met his unwaveringly. "You have called Mr. Beebe's annuity a—a tidy sum. Pray tell me whether it would relieve you of your financial difficulties." She looked away, embarrassed. "The question is dreadful, I know," she said hastily, "but I *must* know the answer. It goes to the heart of whether we can work together. I cannot forget—I *dare* not forget—that you told me you were interested in pursuing me—or, that is, interested in pursuing an heiress—because . . . well, because—"

"Because I need money," George supplied politely. "Certainly. Why else does a man pursue an heiress?"

Olivia took a deep breath. "Yes. Exactly. So I was hoping—"

She seemed to be floundering again. This question was nearly as painful for her as it was for George. Nearly, he reflected, gritting his teeth, but not quite. It was obscene that it had come to this. Disclosing any portion of his fiscal embarrassments to anyone, let alone this particular someone, was humiliation of the keenest order. Anger propelled him from his chair and set him prowling restlessly through the room.

"You thought that Beebe's bequest might be enough for me," he said harshly. "That if I managed to earn my eight hundred pounds per annum, I could abandon the notion of marrying a woman for her purse." His mouth twisted. "What a greedy rogue you will think me! The answer to your question is no. Eight hundred pounds a year is not sufficient for my needs."

He thought fleetingly of what eight hundred pounds *could* give him: freedom from the uncertainty of cards and dice. Freedom from the disgusting maneuvers he engaged in, gulling rich women into losing their jewels and pin money to him. Freedom from the struggle of living with no income at all, and the contortions he performed to hide his insolvency from the Polite World. He was so weary of it all. The annuity could ease his life in a hundred ways, some small and some significant. It was not a fortune, but it was certainly what the world would call a "competence."

Yes, it would ease his life—but his alone. It would do nothing for his tenants. It was not enough money to save Rye Vale.

He knew, because he had gone over it and over it in the past two days, wrestling with the figures, attempting to work out how he could somehow stretch Beebe's annuity to cover the expense of restoring his estate. It could not be done. Even if he sent every penny of it to Rye Vale and continued to live in London, relying on his wits and his skill with cards as he had done for the past twelve years, it would not be enough. He might be able to hire a decent land agent—just. But what could a land agent do with no funds to plow into the land? George could take another route and invest the money, hoping for a windfall at some point in the future—but the three-percents would be too slow, and anything else too risky.

No, there was no easy way out. He would have to marry one of the women on his miserable list. If Lady Olivia Fairfax would give him nothing more than a pleasant flirtation, he had to either discard her and move on to the next name, or change her mind.

He looked at her. God in heaven, he hoped he could change her mind.

At the moment, it seemed unlikely. Olivia had not moved from her seat by the table, so close that he could reach her in three swift strides, but she suddenly seemed very far away. There was condemnation in her clear, silvery gaze, and he felt the distance between them flowing as cold and unbridgeable as the River Styx. It would be wrenchingly difficult to discard his hopes and turn elsewhere, now that he had met her. His gambler's mind knew the odds of finding another rich woman who stirred his blood the way she did: nil.

She spoke then, her voice cool with regret. "I had hoped that we would work together. I had even hoped that you and I might become friends—of a sort."

He forced a smile. "We still may. As I think I have made clear, I am in no position to turn down a guaranteed income. However much it goes against the grain, I will probably swallow my pride and accept it in the end. And you have suggested that I might fulfill the terms of the bequest and yet, somehow, salvage my manhood."

Olivia's attempt at a smile was less successful than his. "I feel sure your manhood will survive. The question burning in *my* brain, at the moment, is whether you will find the task I am about to propose too dull."

"What is it?"

Some of her nervousness had returned. She gestured to the chair and he sat across from her again, but she immediately rose and began pacing. Since she had bade him sit, he remained in the chair, watching her. When she reached the edge of the largest desk, she stood her ground and pivoted, like an animal at bay, looking anxiously at him. "Do you know anything about bookkeeping?" she asked.

The intensity with which she asked such a mundane question made him grin. "Nothing at all. You are right; it sounds dull. But don't you already have a bookkeeper?"

"Yes. Culpepper performs that function for the school." Her mouth set in a grim little line. "I would be glad to—relieve him of those duties."

"Good God. Why? It's hard to imagine Culpepper stealing from orphans."

"Oh, no, no, it's nothing like that!" she hastened to say. "We do not suspect him of any impropriety. But he is very . . . old-fashioned in his views. Quite set in his ways, you know. And we find his attitude extremely trying, at times." She sighed, and rubbed her forehead. "I think I had better tell you the whole."

"Pray do so," said George, his curiosity piqued.

Olivia returned to the chair across from him and sat, steepling her hands before her as she chose her words. "Culpepper was my father's solicitor," she explained. "Despite the disparity in their ranks, they were actually friends—as much as my father could be a friend to one he deemed so far beneath him. Their affinity was really remarkable. In nearly every respect save rank and temperament, they were identical. Culpepper had a more benevolent mien than my father, for my father could be quite harsh. But Culpepper echoed and seconded his every thought. Their attitudes, ideas, opinions, and approaches to life were in complete agreement. It always seemed, to me, that my father's autocratic nature, his mania for control, was actually worsened by his association with Culpepper. No matter how—how *outrageous* my father's fits of tyranny became, Culpepper wholeheartedly approved."

"It astonishes me, then, that you have kept him in your service. Did you not resent his influence?"

"Oh, very much! But he means well. He is genuinely devoted to me, as he was to my father. It is just that—" She sighed again. "Nothing can shake his views. He honestly believes, for example, that women are incapable of rational thought."

George was startled into a laugh. "What! Including you?"

"Oh, yes." She smiled wryly. "Nothing can convince him otherwise. Challenge him and he will prate of phrenology, of the Bible, of the learned treatises on the subject which support his views—all written by men, of course. Women are irrefutably inferior to men. Our brains are smaller, our bodies weaker, et cetera. And we lack the moral sense—did you know that?"

He blinked. "I hadn't heard."

"Culpepper will assure you it is true. Without the leadership and protection of men, women would be not only helpless, but utterly depraved."

George crossed one booted leg negligently over the other. "Fancy that. So I've been wasting my time all these years, trying to lead women astray, not realizing that depravity was your natural bent. What an excellent front you females do put up! How does Culpepper account for that, by the way—let alone your proficiency in what *sounds* like reasoned speech? I understand, now, that you must have learned English much the way a parrot does—"

Olivia choked. "I cannot speak for the parrots, of course," she said, her voice quivering. "But most of the women of my acquaintance have mastered more than a phrase or two. And they do not shout their remarks at random, in the way of a parrot."

"I have known a few that do," mused George.

"We are straying rather far from the point, my lord," said Olivia severely. "Pray allow me to finish my tale."

"By all means."

"It was Culpepper who drafted my father's will. Are you familiar with my family's circumstances?"

"A little." He had researched this, to some extent, when learning what he could about available heiresses. Information on Lady Olivia had been scant. "I know that you are the child of the late earl's second wife."

She inclined her head in acknowledgment. "That is correct. My father's first wife, Blythe, bore him a son who is the present Earl of Badesworth. Blythe died while Ralph was still in leading strings, and my father soon married my mother. She was a considerable heiress in her own right. As part of the marriage settlements, papers were drawn up that would preserve her estate for the benefit of any children she might bear. I was her only child. She passed away when I was seventeen, and I inherited her money. All of it. Outright." Olivia paused, and looked down at her hands. "My father immediately set Culpepper to discover a way to wrest my inheritance from me, since I was underage and female. I will say, in his defense, that Culpepper was disturbed by my father's request. It was the only time I knew him to oppose my father's wishes. His disapproval, however, did not prevent him from working diligently to obey my father's command. Fortunately, he did not succeed. The settlement could not be broken."

She raised her eyes to George's again. Her expression was steely. "I need hardly tell you, I'm sure, that my relationship with my father was . . . strained by all of this."

"I can well believe it."

"My mother had acted as a buffer between the two of us for many years, in ways I hardly understood as a child. With her passing, I saw him as he truly was. I bore the full brunt of his attacks. He was ever seeking to subdue and control me, and I to defy him. It was . . . an unpleasant time."

"It sounds appalling."

"My brother, Ralph, was of no help to me. If anything, he enjoyed the strife and egged us on for his amusement. I found an unlikely champion in, of all persons, Culpepper. He smoothed matters over when he could, and often made sincere efforts—in private— to explain my father to me." She chuckled. "He never tried to explain me to my father, naturally. Culpepper thought it my duty to submit to my parent's demands, reasonable or unreasonable. He merely sought to make submission easier for me."

"How kind," said George dryly.

Humor crinkled the corners of Olivia's eyes. "Well, it was," she insisted. "It was kindly meant, at any rate. The tension between my father and myself escalated steadily, nevertheless. I count myself extremely fortunate that he outlived my mother by only a matter of months. A hunting accident brought him down before I could murder him." She caught herself suddenly and bit her lip, blushing with distress. "I beg your pardon. I should not joke about such a thing."

He smiled. "You may say what you like to me."

"No! It's vile. But thank you for not chiding me." She shook her head, smiling a little. "I should have saved my astringent comments for the next portion of the story. It concerns my father's will."

"Great heavens, don't tell me he cut you out?"

"Nothing so simple." She pulled a face. "He left me an inheritance of some kind—but I have not been told what it is. Yes, you may well stare! Is it not ridiculous? I have an income from it, and a very good one. Culpepper doles it out. It is always the same amount, every quarter. But I have no idea where it comes from."

"Er, have you asked?"

"Well, of course I have! But those were the terms of my father's will: that my inheritance be held in trust—with no information given me as to the actual amount held in trust, nor where it is being held." She gave a mirthless laugh. "Is it all in the funds? Do I own a shipping line, perhaps, or a woolen mill, or a diamond mine in Africa? Can any of it be sold? Might the money be better invested elsewhere? I have no knowledge and I have no control. I have absolutely no idea what my net worth may actually be. And I can do nothing to increase it—or deplete it, for that matter. Unless, of course, I marry." Her voice was brittle with anger. "For although I, as a female, am to be told *nothing* about what I own, Culpepper will be allowed to divulge everything to my husband. Who will then, under English law, own it all himself. *He* will be able to do with it whatever he likes."

George coughed. "My dear Olivia, I would marry at once if I were you, if only to end the mystery. Surely your husband will be good enough to break this conspiracy of silence and tell you something about your inheritance."

Olivia's delicate nostrils flared with scorn. "Since I will no longer own it, I will no longer care." She pounded a fist fiercely into her palm, eyes blazing. "I will *never* marry. Never."

George quelled his impulse to make another irreverent remark or flip suggestion. It seemed the wrong moment. Instead, he kept his expression sympathetic and turned the subject back to her father's will. "Did you not say that Culpepper drafted all this?"

"Yes. But I am sure it was my father's idea. He knew me well. Nothing could be better designed to drive Olivia Fairfax raving mad." Her mouth twisted in a bleak smile. "I daresay I am more like him than I care to think! I was so enraged by it all that I left home at once and have never returned. Ralph was glad to see me go, so I removed to Chelsea with my cousin—and here I am to this day. The instant I received my first payment under my father's will and knew what my income would be, I founded the Helen

Fairfax School with my mother's money. *All* of her money."

"Ah." He looked at her with interest. Her eyes were flashing silver fire, and her cheeks were pink with emotion. She looked magnificent. "So you live on the income from your father's money, and manage your mother's to your willful little heart's content. And this is the secret of your obsession with the school."

A short, unwilling laugh escaped her. "Yes. I'm afraid that is precisely it. I would like to tell you that my interest in its smooth and seamless operation is completely altruistic, but, I am ashamed to say, I take a perverse delight in how extremely *well* I run it! My motives are not entirely unselfish."

He laughed softly. "You're only human, Olivia. And whatever your secret reasons may be, you do run it well—and that is the most important thing. But why do you allow Culpepper to keep the books?"

"Frankly, I am too busy to do it, and he offered, and—well, I did not wish to hurt his feelings. And I do trust him. No, pray do not look so! We must give him his due. He always acts with sincere regard for my best interests."

"Hmm. I suppose he reserves the right to determine what your best interests are."

"He certainly tries, at any rate," she admitted. "That is why I would be very glad indeed for your help in . . . ousting him."

George leaned forward, his eyes twinkling. "Be careful, Olivia! I'm only human, too. I might take a stab at determining what your best interests are—and you might like my ideas no better than you like his."

Her eyes gleamed in response. "Oh, I feel almost certain that I would like your ideas, my lord."

The tension in the room had undergone a miraculous transformation. Amusement lit Olivia's eyes, where anger had burned just a few moments ago.

A slow smile crept across his face. "If you call me

'my lord' one more time," he said provocatively, "I shall demonstrate one or two of my ideas right here and now."

She lifted an eyebrow with mock disdain. "Is that a threat, my lord?" He held up a warning finger and she corrected herself, half-laughing. "George!" she said. "Well? Is it?"

"No." He couldn't resist the obvious retort. "It's a promise."

9

Silver spangles. Olivia had never worn anything so daring. The very sparkle that had enchanted her in the shop, and caused her to exclaim at the fabric's beauty, made her feel decidedly nervous when she saw it draped round her form. The material clung. It definitely clung. And the tiny spangles flashed and glittered everywhere it clung, emphasizing her every curve.

She raised a fold of the gauzy stuff to her face and turned to the other women in the room. "Is it indecent?" she asked anxiously.

"Yes," said Bessie.

"Not at all!" said Edith simultaneously.

The dressmaker was crawling about on the floor with her mouth full of pins and could not reply until she had extricated them. "It's the high kick of fashion, my lady," she said at last, her tone congratulatory. "And a pleasure it is to see you taking an interest in such things! If I do say it as shouldn't."

"Well, I've spent an outrageous sum on it," said Olivia gloomily. "I shall have to wear it, if only to justify the purchase."

"It's beautiful," said Edith staunchly. She was reclining on a sofa, but propped herself up on one elbow to see the effect of the gown being fitted on her sister-in-law. "And what's more, it suits you. Your carriage is so elegant, and you are so wonderfully tall! I wouldn't dare to wear such a gown, myself—"

"It draws the eye," said Bessie critically. "The spangles catch the light, and the gauze hugs your shape. You might as well wear nothing at all! I don't know what's come over you, Ivy. You'll have every man in the place ogling you."

"Oh, dear," said Olivia faintly. "That will never do."

Her dismay was automatic, but it was accompanied by a strange flutter of excitement. The shameful truth was, whatever dismay she felt stemmed largely from a fear that she would look foolish—not that she would overstep the bounds of modesty. In fact, if the effect of the new gown was sufficiently stunning, for once in her life she was ready to throw modesty out the window.

Olivia studied the edge of her reflection, which was all she could make out in the pier glass; if she moved closer she would discommode the woman pinning up her hem. She tried to picture what she would look like in a formfitting ballgown of spangled gauze, but her imagination failed. She had never worn such a thing in her life. Would she look attractive? Or merely grotesque?

"Where are you going in it?" asked Edith. Her voice sounded small and wistful.

Olivia met Edith's eyes in the looking glass and shot her a sympathetic smile. "Vauxhall Gardens. I wish you could go, my dear. It's hard on you, I know, to be a prisoner here."

Edith gave an unconvincing laugh. "Oh, well. I've no desire to be seen with a swollen face and a limp. Being confined to the house is tedious, but I still prefer it to—" She caught Olivia's warning look and stopped abruptly, seeming to realize that it might be dangerous to prattle about her marital woes in the presence of the dressmaker. Instead she asked, "Did you say Vauxhall? I thought it was closed for the season."

"It is." In response to a vigorous gesture by the little dressmaker, Olivia turned to her right. "It has been closed to the public for several weeks now, but this is a special occasion. It's been known for some months that Russian royalty would visit London in September; the Regent requested that Vauxhall Gardens be kept in readiness, and reopened for this one evening." She rolled her eyes comically. "Nothing less than a Russian grand duchess could get me to Vauxhall."

Edith looked surprised. "Do you dislike it? Oh, how can you? I've only been there once, but I thought it was heavenly."

Olivia smiled. "No, I mean that I've never seen it. It's difficult to believe, I know! Pray recall what a sheltered life I have led. I never had a London Season, either—at least, not a whole one. Must I turn again, Jenny, or are we done?"

"That'll do, my lady." The dressmaker struggled to her feet and briskly removed the last of the pins from her mouth, beaming at Olivia. "It's lovely stuff, ma'am. Be a pleasure to work with it."

"I am glad. Pray help me lift this over my head." As the dressmaker assisted her, warning her to mind the pins, Olivia peered through her arms and caught a glimpse of Bessie's frown. "You still do not like it, Bessie?"

"No," said Bessie bluntly. "It's very pretty, I'll grant you. And you'll look lovely in it. It's the party I object to, and the company you'll wear it in. Well! I've said enough on the subject. It's clear I'll not change your mind."

Edith's drooping expression perked up as she glanced curiously from Bessie's disapproving frown to the stubborn tilt of Olivia's chin. The dressmaker departed, the folds of shimmering gauze held reverently in her arms, and Olivia slipped into her wrapper. She tied the belt with a swift, efficient tug and turned to face her accuser. "I'll give you one last chance to change my mind, Bessie," she said. "I have a few niggling doubts of my own, so it's only fair to listen to yours."

Bessie puffed her cheeks in a sigh. "I seem to do nothing but scold and worrit, lately," she admitted grumpily. "I know your patience is wearing thin. And I can't say that I blame you."

"But—?" prodded Olivia.

Bessie's words poured out in a rush. "But it's my solemn duty to warn you, Ivy, and I couldn't live with myself if I saw danger coming to you and said nothing. There, then! I wish you wouldn't go. Not with That Man. And if you insist on going, I wish you would take me along to bear you company, for what other purpose have I in this household?"

"My dear Bessie! You are not a hireling. This is your *home,* and you are talking nonsense! When I first set up on my own, I needed a chaperon and companion—I was barely out of the schoolroom, for heaven's sake! But that was years ago. Do not think me ungrateful, but—"

"Now, don't prate to me of your advanced years," Bessie scolded. "You're a greener girl at six-and-twenty than Edith is at seventeen."

"So are you," said Edith unexpectedly. The combatants' heads whipped round in surprise to see the invalid rise, wincing, to a sitting position. "I may be only seventeen, but I'm a married lady," she announced. "And besides, I shall be eighteen in October."

Since this speech seemed to leave Bessie and Olivia bereft of speech, Edith looked with satisfaction from one to the other. "I suppose if Bessie is objecting, you must be going to Vauxhall with Lord Rival," she said wisely.

"Yes, but not alone," Olivia said quickly. "Had he

asked me to do anything so improper, I would have declined the invitation." He had, in fact, asked her to do just that—but she decided to keep that tidbit of information to herself. After all, she *had* declined the invitation, she reminded herself virtuously. Until he modified it slightly. "Lord Rival's party will include six persons, so I will not be made conspicuous."

Bessie snorted. "In that gown, you'll not blend in with the wallpaper."

Edith stifled a giggle with one hand. "If it's one of the Regent's parties, there will be simply *hordes* of women in revealing gowns—ladies of birth, I need hardly say! If you're afraid she'll start a scandal, I can promise you she won't."

"Hmpf! And how many of the Regent's parties have you attended? None, I'll warrant. I hear he surrounds himself with toadeaters and courtcards—a wild, degenerate set! Young girls have no place among that lot."

"I hope you don't mean to imply that I am a young girl!" exclaimed Olivia. "What may have been unacceptable for Edith in her first Season is a different proposition for a woman of six-and-twenty."

"Take care you don't *receive* a different proposition!" said Bessie tartly, arms akimbo. "You never can tell, with Prinny's set. A parcel of drunken roues, well past their first youth! Why, it makes my hair stand on end just to picture you loose in that crowd. A lamb among wolves!"

"I shall not be unprotected," said Olivia with dignity. "Whatever you may think of Lord Rival—"

"What I think of Lord Rival won't bear repeating!"

"—he will not allow any harm to come to me. Besides, it's not going to be the Regent's *set,* as you call it. This will be a huge gathering. I doubt if I shall so much as set eyes on the Regent, or the grand duchess, for that matter. I will be part of a private evening with a small party. I daresay nothing could be more tame."

"It sounds perfectly unexceptionable," pronounced Edith. "It's the sort of thing anyone might attend."

Bessie pounced on this. "My point exactly! We don't know who will be there. Ivy dear, I don't like to see you go off among a crowd of persons wholly unknown to us. Why, we are not even acquainted with the members of Rival's party, let alone—"

"It's not as bad as that," Olivia insisted. "One of his party is actually a connection of ours, I believe. A third cousin of my mother's. You must have heard of the Cheynes; a very respectable Lancashire family."

Edith giggled. "That sounds dull enough! What can your objection be, Bessie? I was allowed to go to Almack's with a party of persons I barely knew, and I was only sixteen at the time."

Olivia bit back a laugh. Bessie looked as if she would like very much to say something. Olivia could easily guess what it was, and admired Bessie's fortitude in keeping her lips pressed tightly together. Dear Bessie! She did not want to sully Edith's innocent ears with a description of all the ways Olivia's projected party would differ from a chaste evening at Almack's. Olivia felt a certain sympathy for the position her cousin was in; it must be trying—even disturbing—to know someone as well as Bessie knew Olivia, and watch her suddenly change. She was all too aware of how out of character her behavior was of late.

"It's only for one night, Bessie," said Olivia coaxingly. "I promise I will not make a habit of it. Pray do not be angry with me! Lord Rival is an associate of ours now, you know. He's been so gracious about taking over the school's books—a task that galls him, I would think—that the least I could do was accept his invitation."

Bessie's thoughts were immediately diverted into another channel. "If he doesn't care to do the bookkeeping, why, in heaven's name, have you set him on to do it?" she exclaimed, her brow clearing. "I had to

listen to Culpepper's complaints for nearly an hour
yesterday! I tried my best to calm him down, but he's
so deeply offended that I think he barely heard me."

With a sigh, Olivia dropped into a nearby chair.
"Culpepper is a sanctimonious, interfering old busybody, and it's high time he learned his place," she said
crossly. "I had to remind him that I am mistress of
the Fairfax School, and that he works for me. The end
of it was that I dismissed him."

Bessie cried out in horror, and Edith's eyes grew
round with awe. Olivia relented, laughing a little.
"You needn't faint, Bessie! He is still our solicitor. I
only relieved him of his duties at the school."

"Mercy on us!" Bessie sank onto the end of the
sofa unoccupied by Edith, pressing one hand to her
heart. "What a scare you gave me! I knew you
couldn't do anything so cruel. Dismiss poor old Culpepper! Why, he's served our family for as long as I
can remember. He can be irritating, at times, but—"

"Very! Did you know that he believes himself to
be indispensable to the school? That females are too
scatterwitted to keep records and monitor expenditures? His only comfort was that he was being replaced by a *man*! I wanted to box his ears."

Bessie immediately ruffled up in sympathy with
Olivia. "The nerve of him! Well! In that case, I hope
you gave him a piece of your mind."

"I did. Not that it had any appreciable effect."

Edith's forehead creased in puzzlement. "But—if
Culpepper has been sacked, who is teaching Lord
Rival?"

"I am," replied Olivia—with far more aplomb than
she secretly felt. The task had proved amazingly tax-
ing, for reasons she could not quite put her finger on.
She fancied she heard a shocked silence, and hurried
into speech to cover it. "As I say, he's been very good
about it. Such mundane work cannot be his cup of
tea."

Bessie looked at her very hard. "Are you telling us that you—Olivia Fairfax—are turning the worst rake in London into a *bookkeeper*?"

Olivia smiled weakly. "It does sound improbable, I suppose," she admitted.

Edith's eyes were round as saucers. "Gracious! Is Lord Rival a rake?" she squeaked, bouncing upright. "How exciting! I mean—that is—" she broke off, stammering, as Olivia choked back laughter and Bessie bent a minatory scowl on her. "Well, I've never met a rake," she said, with dignity. "Not a real one. My brother Fred fancied himself a dandy—until Papa burned all his waistcoats and threw his quizzing glass in the river. But that's not the same thing at all. Does Lord Rival have a quizzing glass?"

"I don't know," said Olivia, trying to keep her voice from quivering. "Perhaps I shall find out at Vauxhall."

Edith looked envious. "I wondered why Bessie was so anxious to prevent your going off to Vauxhall with him! My mother surely would have forbidden *me* to do such a thing. A girl has to be very careful of her reputation, you know. But you are so old, I daresay it doesn't matter," she added naively.

"Not a whit," Olivia agreed. "A woman as stricken in years as I am may go off with anyone she chooses, and no one can say her nay."

Edith blushed. "I did not mean to call you old," she said apologetically. "I merely meant that you are past the age of trying to catch a husband."

Olivia smiled. "My dear Edith, I knew exactly what you meant. And I agree with you. Since my object is to stay single, it doesn't matter what people say of me. There's no law against a woman befriending a man, is there?" She took a deep breath, trying to steady her suddenly hammering heart. "I am an adult, after all. I can do whatever I like."

She wondered, with some trepidation, to what extent this declaration of independence was true. Could she really do as she chose? Was it possible to break some of the sillier rules decorum imposed upon her? It was most unlike her to snap her fingers at the opinions of others, but lately she could feel her mutinous, reckless streak, a side of her nature she normally tried to keep hidden, festering beneath the surface of her well-ordered life—like a splinter that one cannot dig out however much one tries. She felt that it must either break out soon, or send her into a fever.

For years now, she had been privately growing more and more impatient with the shibboleths and strictures that hemmed a maiden lady in. At her age, by heaven, she ought to be able to think for herself. Explore the avenues that took her fancy. Decide on her own what was right and what was wrong. Encountering George Carstairs had somehow brought these feelings to a head, and she was now openly chafing at her prim little life. She hadn't felt so restless and resentful since Mother died and left her warring with her father over every tiny freedom she tried to seize.

Why this was, she didn't know. Lord Rival certainly did nothing to encourage her rebellion. Since that one day when he had goaded her into riding in the hackney with him, his behavior had been admirably circumspect. In fact, he treated her with the same courtesy she took for granted from other men. He was unfailingly respectful in all their dealings.

It was driving her mad.

The more he kept a polite distance, the crosser she grew. Had he done anything outrageous, she would have instantly upbraided him—but it piqued her that he did nothing outrageous. He showed no inclination to flirt with her at all. The nervous excitement she had felt at the prospect of working with him, anticipating a daily battle to keep his amorous attentions at bay, fell flat in the face of his crushing indifference. And her resulting disappointment forced her to acknowledge just how much she had *wanted* those attentions—

the very attentions she would have spurned, had they occurred!

They met daily in the office of the Fairfax School. She showed him the various books and ledgers and explained the workings and organization of the charity. He surprised her by making excellent suggestions regarding the operation, especially relating to the transfer and ultimate disposition of the assets Mr. Beebe had willed to the school. Lord Rival, against all expectations, had a shrewd head for business. But his burgeoning interest in matters financial did not, unfortunately, extend to her. His attention was completely absorbed by the arcane twistings of the charity's money trail and his detailed—and, really, rather inspired—analysis of which cash repositories were superior, and why.

She wore the new clothes she had recently purchased on Bond Street. He smiled and bowed and showed no interest. She sat beside him and let her arm brush his. He considerately moved aside to give her more room. She deliberately spoke in double entendres. He appeared not to notice. Despite their casual use of Christian names—for she consistently called him "George" when they were alone—no intimacy grew between them.

By the time he extended, in the most offhand way imaginable, the invitation to Vauxhall Gardens, she was wound so tightly that she very nearly sprang at his first invitation—the one that would have placed her in his sole company for the evening. This, of course, would have been wholly unacceptable. It was really shocking, in hindsight, to think how close she had come to saying yes. And even more shocking to realize how much she had wanted to. An evening spent making small talk with a party of strangers would be tedious, but she was relieved that he had offered this compromise at all. She had been half afraid he would make her choose—to go alone with him, or not at all. She would have been strongly tempted to go, and damn the consequences.

It was pique, really, that had spurred her to order this particular gown. She had been thrown into such a temper by her chaotic and confusing emotions, and her overwhelming desire to attract George's interest come hell or high water, that she had selected a fabric more suited for a high-class courtesan than a lady of quality.

She compounded her recklessness by having the gown made up with a décolletage so low that she could not wear stays with it. At her final fitting, her eyes nearly popped in horror. Too late, she realized that she was constitutionally incapable of wearing such a garment in public.

"But you look lovely!" Jenny cried, crestfallen. Since she was a graduate of the Fairfax School who had been apprenticed to one of the highest-priced modistes in London, there was both authority and familiarity behind her protest. "It's the most elegant thing I've ever made."

"Merciful heavens!" Olivia patted her chest distractedly. "If my cousin sees me in this gown, she will shut me in the attic rather than let me go abroad in it. Can we not raise the neckline? I think I could wear stays after all, if the neckline were just a little higher."

"Stays would ruin it," said Jenny firmly. Her expression had taken on a mulish cast. "Only look at the lines, how the dress curves round your bust and falls just so. If you put on stays, my lady, every seam and bone will show through the gauze."

"But I feel so . . . exposed!" Olivia indicated her reflection with a despairing gesture. She looked, frankly, more beautiful than she had ever dreamed possible. But the shimmering gauze that poured down her body and fell in graceful folds behind her, unadorned save for the tiny spangles that glinted in the fabric itself, left little to the imagination.

"I promise you, Lady Olivia, that there is nothing shocking about this gown," Jenny assured her fervently. "Ladies of fashion think nothing of revealing their figures these days. I cannot tell you how happy it makes me to know that *this* gown will be worn by someone whose figure does it justice! And, after all, we have taken great pains to ensure that everything essential is covered." She watched anxiously as Olivia stared broodingly at the pier glass.

Olivia was just about to shake her head in regretful denial when Jenny suddenly brightened, snapping her fingers. "I have it! Stockinette. I will line the body of the gown with stockinette."

"Do you think it will answer?" asked Olivia, torn between doubt and hope.

"Oh, yes, my lady! Stockinette will add a bit of support—and a little warmth, which you may need in the evening air—and the gown will no longer appear transparent. But it will not ruin the effect with bumps and lines, as stays would do. Allow me, ma'am, to assist you out of it. I shall begin work straight away, if I might take it into the next room where the light is better."

Olivia readily consented, relieved that the solution was a simple one. The planned excursion would take place within hours, and her wardrobe contained nothing else that was remotely suitable.

Jenny's careful addition of the stockinette lining proved more difficult than anticipated, however, and as a result there was no time to try on the garment again until Olivia was actually dressing for the evening. By the time Jenny, beaming, pulled the gown into place over Olivia's head, tugging and twitching it expertly to the exact fit she had designed, Olivia's nerves were on the stretch. She turned to face the mirror, dreading what she would see.

She scarcely recognized the exquisite creature staring back at her. As Jenny had promised, the elegant simplicity of the evening gown had been retained. If anything, the folds of material, now slightly heavier, fell more fluidly than before. But Olivia was not entirely sure that modesty had been achieved. The gown was certainly more opaque, and she felt less naked. But the stockinette added its own clingy quality to the thin gauze; her curves were more defined than ever. The sweep of her waist, the fullness of her breasts, even the curve of her belly were nearly as clear as if the dress had been painted onto her rather than sewn.

The little dressmaker was clapping her hands in ecstasy. Olivia's maid was also exclaiming with delight. Their enthusiasm made Olivia wonder if she was, perhaps, being too prudish. Just because she was an old maid, she didn't need to think like one. Thanks to Jenny's artistry, she certainly didn't *look* like one. She stared into the mirror, trying to see the woman reflected there the way others would see her.

Her confidence grew as she studied the glass. *I dare you, Lord Rival. I dare you to keep your distance.*

A wicked smile began to play with the edges of her lips, and the sight of that tiny smile, gleaming back at her from the looking glass, banished the last of her doubts. She took a deep breath, then turned to smile at her audience.

"Thank you, Jenny," she said. "It's perfect. Annie? My diamonds, please."

10

George pocketed the seventy pounds he had won from Nellie Beauchamp two nights ago and deftly straightened his cravat. The stakes tonight were far higher than those offered by little Nellie. If he played his hand well in this game, he might never have to rely on the turn of a card again.

Come to think of it, he had nearly lost the last hand when playing Nellie. George frowned. Was he growing careless? Or merely bored? Bored, probably. It had been so difficult to concentrate in Nellie's company of late that she was beginning to pout and accuse him of inattentiveness.

She was right, of course. His mind was occupied with constant thoughts of Olivia Fairfax and that blasted school of hers—both of which had taken strong possession of his imagination. He chuckled as he studied the smooth-shaven, precisely groomed, expensively dressed rascal in the mirror. Who would have believed that George Carstairs would find his calling while poring over a charity's ledgers? But the columns of numbers and the ups and downs of the financial world they represented interested him. Fascinated him, truth be told. And fired him with ideas—ideas that Olivia seemed to agree were better than any that either she or Culpepper had thought of.

"I'm just a cit in nobleman's clothing," he murmured to his reflection.

The solid thump of a triangular head butting affectionately against his calf made him swear out loud. "Confound it, beast! I wasn't addressing you." He inspected the back of his formerly spotless stocking and grimly removed a bit of black fluff. "Look at this," he admonished Tom, holding it up for the cat's inspection. "What in blue blazes did Beebe see in you? You're more trouble than you're worth."

Tom winked. He always winked when George spoke sharply to him. It was an annoying trait. Doubtless the gesture meant nothing to a cat, but receiving a wink still made a chap feel that he was not taken seriously. The fat, furry nuisance seemed to believe that George was secretly growing fond of him. Which was nonsense, of course.

He heard the clattering of footsteps on the stairs outside his flat, followed by a tattoo of raps on his door. "Damn," said George unemotionally. Since he had recognized the knock, he did not stir from his place before the glass but continued to meditatively make infinitesimal adjustments to his appearance. The door opened regardless, as he had known it would.

"Hallo, Sid," he said dryly. "What do you want now?"

"Hallo, George. I say, that's no way to greet a fellow! Why should I want anything in particular?" Sidney Cheyne sauntered into the room with the familiarity of long acquaintance and dropped, yawning, into a wing chair. "It's cold in here."

"If you don't like it—"

"I know! I can leave." Sid grinned. "My mistake, old man! Your flat is warm as toast." He peered intently at George's cravat. "I say, that's a demmed fine mathematical you've tied there. Very nice indeed. Is that my stickpin?"

"Thank you. And no, it is not."

"Oh, that's right," said Sid without rancor. "Lost it last February or so, didn't I? I must've been bosky to play piquet with you. That sapphire is paste, by the way."

"Yes, I know. I hope you haven't come here to cry off. Have you?"

Sid opened his eyes at this. "You mean Vauxhall? Good God, no. I haven't put on my togs yet, but I'll be there all right and tight. I'm in your debt, dear chap. In fact, I'm much obliged to you for the chance."

George regarded his young friend cynically. "It isn't much of a chance. By the by, the odds are running against you in the clubs these days. The knowing 'uns say that if the Sowerberry hasn't accepted you by now, she never will."

A shadow crossed Sid's features, stealing the rollicking good humor from his cherubic good looks. For a fleeting moment, he looked like the ugly customer he really was. "She'll have me yet," he said shortly. "There's more than one way to skin a cat."

"Dear me! How sinister. I shall refrain from begging you for an explanation of that cryptic observation, and merely point out that there is little scientific evidence to support it."

Sid's laugh sounded a trifle forced. He indicated George's splendid evening attire. "If that's what you will be wearing, the Sowerberry won't look twice at me tonight. Do me a favor, old man, and make yourself scarce once we get there."

"Hm." George seated himself in the chair opposite Sid's. "Is that what you came here for? To request that I keep my distance? You must be feeling even less sure of her than I supposed. But let me put your mind at rest! I have every intention of abandoning my party as soon as I conveniently can—the ideal host, am I not?—which will leave you a clear field, dear boy. You may pursue Miss Sowerberry to your heart's content tonight. I wish you good hunting, in fact."

Sid's relief was as transparent as his hostility. Both warred in his expression as he attempted a careless grin. "Very good of you," he said lightly, and rose to his feet. "I'd place a bet at White's, if I were you, before the odds change. I'm going to win her, George."

George inclined his head in acknowledgment. "In that case, I can only wish you happy," he said, the faintest hint of sarcasm marring his politeness. "What! Are you leaving so soon? Well, well, I shall try to bear up under the loss, and look forward to seeing you later. Briefly, of course."

Sid, already at the door, laughed breezily. "The briefer the better! Although, I must say, I've a great curiosity to see Lady Olivia Fairfax. I was beginning to think her a figment of the *ton*'s imagination."

"Ah. Tried to look her up yourself, did you?" said George, with mock sympathy. "Couldn't get near her, I suppose."

Sid stiffened, an angry flush staining his neck. "More sport in stealing her from under your arrogant nose," he said with false jollity. "Take care I don't cut you out, old man!"

George smiled. "You won't," he promised Sid gently. His tone was pleasant, but Sid's flush deepened.

Sid gave another unconvincing laugh. "Oh, I shan't try. I imagine I'll have my hands full tonight, at any rate, trying to bring Miss Sowerberry round my thumb. Good-bye, then!"

He left as abruptly as he had arrived. George smiled a rather unpleasant smile and regarded the door that Sid had closed behind him. "Quite right," he said softly. "Whatever else you are, Sid Cheyne, you are not stupid."

Tom, who had vanished at Sid's entrance, emerged

from behind the fender and made a sort of peeping sound. George, correctly interpreting this utterance, pointed a finger at his bewhiskered admirer. "No," he said sternly. Tom advanced, clearly intending to spring into George's lap. "No!" repeated George, exasperated. Tom winked at George and then paused, coiling his body in preparation for the jump. George rose, cursing. The only way to thwart the wretched feline was to remove the lap. It seemed to him that in a battle of wills between a man and a pet, the pet ought not to win. Far too often, however, the best George could achieve was a draw.

"Out you go," announced George. He opened a window.

Tom sat on his haunches, looking with mild interest at the gap leading to the rooftops of Mayfair. He did not seem to think that George's invitation was directed to him. Disgusted, George picked up the animal and shoved it bodily through the window and onto the outside ledge. "You want exercise, my pudgy friend," George informed him. "You're getting fatter every day."

Tom sat on the ledge and looked reproachfully over his shoulder at George. "Move your tail," advised George. Tom winked. George, growling, shoved the black-and-white plume out of the way and closed the window. He then removed several hairs that Tom had deposited on his waistcoat while being transported across the room, picked up his gloves, hat, and cloak, and departed for Chelsea.

He paused outside the entrance of his building and looked up. The night was fine and almost warm, far balmier than a September night should be. Stars twinkled in a cloudless sky, and a bright moon bathed London in an ethereal glow. Perfect. He had spent more than a week setting this evening up, lulling Olivia—he hoped—into thinking him harmless. Indifferent to her charms. She had shown signs of pique,

and he had carefully ignored them. She had even cast
out blatant lures, much to his delight, and he had ignored those as well. By the time he invited her to
Vauxhall she was thoroughly miffed, which was just
what he wanted.

Tonight, things would be different. She was primed
to fall at the tiniest push. His practiced show of apathy
had made her unhappy. Tonight, she would tumble
eagerly into his arms, ready to be made happy again.

He had played this game a hundred times.

He sauntered off in the direction of Hyde Park Corner, feeling a pleasant tingle of anticipation. There
was just enough danger in the air to make the game
interesting. One never knew, of course, what a woman's reaction would be, and the uncertain outcome
always added a pinch of excitement to evenings like
this. But this time the game had an entirely different
feel to it. Win or lose, for once he had much more
riding on the outcome than mere pleasure.

A hackney took him to Olivia's town house. She
had suggested that her own coachman drive them to
Vauxhall in a landau. George had not demurred at
this arrangement since, although it was designed to
give Olivia a measure of supposed safety, it also
spared him the necessity of adding Bessie Fairfax to
his party not to mention the expense of providing
the evening's transportation. Upon the stroke of the
appointed hour he alighted from the hackney, paid off
the driver, trod gracefully up the shallow stone steps,
and rapped smartly on Olivia's door. He was in complete control, and his mask of faint boredom was
firmly in place. His quarry must not guess that beneath
the mask he was stretched taut with suspense, as focused as a bloodhound straining at the leash.

Olivia's footman admitted him and he stood at his
ease in the hall, shaking back the folds of his cloak. He
wondered how long he would need to wait. It seemed
unlikely that a woman who had shunned the *beau*

monde for so many years could quickly ready herself for an evening at Vauxhall Gardens. He hadn't given her much lead time, for fear she would back out if she had time to reconsider. He hoped she had not been forced to unearth garments left over from her long-ago presentation. Although she generally dressed well, he supposed he should brace himself for the sight of her in an inappropriately youthful, outmoded evening gown.

No matter what she wore when she eventually appeared, he would have to pretend she looked lovely. He wandered over to a looking glass that hung near the door and absently adjusted the false sapphire he had won from Sidney Cheyne.

"Good evening, Lord Rival." Olivia's low, musical voice sounded on the stairs behind him. George whirled, startled at her promptness, and saw her moving slowly down to him. A half-smile played quizzically across her features.

The suave greeting he had prepared was forgotten. He simply stared at her, his jaw slackening. He thought he had braced himself for anything, but no man could prepare for a shock like this.

Gone was the chaste spinster covered neck to wrist in muslin. Gone was the respectable, no-nonsense director of the Helen Fairfax School for Girls. A dark-haired, smoky-voiced siren was gliding down the stairs, clad in what appeared to be molten moonbeams—and very little else. The candlelight sparkled sinuously along her slender form and flashed from the diamonds at her ears and throat.

Her hair was coiled in shining braids twisted cunningly atop her head, which balanced gracefully on the willowy column of her neck. He had never noticed how long her neck was. He noticed it now, his eye drawn by the twin lines of diamonds suspended from her earlobes and dancing beside her slim throat. But there were many stronger claims on his attention. A glorious expanse of butter-soft skin, hitherto hidden, was spread like a banquet before him. Kid gloves covered her tightly from fingertips to elbows, but somehow they only served to emphasize how thin the veil was that covered everything else. That wonderful neck, those white shoulders, the softly rounded upper arms were bare, and as for the swell of her breasts—s'death, he could see everything! Almost. And what he couldn't see, he couldn't help imagining.

The effect might have been vulgar on another woman. On Olivia Fairfax, it was not. Her queenly carriage, combined with the simple lines and lack of ornamentation on the gown, lent a quiet elegance to the glittering sweep of fabric. She was breathtaking.

He watched, spellbound, as the vision approached and held out her gloved hand. He took it in his, and looked her full in the face. Those extraordinary eyes of hers! Clear as water, bright as moonlight. Platinum haloed with ebony. A man could drown in them and die content.

He was painfully aware that his mask had dropped, and probably lay in metaphorical splinters at his feet. So much for his cherished savoir faire. It was impossible to feign indifference—the most he could do was hold his ground, when he wanted nothing more than to ravish her right there on the cold marble floor.

The best part was, no one seemed to recognize her. Well—actually, the best part had been the expression on Lord Rival's face when she came downstairs. But the *second*-best part was encountering so many people she had met before, and not having to speak to any of them. No one seemed to connect the poised woman in the spangled gown with the coltish little girl who had stumbled and shied her way through half a Season eight or nine years ago. She was able to move along the fringe of the throng, one hand resting lightly on George's arm, and enjoy the beauty of the scene uninterrupted. Her daring costume was nearly as good as a disguise.

It was fully dark by the time they arrived, but the public areas were brightly lighted and paper lanterns glowed in the trees along every walkway, hung in festoons and dancing in the lightest breeze. The effect was magical. Olivia exclaimed when she saw them, impervious to George's teasing about her unfashionable display of enthusiasm. She didn't care. She knew from the moment she alighted from the carriage and saw the splendor of the evening, of the gardens, of the shifting kaleidoscope of well-dressed people, that she was walking into a fairy tale.

The dreamlike quality persisted. She felt wonderful, and completely unlike her ordinary self. The thrill of feeling *beautiful* was completely new to her. As she strolled on the well-kept graveled walkways, Lord Rival at her side, soft globes of colored light everywhere and magic all around her, it seemed to Olivia that this must be the happiest evening of her life. Nothing could possibly surpass it.

He led her through the temples and pavilions, smiling at her unabashed delight, and finally to a little bridge where they could look out over part of the scene. Music drifted up from the Grove, where an orchestra played among the glimmering lights glimpsed through the trees and foliage. Olivia leaned dreamily against the railing before her and drank it all in.

"Everyone should have one night like this," she murmured. "One night, in every life, when heaven comes down to earth. When heaven is so close you can almost touch it."

"The evening has barely begun," he said softly. "We may touch heaven yet."

She was so aware of his compelling presence beside her that she fancied she could feel heat and vitality radiating from him. His hand touched her waist and, for one delicious moment, she surrendered to temptation and leaned against his shoulder. The rough fabric of his coat scraped against her ear and she caught the clean, pleasant scent of his shaving soap. His very masculinity was fascinating—and utterly, thrillingly alien. She moved away, her senses humming from the brief contact.

"Only the angels can touch heaven," she said lightly, if a trifle breathlessly. "I am content merely to glimpse it."

"For now, you mean." He leaned lazily against the railing, watching her.

"For now," she agreed, smiling.

She turned her attention back to the music and the lights, trying to appear unconscious that his eyes were still on her. "Tell me," he said at last, "how it is that you never came here before. I thought everyone managed to end up at Vauxhall at least once or twice during the Season."

"They may, but I avoid the Season. I thought you knew that."

"None better." A grin flashed across his dark features. "You will never know how tirelessly I worked to flush you out of hiding! I know you are a hermit today, but how did you escape the Season during your salad days? You are an earl's daughter. Someone must have presented you at court, given balls in your honor and all that."

She glanced sideways at him, wary as a stalked deer. "Why do you ask?"

"Because I want to know. You may chalk it up to idle curiosity. Come, now! I don't *always* have an ulterior motive."

She laughed at his injured expression. "Very well! There is nothing mysterious about it. I was presented, I was trotted round to a few excruciating parties, and

I attended three and a half balls. I was seventeen, and a late bloomer. In other words, sir, I was still too young and awkward to enjoy it much."

He quirked an eyebrow. "How does one attend half a ball?"

"One attends half a ball when, halfway through the evening, one is called to the bedside of one's dying mother." Her throat constricted and she looked away, vexed with herself. How stupid, to try to speak casually of such a thing. She ought to have avoided the subject entirely. She took a deep breath and hurried back into speech. "My mother was taken ill and left us before morning. It was all very sudden and wholly unexpected. Thus, my one and only Season was abruptly curtailed. I returned home. To my father's estate."

"I'm sorry," he said quietly. "But why did you not return to London the next year?"

"My father died the following March, just before the Season would have started up again."

"Ah." She noticed he did not offer condolences on the loss of her father. Even in the distress of discussing those dark days, she felt a stab of amused gratitude. "And—the year after that?"

"Oh, by then I had started the charity and was a confirmed recluse," she said carelessly. High time to change the subject; they were nearing dangerous ground. She bestowed a bright smile upon him. "At what hour do we join your party?"

He straightened immediately and offered his arm. "Whenever you like."

Relieved, she took his proffered arm and allowed him to lead her toward the quadrangle. But she had not succeeded in diverting his thoughts. He leaned down and murmured in her ear, "You cannot escape merely by snubbing me. I am not so easily fobbed off."

She bit her lip. "Since I have plainly indicated my

desire to change the subject," she said severely, "it would be the height of bad manners for you to pursue it."

"Yes, but I'm such a rudesby that I will pursue it regardless," he said equably. "I am agog to learn how, and why, you became a recluse at the tender age of—nineteen, was it? Yes. You would have been nineteen, certainly no more than that. A bit young to become a hermit, I think. What reason did you have? You are not shy. And it's not that you dislike this sort of entertainment. You are displaying a level of enjoyment tonight that leads me to suspect that you are, if anything, starved for it."

"Nonsense."

"Starved for it," he repeated firmly.

Olivia pasted a determined smile on her face. "How pleasant it is to walk among the trees," she observed. "The paths are very well kept, are they not?"

His eyes gleamed appreciatively, but he disregarded her attempt to ignore him. "Someone must have been rude to you. No, that can't be it. You would not spurn society for such a paltry reason."

"We don't often have such fine weather in September."

"Did the Regent paw you, I wonder? That would be enough to send anyone into hiding."

She choked, but went gamely on. "What a lovely piece the orchestra is playing! Are you fond of music, my lord?"

"Passionately. Let us stop here awhile and listen." He startled her by abruptly dragging her into a side path, much narrower and darker than the main walkway. The foliage grew thicker here, close to the path on either side, and as she followed him, half-laughing, half-protesting, he pulled her along to a small, deserted clearing that seemed utterly private. The place could not be as isolated as it felt, she told herself staunchly. Music was still plainly audible, and lamplight filtered through the leaves. The clearing floor was gravel, neatly raked, so it was obviously part of the public area. But they were quite alone.

"You are a rogue," she scolded him, pulling out of his grip. "What will your party think of us if we do not arrive soon? They will believe you have kidnaped me—and you very nearly have! Where are we?"

He grinned and leaned casually against a tree, looking very much at home. "Every rake in England has a secluded corner permanently reserved at Vauxhall. This is mine."

She did not quite believe him, but his words gave her an odd, disappointed feeling. He had forced her to picture him here with someone other than herself. A host of someones, she reminded herself bleakly. What was unique and magical to her was common in his life, and completely forgettable. He probably did not even remember the kiss they had shared.

Well. She mustn't let that happen again. She folded her arms across her chest as if protecting herself from an onslaught, and fixed him with a gimlet glare. "You are the rudest person I have ever met."

"And the most persistent," he said, with the glimmer of a smile. "It will save time if you simply tell me what I want to know."

Two could play at this game. Her eyes narrowed. "I will answer your question if you will answer mine."

"Done," he said promptly. He looked keenly at her, sympathy writ large upon his face. "Something happened to you the summer after your father died. What was it?"

She lifted her chin defiantly. "If you *must* know, I fell in love."

He straightened, frowning. "By Jove. Why didn't you marry the chap?"

She tried to laugh, but her laughter sounded as hollow as it felt. "I did not marry him, sir, because I discovered he was a fortune hunter."

There. She had said it. Her instinct was to walk away to hide her face, since the rawness of her pain must be visible—but it was more important to see George's reaction. She stood her ground, therefore, and looked him squarely in the eyes.

He looked stunned, but only for a moment. "I see," he said quietly.

Tears stung the back of her eyelids and she blinked furiously to clear them, gritting her teeth. "I am not . . . eager . . . to repeat that mistake."

"No." He paced the clearing restlessly, once, then halted in his tracks and swore under his breath. "I cannot blame you for being on your guard with me. Did you believe he loved you?"

"Oh, yes." Her smile was brittle. "We all believed him. He was so guileless! So frank and open! He seemed to wear his heart on his sleeve, you know. He was utterly, ardently in love with me. He made it all seem perfectly plausible. And I was young and . . . gullible." She shivered. "There is no kinder word for it. I was a fool. I adored him."

"How did you discover the truth?"

"Culpepper found out. And brought me proof." She passed a hand over her eyes, her voice unsteady. "I had rather not dwell on it, if you please."

"My poor Olivia." His voice roughened with what sounded like genuine compassion. She had to fight to keep from casting herself into his arms and weeping down his shirtfront. How absurd!

She took a deep breath and tried to turn the tables on him. "Have you ever been in love?" she asked.

One brow flew upward. He smiled wryly at her. "I did agree to answer your question, did I not?"

"Yes." She smiled faintly. "It's a debt of honor."

"So it is. And I am meticulous in matters of play and pay." He reached casually over and took her hand, drawing her with him into the shadows. "The answer is yes."

Her pulse leaped at his touch. "A dozen times, I suppose you will say! But that is not the same thing."

"I know it." He touched her cheek briefly, then smiled teasingly at her. "I was in love once, and only once."

Olivia decided her best course was to ignore the fact that his hands had moved lightly down and linked themselves behind her waist. She placed her hands against his chest to hold him off—a bit—and asked, as nonchalantly as she could, "Why did you not marry the lady?"

"She was already married."

Olivia stiffened and he shook his head at her, laughing. "Now, be careful, Olivia! You are jumping to conclusions. Clarissa was a paragon of virtue. I was not yet twenty, and incredibly callow. She was a few years older, and the most beautiful creature I ever beheld. I worshiped at her feet—together with half of London, unfortunately. I was one of a gaggle of moonstruck lads who dangled at her shoestrings, writing bad poetry and fighting duels over her and generally making cakes of ourselves. Her husband tolerated it because he knew she had eyes only for him. He was the luckiest chap I ever knew." George shook his head, grinning ruefully. "I maneuvered all Season to get my Clarissa alone, and when I finally succeeded she laughed at me—very kindly and sweetly!—and then scolded me roundly for making advances to a married woman. She thoroughly routed me. As I recall, I actually apologized. A most painful experience."

Olivia could not help laughing. "I wish I could have seen it."

A speculative gleam lit his grin. "Come to think of it, you and she would have gotten along famously. What a pity you never met! She and her husband still make an appearance in town from time to time, but not often. They are too wealthy to care what others think of them—which is another thing you and Clarissa would have in common."

"Oh, you mean that she's as much a snob as I am?"

He chuckled. "You have it backward, my dear. A snob cares too much what others think of him. You and Clarissa are the two most unworldly women it has ever been my pleasure to know."

"And the richest?" she inquired politely.

He flashed a wicked grin. "That, too."

"I sense a pattern emerging." She looked sideways at him, lips pursed. He burst out laughing.

"Touché, my sweet witcracker! Very astute."

Olivia felt absurdly pleased. It wasn't every day she received a compliment out of Shakespeare. "How did you finally manage to fall out of love with her?" she asked.

"I didn't." His smile softened. "Ever since those days, I have found blondes insipid, empty-headed females irritating, and women of loose morals a bore. Clarissa Whitlatch left me with an unquenchable thirst for dark-haired, forthright, intelligent women." His eyes gleamed as they studied her face. "And you are forcing me to add silver eyes to my list of requirements."

She felt her heart skip a beat and had to transfer her gaze to his cravat. She was afraid that a very foolish smile was playing with the edges of her mouth—but, really, it was impossible not to feel fluttered when being flattered by George. He was so awfully good at it.

His arms tightened behind her. "How did you fall out of love with your fortune hunter?" he asked her softly.

I fell for another one. For one crazy moment, Olivia was afraid she had said the words aloud. She had to remind herself to breathe. Then she looked up into George's face with, she hoped, a fair assumption of poise.

"What I loved did not exist," she said flatly. "I fell in love with an illusion. And I think we should join your party now."

11

The supper box where Lord Rival led her seemed, to Olivia, overcrowded. It was designed to hold as many as eight, but when two of the party were as large as Mr. and Mrs. Sowerberry, four persons were sufficient to fill it. The Sowerberrys' ample forms took up fully half the box. Since their daughter and a young friend of George's, Sidney Cheyne, had also been invited, the belated addition of Lord Rival and Lady Olivia was a bit problematic. They did squeeze in somehow, but six persons seated in too-close proximity and pretending to be at ease was not Olivia's idea of a pleasant way to pass the time.

She was unacquainted with anyone other than George. Mrs. Sowerberry, however, immediately attached herself to Olivia and enumerated, in a penetrating voice, all the acquaintances which she supposed they must have in common. Olivia bore this as well as she could, but eventually, in desperation, turned to include Miss Sowerberry in the conversation. Miss Sowerberry was a bony, flat-chested girl with the thick, kinky hair of a sheep. She had a downtrodden look about her, and responded to Olivia's friendly overtures in a monosyllabic mumble. Olivia's irritation turned to sympathy when the reason for this became clear—she caught Mrs. Sowerberry frowning fiercely at her daughter before reclaiming Olivia's attention for her overpowering self.

Within ten minutes of her arrival at the supper table, several unpleasant facts were abundantly clear to Olivia. The first was that Sidney Cheyne—a good-looking lad whom she thought charming for, perhaps, the first three minutes of their acquaintance—was doggedly pursuing Miss Sowerberry. Miss Sowerberry had little to recommend her to a handsome, well-connected young man, so it was plain as a pikestaff that the unfortunate girl was rich. It was equally obvious that Mrs. Sowerberry's opinion of Mr. Cheyne was not high, and that the only reason she had consented to bring her daughter to this party was that she had been promised an introduction to Lady Olivia Fairfax. Olivia was the prize that had been dangled before the Sowerberrys like a carrot on a stick.

She hid her revulsion behind the well-trained wall of politeness her breeding had taught her, but she was deeply angry. That rascal George sat beside her—actually pressing his audacious thigh against her knee!—and smiled blandly at the indignant glances she threw him. She itched to give him a piece of her mind.

Mrs. Sowerberry was the worst sort of mushroom—a pushy, loudmouthed, fawning woman, clinging by her fingernails to the fringes of society and determined to thrust her daughter into the aristocracy. She had her work cut out for her, thought Olivia disgustedly, for although Mr. Sowerberry did little but sit there, silently shoving a fearsome amount of food down his gullet, it was obvious he was nothing but a cit. He must be wealthy indeed for his daughter to attract someone like Sidney Cheyne! But Mr. Cheyne she disliked more than the Sowerberrys. He was a young man of birth and breeding, and, to Olivia's mind, there was no excuse for what he had become.

Had she not been so angry with George, she would

have been grateful when he leaned in and interrupted one of Mrs. Sowerberry's monologues, inquiring whether Olivia would care to try the famous arrack punch.

She shot him a fulminating glare, but kept her voice civil. "I think not, thank you. I believe it is made with strong spirits."

"Rum, in fact." His dark eyes danced with mischief. "I'm sure it would do you good. You look a little pale."

"The air has become strangely oppressive," she told him sweetly. "I hope I am not unwell."

His grin was completely unrepentant. "If you are, my dear Lady Olivia, I heartily recommend the punch. A glass or two, and you will feel wonderfully improved."

Mr. Cheyne chimed in. "Perhaps she needs air, Rival. It's a bit close in the supper boxes." He flashed a careless, overly boyish grin at the Sowerberrys. "I'll be happy to play host while you are gone, dear chap."

Mrs. Sowerberry greeted this suggestion with a hostile sniff, but Olivia was so eager to escape the supper box that she seized on it at once. "If you would not mind, my lord—" she began, trying to sound meek and apologetic.

"Not at all," he said promptly. He immediately rose and discarded his cloak, assisting Olivia with the smoothest of smiles. It was only when she had gratefully risen and taken his arm that it occurred to her: The entire incident was extremely suspect. Was that laughter she saw lurking in his eyes?

Before she could decide, he was bowing and taking his leave of the table, and custom demanded that she do the same. Mrs. Sowerberry hoped, in a disgruntled voice, that Lady Olivia would feel better shortly and return to finish her supper. Mr. Cheyne boomingly assured Lord Rival that the company would be in good hands and that he might take his time without worrying that his guests would be neglected. Mr. Sowerberry grunted, and Miss Sowerberry said nothing at all.

Once again, Olivia found herself strolling off through the gardens on George's arm. Had he planned it that way? As they left the quadrangle and turned the corner onto one of the walkways, placing the supper box out of sight, she stopped in her tracks and rounded on him, eyes narrowed. He looked at her, his brows climbing in an expression of guileless inquiry—but Olivia saw his shoulders shake with mirth.

"I knew it! You did that on purpose," she said accusingly. To her dismay, she discovered that she was fighting a strong impulse to laugh. She bit her lip and glared at him, but it was too late. His wicked grin told her that he had seen the laughter she was trying to suppress.

"I don't know what you mean," he said, assuming an innocent air.

"You deliberately inflicted upon me a party of persons whom you *knew* I would loathe! How dare you use me so?"

"You are too severe," he lamented, apparently deeply injured. "Why would I do such an unhandsome thing? I thought you would be pleased. A simple, family party—"

"Family?"

"Certainly. Mr. Cheyne tells me he is your mother's third cousin twice removed, or some such thing."

She threw up her hands in eloquent despair. "Must you remind me of that?"

"Well, well, one cannot choose one's family," he said soothingly. "If it is any solace to you, he claims a similar kinship to me. I thought his connection to both our families formed a logical link between you and me—adding an air of respectability to the evening."

Her lips twitched. George's air of triumph indicated

that he had thought of that excuse this very instant. "I see. So Mr. Cheyne's presence provided the illusion that, despite my otherwise incongruous presence, your party consisted entirely of family members. Well, *that* ought to keep the scandalmongers silent! Very thoughtful of you. And what relation are the Sowerberrys to me, pray?"

He rubbed his chin thoughtfully. "Let me see. As future in-laws of Mr. Cheyne—"

"According to whom?"

"Mr. Cheyne. Why are you laughing? He ought to know who his future in-laws will be."

"Heavens, yes. There can be no higher authority for that information. Do you know, I am almost disappointed? I thought I was taking a grave risk in coming here alone with you. Instead I discover that I am being chaperoned by all these delightful additions to my family."

George spread his hands deprecatingly. "Exactly. A perfectly tame and logical gathering. I invited our mutual cousin—or whatever he is—to make you feel at ease, and the Sowerberrys to make Mr. Cheyne feel at ease."

She folded her arms across her chest and tapped her foot on the gravel path. "I don't know what you deserve," she said at last, trying to sound stern despite the laughter quivering in her voice. "That frightful woman will trumpet my name to everyone she knows. Even if I escape being hailed as her cousin, I shall figure in her speech forevermore as 'my dear friend, Lady Olivia Fairfax.' "

"She is a friendly soul," he said, sounding pleased. "I'm glad you liked her."

Olivia could not help it; she burst out laughing.

George took her hand and placed it back on his arm, patting it. "Good. You are not truly angry."

"I am *excessively* angry!" she exclaimed, still laughing. "You are the worst rogue I ever met."

"Yes, but your experience is limited," George reminded her, leading her in a leisurely way toward one of the pavilions. "How did you like your newfound cousin?"

"Which one? Mr. Cheyne? He is the second-worst rogue I ever met."

George's eyes glinted down at her in amusement. "So you did see through him. I wondered if you would."

"He is loathsome," announced Olivia, not mincing matters. "Is he truly a friend of yours?"

George paused before answering. "I suppose he is. Fancies himself my friend, at any rate. In a moment of weakness, I actually gave him a key to my flat. I am growing increasingly weary of his antics, however. He doesn't seem quite the amusing fellow I once thought him."

"He sets my teeth on edge. I can't believe you ever thought him amusing! I saw through that false bonhomie at once."

"Oh, I saw through it! I simply—forgave it." He still smiled, but behind the smile Olivia thought he looked troubled. She was sure of it when he glanced down at her and said softly, "He and I are very much alike, you know."

Olivia stiffened in instinctive rejection of such a notion. "You are *nothing* alike!" she said hotly. "How can you say such a thing? No, I will not listen to you— it is absurd! He is the most repellent man it has ever been my misfortune to encounter, and *you*—" She stopped, struggling, and fell silent.

He was laughing again. "Oh, pray finish your sentence!" he begged. "Am I the most *attractive* man—"

"—it has ever been my misfortune to encounter," she finished grimly. She was blushing, but threw him a look of defiance. "I am having a most unlucky September, am I not?"

"And I am having the luckiest." Something in his

smile eased her mortification and almost made it possible for her to smile back at him. She resisted the temptation, however.

They had drawn very near to one of the pavilions, where a small dance orchestra played, planted in an overhanging balcony. The smooth floor of the pavilion was dotted with laughing couples, swirling together in time to the music. Festoons of gently bobbing lanterns had been strung above the dance floor, lending a glow of enchantment to the scene.

It was a pretty sort of dancing, new to Olivia. She had been watching the dance for some time without seeing it, but now it excited her curiosity and claimed her attention. The couples did not dance in a discernable pattern. Instead of sets moving together and apart in figures, each couple seemed to be dancing in isolation. The fact that everyone danced in the same direction was the only thing that kept the couples from colliding. The most arresting feature of the dance was that the dancing couples held each other in a sort of embrace—a stylized embrace, but an embrace nevertheless. She kept expecting them to break apart and form some other figure, but the dance apparently contained none. Some of the couples held each other more closely than others, some danced side-by-side or with the woman revolving gracefully beneath her partner's arm, but all the couples danced in unbroken contact with each other.

It was this that made her realize she was seeing a waltz. She had heard of the waltz. Lurid descriptions of it were a recurring theme in popular discussions of moral decay. The waltz was frequently singled out as providing proof of the decline of civilization. Intrigued, she watched the shifting, circling couples and tried to imagine what it would feel like to dance that way. It was pretty to watch, but she could not picture herself doing it. Certainly not without blushing.

Absorbed in her own thoughts, she belatedly realized that George was soliciting her hand. She looked up at him, startled. "Oh! I beg your pardon; I wasn't attending. Did you—did you say the next dance? If it is a country dance, or even a quadrille, I would be happy to—"

"It won't be. The orchestra's played nothing but waltzes since they struck up. They are all the rage, you know."

"Yes, I know." She returned her gaze to the dancers, concentrating this time on the music. "The music is appealing, isn't it? Very—how would you describe it? Rhythmic."

"Olivia! Is this the first time you've heard a waltz?"

Olivia blushed. "You needn't stare at me as if I were a Hottentot," she said with dignity. "I might very well have heard a waltz before—without knowing it."

"By Jove. You don't know how to waltz." George took a breath, a rather queer expression descending on his face. It almost looked as if he were excited by the news and trying to keep a lid on his exultation. "This is an unexpected development."

"How so? I have already told you that I haven't attended a ball since I was seventeen."

"I think you should learn to waltz."

She chuckled. "I have no need for it! I have allowed you to bring me to Vauxhall for one night, but that does *not* mean I am ready to cast myself into the social whirl! I haven't time for such nonsense. And besides, I would dislike it excessively."

"You won't dislike the waltz," he promised. She felt his hand touch her waist again, and a shock of electricity seemed to pass through his palm and into her body. She looked up instinctively, but it was a mistake to meet his eyes. There was something intimate and teasing in his smile that made her forget to breathe.

"We struck a bargain," he reminded her softly. "I have borne with patience your lessons in bookkeeping, my lady. It is time you submitted to *my* authority for an hour or two. Here is something you need to learn—and I know how to teach."

"Tonight?" she asked weakly.

"Tonight." He grinned. "You'll learn it in no time."

She glanced back at the dance floor, curiosity warring with shyness. "I can't bear it. I shall look such a fool."

"No one will see you. We'll go off by ourselves until you have learned the steps."

She shook her head, laughing. "I might have known! Do you propose to haul me into the shrubbery to teach me the waltz?"

"Curb your suspicion, Prudence! I happen to know that behind that wall to your left, the very wall to which the orchestra's balcony is attached, there is a paved area with a fountain in the center. We will hear the music as well there as if we were on the dance floor. We will be invisible to all the other dancers. And since the waltz is danced in a circular pattern, we can waltz round the fountain." His hand tightened on her waist, drawing her infinitesimally closer as he leaned in to whisper teasingly in her ear. "Trust me."

"I don't know why I should," she said stiffly, trying to sound as disapproving as she wished she felt. She was already perfectly aware that she was about to acquiesce.

He gave her another of his wicked grins. "Then don't. But if you require some token from me to make up your mind, I will pledge to you that, for once, my intentions are honorable. Nothing untoward will happen. May I teach you?"

She studied his face, torn between the impulse to avoid running an even greater risk than she already had, and an even stronger impulse to follow him wherever he might lead. Every instinct clamored out a warning that this man was dangerous, that this night was dangerous, that she was gambling with her heart, her happiness—and perhaps her entire future—by going off alone with him. Of what use was it, to promise herself that she would keep her guard up? That she would not trust him too far? That she would not allow her emotions to run away with her common sense? She had already made those promises to herself, and she was breaking them right and left.

In later years, it seemed to her that this was the moment that forever changed her life. This was the last moment when she could have said "No." Had she refused this one dance, her entire life might have been different.

But she did not refuse.

She looked at the dancers once again, this time picturing herself among them in her shimmering gown, George's eyes smiling down at her, his touch guiding her as they glided on a lilting swell of music. The dream was irresistible.

"Thank you, Lord Rival," she said demurely. "Yes. You may."

12

*H*e hoped she was not already having regrets. As soon as they turned off the main walkway, the light and merriment of Vauxhall Gardens receded, plunging them into a private world. She moved beside him as if in a trance, completely silent, as he led her deeper and deeper into the gloom. The path narrowed sharply near the entrance of the clearing, foliage crowding in on either side until they could no longer walk abreast. He took her hand then, drawing her after him, and at the end of the path held up a low-hanging branch so that it would not strike her as she entered the clearing. She walked gravely beneath his arm and into the clear space. Here, as he had promised, a fountain played and the stars shone down. She halted, looking around her in pleased surprise.

"But—this is marvelous," she said, her voice hushed and filled with wonder.

Luck had favored him once again: The clearing behind the pavilion was deserted. The tall fountain, springing from a waist-high basin, danced and sparkled in the center of the pavement, its tinkling music meshing prettily with the orchestra's strains. His attention drawn to it by the awe in her voice, he also looked around, seeing the place with new eyes. He had to admit, it *was* rather marvelous. There was something deliciously intimate about this space behind the wall, invisible to the world of light and music just beyond it. They shared the enchantment of the lilting strings, the fluting woodwinds, and the filtered glow of lamplight, and yet they were completely hidden, their presence undetected and unsuspected by the musicians and dancers on the other side of the wall. It was a special, secret place. The music and the magic seemed stolen—and somehow sweeter for it.

Olivia walked a few paces toward the fountain, swaying slightly in time to the music, then turned her face up to the stars, stretched out her arms and turned in a blissful circle. "Oh, it's *more* than marvelous," she whispered, laughing softly with delight.

He grinned. Her straightforward enjoyment was touching. It spoke volumes about her naivete as well as her candor. And these guileless displays of enthusiasm seemed to indicate that on some level, and despite everything, she trusted him. Odd, that.

"I'm glad you like it," he said simply.

She dropped her arms and smiled mistily at him. "This is the most wonderful night of my life," she blurted. Then she seemed to catch herself and laughed a little, wrinkling her nose in embarrassment. "Heavens, what a bumpkin! I must sound terribly—*farouche,* I suppose, to a man like you."

He opened his mouth to respond with a polite lie, but stopped just in time. Her honesty deserved better than that. "A little," he admitted, trusting she would see the twinkle in his eyes. "But it's refreshing. Your complete lack of subtlety is so charming, in fact, that I was beginning to wonder whether it was deliberate."

She relaxed a little, leaning lightly against the bowl of the fountain. "No, alas! I have no talent for polite dissembling. And there is something about you. . . . You have a very strange effect on me. I don't know how to describe it." She rested one elbow on the wide

lip of the fountain's pool and tilted her head to one
side, studying him as if his face would provide the
answer.

He strolled forward to join her. "I bring out the
worst in you?" he suggested.

She chuckled. "Oh, I *hope* that's not it! But perhaps
you do. A little."

He smiled. She was such a pretty sight, leaning
gracefully against the fountain, that damnably alluring
gown glittering as if her naked body had been sprin-
kled with diamonds. "If this is the worst of you, Olivia,
I would hate to see the best."

"What do you mean?"

"Remember what you told me earlier? Heaven is
not for mortals." He took her gloved hand in his and
gallantly kissed her knuckles.

She laughed uncertainly. "I think you are flattering
me, but I am not precisely sure," she remarked, pulling her hand out of his. "Never mind! The orchestra
is striking up again. I would like to begin the lesson,
if you please."

"Very well. Shall we begin with the German style,
or the French?"

"I don't know one from the other." She gazed
steadily into his eyes. "Begin with whatever you like."

She sounded a little breathless. The atmosphere had
subtly altered. He looked down into her upturned face
and felt himself tighten with desire.

"I like it all."

"Then teach me everything."

Her voice was husky with a meaning he could not
mistake. He felt his blood begin to pound. She knew
she was treading on dangerous ground. She knew it,
and still she placed herself in his power.

She wanted it, then. She wanted him.

She wants *something,* he reminded himself, fighting
for control. Part of what made this woman so damned
exciting was the contrast she offered to the jaded flirts

he knew. Unlike the bored wives who sought his company, Olivia might not know what it was she wanted.

Desire was not permission. To earn this prize he would have to show her her own desire. Make her name it. Win her consent before he plundered her. George was too experienced a gambler to tip his hand this early in the game.

The night was on his side. He had lured her to the most romantic of settings. The fountain splashed and sparkled beside them; the heady scent of crushed leaves and the rich fragrance of woodsmoke heralded the approach of autumn; the night was fair and cool. Best of all, sweet music swelled and filled the air, seemingly played for them alone. Mother Nature and Lady Luck had joined forces to deal him a winning hand. All he had to do was play it.

Olivia seemed to be holding her breath, waiting, spellbound, for his first move. Inspiration struck. "Take off your gloves," he commanded softly.

There was just enough light to read her expression. Her eyes widened, but she did not back away. "Wh-what?"

"It will be easier to teach you if you can feel my hand." Would she believe him? It was worth a try. He would risk a great deal for a chance to touch that gorgeous skin of hers. He held her eyes with his, willing her cooperation, as he matter-of-factly stripped off his own gloves and laid them on the lip of the fountain. "Come here," he invited. "I'll help you."

She hesitantly held one hand toward him. He took it as gently as if he were holding a baby bird, trying not to break the fragile bubble of Olivia's trust. His ungloved fingers made swift work of the tiny pearl buttons. Then he drew the long glove off her unresisting arm with a sort of reverence. *Beautiful.* Her pale skin glowed like foxfire in the moonlight. Uncovered, her arm appeared almost as white as it had when gloved—but infinitely softer.

He placed the discarded glove beside his own, and, careful not to brush against her ungloved arm, took her other hand. Not until that glove had joined its mate did he dare to touch her newly bared flesh with his. The shock of contact, skin against skin, would surely have broken the spell. She might have forbade him to go further—and he meant to go much further than this.

All gloves were off. It was time to begin.

He took her hand, sliding his fingers intimately across her palm. Olivia's lips parted in shock and he heard the tiny intake of her breath as they touched. Yes. He felt it, too. It surprised him almost as much as it surprised her. Such a small thing, the touching of two hands; such an everyday contact. But this touch was different. Momentous. Charged with temptation and danger.

He had known that touching her bare skin would pleasure him, but it clearly pleasured her as well—and the rarity of such a sensation to Olivia must double its importance to her. Knowing that, and knowing how seldom she had been touched by any man, added unexpected fuel to the fire blazing within him. The mere taking of her hand was charged with sensual electricity.

This was going to be even better than he had imagined.

A smile played across his features as he studied her face. "Step a little closer to me," he murmured.

She was as transparent as water. He read alarm in her eyes, and doubt, battling with desire. He made no move. He knew which of those emotions would prove the strongest, and waited for desire to win. When it did, as he knew it would, she took a tiny step forward. Her breasts nearly touched his coat buttons now. Each could feel heat radiating from the other.

"Place your left hand on my shoulder."

"Like this?"

"Yes."

He placed his right hand on her waist. God help him—she wasn't wearing stays! The fact had been painfully evident to him all evening as he fought to keep his eyes off her breasts, but he had concentrated so hard on that task that he had forgotten what it would mean when he danced with her. Hell's bells! No wonder society demanded that a gentleman wear gloves when dancing with a lady.

No gloves. No stays. One thin, clingy layer of material, insubstantial as gossamer and warmed by her skin, was all that separated his flesh from hers. It was too much; he could not resist. His hand traveled, as if of its own volition, to the small of her back and pulled her body tightly against his chest.

A tiny sound escaped her and her eyes closed for a moment. She looked dazed, completely overwhelmed. Since this was exactly how he felt, seeing her arousal magnified his. He now knew, without a doubt, that if he managed to actually seduce her it would be the best sexual experience of his life—if getting there didn't kill him first.

Her starry black lashes fluttered briefly, then her eyes opened and stared into his. "Close your eyes," he whispered, and she instantly obeyed. Her head fell back, her lips parted as if expecting his kiss, but his gambler's instincts urged him to wait. He inwardly cursed the necessity, but knew his instincts were right. *Not yet. But soon.*

"Listen to the music," he murmured. "Do you feel it?" While Olivia's eyes were safely shut, her head tilted back, he stared drunkenly at her throat, exposed and gleaming, pale in the moonlight. A tiny pulse beat beneath her ear, just where a slender line of diamonds hung trembling from her earlobe and fell back against the dark mass of her hair. "One, two-three. One, two-three," he whispered, mesmerized by her visible, vulnerable heartbeat. "Do you feel it, Olivia?"

"Yes," she breathed, and the movement of her lips

pulled his gaze to her mouth. Before he could tear his eyes away, hers unexpectedly opened.

She had caught him staring at her mouth. He was too drugged with lust to smooth the moment over; all he could do was gaze wordlessly at her with everything he wanted written plainly in his face.

She neither shied away nor blushed. Her eyes drifted shut again and—God save the mark!—he felt her body soften and mold itself to his in blatant invitation.

A haze of pure heat seemed to cloud his vision. He tried to gather the shreds of his cool detachment, and failed. All thought of actually teaching her to waltz fled. Against his better judgment, and still holding her tightly against him, he let her hand go and trailed his fingertips sinuously up the inside of her arm, savoring the feel of her delicate flesh. The sensation caused her to shiver in his embrace, cracking his control still further. He had both his arms around her now.

A crazy impulse to warn her held him off for one last moment. "I'm going to kiss you," he muttered thickly.

"Yes," she whispered.

That was all the encouragement he could stand. He took a ragged breath and covered her sweet, warm mouth with his. Her response was immediate, and staggeringly erotic. He kissed her, and kissed her, and kissed her, until he could no longer hear the music for the roaring of the blood hammering in his ears. She matched his every move. She followed his every lead, matching his ardor with her own. She fit the very contours of his body. God in heaven, she was perfect. It was unbelievable.

Finally, inevitably, his greedy hands strayed too far. For a heartbeat of time she sighed and clung closer, maddening him with lust, but then she caught herself and stiffened in panic. He immediately brought his hands back to her waist, inwardly cursing his idiocy, but it was too late. She broke the kiss and pressed her forehead against his chin, struggling to catch her breath.

"Sorry," he gasped. Since her lips were denied him, he kissed her forehead, then her hair. "Olivia." It felt good just to say her name. "Olivia. Kiss me again." His voice was hoarse with passion.

He moved to claim her mouth again, but she moaned and collapsed limply against his shoulder. "Oh, I can't. I can't. I can't do this."

"Yes, you can." He tightened his arms around her and laid his cheek against the crown of her head. Amid the raging fire of arousal he was aware of something new to him: joy. When had he ever found joy while kissing a woman? Silent laughter shook him as he marveled at it. The answer was simple, he supposed. It was only natural to rejoice when discovering that one's intended bride was passionate about something other than orphans.

She felt him chuckle and moved back to look at his face. "You promised me that nothing untoward would occur," she said, in a small, flustered voice.

"Nothing untoward *has* occurred." He lifted a hand and gently smoothed a stray lock of hair that was ready to tumble into her face. "I told you my intentions were honorable. And they are."

For an instant, she looked confused. Then her features froze in a shuttered expression. "I see," she said quietly. She pulled out of his arms and walked away, crossing her arms in an instinctive gesture of self-protection.

George frowned. He had obviously made a misstep. He studied her, trying to guess her train of thought. She must have known he was hinting at marriage. A stupid thing to do, when he knew her opposition to it—and how many reasons she had to distrust him. He toyed with, and discarded, various ideas for retrieving his false move, then decided it was time for a real gamble. He would risk honesty.

"You know what I want from you," he said quietly. "What is it that you want from me?"

She stood quite still and would not look at him. There was a perceptible pause before she spoke. "Friendship," she said at last. She ventured a glance at him, evidently saw the sardonic expression her response had evoked, and looked away, blushing in the darkness. "It's true," she said defensively.

"You were closer to the truth when you said you wanted—what was it? Spice." He strolled forward and put his arm around her, drawing her back to the fountain, where the light was better. She tried half-heartedly to resist the intimacy, but he shook his head at her. "Come along; I won't hurt you," he said, in the firm tone one used when addressing a child. She gave a resentful sniff, but did not pull away.

He leaned his back against the fountain and locked his hands behind her waist, studying her face. She placed her hands against his chest and stared stubbornly at his cravat, still very much on her guard.

"If you want my friendship, you may have it. You have it now. But I think there is something more between us."

She gave a tiny shrug. "Perhaps," she said carelessly. Her pathetic attempt to sound like a woman of the world failed adorably.

"There's no doubt about it." He tilted his head playfully, trying to force her eyes to meet his. "Do you kiss all the gentlemen of your acquaintance?"

Turning her head this way and that to avoid his eyes, she bit back a laugh. She still would neither look at him nor reply.

"Well? Do you?"

She sighed, and finally glared directly at him. "I am

acquainted with very few gentlemen," she said with dignity.

"If you hand out kisses with such abandon, that will soon change," he remarked. "They'll be swarming like bees by the end of the week."

She looked stricken. "Oh! Surely you wouldn't—" but she stopped as if the words were strangling her.

"Spread the word? Don't be ridiculous," he said roughly. "I was joking." His hands tightened behind her. The image of men swarming around Olivia was oddly disturbing. "I was trying to point out the absurdity of your remark."

She looked relieved, but only slightly mollified. "Hm! I was trying to keep you from puffing up too much in your own esteem." She glanced slyly at him from under her lashes. "Too late for that, I suppose."

He grinned. "Much too late." She was willing to joke with him a little; this was progress. But she grew serious again almost immediately.

"George. I *do* want your friendship. And only your friendship." She clutched at his lapels now, her expression earnest, her words sounding urgent. "I never meant for this to happen tonight. At least— " She hesitated, then bravely finished her sentence. "At least not all of it."

He regarded her thoughtfully. "Really? I meant for it to happen. All of it." And a good deal more, actually—but he needn't tell her so. He leaned toward her teasingly. "Which part did you want to happen? Whatever it was, I will be happy to repeat it. As many times as you like."

She looked both pleased and embarrassed. "No, thank you," she said primly. "I have had quite enough."

She may as well have thrown down a gauntlet. All of George's predatory instincts immediately rose to the challenge.

"Have you?" he murmured provocatively. "Are you certain?" He leaned forward and gently touched his chin to her forehead, then her temple. She appeared too startled to move. He placed his cheek very close to hers, barely grazing it, and whispered in her ear. "I think I need a little more."

Her cheek was so soft. He slid his cheek against hers and bestowed the lightest possible kiss on the edge of her ear. She pulled away, trying to laugh.

"George—" she began, but got no further. He bent to quickly, gently, kiss her lower lip. And stayed there.

"Just a little," he murmured. His whispered words were half promise, half plea. "Just a little more." As he spoke, his lips moved against her skin in the delicate valley between her lower lip and chin. Miraculously, her lips parted. He had not really expected that they would, but they did. This mark of acquiescence sent a rush of power clear through him.

He did not claim those sweetly offered lips immediately. He hung back a little, his mouth hovering over hers, tasting her warm breath, savoring the feel of her submission. Her parted lips and half-closed eyes inflamed him. She must want him badly, to capitulate so quickly. Olivia's desire was headier than opium—and just as addictive. He wanted more. He wanted her to want more.

He would go slowly this time. He would ignore the fact that he had her permission, and coax her a bit. So at first he kissed only her lower lip, running his lips lightly and slowly along the very edge of it, barely sampling her. He felt her body go limp and cling to his, and her arms creep up and around his neck. *Yes.* God in heaven, when had mere kissing felt this good? *Want me, Olivia.*

He kissed her mouth now and she responded eagerly—but as soon as he felt her response he gently pulled away. He barely kissed just the cupid's bow of her upper lip, then the corner of her mouth. She was trembling in his arms, a soft whimper coming from somewhere in her throat. He could not let this gratifying development go unrewarded, so he returned to leisurely kissing her entire mouth. Slowly, slowly. He kissed her as if he had the entire night just to kiss her—nothing more.

Her response was everything he could have wanted. Her bones seemed to melt. And then her lips shifted and clung to his, achingly, with a mixture of tenderness and sensuality he had never experienced.

Against all odds, this green and untouched girl was showing jaded Lord Rival something new. It was a revelation. Reeling, he held her and kissed her and wallowed in the novel sensations washing over him.

Kissing her like this was such a total experience that it was nearly enough. The two of them seemed to be intimately joined, the strange connection he had previously sensed powerfully completed in their kiss. Time had no meaning. The world retreated. He no longer heard the music surrounding them or felt the chill of the night air. He floated with Olivia, linked to her and dreaming, in a silent communion as spiritual as it was physical. For a measureless time, he felt as if he could never get enough, and almost as if he could never want more.

Almost. But he did want more, and not just physically. Drugged with kissing her, he opened his eyes and looked at her, holding her face in his hands. Her eyes were wide and dreamy, their silver depths fathomless. Her mouth was soft and relaxed, her entire face subtly altered and infinitely beautiful.

"Marry me, Olivia," he heard himself say. He hardly recognized his own voice, hoarse with passion, cracking with emotion. "You must marry me."

13

She must have lost her mind. That was the only possible explanation for allowing matters to get so out of hand. Olivia tensed in George's arms, trying to catch her breath, fighting her way back to sanity.

"No," she said, in a strangled voice. And then, more strongly, "No."

He had proposed marriage. He must think her a complete fool. And why not? She had been behaving like one.

He held her close, his lips in her hair. "Olivia," he said gently. "Ivy. My darling girl. This is what you need." He kissed her forehead. "It's what you want. Can't you feel it, sweetheart?" His voice sank to a whisper as his mouth traveled down toward hers. "Trust me," he murmured. "Please, Ivy. Please." And his lips moved to take another kiss.

He sounded drugged with passion, almost as if he could not help himself. As if he had abandoned all his scheming and was acting on instinct alone. As if he wanted her so badly that he was throwing caution to the winds. But she must not forget who he was! Even as she felt her body's traitorous response to his touch, too powerful to deny, it all struck her as too good to be true. He was too good at this. It seemed . . . it must be . . . *practiced.*

Anguished, she jerked herself out of his arms as if

his touch suddenly burned. It wasn't possible to walk away, unfortunately. Her knees had gone a bit wobbly somehow. So she hung on to the ledge provided by the fountain's bowl and struggled to regain her composure, turning her back to George. She felt she would crumble into bits if she looked at him again.

The air was chilly now. She shivered in her thin gown. Her gloves lay before her on the lip of the fountain, their empty fingers splayed in a painful stretch toward nothing. She picked them up and tried, with shaking hands, to put them back on.

"Allow me," said George quietly. Olivia had little choice but to comply. Hating her helplessness, she let him take her hands and work her gloves over her fingers and up her arms, then button them against her wrists.

"Thank you," she said woodenly. She stole a glance at him. His expression was unreadable. His features were harsh and forbidding as he pulled on his own gloves. She felt a ridiculous impulse to apologize, as if she had hurt his feelings with her bald rejection. But that was impossible, of course. He was the hardened rake, she the gullible innocent. His expression probably indicated only anger at himself for misjudging the moment. He had underestimated her resolve. Well! That was not her fault.

Anger stirred within her and she clutched it in relief. "*Why* is it," she asked crisply, smoothing her gloves, "that every time a man kisses a woman he assumes she has tumbled into love with him?" She forced a laugh and tried to look arch. "After all, men are expected to kiss women without losing their heads. Why can't a woman do the same?"

She saw his jaw tighten and knew she had struck a nerve. "No reason in the world," he drawled, as polite and bored as if they were strangers.

Olivia felt her arch smile waver a bit. The contrast between the bliss she had felt three minutes ago and the wretchedness she felt now was dreadful. She shivered again. What a ninny she had been, going off into the night air half-dressed. The zephyr shawl she had brought was back at the supper box.

"You are cold," he observed. She saw his eyes gleam and the mockery return to his expression. "I should have known you would be cold."

It seemed to Olivia that he was referring not to the temperature, but to her nature. Stung, she hugged herself and said stiffly, "The night is chillier than it was a while ago."

"Yes, it is," he said flatly. "And the music is not as sweet."

Her throat suddenly tightened again. She was fighting back tears. Tears! What *was* the matter with her? Furious and frightened, she clutched herself harder. She must stop the shivering before it became uncontrollable. "Nonsense. The music is the same as ever it was," she said bracingly. "I like it."

He was watching her from under hooded eyes, his expression still harsh and unreadable. "How many men have you kissed like that?" he demanded.

The suddenness of his rude question, and its personal quality, shocked her. "I—I don't know what you mean."

"The question is simple enough. Or have you lost count?"

Her brows snapped together as the blessed anger returned to stiffen her spine and rescue her. "You are insolent. I have never been free with my favors. How dare you imply such a thing?"

One brow flew up. His mouth twisted down. "What makes you think I am implying anything? You just said that a woman should be able to kiss a man without emotional consequences. And I agreed with you."

She pounced on this. "Then do not read me a lecture. I would never dream of asking you how many women you have kissed."

"I didn't ask how many you have kissed. I asked how many you have kissed *like that*."

"Like—like what?" She stammered, confused.

"I was admiring your technique, my dear. I never guessed that you felt nothing. You had me completely fooled." He leaned lazily against the fountain, still watching her. "I suppose it takes a great many rehearsals to achieve such a convincing performance."

Her eyes flashed and her chin lifted. "Yes, I suppose it does," she said frostily. "But you would know better than I. I am a rank amateur at . . . feigning emotion." She swallowed hard, willing the tightness in her throat away. She would not cry. She would not.

"Very good," he said admiringly, as if applauding. "Now tell me you have never attempted it before."

"I haven't!" She heard her voice rising in fury. "*I* am not a seducer of innocents! *I* am not a fortune hunter! How dare you sneer at me? The only other man I've kissed was—" She almost bit her tongue in her haste to avoid blurting out his name. Appalled, she covered her mouth with one hand.

George had a gleam in his eye like a cat at a mouse hole. "The man you loved. The fortune hunter. When you were eighteen."

She nodded miserably, then dropped her hand and took a shaky breath. "I am sorry I spoke so . . . sharply," she said unsteadily. "But you made me angry."

His teeth flashed white in the darkness. "I needed to. No, don't scold me! It was the only way to get the truth out of you."

"The *truth,* as you call it, is none of your business!"

"I mean to make it my business." He reached out and carelessly flicked her cheek with one gloved finger. "For a moment there, you had me rattled. It won't happen again."

"What is that supposed to mean?" she demanded.

He grinned. "I believed—fleetingly!—that you might

be rather more experienced than I had originally thought. But you aren't."

"Don't be so sure of that, my lord," she said darkly. "I may surprise you yet."

His grin widened. "Really? I hope so." His eyes flicked over her face and his features softened. "But then, you already have."

The man had a talent for turning her insides into mush. Olivia felt herself blushing and could only hope that the darkness hid it from George. She was steeling herself to suggest that they return to the supper box when his hands closed over her upper arms in a gentle, but inexorable, hold.

"Olivia. Do you know what life is like for a game-ster?"

She met his eyes warily. "Of course not."

He looked very serious. "You and I live by different rules. But I want you to know that although my rules are different from yours, there *are* rules, and I abide by them. I never cheat."

She tried to smile. "I daresay if you did, your career would be at an end."

"Quite right. So I am telling you, my dear, that I am an honest man—in my way. Do you believe me?"

"Ye-es," she said cautiously. "I don't think you cheat at cards, if that is what you mean."

"I also do not cheat at love."

She dropped her eyes, fearing he would see how much his words hurt her. He spoke of love as if it were just another game. A game with rules, where winning was suspect—because winners sometimes cheated. And honest people lost.

But he was right to speak of it that way, she reminded herself drearily. Luke's face, so long forgotten, flashed vividly in her mind's eye. She winced from the image. So sincere. So passionately fond of her. Oh, she had believed it all. He had wept real tears as he held her, begging for her love, and she had given her heart gladly. What a dunce she had been.

But George's steady, soothing voice continued, unaware that its very note of sincerity was ringing alarm bells all through her. "You are so innocent. You may believe that whenever a man and woman touch, sparks fly. You are not experienced enough to know how rare and wonderful this is." His hands—gloved now, thank heaven—moved caressingly over her arms. "There is something special between us, Olivia, and I am loath to give it up."

She did not resist as he pulled her back into his arms. This time, however, she also did not respond. She stood, passive, while he cradled her head against his chest. Bitter memories were flooding her. For the first time in years she welcomed them, not trying to shut them out or turn her mind away from the suffering.

How could she have forgotten? This was what it was to have one's heart stolen. This was how it felt to trust a scoundrel. She remembered. She remembered it all.

She closed her eyes and shuddered. George held her closer, murmuring endearments, but she did not hear them. She heard Culpepper's voice, soft and distressed, begging forgiveness for inflicting pain upon her, protesting that it was for her own good. She was eighteen again, staring in disbelief at the letter he had handed her, Luke's letter, intercepted on its way to his brother. It had been full of idle gossip and mundane matters, with the exception of three fateful sentences:

. . . My courtship of O.F. progresses well tho her family mislikes it and I grow weary of playing the lovesick swain. I cringe when I think of facing those hobgoblin eyes over the b'fast cups for

*fifty years, but heigh-ho! Beggars can't be
choosers. . . .*

The words had burned themselves into her brain.
When she first read them, unmistakably written by
Luke's beloved hand, she had fainted for the only time
in her life.

George must have noticed her passivity. He took
her face in his hands and gently lifted it, trying to
force her eyes to meet his. "What's wrong, sweetheart?"

"Nothing," she mumbled. Her lips were stiff with
cold and suppressed hostility. "I would like to return
to the supper box, if you please. I—I need my shawl."

His brows snapped together in swift concern.
"Something's amiss. What is it? I'll not drag you to
the altar unwilling, if that's what you're afraid of."

"Won't you? You are all consideration, my lord,"
she said coolly. "I suppose you would call such tactics
'cheating,' and therefore beneath you."

"I would." His eyes gleamed down at her. "But I
warn you, madam, that I do not consider it 'cheating'
to try to change your mind."

"I see." She studied his face for a moment. "You
will have to pardon my ignorance, George. I am a
novice at this . . . game. What are the rules of engagement? Or are there any?"

"Rules?" His arms tightened behind her. "They say
all's fair in love."

She nodded. "And war."

He chuckled, apparently not recognizing the edge in
her voice. "Shall I give you the outlines of the game?"

"If you please. I should like to know what the object
is before we go any further."

"The object of the game—of any game—is to win."
His grin flashed. "Reduced to its simplest terms, our
game is this: I want to marry you. You want to stay
single."

"Then despite what you say, your objective is, in fact, to drag me to the altar." She felt another gust of wrath, but his next words surprised her.

"Not quite." He touched her face in a caress that was almost tender. "My objective is to meet you there. To make you *want* to marry me. By whatever means I can."

She resisted the impulse, strong though it was, to lean into the hand that cupped her cheek. "Then my objective must be to repulse you."

"Nothing so simple." He chuckled again. "Your objective is to spice up your spinsterhood—without losing it."

"And for how long do we play this game, sir?" she asked politely. "How will we know when it ends?"

"It ends when one of us wins. I win if you agree to marry me. You win if—" He frowned. "You win if I give up."

"That hardly sounds fair," she pointed out. "We need a rule that will enable me to win cleanly. A time limit, say. If you haven't won my consent, you must retire voluntarily from the lists. I shall give you until . . . Christmas."

"Easter."

Her eyes narrowed as she thought. "Candlemas."

He paused, then nodded, seeming amused by her seriousness. "Five months? If I cannot win you by then, I daresay I never shall. And I've no desire to hang about if there is no hope. Done."

Five months. All she need do was keep herself from saying *yes* for five months. And in the meantime, she would have Lord Rival dancing attendance on her. She could have as many of his kisses as she could handle, all his delicious wooing, everything she wanted. She could glut herself on him, knowing that at the end of five months she would be safe. He would press her no more. The prospect made her dizzy with delight. Five months of heaven!

But he was bending down to her again.

"What are you doing?"

"Sealing the bargain, my dear."

Very well. A kiss to seal the bargain. She could allow one more kiss, having allowed so many. She kept a tight rein on her emotions this time, ensuring that the kiss was brief. Sweet, but brief.

His warm hands cradled her face again, and when he pulled his face back and gazed into her eyes, she could have sworn she saw genuine caring there. "This is a new experience for me, you know." He smiled. "I have never before kissed a woman I intended to marry. It's actually a rather liberating experience—having honorable intentions."

Honorable! She felt her jaw clench. There was nothing honorable about his intentions. It was a game to him. A filthy game, where he tried to make her love him—so he could get his hands on her inheritance. Such marriages were commonplace, and even an unhappy marriage was considered respectable, but a fortune hunter's machinations were *not* honorable. Not by any stretch of the imagination.

He had felt her stiffen as she withdrew from him. "What's this?" he murmured teasingly. "You can't be regretting a stolen kiss or two."

She backed out of his arms, attempting an airy laugh. "Oh, no! I regret nothing. I wanted a little excitement tonight, and you provided it. But the night grows cold, and it's getting late." She smiled brightly at him. "May we go?"

He stared at her in the dim light, head lowered and muscles taut. He seemed to be straining to make sense of her mood. "Certainly. I can take a hint," he said. His tone was carefully casual.

"Good." She turned to walk away, but he caught at her arm, compelling her to face him again. All trace of lightness had vanished from his demeanor.

"Most women who run from a rake's embrace have

excellent reason to be afraid," he said, his voice low and tense. "But you, Olivia, do not. You know I will not seduce and abandon you. I have made plain to you what it is I want."

"Yes, Lord Rival, indeed you have." Her eyes sparkled with unshed, angry tears, and her smile was fierce. "You want my money."

She abruptly pulled out of his slackened grip and fled, blindly, back toward the light and noise of Vauxhall.

14

O n the twenty-ninth of September Olivia, as was her habit, went early and alone to the city. Ignoring the hostile stares and muttered jibes she always encountered in that male bastion, she completed the quarterly banking for the Fairfax School and returned to her home to await Culpepper. This quarterly ritual chafed her. Her defiant trip to the bank was exhilarating, almost like going into battle—which rendered the subsequent interview with Culpepper all the more annoying. He brought her her income punctually, but it was humiliating to wait for him in her morning room, then have her money handed to her in anonymous gold rather than bank notes. It made her feel like a child receiving an allowance.

She always took comfort in handling the school's payroll while she waited, neatly counting out and stacking the money for each employee, folding it into a sheet of foolscap with the employee's name jotted on the front, and noting the date and amount in the payroll ledgers. It was the only set of school ledgers she kept at her home. She handled the quarterly payroll precisely because it gave her a dignified occupation while awaiting Culpepper's arrival with her own income payment. Besides, there was something satisfying about forcing Culpepper to view, quarter after quarter, a desktop full of evidence of her competence at handling her mother's legacy—just as he was doling out pieces of her father's legacy under circumstances that were decidedly demeaning. He generally succeeded in patronizing her, but at least she made it as difficult as she could.

The school had new money this quarter, an infusion into her mother's trust from Aloysius Beebe's estate. She sent up a grateful prayer, smiling as she toyed with the stack of notes. George had suggested that half of it be reinvested while they drew up plans for a modest expansion. His suggestion was excellent and she had taken it, but there was still a tidy sum left over for improvements to the existing facility. New bedsteads for the littlest girls. Wallpaper. A new roof for the east wing. Improvements to the water pipes; they had been a popular experiment. And meat, she decided. The children would have meat twice a week, not just on Sundays and holidays.

And Lord Rival would be paid.

She felt a flutter of excitement and dread as she counted out two hundred pounds and folded it in one of her neat paper packets. What would his reaction be? And what would he do with the money? The man must have frightful debts, if eight hundred pounds per annum was, as he had said, insufficient for his needs. Would he repay his creditors? Or would he gamble the money away? Doubtless that was how he had incurred the debts in the first place; it was an old, old tale, too common among the aristocracy. Odd that the fever would afflict even a man with George's demonstrably sound business instincts.

She was affixing his name to the packet when Culpepper's tap sounded on her door. He came in, his leather satchel pressed firmly beneath his arm and a look of almost painful anxiety pursing his bony face. He hovered uncertainly near the doorway, as if screwing up his courage before approaching her.

Olivia looked up in surprise. "How do you do? Pray come forward, Mr. Culpepper. Is anything amiss?"

"Thank you, my lady," he said stiffly, but did not budge from his stance. "I am afraid there is."

Her first thought was that Culpepper had glimpsed Edith. Olivia set down her quill and looked carefully at him, trying to keep her trepidation from showing. The youthful countess was growing restless, and was careless lately about hiding herself when visitors arrived. Culpepper was the Fairfax family solicitor. He owed Ralph, as the head of her family, stronger allegiance than he owed any of the women. He would not hesitate to betray Edith's whereabouts to her abusive husband.

On closer examination, however, Culpepper's expression seemed to indicate resentment rather than outrage. Olivia's brows climbed. She tried a mild jest. "I hope you were not robbed on your way here?"

"No, madam, I was not." He settled his spectacles more firmly on his nose. "But I fear I have some unpleasant news to impart. It is most vexatious! I do wish that the task had not fallen to me—but there! It is my duty, and I must not shirk it."

Her brows climbed higher. "My word. Pray sit down, and tell me your news without delay."

He complied with the first part of her request, but seemed unable to comply with the second. His mouth tightened until his lips nearly disappeared, and he failed to meet her eyes. "Really, my lady, I scarcely know where to begin. This is most distasteful to me, most distasteful. I am at a complete loss."

She waited in growing alarm while he looked at the ceiling as if seeking inspiration. His cheeks slowly turned a dull pink. Finally he looked back at her, drawing himself upright in his chair. "There is no delicate way to break such news," he announced. "I must simply say it. Please believe that I would not carry such a message to you were I not convinced of its truth."

Dread filled Olivia's heart. "Very well," she said

faintly. The last time Culpepper had spoken so to her, he had handed her Luke's letter. She sensed a terrible blow coming. Her hands tightened on the arms of her chair as she prayed that whatever Culpepper was about to say, it would have nothing to do with—

"The news is about Lord Rival."

She closed her eyes for a moment, bitterness flooding her. Her prayers had not been answered. Then she forced herself to open her eyes and meet Culpepper's agitated gaze steadily. "What have you learned?" she asked, with a fair assumption of calm.

Culpepper took a deep breath, then plunged ahead. "My dear Lady Olivia, we have been deceived," he said impressively. "We have been grossly deceived. You are nurturing a viper in your bosom."

"Go on," she said faintly.

He leaned forward, his voice sinking to a horrified whisper. "My lady, the man is a *rake*!"

"Yes," she said numbly. "And?" She braced herself for whatever revelation would follow.

But Culpepper blinked at her in confusion. "*And?* Lady Olivia, what are you saying? Did you not hear me? I tell you Lord Rival is a rake! A libertine, madam, a bona fide rake, a man whose conquests litter London! He has a most unsavory reputation—and, I may add, a deserved one, for I naturally investigated the matter before sullying your ears with such a tale. I hope you do not think I would credit mere gossip. No, no, my lady, it is true—quite true, quite verifiable."

She stared at him in bewilderment. "What is true? I do not understand."

"Tut, tut! Come now, my lady," said Culpepper testily. "You must know what a rake is. A rake is a seducer, a defiler of women."

"Yes, but—"

"I am telling you, madam—with regret!—that Lord Rival is not a proper person for you to know."

Olivia felt almost faint with relief. "Is that all?" she exclaimed.

Culpepper looked stunned. "All! *All?* My dear Lady Olivia, you have invited this rascal into the school! You have shown him our books! You have—you have *befriended* him! You must cut him loose immediately. You risk becoming a laughingstock. Or worse!"

Olivia collapsed back against her chair. "Heavens, what a scare you gave me! But this is not news at all."

"Not? Not—not news?" He appeared flabbergasted. "Do you mean to tell me you *knew* of this man's reputation?"

She smiled. "Certainly I did. What of it?"

Culpepper looked as if he were about to go off in an apoplexy. "Dear ma'am, you do not know what you are saying! A lady in your position cannot be too careful. A maiden lady, an innocent—why, the tiniest whisper of scandal, the slightest linking of your name with Rival's, could utterly destroy your high standing in the community."

Her smile vanished in annoyance. "My good name should depend upon my own behavior, not the behavior of my friends."

Culpepper gave a prim little snort. "Rightly or wrongly, we are all judged by the company we keep."

She could not argue with his statement, but it did not improve her temper. She straightened in her chair, frowning. "What do you suggest, pray? Am I to suddenly banish Lord Rival from my presence? Dismiss him from his newly assumed duties at the school? I cannot carry on like an overwrought shrew over something I have known all along! That, indeed, would make me a laughingstock—and deservedly so."

"Well, well, there is no need for you to do anything whatsoever," said Culpepper soothingly. "I daresay this all comes as quite a shock to you. To be sure, it came as a shock to me! I can easily imagine that a feminine mind might be quite overset by the prospect.

Your delicate nature gives you a want of firmness, a lack of resolve. Do not disturb yourself, my lady! You may leave it all to me."

"Leave what to you?"

"I shall handle the matter on your behalf. Indeed, it would not be at all proper for you to see the rogue alone, even to tell him that he must not approach you again. I will speak to him; it is my place to speak to him. I merely wished to inform you before I took the liberty of dismissing him."

Olivia held up one hand. "Stop. You do not have the authority to dismiss Lord Rival."

"In such a case as this, my lady, I will gladly *assume* the authority."

"Usurp it, do you mean? No." Her tone was polite, but implacable. "I expressly forbid it."

Culpepper swelled like an angry toad. "What! Can it be possible? Do you not understand the severity of the situation? You—even you!—cannot make light of such a thing. If you care for nothing else, my lady, you care for the school."

Olivia spread her hands in a gesture of reasonableness. "But Lord Rival is valuable to the school. He has proved it a dozen times already. He is a man of intelligence and prudence—"

"Prudence! Of all traits you might ascribe to such a reprobate—"

"Prudence," she said firmly. "I am speaking of financial matters, Culpepper. His private life is not our concern."

"It will quickly become our concern, if Rival's association with the school becomes known! Pray recall that the Fairfax School is a school for *female* orphans."

Olivia's eyes narrowed. "Why, what has that to do with anything?"

Culpepper appeared too distraught to heed the warning signs that he was provoking her. His voice grew shrill with anger. "I am telling you, Lady Olivia, that Rival has neither a heart nor a conscience. And it is known! It is *well* known. You would dislike it more than anyone else, I daresay, should Lord Rival's reputation for debauchery injure your protegées' chances of securing respectable employment."

Olivia's nostrils flared with disgust. "What nonsense you are talking! What *vulgar* nonsense. Mr. Culpepper, I am ashamed of you."

"I am only doing my duty." Culpepper's thin cheeks were reddening again. "It pains me to discuss such matters with a lady of quality. Really, madam, I don't know how to impress upon you the solemnity of this occasion. I tell you most earnestly, *most* earnestly, that you must have nothing further to do with Lord Rival."

"On what cause? Fear of gossip? You are asking me to abandon a friend, Mr. Culpepper. You had better give me a sounder reason than that." Her voice dripped with scorn.

"Good heavens, madam, do not tell me that you hold Rival in affection!"

"Very well, I will not." Olivia was clinging to her temper by the slenderest of threads. "But I *will* tell you that there is no reason why I should not. You disappoint me, Mr. Culpepper. Lord Rival has shown himself to be completely trustworthy where the school is concerned, and I am grateful to him for his ideas and assistance. Why should I not hold him in esteem?"

Culpepper blanched. "I cannot believe my ears. That you should actually defend the man—and knowing full well what he is—why, it is beyond my comprehension! Tut! This is the last thing I expected."

His distress was so heartfelt that Olivia felt a twinge of guilt. It was, in fact, strange that she found herself automatically springing to Lord Rival's defense. She bit her lip. "I beg your pardon. I know that your concern for my welfare is genuine. And I—I do not mean to side with Lord Rival against you. You have been, for many years, my trusted advisor. I have known

Lord Rival for only a few weeks. But you must allow me to be the ultimate judge of what is right, both for the school and for myself. I am not a child."

"You are a female," snapped Culpepper. "Such judgments are not within your sphere."

Olivia was forced to quell a strong, and quite unladylike, impulse to box Culpepper's ears. As she struggled to master her fury, another tap sounded on her morning room door. It opened to reveal Lord Rival standing on the threshold. He paused there for a moment, one eyebrow flying in his typical expression of mocking humor as his gaze flicked from Culpepper's stiff posture to Olivia's flashing eyes. Had these cues not told him enough, the frozen silence that heralded his arrival plainly telegraphed that he was interrupting a quarrel.

Olivia could not deny that she was glad to see him. It might have been merely that George's entrance ended an unpleasant scene, but she suspected that she would have been glad to see him regardless. The mere sight of him fairly made her toes curl with pleasure. She wished, not for the first time, that she might come upon him unawares—so that she might have the pleasure of feasting her eyes on him unseen. Just to *look* at the man was a treat. Today he was impeccably groomed, as usual, in a well-chosen morning coat of nut brown worn with buff breeches and polished Hessians. His dark hair gleamed as lushly as the boots. His linen was spotless. And inside this handsome package was *George,* who would make her foolish heart beat faster no matter what he wore or how he looked. She longed to stare her fill, but courtesy demanded that she forgo that delight.

"Good morning," he said politely. Laughter lurked in his voice. "I hope I am not before my time?"

"No, my lord, you are quite punctual. As usual," said Olivia crisply. "Pray come in. Mr. Culpepper was on the point of leaving."

Culpepper shot his employer an angry glance. "As to that, my lady, I do not feel that our business is entirely concluded."

"Nevertheless, it is," said Olivia. Her tone brooked no argument. "You may leave what you have brought for me here on my desk. Good day."

His cheeks puffed angrily, but he rose and reluctantly dug through his satchel. He almost flung the thick parcel onto her desktop, then sketched a curt bow. "Good day, Lady Olivia. I hope you will not live to regret this day's work. As you know, I must remove from London for the next sennight to assist your brother with his quarterly accounting. I shall not be available to bail you out of any difficulties that may arise."

"Never mind, dear chap," said George, lounging gracefully near the doorway. "Lady Olivia may rely on me."

This reassurance seemed to rob Culpepper of the power of speech. Olivia choked back a laugh and said, her voice quivering, "Thank you, Lord Rival. You have relieved Mr. Culpepper's mind, I am sure."

"Hardly that, my lady, hardly that," muttered Culpepper darkly. "I cannot think his lordship's protection equal to my own." He glared at George, then executed a painfully stiff bow. "Good day, sir!" he barked, and hurried out.

George appeared mildly surprised. "What was that about?" he asked, strolling forward to deposit his hat and walking stick upon a low table. Olivia seized her chance and covertly watched him, relishing the graceful way he moved and the latent power of his muscular form. He turned then and caught her staring, so she hastily looked away.

"Nothing," she said vaguely. "Nothing of importance."

"You're a poor liar, my dear." His wicked grin flashed. "I like that in a woman." He walked to the fire and stretched his hands toward the blaze. "I assume the estimable Culpepper was warning you against me."

Since he had just pointed out what a poor liar she was, Olivia did not attempt to deny it. "How did you guess?" she asked, chagrined.

"It was only a matter of time." He shot her a keen, but rueful, glance. "Whatever his faults, Culpepper cares for you almost as a daughter. I have wondered at his forbearance. Why has he kept silent until now?"

She laughed mirthlessly, toying with the edge of the blotter on her desk. "Because gossip travels slowly to men like Culpepper. Apparently he knew nothing of your reputation until very lately."

"Ah. That explains it." He moved to one of the chairs facing her desk and dropped into it, watching her. "Now that he has, er, perceived my true colors, I suppose he has advised you to cut my acquaintance."

"Yes."

"Will you?" His dark eyes pinned hers, his expression inscrutable.

She met his gaze steadily. "No."

A slow smile spread across George's features. "I should have known," he said softly. "What a reckless creature you are! I pity Culpepper. Or, for that matter, any man who tries to break you to bridle."

"A singularly vulgar expression," she remarked, wrinkling her nose. "And it seems much more illustrative of what *you* are trying to do to me than what poor Culpepper attempted."

He threw back his head and uttered a crack of laughter. "Well said! Although I must protest—I would never try to break you. To bridle, or anything else."

"I am glad to hear it," she said, her eyes twinkling.

He leaned forward on his elbows, his voice low and teasing. "You shouldn't have drawn my attention to it, Ivy."

"To what?"

"The riding analogy. You have started the most wicked train of thought. Shall I describe it for you?"

"Certainly not!" said Olivia, blushing. The wretch never failed to throw her off-balance! "May we move on to more practical matters?"

He grinned and leaned back in the chair. "If we must."

She silently handed him the two hundred pounds she had set aside for him. His face was very still as he stared at the money. Then he raised his eyes to hers again. "Thank you," he said unemotionally, and pocketed it.

She had not anticipated the awkwardness of the transaction. George had said outright that he would dislike feeling subordinate to her, but she had not realized until this moment that she would dislike it, too.

"You've nothing to thank me for," she stammered. "You earned it."

He gave an ironic little bow. "If you say so, my lady. Is this why you summoned me here today?"

"No," she said quickly, glad to change the subject. "Not entirely. I was hoping you would assist me by handing out the payroll at the school. It's something Culpepper used to do, but . . ."

"But you have dismissed the worthy Culpepper and supplanted him with me." His teeth flashed in one of his swift, wry grins. "I was wondering how long it would take for you to regret that."

She frowned. "I do not regret it. You are every bit as competent as Culpepper, and *you* do not patronize me—which he never fails to do!"

"On the other hand," said George smoothly, "you trust him. And you dare not trust me."

She felt herself blushing. "I am about to entrust you with the school's entire payroll, sir—nearly a thousand pounds! If you think that is a small matter—"

"I never think money is a small matter. I suppose

earning your trust in that area is, at the very least, progress."

"Progress? No." She looked down at her hands, unable to meet his eyes. It had to be said, but she could not say it convincingly if she had to look at him. "The word *progress* implies some sort of—forward motion. There will be none. We have had this conversation before, my lord. Kindly disabuse your mind of the idea that you and I have a future together. We do not."

But he leaned forward with disconcerting swiftness and caught her wrist, compelling her to look at him. "I will make you trust me, Olivia," he said softly. "I want your trust in all things."

"What you *want* has nothing to do with it." She forced herself to speak steadily. "You are seeking something you cannot have."

"How can I prove myself to you?"

"You cannot."

He let go of her wrist and sat back, staring broodingly at her. She could not read his expression.

She tried to smile. "We are at an impasse, George, as I have tried repeatedly to make plain to you. But there is no need for anything to change, I hope. I want us to be friends, you and I."

He did not answer for a moment, but studied her, his eyes hooded and his expression inscrutable. Then his smile flickered like lightning, gone almost before it appeared. "Certainly," he said politely. "You and I can be very *good* friends, Olivia. For you do trust me—to a point. And we like each other." The smile flashed again. "We like each other a great deal. Or am I mistaken in that?"

"No," she said, relieved to have matters back on a more familiar footing. "I enjoy your company, George. I—I look forward to seeing you."

"I feel the same." He seemed perfectly relaxed now, but she had the oddest suspicion that he was secretly laughing. He rose, gesturing to the stacks of bills

folded in paper on her desk. "If you will be kind
enough to secure these in some way—"

"Oh! Yes." She rummaged in a drawer and unearthed a satchel similar to the one Culpepper had
been carrying. "You needn't carry the money in your
bare hands."

Bare hands. She wished she hadn't spoken of his
bare hands. She watched as he packed the money
neatly in the satchel, mesmerized by the movements
of his long, strong fingers as he worked. What beautiful hands he had. So masculine. It was sinful to take
this much pleasure in looking at a man, but she
couldn't help it.

Her reverie was broken by the sound of Lord Rival's chuckle. She glanced inquiringly at his face and
was mortified to see his eyebrow climbing and his
mouth pursing slyly, as if he had guessed the direction
of her thoughts. She blushed and looked defiantly
away. But he placed his fists on the top of her desk
and leaned on them, looming over her where she sat.

"Olivia, my dear," he murmured teasingly. "You
will miss me when I am gone."

"Gone?" She looked up, startled. "Wh-where are
you going?"

His face was very near to hers. As always when she
was close to him, her idiotic heart began to flutter and
pound, and she had to remind herself to breathe.

His eyes flicked to her lips, then back to her eyes
again. "If you will not marry me, Ivy," he said softly,
"I must look elsewhere for a bride." His eyes burned;
she imagined she could feel them scorching her. "And
you, I think, will miss me."

He was right. Dear saints in heaven, he was right.
His words forced her to picture losing him, picture the
dark days when George would be some other woman's
husband and she would be alone, back in her safe
little world, a world of good women doing good deeds.
She had loved that world! She had created it herself

and taken pride in its creation. Now her haven of safety and contentment would feel like a prison.

She stared helplessly into his dark, dark eyes, and knew despair. She had told George that he wanted something he could not have; now she knew what a pathetic bluff that had been. It was she who longed for impossible things.

15

"I make it thirty pounds." George tossed his cards lightly onto the table before him and smiled. "My dear Nellie, if you could only see your expression! Should I apologize?"

Mrs. Beauchamp's discontented little face managed to pout and smile at the same time. "La! How absurd you are! After all, it was I who wanted to play." She batted her eyes flirtatiously. "I mustn't complain, must I? I know how dangerous you are. But I can't resist you, George," she cooed.

Her fawning had grown irksome. George, bored, scooped up the scattered cards and riffled them into a deck. "Remember, I told you this would be our last hand."

Her pout intensified. "Yes, but *why*? I suppose it bores you to win so often. But my piquet is improving, is it not?" Her eyelashes came back into play. "It's not fair for you to deny me my revenge. Another week or two and I shall start winning it all back from you."

"You said that a month ago." He smiled to take the sting from his barb. "You should have more pride, Nellie. I'm enriching myself at your expense."

"At Hugo's expense," she retorted, correcting him archly. "He can well afford it." She leaned forward across the narrow table and placed her soft little hand over his. "George," she said coaxingly. "Pray do not withdraw from me. How will I ever amuse myself again?"

"Easily, I should think." He allowed his gaze to travel lazily over the plump cleavage she displayed by leaning deliberately forward into the candlelight. Nellie was a tempting little morsel. "There must be a dozen chaps eager to replace me."

"I don't want them," she complained. "I want you. Why must you be so difficult?"

"I'm turning over a new leaf, my dear." He lifted the hand she had left on his and ironically kissed her wedding ring. "No more trespassing on another man's property."

She lifted one of her delicately drawn eyebrows. "Forsaking your evil ways? You, George? It seems hard to believe."

"Even the worst sinner can repent."

She tilted her head, looking at him through half-closed eyes. "We shall see," she purred. "Come visit me tomorrow morning and test your resolve. Hugo will be at his club any time after ten o'clock."

He tried to hide his annoyance. "You don't take no for an answer, do you?"

Nellie smiled prettily. "In a word? No."

He frowned and pushed back from the table, but her hand reached quickly out and grasped his sleeve. "Oh, George, don't be cross! I can't bear it. You know you must come by to collect your winnings—I don't have thirty pounds with me."

"Very well," he said curtly. "I shall call upon you in the morning, Nellie, and we shall bid each other farewell and good fortune. Forgive my abruptness, but I see Daventry in the other room and must speak to him tonight."

She pulled back, sulking. "Go, then."

He rose and bowed. "I thank you. Good night— Mrs. Beauchamp."

He felt her resentful eyes upon him as he left the

little anteroom where they had been closeted for their game and reentered the noisy salon. It was unlike him to break off his alliances so crudely, but Nellie had been an irritant in his life for some time. "Thanks be to God and Aloysius Beebe," he muttered to himself as he headed for the door. What a difference a little money made. He was free of her—her, and all the women like her.

Whatever the outcome with Olivia Fairfax, he vowed, he would not return to fleecing the bored and lonely wives of rich men. At least, not permanently. He had to admit that if his courtship of Olivia ultimately failed, it might not be possible to hang about and earn Beebe's annuity. He might need Nellie Beauchamp and her ilk to tide him over while he sought a different bride. But he would cross that bridge when he came to it. In the meantime, he must not entertain the possibility that he could fail. All his energy, all his drive, must be concentrated on winning.

Olivia did not trust him. She had good reason not to. Earning her trust bit by bit might take years, and she was only giving him months. Very well; he would abandon the attempt.

She would marry him, by God, whether she trusted him or no.

If there was one thing Lord Rival knew, it was women. Many of his conquests had been reluctant—initially. Women, in his cynical opinion, generally underrated their capacity for lust. That made them easy to astonish. Many a female had fallen for him, and fallen hard, simply because he had tapped into some overlooked well of desire. Make a woman want you badly enough and she would ignore her own common sense. A man could rely upon that, like summer following spring.

Olivia Fairfax was a woman of uncommon strength of mind, and it would take a great deal to make her ignore her better judgment. But Lord Rival was not one to shrink from a challenge. After all, he reminded himself, the mistrustful, suspicious women had eventually tumbled into his bed just as the dupes had. A marriage proposal couldn't be that different from his usual proposition. Could it?

Rake Rival was experiencing uncharacteristic doubts.

It was tricky to accomplish this delicate seduction while grappling with his own headlong rush of desire. So far, the strength of his attraction to Olivia, welcome as it was, was more of an impediment than a help. It clouded his judgment. His usual trick of backing off, feigning disinterest, and distancing himself from his intended target was meant to drive the woman mad with longing. This time, it was George who seemed to be going round the bend. It was George who paced the floor, a prey to feverish fantasies. It was George whose every thought seemed to revolve around Olivia, and with no clear idea whether his obsession was reciprocated. He longed so intensely to see her again that, when he finally did, he fought an urge to crush her in his arms the instant she came into view.

Now, this happened to be the very effect he was trying to create in Olivia—but he was so distracted by his own overpowering reaction to her that he had little attention to spare for *her* reaction to *him*.

He was actually rather disgusted with himself. The only explanation he could divine for his bizarre loss of control was the heightened significance of the connection he was trying to form. Marriage was naturally more important than a liaison. Perhaps it was normal to lose a little sleep, get a bit keyed up, when contemplating such a step.

His impatience to see her drew him to her home one fine morning in October, ostensibly to show off the curricle he had just purchased. Olivia's housekeeper had fallen into the habit of treating him almost as one of the household, so she beamed and bobbed and shooed him upstairs to announce himself. George ran lightly up the stairs, hat in hand, feeling an almost boyish flutter of anticipation. He knocked on the door of Olivia's morning room, then entered.

His sense of anticipation was rewarded. She was alone, writing at her desk, and greeted him with a flush of delight that could not have been feigned. "George!" she exclaimed, rising to her feet in pretty confusion. "I did not expect to see you today."

He set down his hat and moved to shake her hand. "How do you do? I hope you will forgive the intrusion."

"Nonsense, I'm always happy to see you. Besides, I was trying to write my brother—a shockingly difficult task! I'm glad of the interruption." She seemed to notice that he was touching her rather longer than necessary, and turned a most becoming shade of pink. "Won't you sit down?"

"If you will sit with me."

She tried unsuccessfully to pull her hand out of his. "Don't be absurd. George, for heaven's sake! The door is open."

"That's easily remedied." Pulling her by the hand, he returned to the door and audaciously closed it. Olivia stared at him as if he were a madman. He grinned at her dumbfounded expression. "How long has it been since I've kissed you?"

Her jaw slackened. "What?"

He answered his own question. "Too long." He leaned in and ambushed her by kissing her soundly. She responded—briefly—then pulled her face away, laughing and holding him off, her palms flat against his chest.

"George, you'll be the death of me. Only think of the scandal, should anyone come in!"

"Yes, how shocking. You would have to marry me." He bent to take her lips again, but she placed one hand over his mouth.

"You may stop right there, sir," she said firmly.

He kissed her palm; she snatched her hand away. "I may," he said teasingly. "And, then again, I may not."

Her eyes widened in amusement as she recognized her own words flung back at her. "Rogue! Have you no shame?"

"Very little." He smiled down at her, rosy and laughing in his arms. "You know, you're really rather adorable."

"For an heiress," she murmured provocatively.

"For anyone," he averred, his arms tightening around her. "On any terms. I'm a lucky chap."

Now she looked cross. "You take too much for granted. I am not yours."

"You will be." He saw anger sparking in her eyes and stole it from her by whispering, "And I will be yours." Then he bent his head and really kissed her, his mouth lingering tenderly on hers. She went limp and pliant, picturing, as he knew she must, a life where he belonged to her. A life where their kisses did not need to be furtive affairs, stolen in moonlit gardens or behind closed doors.

He ended the kiss and looked at her. Her eyes were shut and her face had gone soft and dreamy. It occurred to him, not for the first time, that marriage to Olivia would offer him more than mere monetary gain. It would, in fact, be extremely pleasant to kiss her like this whenever he wanted to. "Marry me, Olivia," he urged her softly, "so I can kiss you in the daylight."

Her lips curved in a smile. "That would be lovely," she sighed. Then her eyes opened and some of the laughter returned to her face. "You're a persuasive rascal, George. Well! I can't say I wasn't warned."

"I warned you myself, as I recall. What a wooden-headed thing to do."

"Yes, it wasn't very clever of you," she said, with mock sympathy. "Poor George! But I expect you'll do better next time."

"Next time?"

"The next time you court an heiress."

"Ah." He tapped her nose with his fingertip. "There won't be a next time, minx, because I am going to marry you."

The challenge glinted in her silver eyes. "You won't marry me, George, so you had better consider your options."

She slipped out of his grasp and pointedly opened the door, then walked sedately back to her rosewood desk. "To what do I owe the honor of your visit? You couldn't have come all the way to Chelsea just to kiss me."

He suddenly realized that that was exactly what he had done. The new curricle was just an excuse. He grinned ruefully; if he told her the truth she'd think he was joking. Or worse.

"Well," he said thoughtfully, "It's a very fine morning, and I *do* have a new curricle. I thought you might like to see one of the items on which I'm squandering Beebe's money."

"A curricle!" She looked impressed. "My word. How extravagant."

He grinned. "You've lived in the lap of luxury all your life, my dear girl. You don't know the difference between an extravagance and a necessity. A vehicle, I'll have you know, is a necessity—one that I have done without for far too long."

"A sporting vehicle is hardly a necessity." She tried to look severe, and almost succeeded.

He placed one hand on the back of a chair and leaned forward, addressing her in the whispered tones of a conspirator. "If you *must* know, I had originally looked no higher than a humble whiskey."

Her lips twitched. "Very proper."

"However, I am happy to say, this particular curricle cost no more than the whiskey. I was able to purchase it dirt cheap from a crony of mine who was, er, strapped for cash."

Her smile warmed. "Oh, I'm so glad! That is—well, of course it's none of my business, but—"

"But you are glad I'm not the wastrel you thought me."

"Yes. Oh, dear!" She bit her lip, laughing as if vexed at herself. "As if any of this were my affair! It's also not my business to feel *glad* that you were able to purchase something you wanted. I beg your pardon! I'm not usually such a busybody. My only excuse is that—"

"You need no excuse." He gave her a sly smile. "A lady naturally wants to understand the character of the man she is about to marry."

"Humph! I suppose you think that is funny."

"Not at all. But tell me—have I tempted you sufficiently? Will you leave your writing desk for half an hour and let me tool you about? It would give me great pleasure."

She did, indeed, look tempted. "I wish I could. But—"

"Let me show it to you." He walked boldly up behind her desk and placed his arm around her waist, drawing her to the window where they could see his carriage being led up and down. "There. That handsome black equipage with the brass trim. Now, how can you resist being seen in such a stylish turn-out? You'll be the envy of Chelsea."

"Gracious. Indeed I would. That curricle is beyond stylish; it's— it's practically decadent."

"Suits me, doesn't it?" he agreed.

She chuckled and relaxed a little, leaning so slightly against his body that he might have imagined it. "But I don't need to be the envy of Chelsea." She turned her face up to his. He had to fight the urge to kiss her again. Her eyes were as soft and silvery as the sea mist that drifted through the trees of Rye Vale. "Thanks to you, I now have everything I ever wanted," she said, her low tone blending amusement and warmth. "I have everything I had before, plus your company to enliven my humdrum existence. My life lacks for nothing."

"Then I need to make you want something more," he said huskily. "I need to make you a little less contented, my sweet. For there is something I want, something only you can give me. And I want you to want it, too."

Heedless of the open door behind them, he pulled her body tightly against his and pressed his mouth hungrily against hers. Her response was swift and instinctive. How could she not want more? He wanted more. Damn her innocence! She must not know what she was missing.

"Olivia." He held her face between his hands. "Can't you feel it, sweetheart? Can't you tell that there is more to want, so much more than you ever dreamed of? What we have together is rare—this spark, this fire." He kissed her again, passionately, but she struggled to break free.

"No," she moaned. "No. Don't you see, George? It doesn't matter what I feel—"

"Then you don't feel enough. Yet."

It was confoundedly hard to let her go, but holding her against her will would serve no purpose. He dropped his hands to his sides. She appeared confused, struggling, but it was impossible to say what she struggled against, or why. He was too close to her. That was the chief difficulty. He had no perspective; his own emotions loomed too large. He could not see past them.

She lifted a wavering hand to straighten her hair and gave him a tremulous smile. "You certainly know how to interrupt a lady's morning."

Out of the corner of his eye he thought he saw movement. He swung round to look at the open doorway. Whatever it was, it had whisked out of sight.

Olivia walked back to her desk as if retreating to a safe harbor, and seated herself a bit shakily. "I really must decline your obliging offer and finish my letter. Perhaps—another time?"

"Tomorrow, then."

"Very well. I would be glad to drive out with you tomorrow."

"Early."

Some of her sparkle returned. "As early as you like."

He placed one hand on her desk and leaned teasingly over her. "Wear your bonnet to breakfast, my dear. I'll be waiting on your doorstep when you awaken."

He then picked up his hat and sauntered out, her soft laughter following him.

George was halfway down the stairs when he heard a rustle in the darkness behind him. He whirled, his well-honed instincts bringing up his fists without conscious thought. His pursuer gave a terrified gasp and ducked, falling to a sitting position three or four steps up.

It was a young girl. She looked like she might yet be a schoolroom miss. He had no idea who she was; he had certainly never seen her before.

"Good God! Are you hurt?" He reached out to help her but the girl cringed, recoiling from his quick movement. He dropped his hand to his side. "I beg your pardon. You startled me, but it seems I startled you more."

"Yes. Oh! I'm s-sorry." As she recovered from her overreaction she seemed appropriately mortified. This time she did not shrink from his hand but took it, letting him pull her to her feet. "How stupid of me."

"Not at all," he said politely.

"I think—I think you must be Lord Rival?" she said tentatively.

He bowed. She was blushing furiously and the stairwell was unlit, but he could see that she was a pretty thing, with the blue eyes and whitish hair of a porcelain doll. Not at all to George's taste, but some men admired the swan maiden type.

The girl clutched the banister anxiously. "You must think me a complete ninny. I am Miss—I am Lady Badesworth," she said.

George's brows flew upward. So this was Badesworth's child bride. She really must be a ninny.

"How do you do? I hope you can forgive me for frightening you. Shall I escort you to one of the withdrawing rooms? Or summon assistance?"

"Oh, gracious, no. I'm perfectly well," she assured him. "It was quite my own fault, you know, for following you so closely."

It was, of course, but it would be impolite to agree. "I'm sure you had a good reason for doing so. May I ask what it is?"

Lady Badesworth looked ashamed. "I'm afraid I was planning to—to accost you, my lord. And perhaps beg a favor from you."

George was mildly astonished. "Dear me. You know, I think we ought not to converse on the stairs. It strikes me as awkward. And a little unsafe."

"Oh, yes! Pray follow me, sir."

Lady Badesworth passed him—skirting him a little nervously, he noted with amusement—and led him to the small library that opened off the entry hall. She seemed strangely at home in Olivia's house. He wondered briefly why Olivia had not mentioned to him that her sister-in-law was visiting her, but dismissed the thought with an inward shrug. No reason why she should, he supposed. After all, it might be awkward for her to introduce him to her near and dear. He was used to that; most women were anxious to keep their families in the dark regarding their friendships with him.

He observed the furtive glance Lady Badesworth cast around the hall before slipping into the library. The girl plainly did not want to be seen with him, and yet she was "accosting" him. Interesting. Once she had him alone, she pressed her hands together and breathlessly confided that she had overheard a portion of his conversation with Olivia.

"I hope you will not think me an eavesdropper, Lord Rival, for I was not listening on purpose—but I think you wanted Lady Olivia to drive out with you. In a curricle. And I think she told you she could not. And I realize that you and I have not met before, but I was wondering—"

She broke off and gulped, evidently realizing the awkwardness of requesting favors from strange men encountered in other people's stairwells. George suppressed his natural inclination to laugh and managed to keep his expression grave. "I daresay you are in need of transportation?" he prodded helpfully.

She threw him a grateful look. "Yes, my lord. That is exactly what I need. I suppose it sounds strange to you—"

"Hardly that. Perhaps it would ease your mind to know that I am quite in the habit of being accosted by females and requested to perform odd services. Little things, you know, that a lady doesn't like to ask of her husband. I generally am happy to oblige. Where do you wish to go?"

"Oh, anywhere!" she said impulsively, then blushed and fidgeted. "You see, I have been—I have been a bit unwell, and I have been cooped up indoors here for simply ages, and I just—I would like very much to go out in the sunshine, even for a *little* while. And besides, Lady Olivia has been excessively kind to me and I would like to buy her a present of some sort. To thank her."

It sounded peculiar, to say the least. Why ask a stranger? He could not help wondering about her relationship with the choleric Lord Badesworth, since it seemed that a husband would be the logical companion for this harmless errand. But, of course, Badesworth couldn't possibly have won the heart of this tender bud. The unfortunate child must have been sold to the highest bidder. She began to arouse his chivalrous instincts as well as his curiosity.

At any rate, solving the mystery would provide him with a morning's entertainment. He therefore acceded without a blink to her strange request. She thanked him profusely and ran upstairs with a bright face, promising excitedly to return in a trice. When she rejoined him she had donned a blue pelisse and a hat with a thick veil. The veil amused him, since this evidence of an anxiety to avoid being recognized would unerringly draw all eyes to her, but he said nothing. She was very young.

The mystery deepened as he tooled Lady Badesworth briskly through Chelsea. It was clear that she had not seen it before. She gawked like a day-tripper, peering eagerly through her veil at every new sight, craning her neck and exclaiming. When not commenting on her surroundings she prattled artlessly about herself, volunteering a wealth of boring information about her school friends, distant relatives, dear little doggies she had known and loved, and her early home life.

He would have found her uninterrupted stream of chatter profoundly tiresome had her *omissions* not been so interesting. She said nothing whatsoever about her present life—neither her husband nor her visit to Lady Olivia were mentioned. Her abundant energy also cast doubt upon her tale of recent convalescence. There was something very odd at work here.

After twenty minutes or so, George casually asked, "Should I take you back now?"

Her face fell, almost ludicrously. "Oh, no! Why? I mean—that is—I am so sorry! I daresay I am trespassing shamefully upon your time."

"Not at all. But I shouldn't like to make you ill."

She appeared astonished. "Ill? Why would it—? Oh." She bit her lip in confusion. "I did say I had been unwell, didn't I?"

"Yes, you did."

"I ought rather to have said I was—injured. But that was *weeks* ago, and I am completely recovered. Or as near to it as makes no odds."

"Injured? I'm sorry to hear it. Nothing broken, I hope?"

"Only my finger. It's a bit stiff yet, but much better than it was." She held up her left hand, demonstrating the movement she had regained. "I tape it up at night."

He studied her guileless face, wondering if he imagined the greenish tint of healing bruises behind her veil. "I see."

He began to think he did, in fact, see. *Injured.* He remembered the way she had ducked on the stairs, expecting to be hit. He had observed the way she flinched and shied at sudden movement. He was no stranger to this evidence of an unhappy marriage. His sister Susan had begun developing similar symptoms shortly after her wedding.

His sister Susan was dead.

He rarely thought about Susan. Every time he did, a thick fog of unpleasant emotion rose up to cloud his vision. He blinked the miasma away with an effort and forced his mind to return to the present. He would try for another piece of the puzzle.

"The drive seems to be doing you good. Why has no one brought you out to take the air? I should have thought that Lady Olivia, or perhaps Lord Badesworth, would have done so, now that you are so nearly recovered."

She laughed nervously. "Oh, I have been overly cosseted and protected. Most unnecessary! Although everyone means it kindly, so it's wrong of me to say so. Is that a confectioner's shop? Would you mind terribly if I ran in and bought something? For Lady Olivia and Miss Fairfax. They have been excessively good to me."

"I am entirely at your disposal, Lady Badesworth."

Nellie Beauchamp stopped in her tracks, her eyes narrowing into a squint as she stared across the busy street. That was Lord Rival driving that showy curricle, no doubt about it. But who was the new conquest? Veiled! How theatrical. Nellie's lip curled in a sneer.

Anger licked through her. Had George bought that curricle with Hugo's money? The money he had won from her? She wouldn't care a jot, had she been the lady at his side. But the thought of George using her money—or even a portion of it—to squire some other female about, definitely stuck in her craw. That had always been a possibility, of course. Even a probability. She wished bitterly that she had thought of it before.

George was pulling up, tossing a coin to a lad who dashed to hold the horses' heads. He stepped easily down from the curricle's high perch and turned to assist his companion. Nellie, half ashamed of herself, turned her back to avoid being seen. She watched closely as the little pantomime played out, reflected in the shop window beside her.

There was definitely something familiar about that figure in the blue pelisse. Nellie had always had a keen memory for faces. She would recognize the lady in a moment.

Blond hair peeped from beneath the hat. Was it Chloe Gilliland? No. Too slender, and a little too tall. Then the lady hopped down from the carriage in a way that somehow revealed her youth, and for an instant her veiled features turned directly toward Nellie. Nellie caught her breath, astonished. Lady Badesworth! Lady Badesworth, by all that was wonderful! She'd know her anywhere, veiled or unveiled.

Nellie spun round to stare. George and her ladyship, oblivious to the fascinated gaze riveted upon them, disappeared into the shop—but not before Nellie was absolutely sure. It *was* Lady Badesworth.

A catlike smile slowly curved Nellie's lips. What tasty fodder for the gossip mill. Bad Lord Badesworth cuckolded by Rake Rival! She could hardly wait to spread the tale.

It was high time George learned a lesson. Well! Badesworth was the very man to take arrogant Lord Rival down a peg.

16

*T*hese were the best times. Sitting beside George on the high, narrow bench of his curricle, pale October sunlight warming her and a crisp breeze fanning her face, pressed against him from hip to knee, was Olivia's idea of paradise. Here, and only here, could she spend time alone with Lord Rival and risk neither her reputation nor her sanity. She could have the happiness of touching him, without worrying that the situation would slip beyond her control. Even when his banter became laced with double entendres, causing her blood to warm and her toes to curl, she need not fear that anything would come of it. There were few pleasures greater, she found, than the enjoyment of what *felt* like danger—so long as one knew one was safe.

Lord Rival called for her promptly every morning, and the ritual of their daily drive had quickly become the favorite part of her day. She looked forward to it with keen anticipation, and was ridiculously disappointed when inclement weather interfered with her precious hour alone with George. Thus far, it had only rained once—but the sharp disappointment she felt made her wonder nervously whether her feeling of safety was, itself, illusory. It was such a relief to relax and enjoy George's company that perhaps she was relaxing a bit too much. True, one need not worry about improper advances while being driven in an open curricle in broad daylight—but it would not do to let her guard down entirely. Matters were bad enough already.

Lord Rival was making inroads in her heart, however diligently she tried to guard it. In fact, she was terribly afraid that she was falling fast and hard for the last man on earth she wanted to love. It wasn't just his appearance—although that, in itself, made her weak in the knees. It was his intelligence, and his humor, and the kind heart she glimpsed behind his suave facade.

As she sat beside him one sparkling morning in the second week of October, she studied his strong profile and fell into a reverie. She wondered if Lord Rival knew what gentlemanly instincts ruled his secret being. She rather fancied he didn't. He seemed to think of himself as hardhearted and cold. She had seen through this charade almost immediately, of course, and once she had picked up on what she persisted in believing was his true nature, a thousand little clues presented themselves, confirming her views.

Feeling her eyes upon him, he glanced down at her, quirking one eyebrow in amusement. "You're very silent this morning."

"I am pondering your character, Lord Rival."

He looked startled. "Good God. I must find a way to distract you."

"Why? I am not thinking anything offensive."

"Indeed! What are you thinking?"

She smiled. "That you underestimate your own goodness."

His expression became sardonic. "In that case, my pet, I had better interrupt your train of thought—before you have a chance to weigh all the evidence."

She chuckled. "Speaking of pets, George, how is poor Tom?"

"Fat as a flawn. Fatter every day."

"Now, *that,* sir, is evidence," she said teasingly. "Overfeeding a pet you claim to despise! You have a soft heart."

"A soft head, more like," remarked George, deftly rounding the corner of her street. "That confounded cat rules me with an iron paw."

"Have you trained him not to bother you while you sleep?"

"On the contrary! He has trained me. I now sleep soundly, but every morning I awake to find him at the foot of my bed—so I cannot flatter myself that my efforts to rebuff him have met with success. It is Tom whose will has prevailed."

She was still laughing at his lively descriptions of Tom's tyranny as George pulled to a halt before her house. "Oh! Are we back so soon?" she said wistfully. She always felt a pang at ending their brief time together.

His dark eyes glinted down at her. "Come now, Lady Olivia. You are a busy woman, remember. You haven't time to waste dallying with the likes of me."

"Very true." A tiny smile played across her features. "But I can't help wishing I did."

His eyes seemed to darken further, turning her a bit dizzy. She felt his arm slide daringly round her waist. "When can I get you alone?" he murmured.

"Why—tomorrow morning, of course." To her annoyance, her voice was pitched higher than usual.

He shook his head. "Not in a curricle. Not in public, my sweet. Alone."

She knew she ought to tell him flatly that he couldn't, but somehow what came out was a weak and whispered, "I—I don't know."

"Let me take you to the theater."

"Oh, no—you're joking. Alone? Vauxhall was bad enough. The theater would cause a scandal."

His eyes bored into hers. "Dinner, then. Somewhere private. We can't start a scandal if no one sees us."

"I daresay you know just the place." She managed a queer little laugh. The thought of him with other women always acted upon her like a dash of cold water, momentarily stiffening her spine. "No," she said, more firmly. "You know my answer must be no."

Her footman opened the door and darted down the steps to help her alight from the curricle. She turned to him with relief, glad for anything that would break Lord Rival's spell. After she clambered down, however, she turned to shake George's hand. "Until tomorrow, then."

He took her hand, and held it tightly for a moment. His eyes locked with hers. "We shall revisit this discussion, my lady. You may rely on that."

Her heart beat faster, whether with fear or excitement she could not say. "Tomorrow," she repeated faintly.

He smiled, touched his hat to her, and drove off. She stood for a few seconds as if in a daze, watching his tall, elegant form recede. She felt a pang of heartache every time he left her, even for a day. It was tearing her apart, telling him no, over and over—when she longed more and more to say yes.

She had barely entered the house when her housekeeper, Mrs. Pratt, pounced on her. "My lady, a word with you," she begged, jerking her head in a sharp gesture toward the library.

"Good heavens, what is amiss? You nearly frightened the wits out of me." But Olivia's teasing smile faded as she perceived the housekeeper's genuine agitation. She walked quickly past the door Mrs. Pratt was holding open for her. "What is it?" she asked, in quite a different voice.

Mrs. Pratt closed the door quietly behind her and stepped forward, folding her hands at her waist. "It's Lord Badesworth, madam. He's here."

Olivia's hand instinctively crept to her throat. "Here? In Chelsea?"

"Upstairs, my lady. He's waiting for you in your morning room. I thought you would want to know before you went up."

Olivia felt herself turning pale. "Where is Edith?"

"She's above, madam, safe in her chamber. With the door securely locked, have no doubt. Miss Fairfax is with her. It's they who wished me to intercept you on your way in."

With a soft exclamation, Olivia began pacing the room, thinking furiously. She was conscious of an absurd impulse to run and call Lord Rival back again, although she couldn't think of a blessed thing he could do. It was utterly irrational to feel that having him at her side would somehow lend her strength. "How long has Ralph been here?"

"Twenty minutes or thereabouts. We told him you were not at home, my lady, but at first he did not believe us. He actually forced his way in—threw my Joe aside as if he weighed nothing at all."

The aggrieved note in the housekeeper's voice did not escape Olivia. "I am sorry I was not here to deal with him myself, Mrs. Pratt," she said quickly. "I hope Joe was not hurt?"

"No, my lady," said Mrs. Pratt, mollified. "And as for hanging about here on the off chance that Lord Badesworth might drop by, I'm sure there's no reason why you should. We all know our duty. We had to let his lordship in, and he insisted on waiting for you, but he's none the wiser for all that. The poor mite is hidden away, and we trust she'll stay so."

"Thank you, you are very good," said Olivia automatically. She pressed one hand to her forehead. "Did he seem . . . angry? Yes, I suppose he was, or he would not have manhandled poor Joe. I wonder how on earth he learned that Edith is here?"

"Well, we don't know that he did," said Mrs. Pratt comfortably. "Lord Badesworth didn't mention her. He asked for you, not for his wife."

Olivia halted in her pacing. "Did he? Let us hope, then, that he does not know she is here. Or at least that he is not certain! At any rate, I had better go up without further delay. He will have seen my arrival through the window."

Mrs. Pratt permitted herself a satisfied smile. "As to that, my lady, I took the liberty of tightly closing the shutters."

"Oh, well done." Olivia gave her a grateful smile. "If he has not torn the house apart, then, he does not know that you have warned me. Heavens, if only I knew what to do!"

Mrs. Pratt's kindly face was troubled. "Have we the law on our side, my lady?"

"No," said Olivia in a low tone. "I fear we have not." She sighed. "There is nothing for it but to tell him the truth. We knew this day would come. I have been thinking that we might negotiate some sort of settlement. Marriages of convenience are so common among our class, and so few of them succeed, that many husbands and wives eventually agree to live apart." Even to Olivia's ears, her optimism sounded forced.

The housekeeper, who had served the family all her life, looked skeptical. "Master Ralph was never one to let go of anything that was his. Not unless it was took from him by force."

This was true, and Olivia knew it. She took another hasty turn about the room, thinking aloud. "I must think of something. I must *try*. I cannot agree to let Ralph set Edith up in the dower house. She will never be safe so long as he knows where she is. But perhaps he will allow me to keep her here, for a price."

Mrs. Pratt gave a satisfied nod. "If you'll pardon me, my lady, I'll just step up and let the ladies know you are home, and that all's well."

All was far from well, but Olivia waved her off absently, still thinking. A few moments later she took a deep breath to steady her nerves, then walked upstairs with a straight spine and a reasonably firm tread. *This is my house,* she reminded herself. *Ralph has no power here.*

She pasted a pleasant expression on her face, opened the door, and entered her morning room. "Ralph, how do you do?" she said cordially, walking forward with her hand extended. "What brings you to Chelsea?"

He was standing by the fireplace and did not move to greet her. His belligerent scowl put her instantly in mind of their father. Ralph looked more like him every year. His hair was thinning rapidly, and the thickness of his body was no longer due to muscle, but to fat. *Poor Edith,* she thought with an inward shudder.

"Cut line," he ordered brusquely. "I'm searching for Edith. She ran off. Left me without a word of warning. I've only one question for you, Olivia. Did you know?"

Since he obviously was not going to shake her hand, she dropped it to her side. "Yes," she said simply.

Ralph's face flushed with anger. "I'll warrant you did, begad!" he shouted. "She's been spotted in Chelsea. Chelsea! I could scarce believe my ears when I heard it." He shook his fist at her in impotent fury. "Have you conspired with her all these weeks, Olivia? Did you help her run away from me? Was it your idea? By thunder, I wouldn't be surprised if it was! You've never cared tuppence for the family name—"

"It was not my idea," she said crisply. "Control yourself, brother, and kindly remember where you are. If you cannot speak civilly to me, I shall ask you to leave this house."

Her words, not unnaturally, sent him into a tirade. While Ralph stomped about, cursing and hurling abuse at her, Olivia calmly removed her hat and gloves, setting them on a small table near the door.

She then seated herself in one of the wing chairs and regarded her brother impassively, waiting until he shouted himself to a standstill.

"That temper of yours will be the death of you one day," she observed. "Pray sit down and behave like an adult—if you can! Throwing a tantrum will not achieve your ends."

"How dare you?" he spluttered. "How dare you take that tone with me, you insolent chit? I'm the head of the family, by God!"

"You are not the head of anything here," she informed him sharply. "You are a guest in my home—an unbidden guest, I might add—and fast wearing out your welcome. Come down off your high ropes, Ralph. You can't bully me."

He couldn't, because years of practice had taught Olivia to hide her fear when dealing with him. She had long been thankful that the spread of years between their births had protected her, to some degree, from what might have been a childhood filled with terror. Ralph had always had a cruel streak and a hot temper, but he had been away at school most of the time when she was small.

He glared at her, eyes narrowed and head lowered like an enraged bear. "The baggage ran away," he growled. "Ran away, d'ye hear me? She's made me a bloody laughingstock. It's impossible to keep such things a secret. The state of my marriage is the talk of the town. I would have suspected you had a hand in it, but I thought you barely knew her."

Her nostrils flared with disdain. "Yes, that sounds like you. If the thought had only crossed your mind, you would have suspected me—with evidence or without it. It is your nature to blame others for your failings."

"You were ever eager to do me a bad turn! I would not put it past you to plot the episode yourself. You would engineer my humiliation if you could."

"I have better things to do with my time." She again indicated a chair and he finally sat, scalding her with a look of pure hatred. Olivia, armed with the knowledge that her servants hovered watchfully nearby, addressed him with her customary calm. "There is no dark plot brewing against you, Ralph. Edith ran away because you beat her."

"Hah!" he barked. "Then you have spoken with her. I thought as much. Is that what the jade told you?"

"She did not need to tell me. I saw the injuries you inflicted." Olivia's voice was even, but her hands curled into angry fists in her lap. "They were beastly. She still has not fully recovered."

"Ho, she hasn't, has she? She's feeling well enough to jaunt about the town with her paramour! But you wouldn't know anything about that, of course." Ralph's voice dripped sarcasm.

Olivia was bewildered. "Paramour? You're mad. Edith has no paramour."

His mouth twisted in an ugly sneer. "She left me for another man. Pretty picture, ain't it? Did she enact you a tragedy? Portray herself as Innocence Wronged? Cunning little trollop! I make no doubt she did—and you fell for it. You fall for every hard luck story you hear."

Olivia laughed with angry amazement. "Next you will tell me you never raised a hand to her."

"I raised my hand to her, and I'd do it again," he snapped. "I was within my rights. A man must have discipline and order in his home. She earned that punishment. Aye, and worse! It would have gone much harder with her had I known she was seeing Lord Rival on the sly."

"What?"

"Come now, Ivy! Don't pretend to be stupider than you are. You must have seen them together. They tell me that rakeshame is forever hanging about your precious school these days. It must be my wife—my wife, God rot her!—who brings him there."

Olivia pressed her hands to her temples. "I don't know whether you are running mad, or I am!" she exclaimed. "Lord Rival's presence at the school has nothing to do with Edith. They have never even met."

"So say you!" spat Badesworth. "The rumor is that my blushing bride is living under Rival's protection."

"Why, then, I can nip that rumor in the bud. She is living here with me." The relief flooding Olivia's soul showed her how frightened she had been by the terrible suggestion, however silly, that George and Edith had been . . . but no. It was all gossip and rumor. "I wonder how these preposterous stories get started?"

Relief did not seem to be Ralph's predominant emotion. His face slowly turned almost purple with rage as the realization sank in that his half sister had been sheltering his errant wife. He sprang out of the chair in a rage, and Olivia was afraid for a moment that he was going to throttle her. Fury robbed him of speech for a few seconds, but then he launched into a blistering, profane, and largely incoherent indictment of women in general and Olivia and Edith in particular. His opinions were couched in such filthy language that Olivia had difficulty following them, but the gist of his remarks was clear enough.

"Stop! Stop!" she cried at last, covering her ears with her hands.

"Do you have her here?" bellowed Ralph. "Is she in this house at this moment? By God, Olivia, I'll have the law on you!"

"On what charge, pray? Theft?" she retorted. "This is not the middle ages, brother, and Edith is not your chattel."

He stalked over to her, menacing her with his sheer physical power. Ralph Fairfax was a large man, and however strong she appeared on the surface, his tantrums had frightened her since she was a child. His eyes bulged with temper, their gray irises seeming to glow eerily in his red face. Olivia swallowed hard, but managed to keep her chin high.

"I ought to throw you against the wall," he told her, the sudden flatness of his tone filling her with terror. "I ought to horsewhip you. Teach you a lesson, by Christ. Teach you to respect the head of the family."

Abruptly he straightened and strode toward the door, then flung it open and burst onto the landing. She saw in a flash that he meant to hunt Edith down. If he found her while in this mood, something dreadful would surely happen. Olivia ran after him crying, "Joe! William! Help, help!"

It seemed that her entire household had gathered at the foot of the stairs and was anxiously watching the landing. A sea of upturned faces parted as her footman and kitchen boy raced to answer her frantic call. Ralph tried to dash farther up the stairs, roaring his wife's name, but Olivia's manservants intercepted him. The kitchen boy, Joe, tackled Lord Badesworth with relish. William joined the fray more gingerly, but the two servants, uniting their efforts, were able to hold the earl.

"For shame! For shame, Ralph! Calm yourself," Olivia exclaimed, scarce able to make herself heard above Ralph's curses. "Must we summon the Watch? For heaven's sake, think! Remember who you are."

He struggled like a demented beast, glaring at her. "Hand her over," he panted. "She's mine."

"I cannot let you see her, let alone take her away, so long as I fear for her safety."

"That's my affair, not yours. Edith is my wife, for God's sake! You're interfering in the private business of a man and his wife—something you know nothing about." He shook off William's timid hand and turned, snarling, to Joe. "Unhand me, sirrah."

Joe's chin jutted pugnaciously, but Olivia nodded her assent. The lad backed off with obvious reluctance. Ralph brushed off his coat sleeve contemptuously and stomped back into the morning room. Olivia gave a brisk nod to her gape-mouthed staff and they scuttled off to their various tasks. But to Joe and William she said, in a low tone, "Thank you. Please stay within earshot." They nodded grimly. She felt a bit safer knowing that after she closed the door, they would remain on the landing outside.

Once within the morning room again she faced Ralph squarely. "Let us discuss this matter like rational creatures. You have been married for less than a year, and already it is clear that you and Edith cannot live peaceably together. Why not agree to live apart?"

He uttered an ugly bark of laughter. "I didn't marry for a life of peace. I married because I need an heir."

"Well, you won't get one this way," said Olivia with asperity. "Had Edith been increasing a month ago, the beating you gave her would have induced a miscarriage."

"Much you know about it," jeered Ralph. "At any rate, I'll be damned if turn a blind eye while she's cuckolding me. She's not even discreet, blast her! Some men may wink at their wife's indiscretions; I never will. There will be no mongrel blood in the Fairfax line. I'll lock her up if I have to."

"But this is all nonsense! Edith has no paramour. I promise you, brother, you have been misinformed."

"Faugh! Edith was seen hanging on Rival's arm in Chelsea. Whispers had already started when she left me. Now the rumor is all over town that she left me for Rival. I come hotfoot to London and where do I find Edith? In Chelsea, just as the talemongers said I would!" He ground his teeth. "That little bitch is dragging my name through the mud. Aye, and yours! But you don't care for that."

"No. Frankly, I don't."

The door opened and Bessie walked through it, her sharp eyes taking in Olivia's tense, wary face and Ralph's menacing stance. "Well, well," she said equably. "Here's a pleasant family gathering. How are you, Ralph? But you need not answer. I can see for myself."

Ralph's thick lips curled in an ugly sneer. "I forgot about you," he said rudely. "I suppose you've been in the thick of things as usual, meddling in matters that don't concern you."

Bessie's brows drew into a fierce line above her short nose. "If you mean protecting Edith from you, you brute, indeed I have. And I'm here now to see that you don't browbeat Ivy."

The top of Bessie's head barely reached the middle of Ralph's chest, but she was a formidable ally nevertheless. Dear Bessie! Olivia felt a rush of gratitude and affection for her cousin. She was always on Olivia's side, come what may.

The two women formed a united front, summoned their patience, and bent all their persuasive skills to the task of soothing irascible Lord Badesworth. It took a little time, but they calmed him down sufficiently to achieve a grudging acceptance of reality, which was that Edith would not return to him unless she could be convinced, at the very least, that it was safe to do so. The longer they spoke with him, however, the more uneasy Olivia felt. It seemed clear to her that Ralph could not be trusted. Contempt simmered beneath the surface even as he pretended to agree, and she suspected that he was merely humoring them in order to get his hands on his wife again. Once he had spirited Edith away, there was no telling what he might do.

It was, therefore, with a heavy heart that Olivia eventually climbed the stairs to Edith's chamber. It was time to add Edith's voice to the negotiations regarding her future, but Olivia wanted to summon her personally rather than entrust the task to a servant. In the first place, Edith might very well refuse to come down—and in the second, Olivia wanted to warn her that whatever bargain they struck with Ralph, Edith should arm herself against the day when he would break it.

She tapped softly on Edith's door. "Edith, dear. It's Olivia." She waited for a moment, then knocked again, louder. No answer. She frowned and tried the handle. The door was locked. "Edith, don't be a goose. There is no one else with me. Ralph is downstairs. Open the door."

No answer. Indeed, not a sound. Olivia did not know whether to feel alarmed or merely irritated. She rattled the iron doorknob and knocked again, beseeching her sister-in-law to let her in, but all her efforts and pleadings met with cold silence.

A few quick strides took Olivia back to the landing, where she called for assistance. Mrs. Pratt and Joe came up. Olivia convened a hasty council. Mrs. Pratt disclosed that she had given her only key to Edith, so it would not be possible to unlock the door from the outside. Joe offered to break the door down, but Olivia assured the boy that such drastic action would not be necessary. At this point in the strategy session Ralph stumped up the stairs. Bessie puffed in his wake, vainly imploring him not to rush to judgment, and the group massing outside Edith's door swelled to five persons.

As soon as Ralph's suspicions were confirmed—that Edith had locked the door and was not emerging voluntarily from her sanctuary—he put his shoulder to the door and, ignoring the clamor of protests from everyone else, summarily broke it off its hinges.

The entire company spilled into the darkened room. It was empty.

17

"*E*dith!" cried Bessie, running to check the dressing area that opened off the bedchamber. But Ralph strode immediately to the window embrasure and flung back the floor-length draperies in one fierce movement. Behind the folds of heavy material, the window was open.

Olivia gasped. "Merciful saints! Surely she could not have left through the window?" She ran to peer out, unbelieving, and half afraid that her sister-in-law's lifeless form would be lying on the pavement below. The pavement was bare, however, and Edith was nowhere to be seen. Something that looked like wrung laundry lay in a tangled twist on the paving stones. Her eyes could not make sense of it.

Ralph apparently recognized this object, however. Snarling, he turned away from the window and crossed to Edith's bed, where he yanked open the bedcurtains. The bedclothes were missing.

"What on earth—!"

"She made a rope," snapped Ralph. "Knotted the sheets and pillowslips together. Looks like it didn't hold her all the way to the ground this time. I hope the bitch broke her neck."

"Ralph, how can you?" cried Olivia. She ran back to the window, terrified that a closer examination would reveal blood on the ground, but she could see nothing. "Oh, why would she do such a desperate thing?"

Bessie joined her, her features drawn and worried. "Because she felt desperate, poor lamb. She thought we would hand her over to Ralph."

"But where could she have gone?"

A crashing oath behind them made the two women turn round, startled. Ralph stood by Edith's dressing table with a note in his hand. It had been folded and addressed on the outside to Olivia, in large enough letters to be read across the room. Joe and Mrs. Pratt instantly converged on Ralph from one side and Olivia on the other, exclaiming in outrage that he would so cavalierly read a message not meant for his eyes. He held it up above their heads, however, staring at it, then crumpled it in his fist and threw it to the floor. He was livid with rage. Bessie pounced on the crumpled note as Ralph headed for the door. Olivia seized his arm but he shook her off, cursing.

"Where are you going?"

"Brighton," he said through his teeth, and started down the stairs.

Edith must have foolishly disclosed her destination in the note. Olivia ran out into the passage and called after the earl's retreating form. "Wait! Ralph, what will you do when you find her?"

"Kill her. And that whoreson Rival," he shot over his shoulder.

Olivia, stunned, pressed her hands to her cheeks. Ralph always said such things, terrible things, when he was angry. Of course he wouldn't really kill anyone. Not his own wife. People didn't do such things. And certainly he would not harm Lord Rival. It was absurd. Why would he? George had nothing to do with this.

Even so, half-formed fears chased madly through her brain. Ralph's apparent certainty that George was aiding in Edith's escape, and that when he found Edith

he would find George with her, frightened Olivia on
some deep and primal level that she hardly cared to
acknowledge.

She heard the front door slam, far below, and the
sound seemed to break her trance. She would think
about the implications later. She would worry later.
Now was the time to act, not think. She spun round
and flew back into Edith's bedchamber. Bessie tried
to hand her Edith's note, but Olivia was intent upon
Joe Pratt.

She grabbed the lad by his shoulders and turned
him to face her, speaking urgently into his startled
face. "Joe, I need you to take a message to Lord
Rival. At once. You will probably find him at the
school. If he has left there, you must seek him at his
home in Mayfair. Take a hackney; it's the fastest way.
Ask his lordship to return here to me *immediately*.
Warn him that—that Lord Badesworth has taken a
foolish notion into his head and means to do him a
mischief. Do you understand?"

"Yes, my lady," said Joe eagerly. He wasted not an
instant, but pelted down the stairs.

"What does Edith's note say?" asked Olivia, finally
taking it from Bessie with a trembling hand.

"Not much," admitted Bessie. "She wrote so hastily,
I can barely make it out. Why is Ralph angry with
Rival?"

"Because Ralph is a lunatic," retorted Olivia, praying that this was, indeed, the only reason. Her eyes
scanned Edith's note, concentrating on the scrawled
words. They did not shed much light. "Brighton," she
murmured, bewildered. "Why did he think she was
going to Brighton?"

The note said merely,

*Dear Olivia and Bessie, pray forgive me but I
cannot stay. You have been more than generous and I am very greatfull. Pray accept the candy*

*I was going to give you but now there is no
tyme. Lord Rival* [illegible].

*I am so sorry to inconvince you but I must go
and it is better that you not know where, I
promise you I will be safe for I go to one who
loves me. I should have gone there at once but
it was to far. I shall writte to you when I am
safe. Edith.*

Olivia read it. She read it again, her unease growing.
That was surely *Lord Rival* in the center of the note,
but what came after? She pointed to the phrase, holding the note toward Bessie. "What does that say?"

"Inconvince. She means inconvenience."

"Yes, yes, but what comes before it? Something
about Lord Rival."

Bessie stared hard at the crumpled paper, then
shook her head. "I don't know. Did you see the basket
of marzipan she left us? Poor little poppet! It was a
sweet thought."

"Never mind that," said Olivia impatiently. She
read Edith's note again, straining to understand it.
"Why does her note mention Lord Rival? How does
she know him?"

"I didn't even think of that. Mercy! It's odd, isn't
it?"

"Yes. Ralph taxed me with it a half hour ago, and
I promised him that Edith and Lord Rival had never
met. But apparently they have."

"Well, he can't think she meant Rival by that *one
who loves me* rubbish! Is that what sent him flying up
into the boughs?"

"Perhaps. There's no knowing what may be in
Ralph's head." Olivia suddenly realized that the
housekeeper still hovered nearby, her forehead knotted with concern. "Mrs. Pratt, kindly see to it that
bandboxes are packed for Bessie and me, suitable for
an overnight stay. Immediately, if you please."

"Yes, my lady."

Mrs. Pratt vanished about her business, but Bessie's eyes narrowed in suspicion. "Bandboxes! Ivy, what are you thinking?"

Olivia's face set in stubborn lines. "That you and I must needs go to Brighton. If Edith is truly headed there—for whatever reason—and Ralph is on her trail, we must catch her before he does. Or soon enough afterward that he won't have time to harm her."

"How are we to catch her?" demanded Bessie. "Ralph seemed to know where she was going, but we do not."

"Actually, we needn't catch Edith if we succeed in catching Ralph. I know it can be done; one hears of runaways being caught after much longer head starts than this. At any rate, Lord Rival will advise us."

Bessie looked as if she might pop. "Lord Rival! What has he to say to anything? I hope you do not mean to air our family's dirty laundry with—"

"Bessie, for heaven's sake, Ralph said he meant to *kill* the man! Even if it's just bluster, we must, at the very least, warn him."

"Joe Pratt will warn him," said Bessie patiently. "Ivy, be reasonable! If you truly mean to set out after Edith, we can't wait for Rival."

Olivia's chin jutted stubbornly. "I shan't leave without him."

"Then it's a fool's errand," Bessie grumbled, but Olivia was adamant. Irrational or not, she wanted George by her side. It wasn't so much his counsel that she wanted, it was his presence. She would know no peace until she saw him walk through her door—not, she was ashamed to admit, because she was afraid that Ralph would do him an injury. She was privately sick with fear that Ralph was right.

Part of her was bracing for the possibility that Joe Pratt would return without George, saying that he could not be found. If Ralph was right, then Edith had not hurt herself when the makeshift rope let go because Lord Rival waited beneath her window. The mental picture of Edith tumbling into George's arms made Olivia feel as if the room were spinning. If Joe returned without him—if George and Edith were even now on their way to Brighton together—dear God, could she bear it?

When Bessie left to supervise the packing of her bandbox, Olivia was left alone in Edith's empty bed-chamber. There, her private demons stalked her. She tried in vain to fend them off, busying herself with a perfunctory inventory of Edith's room. She fought down her rising fears by searching for clues.

A few of Edith's toiletries seemed to be missing. Her clothing had been tossed about in her dressing area. This indicated hasty and abbreviated packing. But Olivia could not concentrate. Her demons hovered and circled like vultures, pouncing whenever her thoughts paused. They gnawed and tore at the tender edges of her mind.

The demons whispered that Edith had appeared on her doorstep the very night before George entered her life. Was it coincidence? Or had Edith, as Ralph had told her, left her husband for George? Had George and Edith been meeting on the sly all along?

It would not be the first time Olivia's gullible heart had trusted and been betrayed. It was her worst night-mare, to relive that particular pain: discovering that someone you loved was deliberately playing you for a fool. Or, in this case, two someones.

Imitation friendships were the chief hazard of wealth. In small ways, with casual acquaintances, it did not matter when people smiled and fawned and flattered. One usually heard the false note, spotting the insincerity before it had a chance to hurt. But in great matters—to be wrong about friendships that mattered to you—to show kindness to someone the way she had shown kindness to Edith, and be despised for it—that hurt. And it hurt worse, it hurt unbearably, to dream about a certain man, to melt at his touch, and then discover that he secretly laughed at you.

Olivia steeled herself to meet that pain again.

Giving in to the demons, bracing herself to learn that George had spirited Edith away, she worked herself into such a state that when she heard a familiar baritone voice and quick, firm tread below, she could not, for a moment, credit her own ears. She froze, holding her breath, then let it out in a whoosh. The relief was so overpowering that she grabbed the bedpost to keep her knees from giving way. She heard his footsteps taking the stairs two at a time and then, like a miracle, George stood in the doorway before her. He was still wearing his many-caped driving coat and his tall, broad-shouldered bulk nearly filled the door frame.

His gaze flicked over her and his expression altered. "What's wrong, sweeting?" He crossed to her in three quick strides and gripped her shoulders, his eyes filled with concern.

Belatedly, Olivia realized she was still clutching the bedpost. She gave a shaky laugh and let it go, smiling mistily up at him. "Nothing. My foolish fancies were getting the better of me."

His grin flashed, although his eyes were still serious. "Excellent. I hope you count me among your foolish fancies."

He had misunderstood her, but it didn't matter. She smiled up at him, giddy with relief. "Oh, yes. You are the most foolish of my fancies. But thank you for coming so quickly—indeed, there is not a moment to be lost."

One brow shot up. "Are matters so urgent? Where is Lord Badesworth? Joe Pratt tells me he is making threats. I have come here to make sure that whatever threats he makes, he makes against me, and me only."

He cupped her cheek briefly in his hand. "Is that what distresses you, Ivy?" he asked, his voice rough. "Has he threatened you? Tell me."

"Threatened me? Not really. He would certainly blame me if he could, but I was with him when Edith disappeared. He knows I had naught to do with it—today, at least, although he may persist in thinking I helped her run away the first time. Ralph spews so much bombast that there is no telling what he truly believes."

He returned both hands to her shoulders and leaned back, holding her at a distance as if trying to bring her face more sharply into focus. "I think we are speaking at cross-purposes. Who is Edith?"

Her eyes widened. "I beg your pardon. Lady Badesworth. Edith is my sister-in-law." It seemed he did not know her name. This was reassuring.

His air of bafflement increased. "Now, look here—I was told that your brother is hunting for me, breathing fire. I assumed he discovered our friendship and means to end it if he can."

Olivia gave a startled little laugh. "No! Ralph wouldn't care what becomes of me. He thought you had formed a . . . a connection—an illicit relationship with his wife."

It was George's turn to look startled. "The deuce you say! What put such a cork-brained notion into his head?"

Olivia began toying with the edge of one of his greatcoat's capes, still watching him out of the corner of her eye. "Why is it a cork-brained notion? I thought you had a history of—of stealing the affections of married women."

"Certainly I do," he said promptly. "But only when it serves my own interests. Ivy, you wound me! I may be a lascivious chap, but I am not an idiot."

This callous speech should have made her think less of George. Somehow, it had the opposite effect. She beamed. "I hadn't thought of that," she confessed, relaxing happily. "I suppose it would be rather stupid of you to seduce Edith. Under the circumstances. But, well, Ralph told me that she left him for you."

"Poppycock. Don't tell me you believed it." He tilted her chin up with one hand, studying her face in unabashed amazement. "You did believe it. Why?"

"She's run away! Didn't Joe Pratt tell you?"

"No." He frowned. "Why should he?"

"She left a note." Olivia's voice faltered a little. "It mentioned you."

George looked thunderstruck. "But her note didn't say she was eloping with me!" he exclaimed. "It couldn't have."

"No."

"Well? What did it say?"

Olivia felt a little foolish. "We're not entirely sure," she admitted. "No one can read it."

After a moment of stunned silence, George threw back his head and laughed out loud. Olivia was sure now that her fears had been completely silly. "I ought to have known there was something strange about all this," she confessed, delighted. "After all, you never met Edith."

"Yes, I did," said George unexpectedly. "She ambushed me one day and bade me drive her to a confectioner's shop."

His reply was surprising, but its straightforward delivery was further evidence that Ralph had frightened her for no reason. Olivia leaned back against George's strong arms and shook her head, mystified. "Well! I have a thousand questions, but I suppose they will have to wait. Edith must be found without delay."

George glanced idly round the room. "There's the basket of marzipan she purchased. I'd know it anywhere; those infernal ribbons flapped in my face all the way here from the shop. Where is her note?"

"I have it." She pulled it from the pocket of her round gown and handed it to him. "Ralph read it and concluded she was heading for Brighton, although I see nothing about Brighton in it."

He gave it a cursory inspection. "She has a grandmother in Brighton," he said absently. "Well, what a goosecap! She does mention my name, but I fancy she is still nattering on about the marzipan. Fatal, to put my name in a farewell note when running away from her husband! No matter how innocent the context, my name has a rather—er—inflammatory effect on married men. I don't wonder at Badesworth's jumping to conclusions. Cooler heads than his have fired up with less cause." He handed the note back to Olivia. "Why did you send for me, my dear? Would you like me to chase down the runaway for you?"

"Not for me. *With* me." His casual mention of Edith's grandmother gave her a jolt—how well *did* George know Edith?—but she must not stop to inquire now. "I wish to accompany you. Please."

His eyes gleamed down at her. "This gets better and better. That curricle was the cleverest purchase I ever made."

She stuffed Edith's note hurriedly in her pocket, still anxiously studying his face. "Can it be done, George? Will we catch them?"

"How long ago did they leave?"

"I don't know when, exactly. Edith left, I think, at least an hour ago. Ralph has been gone for nearly that, but he always travels in his own coach. He will have gone back to his hotel, I daresay, to make arrangements. I would not be surprised if he is there yet, or at the very least, has barely left."

"In what sort of coach?"

"An old-fashioned traveling coach—a berline, I think. He prefers comfort to speed. And he always hires a guard to sit on the box with the driver, so assembling his party may take a bit of time."

"Good. How do you suppose Edith is traveling? On foot?"

The absurdity startled a laugh out of her. "I hope not! But I hadn't thought of that. I don't know."

"Does she have any money? Any luggage with her?"

Olivia thought swiftly. "Yes, she has money. And she has taken a few belongings, although I don't think she has taken much. She knew Ralph was in the house when she left—well, that's the reason why she left!—so I suppose she will use whatever money she has to buy speed."

"A post chaise, then. I can't imagine little Lady Badesworth riding *ventre à terre* to Brighton." He rubbed his chin thoughtfully. "Brighton. What a pity her grandmother lives in Brighton."

"Why?"

He flashed his wickedest grin at her. "Because I'd rather take you to Scotland, my sweet. And spend several nights on the road."

18

*I*n the end, they did take Lord Rival's curricle—for the sake of expediency. But it was hardly the most practical equipage for three persons on a cold day. Bessie staunchly insisted that neither her comfort nor her dignity be considered in this emergency, so their objections to placing her on the hard little bench meant for a groom or tiger were overruled. Perch there she did, sitting very upright and gazing straight ahead, a thick rug tucked round her to ward off the chill. The ladies' bandboxes were strapped to the back of the curricle, Olivia was handed up to sit beside George, and off they went, still earnestly discussing at which towns they should change horses and where to obtain shaving tackle and fresh linen for George, since it seemed probable they would spend the night in Brighton.

"And please do not protest at my expenditures on your behalf," begged Olivia. "We are deeply in your debt for escorting us, and I will do whatever I can to minimize your discomfort and inconvenience. It is the least I can do, sir, after presuming upon your good nature in this unconscionable way."

"Very well," said George affably. "I've no objection. Be as generous as you like. It will compromise me, of course, to accept expensive presents from you, especially items of a highly personal nature. But I rely

upon your sense of honor and fair play. I am confident
you will offer me marriage after you have ruined
me—"

Olivia choked. "And I suppose you intend to accept
my offer."

"Certainly I will accept it. With unbecoming alacrity. I can barely contain myself, anticipating the moment when you kneel and request my hand."

Olivia was acutely conscious of Bessie hovering
watchfully behind their heads. Her seat, meant for a
servant, was positioned high enough so that she could
not well overhear their conversation if they kept their
voices low, but Olivia felt uncomfortable enough iso-
lating her devoted chaperon without falling into the
rudeness of a murmured, exclusive conversation with
George. She gave him a warning look, therefore, and
turned the subject away from their nonsensical banter.

"How long will we be on the road, my lord?"

George shrugged lightly, his eyes on his team as he
skillfully threaded them through the congested streets
of London. "That depends, I suppose, on whether we
overtake our quarry en route. If we do not, and must
look up Lady Badesworth's grandmother in Brighton
at the end of our journey, I daresay we have an ardu-
ous day ahead of us. Especially if none of us knows
Lady Badesworth's grandmother's name or direction."

"Oh, dear. But are we likely to overtake them on
the road?"

He shot her an amused glance. "I failed to bring my
crystal ball. But I would say we stand a good chance of
overtaking Lord Badesworth, at least. I'm a very good
driver—or was. I may be out of practice."

They were forced to keep a sedate pace while still in
the metropolis, but once they were past Westminster
Bridge the traffic thinned and Lord Rival was able to
test his skill. Olivia was pleased to discover that his
expertise had not, after all, deserted him during his
years without a carriage. The horses were hired and

therefore strange to him, but he coaxed them effortlessly into a strong and lively pace that soon had them
bowling along at an astonishing rate of speed. Olivia,
unfamiliar with the attributes of sporting vehicles,
marveled at how quickly Lord Rival's curricle covered
the ground.

"I would not be surprised if we caught Ralph within
the hour! Bessie, is this not delightful?" One hand on
her hat, Olivia turned to direct her question at Bessie
and saw, to her dismay, that her cousin's expression
was more strained than delighted. She was hanging on
for dear life.

"At any rate, the faster we go the sooner it will be
over," said Bessie stoically. Her voice chattered as the
curricle rattled beneath her. "No, no, do not slacken
the pace on my account," she admonished, as Olivia
seized Lord Rival's arm in concern. "I shall do."

"But we are villains to make you so uncomfortable," said Olivia remorsefully. "We should have
hired a closed carriage after all."

"Rubbish," scoffed Bessie. "No time for that. But
I'll tell you this, Ivy—I wouldn't be a tiger for any
salary you could name. Mercy! It seems a great distance to the ground from up here."

Once they were well and truly on the turnpike, they
paused briefly at each tollgate and every likely posting
house to describe, with as many details as Olivia and
Bessie could recall, Lord Badesworth's traveling
coach. They could not inquire whether Edith had
passed because they had no inkling how she might be
traveling. Every inquiry was answered in the negative,
however, until they reached Croydon. There, one of
the ostlers at the King's Head recalled a red-faced
gentleman in a crested coach. He had caught the lad's
attention by abusing a waiter at the top of his lungs.

This information so precisely described Lord Badesworth that it earned the ostler a handsome tip. Unfortunately, it was all the information they were able to

obtain. The other ostlers, spying the largesse bestowed upon their compatriot as a reward for his feats of memory, gathered like a flock of hungry birds and chimed in with their own offerings when additional questions were asked. An argument broke out when the lads tried to recall exactly how long ago the incident had occurred. Nothing could be ascertained from their conflicting accounts of the time the earl had arrived, how long he had stopped, or the time he had departed. When the change of his own horses had been completed, therefore, Lord Rival elected to go forward rather than wait for the ostlers to sort it out.

"After all, it might discourage us to learn how far behind we are," remarked Lord Rival, giving his new team the office to start. "But we'll make up time now that we needn't stop in every hamlet. He won't change horses again until Horley, I imagine."

Olivia had been half afraid, when their previous inquiries had met with no success, that they had somehow flown from the scent—or, worse yet, gotten ahead of Ralph. With this concern alleviated, she was able to relax a little and take note of her surroundings. It would have been a pleasant trip, had they not been worried and pressed for time. The scenery was interesting and varied, even beneath a bleak autumnal sky. Despite the coldness of the day and the anxiety of the moment, Olivia was secretly enjoying herself.

A large part of this furtive enjoyment, she had to admit, derived from her forced proximity to Lord Rival. Even Bessie's quelling presence could not alter that. The heat of his body warmed her, and the rocking of the carriage brought them into repeated contact. He sat very much at his ease beside her, his keen gaze fastened on the road ahead. George handled his team with a stunning display of nonchalance, but Olivia was not deceived. Driving unknown horses headlong down one of the busiest turnpikes in England must be both difficult and tiring. She could not help admiring his manifest skill and stamina, and found them more impressive the more indifferent he appeared. As the hours went by, he seemed not to tire at all.

Olivia did not like to distract George from his concentration on the road, and Bessie was fully occupied in keeping her precarious seat, so conversation was desultory. As they wound across Eastwood Common, however, George did spare Olivia a glance and a smile. "Tell me, my pet. Why are we chasing Lord and Lady Badesworth? I don't wish to seem vulgarly inquisitive, but if I should have to explain myself to a magistrate at some point in the not-too-distant future, I would like to have some ready answer for the chap."

Olivia slewed round to stare at him in amazement. "Don't you know?"

He coughed apologetically. "Well, no. I know that Lady Badesworth has run away, and I can understand her husband's natural anxiety to recover her, but what you and I—and, for that matter, Miss Fairfax—have to do with the matter, I don't quite see."

Her jaw dropped. "Do you mean to tell me that you have driven me halfway to Brighton at a moment's notice without knowing the *reason*? I beg your pardon; this entire escapade must seem perfectly demented to you! Why did you agree to help us?"

His eyes lit with laughter. "Because you asked me to."

Olivia was momentarily speechless. Bessie's voice, warm with approval, chimed into the silence. "Very obliging of you, my lord, I am sure," she said. "And if we bring matters to a tidy conclusion, I daresay none of us will be called before a magistrate."

"Thank you, Miss Fairfax. You relieve my mind."

Olivia knew she must have a very queer expression on her face. She hastily turned away from George and stared blindly at the horses, her emotions in a jumble. It had struck her like lightning that there was something rather wonderful about having a man in her life who would leap to her aid with no questions asked.

"Well, I never!" she said at last, her voice quivering with laughter. "I'm very grateful to you, of course. But of all the rash, heedless, reckless starts—"

"No such thing," said Lord Rival, sounding injured. "Miss Fairfax assures me that I may not even be arrested."

Olivia choked. "If all goes well," she reminded him.

"If anything, my lord, we may *prevent* a crime," added Bessie. "Ivy, dear, pray explain it to him."

She did, with some hesitancy. She watched George out of the corner of her eye as she described the unbridled rages she had witnessed in Ralph since childhood, and the state Edith was in when she arrived on Olivia's doorstep last September. One never knew, with gentlemen. Many men felt that a husband's legal right to discipline his wife extended to just such a beating as Ralph had inflicted upon his bride.

As she carefully told the tale, glossing over some of the harsher details, she saw George's expression harden into grimmer and grimmer lines. He said nothing. It was impossible to tell whether he disapproved of Ralph's behavior, found the subject distasteful, or was simply angry that she had tricked him into involving himself in a domestic dispute that was none of his affair.

Before she could probe George's reaction they reached Horley. Olivia fell silent as George, still frowning abstractedly, steadied his nearly blown horses and negotiated the crowded approach to the Chequers at a trot. This inn was probably the most popular stop on the Brighton road, so they were not surprised to learn that none of the busy ostlers or beleaguered waiters recalled Lord Badesworth or his old-fashioned coach among the many vehicles they had attended in the past few hours.

Bessie and Olivia alighted from the curricle and stretched their legs while a fresh team was brought out. Bessie was limping, and admitted that she had "stiffened a bit" during the journey, but she steadfastly refused to exchange places with Olivia, even for one stage. "Think how ludicrous we would look!" she said, and, upon reflection, Olivia had to agree. The sight of elegant Lord Rival squiring a middle-aged dowd in an open carriage, with Olivia playing propriety in the tiger's seat, might be ridiculous enough to draw unwelcome attention to their expedition. Olivia, however, was guiltily aware that the bone-jarring journey in an uncomfortable seat was much harder on her older cousin than it would be on herself. She insisted on purchasing a cushion for Bessie—at an exorbitant price—from the enterprising management of the Chequers. The inn had quite a supply of these; they had evidently encountered many a weary traveler whose seat had proven unexpectedly uncomfortable.

The sun was low in the sky by the time they left Horley. Lord Rival had fallen into a brown study. His gaze fixed broodingly on the road, he seemed to move automatically as he drove, his mind busy elsewhere. Olivia felt a certain shyness about interrupting his thoughts despite the painful questions crowding her own. Nevertheless, she was plucking up her courage to ask him directly about his acquaintance with Edith when he muttered a soft exclamation. She looked inquiringly at him and saw that his gaze had sharpened and focused, as if something had startled him back to the here and now. Following the direction of his gaze, she saw a sleepy village ahead with a gabled posting inn beside the road. Beneath a spreading tree in the yard before it sat, unmistakably, Ralph's traveling coach. Olivia and Bessie cried out almost simultaneously, and Olivia instinctively grasped George's arm.

"I see it," he said curtly, and in a very few seconds

he had drawn his curricle neatly to a halt beside the
dusty berline. A boy ran out to take the horses' heads
and George jumped lightly down from the curricle.

He turned to Olivia and took her hand, speaking to
her in a low, urgent voice. "Forgive me, but I must
leave you to be handed down by the staff."

"Why?"

"It's better that I enter the inn ahead of you. If
Lord Badesworth has not recovered his temper—"

He broke off suddenly and, before Olivia registered
what was happening, George's quick reflexes had
taken him halfway to the door of the inn. She heard
it, then—a muted scuffling sound coming from inside
the building. Some sort of physical struggle was oc-
curring in one of the rooms near the open doorway,
and George was racing toward it.

A stifled exclamation escaped her. Scarcely knowing
what she did, Olivia slid from the curricle on her own
and stumbled past the surprised servant who was holding out his hand to assist her. As she ran toward the
inn she heard Bessie's querulous voice behind her,
scolding the lad for his slowness and demanding that
he help her down at once, at once, for heaven's sake!

Just as she reached the entrance to the inn a tre-
mendous crash sounded from a room to her left. She
darted toward it and paused on the threshold, her
hand unconsciously creeping to her throat. Her frantic
gaze took everything in at a glance; before her was a
small private parlor containing three persons. Lord
Rival stood near the window, his feet planted wide
apart and his hands curled into purposeful fists. He
seemed completely oblivious to the fact that Edith was
pressed tightly all along the length of his body as if
seeking to hide herself among the folds of his greatcoat. Her face was buried in its lapels. George's attention was entirely focused upon Ralph Fairfax, Lord
Badesworth, who lay sprawled on the floor before
him, insensible.

She must have made some sort of sound. George's head swung round to face her. The expression on his face almost caused her to take a step backward, so frightening was it. She had never seen such bleakness in a pair of human eyes, nor such blazing ferocity. But as his gaze fixed on her, his clouded vision seemed to clear, as if the sight of Olivia called back his sanity. He even managed a strained smile.

"I beg your pardon, my dear," he said, with a fair assumption of his usual aplomb. "It seems Lord Badesworth and I have made rather a mess of this room. Perhaps the ladies should be taken elsewhere."

She started forward in alarm. "Are you hurt?" she asked anxiously.

His eyes suddenly twinkled at her. "What! No concern for your nearest and dearest?" Edith's shivering body glued to his prevented him from actually moving, but he jerked his head toward Ralph's prostrate form. "I fancy your brother received the worst of it."

She glanced down. The earl's stocky body lay as if flung, sprawled across the hearth rug. He had apparently clutched at a tablecloth on his way down, since a wooden table was upended beside him and he lay amid a tumble of scattered pewter mugs and candlesticks. She made a little moue of distaste and stepped gingerly over his booted feet to stand beside George and Edith. "I daresay he'll live."

"I trust he will. It was not my intent to murder him." George paused. "Not that I wasn't tempted, of course."

"Lord ha' mercy!" Bessie's astonished gasp drew George's and Olivia's eyes to her. She stood, slightly out of breath and with bonnet askew, in the entrance to the room, pressing her plump hand to her heart. "What has happened here?"

Edith suddenly let go of George and, with a loud wail, flew to Bessie. Bessie folded the terrified countess protectively in her arms, glaring fiercely at George.

"Lord Rival, I would be obliged to you if—hush, lamb-kin! You're safe now, dearie. Nothing bad will happen to you."

Edith's tearstained face emerged. "I won't go back to Ralph! I won't! I cannot!"

Bessie patted and murmured soothingly, and Edith subsided back into her shoulder. She returned her gimlet gaze to George. "As I was saying, my lord, I would be obliged to you if you would furnish an expla-nation of what has transpired in this room, although it's plain as a pikestaff that whatever occurred, it ended in fisticuffs. I do not approve of fisticuffs, my lord, and I take leave to tell you that such goings-on would send any gently nurtured female into hysterics! Lady Badesworth has had a very trying day—"

"Oh, Bessie, *pray—!*" Edith lifted her head once more from her protector's shoulder. "It was not Lord Rival's fault. Everything happened so quickly—and, oh! When Lord Rival appeared, I was never so glad to see anyone in my life!"

By this time, George had entirely recovered his cus-tomary poise. He bowed gracefully in the direction of the ladies. "Miss Fairfax is quite right, Lady Bades-worth. I ought to have asked your husband to step outside with me before—ah—expressing my opinion of his behavior in so decided a fashion. Decking a gentleman in the presence of his wife is very bad *ton*. My only defense is that the provocation was"—his face hardened—"extreme."

"Do not apologize," said Olivia roundly. "I am al-ready persuaded that whatever treatment you handed my brother was well-deserved."

A deep groan sounded from the prostrate earl. George raised one eyebrow. "At any rate, Lord Bades-worth is regaining consciousness," he remarked. "If he comes to his senses in a figurative sense as well, I shall refrain from further demonstrations of—what did Miss Fairfax call it? Fisticuffs. But as we can place no dependence upon his lordship's self-control, I repeat my suggestion that the ladies be escorted to another room. You, there"—he nodded toward a cluster of figures huddled, openmouthed, in the hall just outside the door—"if this inn has another private parlor—"

Ralph muttered a foul expletive into the hearth rug. Olivia skipped instinctively backward at the murderous note in his voice, as if expecting the hem of her skirt to be stained by the language spilling from her brother's lips. George's arm shot out to steady her and she clutched it gratefully.

"Just so," said George pleasantly, a most unpleasant smile curling his mouth. "You are in the presence of ladies, Lord Badesworth. Kindly contain yourself for a few moments more. I shall then be entirely at your disposal."

A harassed-looking individual in an apron was shepherding Bessie and the still-shivering Edith out the door. Olivia stood her ground, her eyes flashing, only dimly aware that she still clung tightly to George. "I won't go," she announced. "I won't sit tamely in a coffee room somewhere while my detestable brother tries to do you an injury."

George looked down at her, laughter lurking in the dark depths of his eyes. "Thank you. Believe it or not, I am fully capable of protecting myself."

"You don't know him," said Olivia stubbornly. "He cheats."

"Yes. I gathered as much during our brief, but illuminating, interaction a few moments ago."

Ralph emitted another groan and rolled, with difficulty, onto his side. He seized his head as if trying to hold on to consciousness by physical force. "You dog," he muttered thickly. "I'll teach you. Unhand my wife."

"Your wife is long gone, Lord Badesworth," said George crisply. "Do you recall where you are?"

"Yes, damn you. Inn. Road to Brighton." He struggled and swore and managed to sit up, still holding his head. "I'll kill you for this, Rival. I'll kill you."

"I think not," said Lord Rival dryly. "But you are welcome to try. Are you always this fond of hyperbole? What a nuisance your family must find it." He reached gracefully down to assist Lord Badesworth to rise, but the earl only glowered at him, panting. George shrugged and straightened. "Suit yourself. We can have this conversation as easily with you seated on the floor, I suppose."

"What conversation?" Ralph's bleary eyes focused on Olivia. "Confound it, Ivy, what the devil are you doing here?"

"Lord Rival brought me."

The earl's features, never handsome in the best of conditions, twisted into a hideous sneer. "Well, I'll be damned. I knew Edith was a lightskirt at heart, but I never thought my dried-up sister would turn whore."

Olivia was still holding George's arm, and felt his muscles jump and bunch beneath her fingers almost before the ugly words left Ralph's mouth. She could feel the effort it cost him to keep from hitting Ralph again.

"I can't strike you while you're down," he said between his teeth. "But I can tell you to shut your filthy mouth. Your sister asked me to bring her here because she feared you would do your wife an injury. And you were on the point of doing so, my hotheaded friend, when I arrived and caught you in the act. Under the circumstances, I suggest you keep a civil tongue in your head. You've done enough damage for one day."

A timid cough sounded from the doorway. The aproned individual stood there, still looking rather harried. "I beg pardon, gentlemen—oh, and yours, milady—but I've shown the other females to the coffee room as you bade me, and my good wife was wondering if you was all staying to dinner. Or if you was wanting rooms," he added, brightening a little at the thought.

"Both, I think," said Olivia. "It's growing quite late." She bestowed a reassuring smile upon the nervous landlord, indicating her brother with a wave of her hand. "Lord Badesworth will pay for any breakage or damage sustained to this room. And we do beg your pardon for whatever trouble we have caused."

The landlord looked relieved. "Thank you, milady, I'm sure. My wife was fair bewattled, thinking the gentlemen would murder each other right here on the premises—which, I'm sure you understand, is not the sort of thing we are accustomed to."

"No, certainly not," said Olivia sympathetically. "Anyone can see that you run a respectable establishment."

The landlord bowed, seeming much mollified. He then cast an uneasy glance at Lord Badesworth. "I hope the gentleman is not injured, ma'am. Should I call for a surgeon, or—or anything of that nature?"

"I think not," said George, flicking an imaginary speck of dust from his sleeve. "What this country needs, of course, is a police force. But absent that—"

The landlord looked shocked. "Police? Oh, no, sir, begging your pardon. This is England."

He scurried off to order their dinner and George drew a chair up to where Ralph still sat on the floor. He placed one booted foot on the seat of the chair and leaned one arm on his knee.

"Now, then," he said pleasantly, looking down into the truculent face glowering up at him. "We are going to discuss your marriage, Lord Badesworth. None of my affair, you will say, but you have seen fit to make it my affair. You have dragged my name into it, Badesworth, and I want an explanation. And while we are discussing your marriage," he added, "we may as well discuss its future. I don't think Lady Badesworth will be returning to your care, sir." His voice became silky. "In fact, I will personally guarantee that she does not."

19

She had been expecting a miserly little hip bath. Instead, one of the largest bathtubs it had ever been her pleasure to encounter had been carried to her room and filled for her. Olivia sank nearly to her chin in the steaming water and sighed with bliss. There was nothing quite like a hot bath at the end of a long day, particularly a day spent traveling in an open carriage. Olivia had lavishly ordered baths for everyone in her party. The expense would be well worth it. Bessie's stiff muscles would be soothed, Edith's anxiety would melt away, and George—oh, dear. The bath seemed to grow hotter when she thought of George.

The inn had only had three rooms available, and one private parlor. Ralph had immediately removed himself from the premises and headed back toward London rather than share a room with Lord Rival, and Olivia was hopeful that they had seen the last of Ralph for the time being. Bessie seemed to have a calming effect upon Edith, so Edith and Bessie were sharing the largest of the three rooms. Olivia's room was two doors down from theirs. George had been placed, with the landlord's profuse apologies, in a small and noisy room over the kitchen. He assured the landlord that he was inured to hardship and could sleep through anything. Remembering that, Olivia chuckled. Lord Rival did not have the appearance of one who was inured to hardship. She supposed he equated Tom purring at his feet with the racket of a public kitchen.

She rested her head against the rim of the tub and let her eyes drift shut. Steam curled around her, fragrant with the scent of lavender. One by one, her muscles seemed to loosen. This, she thought lazily, was the best moment of the day. Unless one counted all the moments when she had touched George. They had touched frequently today, and each tiny contact seemed to brand itself into her skin. She wondered for a moment what it would be like to combine the two experiences . . . a hot bath and George Carstairs. What would happen if George walked into her room right now? At any other time, lascivious thoughts about Lord Rival would make her blush. Here in the bath, warm and loose and safe, such imaginings made her smile.

She lifted one leg out of the bathwater and regarded it, arching her foot. Water streamed down her calf in little rivulets. She had always wished that fashion allowed a lady to show her legs. Hers were long and slim and smooth, prettily shaped, and—so far—utterly wasted. No man had ever seen them. She wondered now whether Lord Rival one day would. The thought frightened her a little, and not just because it was outrageous. She hated the idea of exposing her pathetic claims to beauty to a man who had viewed the charms of so many women. So many beautiful women.

She submerged herself again, shivering a little. Spicing up one's life was all very well, but one had one's pride. She must never make herself that vulnerable to George.

Was she winning the strange little game they were playing? She supposed she was. He had enlivened her existence, just as she had hoped. Rather more than she had hoped, actually . . . but the sense of growing danger added to the excitement. And she had *not* agreed to marry him. So she must be winning.

The problem was, some mad corner of her being wished that she would lose.

What a masterful man he was, she thought dreamily. She generally disliked the masterful types, but George—ah, George broke all the rules. And after today's experiences, the advantages of having such a powerful man at her side were glaringly obvious. Ralph would never have let three mere women shame him into civility. He had left in a huff, but he had left—and without his wife. For that, they had George to thank. It was the force of Lord Rival's personality, his rank, and probably his proven ability to land a solid punch, that had won Ralph's grudging cooperation. Really, it was marvelous. Bad Lord Badesworth had not only left without injuring Edith, he had agreed to stay away from her until some formal arrangement could be made for her protection. Edith had actually wept with gratitude; it was all Olivia could do to prevent her from kissing George's hand as if he were a saint.

A small frown creased Olivia's forehead as she replayed that scene in her mind. She had to admit, she disliked the idea of Edith physically demonstrating her gratitude to George. She didn't want Edith kissing his hand—or any other part of him. It had been upsetting enough to see Edith pressed against George after he had knocked Ralph senseless. She had no wish to witness such a spectacle again. Ever.

Not that there was anything she could do about it.

Olivia moved restlessly in the water, mulling over that unpleasant thought. She had no right to complain, whatever George did or whoever touched him. George was offering her the right, but she had steadfastly refused it. At some point—some not very distant point—he would leave her and move on to the next heiress on his list. He had made that brutally clear. He would soon be dancing attendance on some other lady. Some other lady would enjoy his smiles, his attentions, his delightful company. His kisses. Would she mind?

Yes, she would mind. Terribly. Olivia's frown deepened and she sat up, wringing her washcloth with a vicious emphasis. There was no blinking the fact. She was going to hate it when George moved on. And she was going to hate the lucky lady he moved on to.

The water had grown cold, as bathwater inevitably does. Olivia shivered as the air hit her. She began scrubbing herself in a brisk and businesslike manner. High time she finished her bath and dressed for dinner. She had been lolling about, indulging dangerous trains of thought, for too long.

Dinner had been ordered for her party in the very room where George had felled Ralph just a few hours ago. Olivia was the first to arrive. The table had been righted and fresh linen spread, and the landlord, eager to do justice to the occasion—since it was rare for his little inn to house members of the peerage—had whisked all the pewter accouterments away and replaced them, somehow, with a decent grade of porcelain. He bowed Olivia nervously into the room, begging her to excuse the candlesticks, which did not match the dishes. She smiled and promised him that everything looked lovely. He then began making apologies for the dinner he was about to set before her, since, on such short notice, his wife had been unable to acquire or prepare the elaborate dishes she deemed appropriate for persons of their rank. He would have enumerated all the courses that awaited, and confided far more than she wished to know about their procurement and preparation, had the door not opened to admit Lord Rival. At that moment, either the landlord fell silent or Olivia no longer heard him.

George was clad in his morning costume, less the driving coat, but he had apparently had his clothing brushed clean and pressed for him, and his boots polished to a high gloss. And somehow, he had procured fresh linen. A clean shirt and neckcloth gleamed white at his neck and wrists. His appearance was immaculate, and he carried himself with an elegant poise that made the wearing of morning clothes to dinner seem *de rigueur*.

Dear saints in heaven, the man was handsome. More than handsome. There was that certain something about him that simply brought her to her knees—metaphorically speaking, of course. Did he have this effect on every female? She supposed, rather forlornly, that he did.

Well. Even if she *were* inclined to marry—which, of course, she was not—the last man on earth she would want to marry would be Lord Rival. Fancy having to live with a man that handsome! He simply could not help attracting women the way honey attracts flies. His bride's life would be a torment. An absolute torment.

On the other hand, Olivia's life was a torment now.

Then he strolled forward, a light in his eyes that seemed to be for her and her alone, and Olivia felt her breath catch in her throat. A very foolish smile trembled on her lips. Hating herself for her weakness, she allowed him to bow over her hand. As he bowed, his eyes twinkled with sly mischief.

"Alone at last," he murmured, low enough to escape the landlord's hearing.

She blushed and pulled her hand away. "How absurd you are. The others will arrive at any moment."

"On the contrary." He turned to indicate the landlord, who, in his capacity as waiter, was busily clearing half the dishes off the table. "It seems Miss Fairfax and Lady Badesworth have sent their regrets, and requested that trays be sent up to their room. Your sister-in-law is still feeling a trifle overset by the events of the day, and Miss Fairfax looked all in when I saw her last."

"Yes, she did. Poor Bessie. What a miserable journey that must have been for her." Olivia was glad to hear that her voice sounded quite normal, not flustered in the least. She was feeling decidedly flustered. Dinner alone with George was not what she had bargained for. In fact, she suspected that dining alone with a single gentleman was indecent. Since the gentleman in question was George, it was almost assuredly indecent. She glanced uncertainly at him. "I wonder if we ought to follow their example, my lord?"

Devils danced in his eyes. "Have our dinner sent up to your room? Certainly, if you insist."

She bit her lip and threw an agonized look at the landlord, but it was clear he had not heard George's sally—thank goodness. Occupied in balancing his dishes, he was bustling back out the door.

It struck her that the landlord, an eminently respectable man, seemed to think nothing of her dining alone with Lord Rival. Perhaps she was making a mountain of a molehill. She tapped her foot against the wooden floor, thinking hard. Could she justify dining with George? Did she even want to? The risks were high . . . on several levels . . . but it might be worth it.

The door closed behind the landlord. She was alone with George. She cast him a sidelong glance. He was, predictably, completely at ease—and laughing at her. Olivia sighed and rolled her eyes. "I know I am being missish," she observed crossly. "I can't help it. As a female, I can't afford to ignore the proprieties the way you do."

"When you are eighty, my dear Olivia, and look back on your life, you should have a few racy memories to warm your heart." He winked. "I'm here to provide them. Don't waste your opportunity."

An unwilling smile tugged at her lips. "This very morning—my word, how long ago it seems!—you proposed dining alone with me, and I refused you."

"Yes, you have a habit of refusing my proposals.

But I'm a persistent chap." He walked to the table and pulled a chair out for her. "Pray sit down, dear lady, and give me the pleasure of your company. I promise to do nothing outrageous."

She moved forward and allowed him to seat her. "Your notion of outrageous and mine probably do not coincide," she said ruefully. "But I suppose it would be shabby to refuse you, after all you have done for me this day."

"In that case, I won't tell you what a pleasure it was to help you." He strolled over to the seat across from her and sat down.

"It is your kindness that makes you say so. It can't be your idea of pleasure to be . . . *commandeered* and forced to drive to Brighton! With no luggage, too. And then to have to deal with Ralph at the end of it! I am quite sunk with shame when I think of the trouble I have caused you."

He eyed her with amusement. "Chalk it up to my service to the school."

She looked away, uncomfortable. She disliked recalling that she held that power over him. "I will, if you wish," she said lightly, "but I don't believe either of us were thinking of the school when I brazenly dragged you into my family squabbles."

"Never mind. I found it instructive—furthering my acquaintance with Lord Badesworth." His mouth twisted wryly. "I have not forgotten the tales you told me about your father. If your opinion of the male sex is based on these two specimens, I obviously have a hard row to hoe."

She smiled. "It's true that old impressions die hard. But I have come to realize, over the years, that the men of my family do not represent the entire spectrum of manhood."

Unexpected emotion suddenly choked her as she mentally compared Ralph and her father to the knight in shining armor seated across the table from her. She suddenly felt that her cynical view of his motives was mean and petty, and had blinded her to his innate heroism.

She leaned forward impulsively and touched his hand. "All joking aside, George—I don't know how to thank you," she said softly. "I don't know what we would have done without you today. I don't care why you did it. You rode to my rescue without a backward look or a second thought, and I will never forget it."

His hand covered hers for a moment, all amusement wiped from his expression. Although he was touching her, he looked away. It seemed to her that the remoteness she had seen in him earlier returned, as if he were listening to faraway voices. He frowned, and seemed to speak with an effort. "You needn't thank me. It is I who am grateful. You have given me a chance to . . ." His voice trailed off. "To lay some old ghosts to rest."

Olivia almost stopped breathing; she was so afraid of shattering this moment. Would he confide in her? She longed to know something about him. It occurred to her that she had fallen into the habit of thinking she knew him well when, actually, he was an enigma. She knew nothing whatever of his past, and little of his present. But for the places where his life touched her own, she did not know him at all.

His urbanity, as always, surfaced quickly and he smiled at her again. "You haven't even asked me why I flattened your brother."

"Half brother," she responded automatically. "I assume he insulted you. Or offered you violence."

"No," said George quietly. "I'm afraid I haven't that excuse." She looked inquiringly at him and he gave her a wry smile. "Most people, I suppose, have hidden triggers that cause an explosion when pulled. Lord Badesworth unwittingly pulled one of mine."

"Heavens. How did he find time to pull a trigger? I arrived barely ten seconds behind you, and Ralph was already on the floor."

"It's a hair trigger," George explained. "Fires immediately when touched."

"I see." She smiled a little. "Perhaps you should tell me what it is before I inadvertently run into danger."

He gave a short laugh. "You won't. What fires it is seeing a bully terrorize someone weaker than himself." His features hardened. "When I arrived on the scene, Lord Badesworth was attempting to gag his wife. He was stuffing a piece of cloth in her mouth—a handkerchief, I believe. He had pinned her into a wooden chair with his knee, and was stuffing the cloth in her mouth with one hand while pulling her hair with the other. Pulling her hair to force her chin up, you understand." He paused, then spoke very softly. "I'm afraid I lost my temper."

"Merciful saints," whispered Olivia, horrified. "I would have, too. What did you do?"

"I'm not sure." His eyes lit with dark humor. "Whatever action I took, it was apparently prompt and effective. But I fear it may not have been gentlemanly."

"Gentlemanly? It was heroic," exclaimed Olivia. "I am more grateful to you than ever. I think it was perfectly *splendid* of you to rescue Edith. Why, you barely *know* her!"

"True." His urbanity once more slipped a little. "But I have known—others in her predicament." The rueful smile flashed again. "These triggers in a man's soul do not appear at random. They are created."

Olivia felt that she had caught a glimpse beneath the polished veneer that Lord Rival showed the world, and she craved more. However, the landlord entered with the soup tureen and their conversation shifted, perforce, to more general topics.

Yet the sense of new intimacy they had established

remained. Olivia tasted little of her dinner, so absorbed was she in her conversation with George. Dishes were brought, dishes were removed, glasses filled and emptied, but the two of them seemed as alone as if they sat together on some private island. The table was drawn near the hearth, where a wood fire popped and crackled, warming them. Candlelight sparkled in the cut glass, making the wine glow as if lit from within. And across from her sat the embodiment of all her fantasies, separated from her only by the width of the narrow table. As they talked and laughed, the evening took on a dreamlike quality. Olivia could never afterward recall what they had talked about over that meal, but she never forgot the way George looked and moved and sounded. Sometimes he leaned back in his chair, toying with the stem of his wineglass, a half-smile playing across his features. Sometimes he leaned forward, resting an elbow on the white cloth, his dark eyes mesmerizing. Always, a sense of delicious promise was in the air, a tingling connection between them that grew stronger as the evening progressed.

Time passed unnoticed. Eventually a log fell in the fire, sending up a shower of sparks and momentarily brightening the light. Olivia blinked as if waking from sleep, and looked round her in surprise. The dinner had been cleared away and the fire burned low. She had a sudden sense that the hour had grown late. "How long have we sat here?" she asked, surprised.

"I don't know." He smiled. "Are you going to withdraw now, and leave me to drink my port in solitary state?"

"Oh, dear! I have the most lowering suspicion that I should have done that long ago." She started to rise, but his hand shot out and his long, strong fingers closed around her wrist.

"Don't go," he said softly.

She froze in place. Their hands were ungloved and,

in her dinner dress, her arm was bare. His grip was light, but the contact of his skin with hers was so precious to her that she could not force herself to break away. She stared down at her wrist covered by his hand, savoring the feel of his touch—and knowing it must end.

"I must go," she whispered, but she did not move. A tiny, rebellious voice inside her cried *No!* when he broke their contact and removed his hand—then sighed with relief when he rose and walked around the table to her. He was going to try to make her stay. Joy warred with panic. She stood and lifted her eyes to his, terrified of what she would see there, dreading his desire—but dreading his indifference even more.

Whatever she saw in his eyes, it was not indifference. He regarded her with great seriousness, as if her decision to leave the room was a matter of importance. "Do you want to go?" He reached out, gently, and closed his hands around her upper arms. He held her lightly, his touch caressing. The warmth of his hands against her cool flesh made her shiver with longing.

"I don't know what I want," she blurted. Her voice was ragged with pain. She bent her head weakly and rested the top of her head against the hollow of his shoulder, as if butting him away. "Don't torture me," she said to the floor between his boots. "Please, George. Don't."

"Never, sweetheart." He pulled her gently into his arms and cradled her like a child. "Never that."

Her arms slipped around his back and she sighed, pressing her cheek against his lapels. Bliss. She could not refuse this chaste embrace. It was heaven to feel George holding her close to him, folding her in his arms. She closed her eyes and listened to his heartbeat, strong and slow. But the sweetness of the moment was tinged with sorrow. Her throat tightened with the threat of tears. She ought to enjoy this. What was this strange, stupid heartache she felt?

But she knew what it was. It was the ticking of the clock that made her sad. It was the knowledge that these halcyon moments were numbered. This sweetness was only borrowed; it was not hers to keep. How long until Candlemas? Four months? She had struck a fool's bargain. She would have George just long enough to spoil her. The empty years that yawned before her would seem drearier than ever once these few months in paradise were over and gone.

His arms were so strong. His body was so powerful. It was ironic that his touch made her feel secure and protected, as if she had somehow come home, when reason told her that the opposite was true. It was irrational to feel that George's arms were the safe harbor she had secretly longed for all her life, when she knew perfectly well that her feelings for him were putting her entire future at risk.

A fortune hunter, she reminded herself listlessly. It's not Olivia Fairfax he is holding so tenderly. It's her money.

Ugly, agitating memories stirred. Useless memories. She fought to repress them. She did not need to remember Luke. She remembered the lesson he had taught her, and that was enough. Her wealth was the only thing she had that might attract a man as desirable as George Carstairs. The humiliating phrase *hobgoblin eyes* whispered evilly in the back of her mind.

George's voice broke in to her chaotic thoughts. "You fit perfectly in my arms," he murmured. "As if you belong there."

He sounded so sincere! *Just as Luke had.* The thought stiffened Olivia's spine. She pulled back from him, smiling tensely. "Prettily said, my lord," she said brightly. "I almost believe it."

He looked startled. Then his expression went blank

and shuttered, as if she had hurt his feelings. My word! What an actor. Still, the impression that her words had caused him pain—even as she reminded herself how impossible that was—cost her an answering pang. She couldn't bear to hurt George.

Before she could stop herself, her hand automatically fluttered up to caress his cheek. His eyes darkened with some emotion she could not fathom, and his hand reached up to cover hers and hold it there against his face.

"Believe it," he whispered. "There's something more than friendship here." He turned his head and kissed her palm. The feel of his warm mouth against her flesh sent a rush of heat clear through her. She closed her eyes, struggling not to succumb to it.

"Don't fight it, Olivia." His mouth moved lower and kissed her wrist. Her pulse leaped and hammered in response. "You know it's true. You can feel it for yourself."

"I don't know what I feel," she whispered, agonized. "I don't know what is true."

"Yes, you do."

She opened her eyes, confused. They met his. His eyes were so close to hers, so compelling, so filled with certainty that she felt her own will wavering. His lips curved in a half-smile. "You don't want to feel what you are feeling. But we both know you feel it."

A tiny frown creased her forehead. She pulled her hand out of his. "You don't know what I'm feeling," she said crossly. "And whatever I'm feeling, it doesn't matter. Feelings can't be trusted."

An arrested look crossed his features. "Interesting." His hands came up to cup her face. "Another fascinating insight. What opposite lives we have led, you and I."

"What do you mean?"

He quirked an eyebrow at her. "You deny your desires. I live entirely for sensation. You immerse yourself in serving others. I quell every good impulse—when I can." Mocking devils danced in his eyes. "We have much to teach each other."

"What you intend to teach me, I do not wish to learn." Even in her own ears, her protest sounded more stubborn than noble.

George's smile softened. "Oh, Olivia," he murmured. "You are crying out for it." His mouth hovered over hers. "I hear you," he whispered, "even in my sleep."

Irresistible. He was irresistible. She could no longer even rail against her own helplessness. Her mouth reached up to answer his whether she consciously willed it or no. He was her drug and she a mindless addict, wallowing in the very sensations that threatened to destroy her. Her eyes drifted shut.

But he didn't kiss her. She felt his breath quicken and her bones melted in response to this mark of his desire, but still he did not kiss her. Olivia's wits had completely fled, taking her willpower with them. She heard a soft, pleading moan and knew it had come from her own throat. Shameless, shameless. She didn't care.

"Please," she whispered, lifting her lips to touch his.

His voice was low and rough, ragged with strain. "Tell me I'm right."

"Yes." *Anything. Yes, you are right. Yes, I will marry you. Yes, the world is flat and I'm a kangaroo. Anything, anything you say.* "Just kiss me."

This time the groan came from him. But he was laughing, too, either at her or himself. Instead of kissing her, he nuzzled his face against her cheek, her nose, her forehead. "I'll kiss you, sweeting," he teased her. "I'll kiss you senseless. But not if I'm wasting my time."

"What?" She opened her eyes, dimly aware that if she weren't so intent on that wicked mouth of his, she'd be seriously annoyed by now.

He grinned at her. "It seems to me that I have no trouble awakening your—er—primal instincts. The difficulty I face is in getting you to acknowledge it, once the moment has passed."

If he only knew! The moment never passed. She wanted him every minute they were together, and every minute they were apart. Thank God he had not tumbled to that fact. She rallied her senses and managed a haughty sniff. "What nonsense you talk."

"There. You see? You are already doing your best to forget what you felt ten seconds ago." The corner of his mouth turned down. One eyebrow flew up. "I suppose I will have to remind you."

He leaned in again, but this time Olivia was ready. She placed her hands hastily against his shoulders before he could get close enough to steal her wits again. "I remember very well, thank you. But what I feel, or whether I feel, is not the point. Feelings lie."

"Only people lie." The arrested expression returned, and he straightened, studying her face keenly. "Just as you expect me to lie." He said it as if it were a revelation. "You dissect my every statement, hunting for the lie you believe it contains."

She gave him a rather wan smile. "Yes, I suppose I do." It was a dreary thought. It was also an insult, she realized, feeling rather ashamed of herself. But it was true. "Does that disturb you?"

"A little." The mocking gleam returned to his eyes. "But not much."

His admission startled a laugh out of her. "Really? We *are* different. I would be distressed if someone thought I was untrustworthy."

"Naturally. You aren't accustomed to it. I, on the other hand, am mistrusted by nearly everyone." He said this without a touch of rancor. He even smiled in that self-mocking way that made her go weak in the knees. "Mind you, I do find it ironic that you, of all women, expect the worst of me, since I have made a fairly valiant effort to behave honorably—for once. But you have very good reasons not to trust me. And I'm not the sort of sapskull who expects to change your mind in the twinkling of a bedpost."

"I am glad to hear it," she said primly, trying to feel glad. "You told me at the outset that you sought to marry money, and all the world knows your checkered past. I like you very well, George, and I admire you on many levels. But you cannot earn my trust merely by befriending me for a few short months."

"Quite right. Only a fool would trust me on so little evidence. And you're no fool."

Olivia felt a little disoriented. He sounded perfectly calm and reasonable. But, surely, he was telling her that the game was over—and that she had won. She cocked her head, puzzled. "Are you withdrawing your suit?"

He linked his hands behind her waist and flashed her a wicked grin. "By no means."

"But . . . but . . . we have just agreed that I do not trust you—and that you do not even *expect* me to trust you."

He touched her nose playfully with the tip of his index finger. "You may not trust me wholly, my pet, but you trust me in some respects. That will have to suffice. For you will marry me, my sweet Ivy, whether you trust me or no."

"You're daft," she said, with conviction. "Why would I marry a man I do not trust?"

"This is why," he said softly, and bent to take her lips.

It was absurd for him to think he could change the subject so easily. It was ridiculous, and insufferably arrogant, that he believed he could turn her from skeptic to slave by merely kissing her. But he could. Heaven help her. The instant his mouth touched hers she was lost.

She knew she was proving his point, and still she

could not rebuff him. She wanted him too badly. The long day of emotional ups and downs, the cumulative effect of all the little touches they had shared, the excitement of knowing how many of those tiny contacts had been secret and stolen, the hours of intimate conversation, everything she had felt and thought and experienced today seemed to culminate in this moment, making the effect of his kiss, too long postponed, electric.

A soft moan rose in her throat, desire and despair sounding with one voice. His arms tightened, sliding behind her back to hold her closer while his kiss deepened, demanding more. And she responded despite herself, with a wanton eagerness that proved to both of them—had any shred of doubt remained—how much she wanted him. Oh, it was terrible. It was wonderful. It was humiliating. It was heavenly. Tears stung the back of her eyelids and still she kissed him, aching with need.

20

S he was so sweet. He held her close, kissing her with all the gentleness he could muster, given the raging lust he was battling. Did she know what she did to him? Probably not. The needs that drove men were completely beyond her ken. And besides, she was preoccupied with her own confusion. He understood that. The innocent ones were always bewildered by their first taste of passion.

He forced himself to slow down. The last thing he wanted to do was frighten her. Nothing must distract her from the discoveries she was making. Luck had favored him once again, and he was determined not to waste the opportunity. Against all odds, in an almost incredible stroke of good fortune, he had her all to himself. They were shut up together in an inn, for God's sake. If he couldn't win her tonight, he never would.

He softened the kiss, pulling back to a series of light, cherishing movements against her lips. She shifted slightly in his arms, pliant and sighing with unmistakable longing. This evidence of her desire maddened him. He wanted her badly. A sound escaped him, half groan, half laugh. How badly did she want him? Enough? He dared not miss his timing. He had to know. He tested her, lifting his mouth from hers and hovering there, suspended above her lips.

She immediately followed, reaching up to press her mouth against his, mutely asking for more.

Excellent.

He gave her more. And more. And then he swept one hand down behind her thighs and lifted her. She gasped, startled, and pulled her face back to stare at him. Her silver eyes were huge, but she neither struggled nor objected. She clung to him, arms around his neck, and he carried her to a low sofa that faced the fireplace.

He set her on its velvet surface and slid down onto it beside her, sweeping her into another kiss before she could protest—just in case. But protest seemed to be far from her mind. He pulled her knees across his lap, nestling her body snugly against his, whispering encouragement.

She shivered, pulling her face away. "We mustn't. The landlord—"

"Won't come in." Since her mouth was denied him at the moment, he buried his lips in her hair, then moved down to kiss the side of her neck. She gasped when his lips touched her throat, and arched her neck instinctively to give him better access. Dear God, she was sweet. He'd been dying to kiss her throat for weeks. The delicate skin beneath his lips felt warm and soft and . . . untouched. Just as he had imagined it would.

"How do you know?" Her voice sounded strained and breathless. *Hallelujah.*

"Greased him in the fist," George muttered thickly. He moved his mouth against her throat, kissing his way down and around it, glorying in the feel of her. She panted and squirmed in a very gratifying way, but still pressed her palms against his shoulders as if trying to hold him off.

"What?" she managed to utter.

He lifted his head and looked at her. His senses cleared briefly and he realized she had not understood his cant expression. "Tipped him," he croaked. "Told him not to disturb us. He won't come in, sweetheart."

He saw consternation in her expression and kissed it away, guessing that she was worried, womanlike, about what the innkeeper thought. But there was something else disturbing her. She kissed him back as if she could not help it, but he sensed that her enjoyment was tempered with anxiety.

He could not ignore her fears. He wanted her wholehearted. Eager. Taking her maidenhead—if it came to that—would profit him nothing unless he shattered her world along with it.

Inwardly cursing the necessity, he ended the kiss and looked at her, cradling her face in his hands. "I told you once that I do not cheat at love. Do you remember?"

"Yes," she whispered. Her silver eyes were wide and vulnerable, completely opened to him.

"Do you know what I meant by that?"

"No." She swallowed. "Not—not exactly."

He studied her face, pushing a wayward tendril of her dark hair off her forehead and tucking it gently behind her ear. Olivia was too intelligent to believe he might force himself on her, but she might, nevertheless, be frightened of the act itself. Or she could be worried about the consequences. One never knew, with virgins. If what he had in mind was a brief liaison he could have treated the subject delicately, but this was the woman he intended to wed. He did not want to spend a lifetime talking in circles to protect her sensibilities. He decided to err on the side of frankness.

"I'll give you an example. I will not compromise you. That would be cheating." He found another strand of escaped hair and carefully replaced it among those bunched at the base of her neck. "Whatever we choose to do together, no one will know. Miss Fairfax and Lady Badesworth will surmise that we have dined

together, but that is all they will surmise. No one outside this inn will learn even that much. You won't be
forced to marry me to save yourself from scandal.
There will be none."

She gave a brief, tiny nod. He returned his eyes to
hers. "You may think that getting you with child
would serve my ends. It would, but I won't do it." He
returned his hands to her face and placed his palms
gently against her cheeks, smoothing the delicate arch
of her eyebrows with his thumbs. "I want you," he
told her softly, "but I want you willing. Not compelled."

She closed her eyes under the soothing strokes of
his thumbs. "I wish I could make you understand,"
she whispered. He felt her brows contract. "Whether
you win by fair means or foul, the result would be the
same. Marriage. And it is marriage itself I am
avoiding, not specifically marriage to you." She
opened her eyes. The expression in them was troubled, almost pitying. "I honor your forbearance, and
I'm grateful for it. But if you will not take unfair advantage of me, George—you cannot win."

It sounded almost like a dare. His brows climbed.
"My dear, you underestimate me." He slid one arm
behind her and pulled her closer, locking his eyes with
hers. "No matter the game," he murmured, "you
should always bet on the more experienced player."

Anger sparked in her platinum eyes, but she veiled
them swiftly with her lashes. "Have you never heard
of beginner's luck?"

He chuckled. "That's the dandy. You go ahead and
rely on your beginner's luck." He leaned in and nuzzled her neck. "In fact, let's raise the stakes. What do
you say, Ivy? Double or nothing." Whatever that
meant.

"The stakes are already high enough, thank you,"
she said a little shakily.

"Higher than you know." He lifted her hair and leaned further in to kiss the nape of her neck. He felt her tremble at the sensation his lips evoked. What power. What power she gave him. Her immediate response to his every touch was intoxicating. "Come here," he whispered against her neck, and pulled her all the way onto his lap. She uttered a weak protest but he stilled it, murmuring soothingly and nestling her against his chest. She sighed and snuggled, resting her head on his shoulder.

He needed one more piece of the puzzle before he could proceed—even if it meant wasting additional minutes in conversation. He kept his voice low, inviting intimacy. "Tell me what you have against marriage."

"I should think it was obvious."

He pondered this for a moment and concluded that it wasn't. "Are you going to make me guess?"

She blinked up at him in what seemed like genuine surprise. He grinned. "Most women are, if anything, eager to tie the knot. What makes you different?"

She uncoiled herself from his arms and sat up indignantly. "I can't believe you are asking me this. You're a sensible man. Think! You know me well, do you not? What do you suppose I value most in life?"

George studied her tense face, the blaze of intelligence and anger in her eyes contrasting oddly, wonderfully, with the softness of her. She really was a remarkable creature. He had no idea how to answer her, so he resorted to cheek. "Me?"

As he had hoped, her features relaxed and lit with laughter. "Wretch! You have it backward—that is what *you* value most."

"Ah. I knew one of us did."

But she was not so easily distracted. Some of the earnestness returned to her face, sobering it. "I value my independence. Freedom is a blessing enjoyed by very few women, even women of my station. I order my days as I see fit. I answer to no one. I am the unquestioned head of my household and my business. How many females can say that?"

"Not many. Few men can say it, either."

"I would be a fool to relinquish my precious freedom to a husband." She gave him a rather crooked smile. "It isn't only that I don't trust you. I don't trust any man enough to make him a present of myself, my fortune, and my future. Marriage confers upon the husband absolute authority over the wife. A woman must be desperate, I think, to agree to such a bad bargain."

"Desperate for what?" He smiled at her puzzled expression. "I am perfectly serious. Approach the question intellectually. The way you have stated it presents a logic problem. After all, women agree to marry men every day. Why do you suppose they do it? Theoretically."

"Most women require financial support. I do not."

"Very well. But you are not the only rich woman in England. It seems to me that rich women marry as readily as poor ones. Why?"

She looked thoughtful. "Perhaps they act without thinking. We are forever told that marriage is our destiny. I suppose many women come to believe it, and simply follow like sheep."

"Not all rich women are stupid."

"I didn't say that!"

"No? Then some rich women are clever. Why do the clever ones marry?"

She frowned. "To please their families. Or simply to do what the world expects of them."

His brows climbed. "What! Marry to please others? These rich, clever women must be morbidly devoted to their families, to sacrifice themselves like so many lemmings! Which leads to another question: Why would a loving family press a daughter into the slavery you describe?"

She tilted her chin at him. "You know very well why. Marriage brings children."

Something in her voice made him look at her more closely. She appeared flustered and resentful, but he detected a vulnerability beneath it. He was hitting a nerve.

Of course! Olivia had devoted her life to helping orphans. Her choice of charity was a clue to her heart's desire. It told him what was missing in her life.

He reached to cup her cheek in his palm. She did not pull away, but there was wariness in her eyes. "Are children a boon only to their grandparents?" he asked her softly.

Her eyes filled with pain. She pulled her face away from his hand, blinking rapidly. "No," she said in a muffled tone. "I suppose women sometimes marry because they—because they want children."

"Then marriage does have its compensations. Even for rich, clever women." He pulled her roughly against him, startled by a fierce wave of unexpected emotion. When he spoke again, his voice was husky with it. "My darling girl, I've tempted you at last."

Her arms went round him and she uttered a sound somewhere between a sob and a laugh. "I suppose you have. It's not *fair*," she told his waistcoat. "I do wish a single woman could bear a child without ruining her life."

He smiled against the top of her head. "It is typical of you, my dear, that the prospect of a lonely old age leaves you unmoved, that my kisses fail to bring you round my thumb, that you have no real need for my advice, my assistance, my protection, or my company, but one mention of children and you crumble like an overbaked biscuit."

She sniffled and sat defiantly upright, wiping her eyes with the heel of her hand. "Not quite," she said bracingly. "For I do have children. Plenty of children. Dozens of them."

"They are not yours," he said quietly. "They are not ours."

Ours. A burst of pure wonder shot through him, an emotion he had not felt in so long that he had almost forgotten its power. It startled him. He had been so concentrated on the task at hand, so busy attuning himself to Olivia's reactions, so preoccupied with besting his opponent, he hadn't entertained this obvious thought: If he won, Olivia would bear his children.

George had spent twelve years adroitly dodging his memories and his dreams. He had become a master at avoiding both. Neither the past nor the future had any place in his hedonistic existence. Now, suddenly, his past and future rushed together and met in this moment.

His arms went swiftly round Olivia and a dizzyingly vivid picture of Rye Vale, lush with grass, fresh with sea wind, flashed before his eyes. *Home.* This particular woman at his side. Dark-haired, fair-skinned children, innocent and wild, faceless but infinitely dear, running, laughing, through the sweep of windblown grass. *Home.*

Olivia would make it all possible. Olivia and her heaven-sent money. And he would be so grateful that he would care for her and protect her all her days. He would do everything he could to make her happy. It would, he realized, be a pleasure to make her happy.

He knew he was holding her too tightly, but he couldn't help it. He kissed her hair, hard, then turned and pressed his cheek tightly against the top of her head. "Olivia. Marry me. For God's sake, marry me." He felt her sob, just once, and couldn't wait for her answer. He knew it would be *no,* and he didn't want to hear it. He turned up her face and kissed her ferociously, willing her to not say no. Not yet. He wanted to hold the dream a little longer.

Those were tears on her cheeks. He tasted salt and

groaned with frustration. He had done it again. He had lost sight of his goal and overshot the mark. Hell and the devil confound it, the wench was weeping! Fighting for control, he ended the kiss, breathing as raggedly as if he had just run a race. He pressed his head to hers and gasped out an apology.

She shook her head, then tucked herself down to bury her face in his neck. She had somehow ended up back on his lap, twisted in his arms and plastered against his chest. She mumbled something into his cravat.

"I can't hear you, sweetheart."

She lifted her head. "Don't call me *sweetheart,*" she said with dignity. "It muddles me."

"Good," he muttered, making a mental note to call her sweetheart as often as possible. "I want you muddled. I need you muddled." His cravat had worked itself loose and seemed to be resting mostly on his shoulder. He tugged it impatiently away and tossed it onto the sofa beside them. "Tell me again what you said a moment ago."

But Olivia seemed temporarily to have lost the power of speech. Her eyes widened as she leaned back and stared, fascinated, at the bare skin revealed by the removal of his cravat. He bit back a laugh. It was enough to make a man vain to see the look on her face. "What's the matter?" he asked. "Haven't you seen a man's throat before?"

Her eyes slowly lifted to his, wide and luminous. "Not your throat," she whispered.

His heart lurched. "Look your fill," he said hoarsely.

She did. Her eyes traveled slowly, dazedly, over his neck and throat. Her innocent amazement was both touching and arousing. When her eyes reached the juncture where his skin met his shirt, they stayed there.

Did she want to see more? Well, George was always

happy to oblige a lady. He reached up and unbuttoned his waistcoat.

She watched his fingers move, apparently mesmerized by the sight of each button working loose. When the waistcoat was unbuttoned he dropped his hands passively to his sides and waited. *Your move, Ivy.*

Olivia slowly slipped her hands inside his unbuttoned waistcoat, parting it. And still she stared, drinking in the sight of him in the clean linen shirt he had bought from the landlord that day. She ran her hands worshipfully over his chest, seeming only half-aware that she was breaking every rule of propriety and decorum. Her eyes, wide with wonder, followed where her fingertips led. Under her exploring hands the shirt's wide neck fell open nearly to his waist. He was careful not to move. He lay passive, half-reclining while she stared and touched at will.

"Gorgeous," she murmured reverently. She sounded drunk.

He chuckled. "Spare my blushes, sweetheart. I think you need more light." He sat up, kissed her lightly, and rose, casually discarding his waistcoat as he did so. He walked to the fireplace and added another log to the dying fire. If his intended bride liked to look at him, she was welcome to do so. He hoped to be looking at her soon, so he wanted light for his own selfish reasons.

He turned and straightened, letting the fire backlight him and reveal his form through his shirt. The effect must have pleased her; he could see the quick rise and fall of her breasts as she sighed.

"I'll be happy to remove anything else that is in your way," he offered teasingly.

She seemed to return to her senses somewhat. "Oh! I'm—I'm sorry," she blurted, shamefaced. "I don't know what came over me. I shouldn't stare at you."

"If it gives you pleasure, I've no objection." He leaned one hand on the mantelpiece, letting the light outline the muscles in his arm for her. "But, I would remind you, turnabout is fair play."

The leaping firelight revealed her blush. "Oh, dear. No. Please. I hate being stared at."

He strolled back to the sofa and stood smiling down at her. "You won't hate it," he promised softly. "Not if I look at you the way you are looking at me. And I will."

He stood over her for a long moment. She was beautiful. The dark blue silk of her dinner dress set off the pale perfection of her skin; her silver eyes were complemented by the gleam of silver at her neck and earlobes. He smiled, reveling in the sight of her, knowing that it would only get better. "I suggest we start with the jewelry."

21

*H*e never spoke of love. Had he said the words, she knew she would not have believed him. Even so, their omission hurt her heart.

He did say other things. Oh, he was good with words. He whispered things that set her on fire, touched her and teased her and whispered to her until she writhed, gasping, in his arms, panting out mad words of her own.

And one thing he had promised turned out to be true—she did not mind him looking at her. Strange, that. Inhibitions evaporated under the heat of his gaze. He made her feel beautiful. Seeing herself through his eyes, her modesty transformed into a glorious excitement. She could not mistake what she saw in his face, what she heard in his voice. If it was not love, it was something nearly as wonderful. He desired her—her, the woman—and for once she was absolutely sure that money was the farthest thing from his mind. Had she been wrapped in ten-pound notes, he would have torn them off and flung them aside without a backward glance.

She had not intended to give so much of herself when she dared not trust her heart to his keeping. But it did not seem possible to deny him aught he asked. Since she did not know what she herself wanted, and he seemed confident of both his desires and her own, it was easy, it was natural, to relax her guard and follow his lead. It was almost like dancing. The dance was new to her, but her partner was very sure of his steps. So she clung to him and he commanded—and she followed, followed, followed.

At times, the intensity of what she felt, of what he made her feel, frightened her. He would sense her bewilderment and find some way to reassure her, then goad her into further madness. After a time, she lost the ability to think. Her rational being splintered and scattered to the winds. Language itself seemed to leave her. He was the center of the world, the only thing that mattered, and she was frantic with some nameless need. It was all bound up in him, the desire to please him, the desire to be pleased, a growing urgency for she knew not what. He was touching her in places she had never been touched, places she never knew existed, igniting her. She was on fire. She wept and gasped and arched her back, straining toward his touch.

And then his face loomed over hers, filling the universe. His eyes burned like coals—as dark, as hot. "Marry me," he urged her. "Say it. You will marry me."

For a moment she could not understand him. Then inarticulate rage filled Olivia, fury that he would intrude this command upon her at this moment, fury that he would force her to *think* at such a time. She could not think! She could not even form the words to tell him what she thought of him. She twisted her head from side to side, panting, agonized. Wanting. Angry. Adoring.

His head dipped lower. His mouth touched her skin, moving sensuously, driving her to the brink. "Say yes," he crooned against her body. "Say yes, Ivy. Say it now."

She couldn't. Dear God, what was he *doing* to her? She would die of it soon. He lifted his head and his eyes held hers, compelling. Understanding. Promising impossible things. Promising release. "Trust me," he urged her softly. "Let go and trust me. Say yes, sweetheart."

Desperate, she closed her eyes and did exactly as she was told. She trusted him. It was a terrific relief to trust him. *"Yes!"* she sobbed, and immediately the world turned upside down, tumbling her over the brink and into rapture.

"Was that . . . everything?"

He chuckled, deep in his chest. "Not by a long chalk."

She had thought not. There must have been little reward for him in what they had done; all the pleasure had been centered on her. She pondered this, and realized that had the tables been turned there would have been reward, of sorts, in pleasuring him without sparing a thought for herself. Interesting.

But then, she loved him. And that was doubtless the essence of love. Since he did not share her feelings, selfless devotion to her pleasure must leave him feeling cheated. She raised herself on one elbow, studying him. "You are not satisfied," she said gravely.

He smiled. There was heat in his smile, but no loss of control. "I am satisfied enough. I have long suspected that a superbly passionate woman lurked beneath that proper facade of yours. I was right, and that's satisfaction enough. For this night."

Desire still burned in the depths of his eyes, but he was keeping the fires carefully banked. She could scarcely imagine the power such an effort must require; surely she would never have that much strength. She had failed the test miserably. His touch instantly reduced her will to rubble. Why did her touch not have a similar effect on him?

Perhaps it could. She reached out, experimentally,

and ran her fingers caressingly over his body. To her delight, she felt his muscles tighten and heard his breath hitch.

"You told me, earlier, that turnabout was fair play," she reminded him softly, and was thrilled to see that her fledgling efforts were crumbling the edges of his control. The flames leaped and danced in his eyes and he gave her a slow, hot smile that reawakened her own slumbering senses. A knot of fierce desire suddenly formed in her belly and the game became deadly serious. "Teach me," she whispered, and lifted her mouth to his again. "Teach me how to please you."

Had she agreed to marry him? Had she really agreed to *marry* him? They were in her bed now. She had agreed to that much, at least, and that in itself was madness. But surely she had never said she would marry him. Not in so many words.

Perhaps she should clarify that point.

"George."

"Mm."

"I didn't say I would marry you."

He opened one eye. There was just enough light from the low-burning candle to see the arch of his eyebrow. "Yes, you did."

She frowned. "But—"

Quick as thought, he rolled over and pinned her to the bed with his powerful arms, growling playfully in his throat. "Stop right there, madam. You gave me your word."

"I certainly did n—"

"You said yes. Yes is a word."

She stared at him, nonplussed. Was he laughing? "You can't be serious. You won't hold me to—to words spoken in the heat of the moment." She knew she was blushing. She glared at him. "I would have said yes to anything. You could have asked me to stand on my head, or mew like a kitten, or cut off my hair and join the army."

He was definitely laughing now. "How gratifying! You were putty in my hands, in fact."

She tried to keep a straight face, but failed. His grin was too infectious. "You know I was. Wretch."

"Was?" he murmured teasingly. He relaxed his body against hers, inch by inch, and she sighed in surrender at the delicious intimacy.

"Am," she agreed, too happy to pretend otherwise. He rewarded her with a kiss that, incredibly, stirred her desire for him yet again. She moved beneath him in instinctive invitation and he paused, lifting his head from hers.

"Shall I take you this time, Olivia?" he asked her huskily. "Would you like that?"

Hazy with longing, she wasn't sure what he meant. Then she thought she knew. She opened her eyes and looked dreamily into his. Oh, yes, she believed she would like it. She would like it very much.

Before she could marshal her wits enough to answer him, he slid one hand between their bodies and touched her in a way that entirely robbed her of the ability to speak. "You are a virgin, sweetheart?"

She nodded, gasping. His fingers stilled. For a moment he seemed to be wrestling with a decision. Then he rested his forehead against hers for a second and, with a sigh, removed his hand and rolled away from her. "We'll save that, then. For our wedding night."

Bereft, she lay still for a moment. Then his words sank in. Wedding night! She caught the sheet around her and sat up, blinking as if startled out of sleep. "George, no!" she blurted, anguished. "I don't want to be married. And neither do you."

She seized his hand and looked earnestly into his lazy, mocking, dangerously seductive smile. Words suddenly tumbled out of her. "You have been thinking

that marriage to me would put an end to all your
worries. But money isn't everything, George. Your
troubles would have just begun."

Both his eyebrows flew up. "Oh, are you a shrew?"
he inquired mildly. "This is news."

"I would be no complaisant bride, willing to put up
with all your vagaries," she warned him. "I would
make your life a living hell. Don't doubt me, George!
Because I am a woman you may think me powerless,
but I have powerful friends. I'll not endure the mortification of a faithless, straying husband."

He looked startled. Good. She was making him
think. She dropped his hand and pressed her palms
together beseechingly. "Do you see? You have not
thought beyond the financial rewards. You have not
pictured what it would be like to tie yourself to one
woman for the rest of your days."

He raised his arms and linked his hands behind his
head, staring thoughtfully at the low-beamed ceiling.
"No, I suppose I hadn't," he admitted. "But I'm picturing it now."

Judging by his expression, the picture was a surprisingly pleasant one. But Olivia dared not leave it at
that. "Well?" she demanded, trying not to look at the
breathtaking display of muscles his position revealed.
"What, exactly, had you been picturing? Going directly from our wedding to my bankers, no doubt, and
blithely spending my money while I waited in vain for
you to remember my existence." She gritted her teeth.
She was working herself into a fine rage. "Marriage
to a man like you would be a life of loneliness—and,
all too soon, poverty. Forgive me if I speak too
bluntly, but what I am saying is true. There is not
enough money in the world to keep a hardened gamester rich."

She was annoyed to find that a quaver had crept
into her voice. But this sign of her vulnerability was
not what was causing that arrested look on George's

face. He stared at her as if seeing her for the first time. "I see," he said slowly. "No wonder you've resisted the notion of marrying me. What a grim life you've been imagining." He quirked an eyebrow at her. "As for my character and my motivations, I'll pass over the unflattering portrait you have drawn and cut to the crux of the issue." He reached over with one strong arm and pulled her, despite her halfhearted resistance, on top of him. He held her there, smiling lazily at her ruffled expression. "Item one: I have no intention of gambling your precious money away."

"No," she said bitterly. "A gamester never intends to lose."

"That's right," he said equably. "But I am not, despite every appearance to the contrary, a true gamester. It is a matter of complete indifference to me whether I ever play another hand of piquet, and I don't care if I never see the inside of another gaming hell. Ssh!" He held a warning finger over her lips. "Don't tell a soul. You'll ruin me."

She tossed her head crossly, dislodging his lean fingers. "Do you expect me to believe that? You're a peer of the realm. You can't be jailed for bankruptcy. What do you need the money for, if not to pay gambling debts?"

"Oh, I do need it to pay gambling debts. But not my own. Once paid, no more such debts will be incurred. But we digress." His mouth was serious but his eyes were laughing at her. "Item two: I intend to be a faithful husband."

Her heart gave a queer little lurch. Speechless, she could only stare at him. He chuckled. "Surely you've heard the old adage. A reformed rake makes the best husband."

"The catch is," she informed him tartly, "that there is no such thing as a reformed rake."

He scooped his hands, splay-fingered, into the dark hair that tumbled around her face and cradled her skull in his palms. "Olivia," he said gently. "I do not make light promises."

It was true. Her own honesty compelled her to recognize it. George did not, in fact, make light promises. Had he been willing to say easy words, he would have told her that he loved her. And that was just the first example that occurred to her.

Her anger faded as she struggled with this new thought. It did not square with her picture of him as a hardened gamester. Any gamester—hardened or not—knew how to hide the truth. She had every reason to believe that George would make a convincing liar. Yet he had had any number of opportunities to win her with lies, and still had spoken nothing but truth to her. Even when lies would have served him better.

She hesitated, searching his eyes, and saw no evasion there. He met her gaze levelly. But she dared not trust it; he might mean what he said and still fail. The temptations thrown in his path, especially after a period of practicing humdrum virtue, might prove stronger than even George's iron will.

"Can the leopard change his spots?" she whispered, forcing the words past a lump in her throat. "I think not."

He seemed to choose his words carefully. "I would say it depends upon the leopard. I am one leopard who no longer feels comfortable in his own, lamentably spotted, skin. I begin to wonder whether nature truly intended me for a leopard after all." His eyes lit with humor. "A bit late for this soul-searching, you may say, after I have savaged half the village."

"Let us speak English! Are you saying that you would change your ways if you married me?"

"Not if. When." He swept her firmly into a bear hug and rolled her onto her side, where their eyes met at an equal level. "Is that so hard to believe?"

"Yes," said Olivia frankly. "Why would you?"

"Ah. You think I lead an exciting life."

She raised an eyebrow. "That is, certainly, what one hears."

"You should never listen to gossip."

"Gossip, indeed!" said Olivia indignantly. "Why, you told me yourself that you are a rake and an adventurer, and you boasted of your skill at piquet. Among other things."

"Yes, but the life of a rake and an adventurer is highly overrated." He raised himself on one elbow and looked down at her. The candlelight edged his face with warmth. Had she not known better, she would have thought his expression tender. "Olivia, sweeting. There is nothing duller than sin. You may trust me on this, for I know whereof I speak. I am intimately acquainted with sin. I have wallowed in it for years. Whatever thrills it once held faded long ago, and lately I have continued my way of life only because I did not know how to stop. It finally occurred to me that there was nothing stupider than to waste one's life simply because one could not think of anything better to do."

She pretended to look thoughtful. "So you thought you would try something a little different, and marry an heiress. Just for a change of pace." Her voice was sharp with hurt.

He frowned. "That's what I planned," he admitted. "But I had good reasons. And my reasons were not entirely selfish."

"Spare me your reasons!" she flashed. "You have humiliated me enough for one night." She buried her face in her hands, furious to think he might see the naked emotion there. "Go away. Try your tricks on some other heiress."

"No," he snapped. She felt his arms go around her. She stiffened, fighting the urge to respond. She was so damnably weak where he was concerned! She kept her hands over her face and refused to budge, even when she felt his lips in her hair.

"You have said you will marry me, and I am holding you to your word," he said. His voice was quiet, but implacable.

"You tricked it out of me!" Her voice was muffled in her hands. "For shame! You said you would not cheat."

"I didn't cheat." Laughter rumbled in his chest. "I said I wanted you willing. You were more than willing."

She gave an inarticulate cry of frustration, muffled against his chest. He hugged her to him, laughing, then pulled her hands away from her face. She glared at him. His eyes were still twinkling. "It is you, Olivia, who has not thought what marriage would mean," he said softly.

"I have given it a great deal of thought!" she exclaimed, stung.

He raised a warning finger, then lightly tapped her nose with it. "You have accused me of considering only the financial aspects of marriage. I say that's the pot calling the kettle black."

She stared at him. He smoothed her hair back from her brow and caressed her shoulders soothingly, smiling his mocking, maddening smile. "As you so wisely pointed out not so long ago, money isn't everything." He kissed her to make sure she understood his point.

She pulled away, incensed. "That is the most cold-blooded insult you have handed me yet. Are you proposing to trade your—your sexual prowess for my money?"

His brows rushed together in a quick frown, but he did not seem to feel nearly as insulted as she did. "I am merely pointing out that marriage is something more than a contract. The rewards it offers are more than monetary, and they are not altogether one-sided." He nuzzled her cheek, whispering. "We will share a home, my sweet. And a bed." He kissed her ear, making her shiver. "And children."

She closed her eyes, awash in sensation. His mouth was wreaking havoc once again with her common sense. But he was right, she told herself weakly. Oh, dear. He was right. The prospect of sharing a home, let alone a bed, with this impossibly desirable man was enough to turn any woman's head.

And children. The tantalizing, terrifying hope, borne on his whispered words, danced on the edges of her consciousness. She quashed it automatically, from long habit. Then she realized she need not repress that longing anymore if—

—if she married.

And for the second time that night, Olivia Fairfax, mistress of her own fate, queen of her own destiny, careful and commonsensical creature that she was, looked danger directly in the face and smiled. This time she even said it with her eyes wide open.

"Yes."

22

Sunlight poured across the table linens and flashed and sparkled in the water glasses. The little coffee room looked surprisingly beautiful in the clear light of morning. Olivia hadn't slept much that night, but she felt remarkably well and wide awake. It was, in fact, a glorious morning, and she was in a mood to notice it and rejoice. Humming under her breath, Olivia spread jam on her toast and waited for her announcement to sink in.

Bessie dropped her fork onto her plate with a clatter. "*What* did you say?"

But Edith flew from her place with a shriek and pounced on her sister-in-law, throwing her arms round her neck. "Oh! Oh! Oh, I think it's wonderful!"

Olivia laughed and coughed and tried to push Edith away. "Thank you, but pray do not choke me! It can't come as that much of a surprise."

Edith bounced back into her chair, chattering merrily. "Oh, but it does! It is! Why, you have always insisted that you would *never* marry. Everyone says that of you, and I have heard you say it with my own ears! I don't know how many times you have told me how glad you were to be single. Oh, you sly thing!"

"I wasn't being sly," Olivia began, but Edith was still speaking.

"And all the time, you were setting your cap for

Lord Rival! I never guessed. Especially since he seems the last man on earth you would choose! Although, I must say, he has certainly seemed attentive—and in a *respectable* sort of way, which, considering the tales one hears of him, makes this doubly surprising. Of all the unlikely matches! What a seven-day wonder it will be! The town will talk of nothing else. Rake Rival and Lady Olivia Fairfax—the most confirmed bachelor in London and the most dedicated spinster!"

Edith broke into a peal of laughter which Olivia found herself unable to share. She set her toast back down on her plate. Her appetite had unaccountably diminished. She stole a glance at Bessie, who looked as if she had been turned to stone. A shadow crept across Olivia's bright morning.

But then the door opened and George walked in. The sight of him shot a swift, visceral flutter of nerves through Olivia, making her feel almost lightheaded. The combination of weak-kneed desire and giddy fear clashing within her was, to say the least, unsettling. He looked as beautiful as a jungle creature, and every bit as lethal. Her agreement to marry this powerful, dangerous man suddenly seemed impossible. Deranged! Had she lost her mind?

Then he smiled at her, and she knew she would do anything to keep him at her side. She had not only lost her mind, she had lost her heart. He hadn't tricked her into saying yes; she had been dying for an excuse to say yes. *Too late now, too late,* hammered mournfully in her brain as she extended her hand to him, blushing and smiling like any other bride. She would save her regrets for later. With George bowing over her hand, all she could feel was idiotic happiness.

He shot her a secret smile that intensified her blush. "Good morning," was all he said, but the way he said it cast her into confusion.

"Good morning," chirped Edith. "And congratulations! Or is it felicitations we should offer?"

"To me? Congratulations, I think." He bowed. "I am a lucky man."

Edith beamed. "Well said, my lord. I daresay that wishing you happy would be redundant."

He gave Edith an amused glance as he seated himself beside Olivia, not waiting for an invitation. "I had thought, Lady Badesworth, that you would have a rather jaundiced view of marriage at the moment."

"Oh, no! Not I. Despite my own troubles, I approve of marriage in general." She giggled as her gaze slid from Lord Rival to Olivia. "It was my sister-in-law whose opinion of matrimony was poor. I'm glad you have been able to change her mind."

"So am I," said George agreeably, reaching for the coffeepot.

Olivia felt as if she were suffocating. "My opinion of marriage has not changed," she said, as firmly as she could. "It's just that . . ."

Her voice trailed off as she gazed helplessly round the table. All eyes were on her, and she could not find a way to finish her sentence. George looked amused, Edith surprised, and Bessie still had that queer, stonefaced expression. George spoke smoothly into the silence, finishing her sentence for her.

"You and I will be the exception that proves the rule." He took a calm sip of coffee. "Unlike the majority of husbands, I shall not dominate my wife."

Olivia choked at this patently false assertion. George dominated every room he entered, simply by the force of his personality! The thought of him dwindling into a meek and deferential husband was ridiculous. She shot him a fulminating glare, which he met with his blandest smile.

Bessie spoke at last. Her voice was thick with suppressed emotion. "I do wish you happy, Ivy. I do." She whisked a handkerchief out and blew her nose fiercely. "It comes as a bit of a shock, but if it must be—"

"It must," said George.

"Then I wish you happy. I wish you *both* happy. There!" She gave a last sniff and began nervously wadding her handkerchief. "I am sorry to be so—so overset. The news has taken me by surprise, is all. I never dreamed—but never mind. I shall come about." She straightened in her chair and assumed the determined expression of a soldier resolved to do his duty. "I've a high opinion of you, my lord," she announced unexpectedly. "I didn't care for you at first, as you may have surmised. But I've come to see that you are a man of honor. After yesterday's events, I am inclined to think that the world has painted an undeservedly black picture of you, and I mean to correct it if I can. You have the makings of a hero in you, my lord, and I shall tell whoever will listen."

George looked both surprised and touched. "Thank you, Miss Fairfax. But pray do not imagine that the world has wronged me. I earned my sordid reputation, and you were quite right to view me with suspicion." The glimmer of a smile lit his features. "You are also right to abandon that view now, however, and I hope we will be friends."

Bessie gave a brisk nod. "Very good, my lord. I hope so, indeed." She looked from George to Olivia and back again. "What are your plans?"

"Plans?" asked Olivia blankly. She had no plans.

George, however, apparently did. He helped himself to the buttered eggs, his demeanor still unruffled. "First, I think we will ask you to return to Chelsea with Lady Badesworth, Miss Fairfax. If you will be so good."

"Oh, yes!" said Edith quickly, turning beseeching eyes upon Bessie. "Pray do not leave me, Bessie. I feel so much stronger with you at my side. What if I should encounter Ralph again? And—oh, dear, what will I say to Culpepper?"

"Nothing," said Bessie staunchly. "I've known Cul-

pepper longer than any of you. His fussing and moralizing won't bother me a bit. I'll speak for you, Edith,
never you fear."

"Excellent. I'm sure you will represent Lady Badesworth's interests admirably. I have a suggestion, if I
may be so bold." George looked inquiringly at Bessie
and she gave him a brief, wary nod. He returned his
attention to leisurely salting his eggs. "I hope you and
Lady Badesworth will discuss your future jointly, prior
to meeting with Culpepper. Whatever decisions are
made regarding her future living arrangements, it
would be unthinkable for her to live alone."

Edith immediately voiced her enthusiastic assent
and cried that Bessie must, really *must*, come to live
with her. Bessie flushed with emotion—emotion that
Olivia had no difficulty in recognizing as gratitude and
relief. It gave her a queer little pang to see that
George had correctly divined the origin of Bessie's
stonefaced expression, and that she, Olivia, had utterly
failed to perceive that her marriage would leave Bessie homeless.

"I'll send for the old rascal the instant we return—
before Ralph has a chance to bend his ear," declared Bessie.

"And while you are driving a hard bargain with
Culpepper," continued George, returning the salt cellar to the center of the table, "you may direct him
to place a notice of Lady Olivia's betrothal in the
London papers."

Bessie chuckled. "That ought to distract him. I'll
tell him just as he works himself into a fine hand-
wringing over Edith leaving Ralph."

Olivia felt as if she were being swept along on a
strong tide. Her chin took on a stubborn tilt. "Have
I nothing to say in any of this?" she demanded. "Why
should Bessie meet with Culpepper? He is my
employee."

"You will be busy elsewhere," George informed

her, still with that irritating calm. "I think we can safely leave Lady Badesworth in your cousin's care. Miss Fairfax seems quite capable."

Olivia was speechless. Bessie was pink with gratification and Edith was beaming with approval. Her new fiancé seemed to have effortlessly removed the reins from Olivia's grasp and taken complete mastery of her household. Already.

He spoke over her head as he addressed Bessie again. "There is some advantage, I think, in your meeting with Culpepper before Lord Badesworth does so. I shall bespeak a chaise to carry you and Lady Badesworth to Chelsea with all possible speed. How soon could you be ready to depart?"

"Within the hour, my lord."

"Very good." He picked up his fork. "The chaise will be waiting for you. Lady Olivia and I will depart at roughly the same time, but we are taking my curricle to Sussex. I shall return her to you safely in a day or two."

Olivia found her tongue. "Oh, you will, will you?" she said rudely.

"Certainly I will." His eyes laughed at her over the rim of his coffee cup. "But first, I am showing you Sussex."

Her eyes flashed. "What is in Sussex, pray?"

"Your new estate," he said softly. His smile burst her bubble of anger, but his words paralyzed her.

Estate. What a dunce she was. He was a baron; of course he had an estate of some kind. Had she been thinking—but, of course, she had not been thinking—she would have realized this. Most females had the good sense to find out all the particulars before they entered into a marriage contract. Even the sillies who fell for a handsome face, as she had obviously done, usually had prudent guardians to find out the particulars for them. But Olivia Fairfax, who prided herself on needing no guidance, who scorned advice and

made her own decisions, had blundered into love like
a green girl and recklessly promised herself to a man
of whom she knew almost nothing.

A man with an estate. In Sussex.

Olivia heard no more of the conversation enlivening
the breakfast party. She eventually left the table, her
food untasted, and climbed the stairs like a sleep-
walker to oversee the packing of her bandbox. Her
mind grappled with her new situation, trying to understand how her circumstances could have altered so
radically overnight. She felt as if her brain had turned
to sludge.

Sussex. He was taking her to Sussex. He would
show her his home. He would doubtless expect her to
live there, on his estate. And where would he live?
Back in Mayfair, gambling away her inheritance? Dallying with the bored sophisticates of the *ton* while his
dupe of a wife cried into her Sussex pillow, far from
everything she knew and everyone she loved?

The thought seemed to dash cold water in Olivia's
dazed face. She inhaled sharply, then suddenly rushed
from the room and pounded on the door of Bessie's
bedchamber. There was no answer. She flew downstairs to the front hall, arriving just in time to see the
cloud of dust on the horizon left by the departing
chaise. Bessie and Edith were gone.

Olivia sank numbly onto a narrow wooden bench
that faced the open door. Bessie had gone, and when
she arrived in Chelsea she would immediately send
for Culpepper. A notice of Olivia's engagement would
appear in the London papers within the week. What
a calamity. Once the notice appeared, breaking the
engagement would cause even more talk than the engagement itself.

Olivia pressed her hand to her cheek and tried to
think. Weathering a scandal would be most unpleasant, but however much she dreaded gossip, she could
not, would not ruin her life simply to silence a few

wagging tongues. What should she do? She had seldom felt more alone in her life.

A booted step sounded behind her. She did not turn to look. She knew it was George. Her every nerve seemed to vibrate whenever he was near, signaling his proximity before her ordinary senses alerted her. She felt him stop beside her, and still she did not move to acknowledge him. She simply stared, expressionless, at the point in the distance where the chaise had last been seen. Even the dust cloud had settled by now.

"Olivia." His quiet voice sent a tremor through her, whether of fear or lust or love or resentment she had no idea. She could no longer sort out what she felt. She only knew she felt, and felt keenly.

"Olivia." When she still did not move, he stepped into her field of vision and dropped to one knee before her, taking her cold hands in his. Even on his knees, she thought detachedly, he lost not one whit of his composure or authority. He made the posture of supplication look graceful and natural.

"You are afraid," he said softly. "I have joked with you overmuch. Forgive me, sweetheart. I am new at this, but I shall improve as time goes on." He smiled. "I can't promise you that I will always be serious, but I think I can manage to drop my habitual flippancy from time to time. When the need arises."

She looked at him, wishing he would make some magical gesture that would set everything right and give her back the giddy happiness she had had an hour ago. What that gesture could be, she had no idea.

"I am afraid," she said slowly. "But no amount of plain speaking will repair matters. I agreed to marry you, and I don't know why. I barely know you." Her voice sank to a bewildered whisper. "I think you have bewitched me."

His swift grin flashed. "If I could have, I would have. But I never studied the black arts." He rose lightly to his feet and offered his arm. "Walk with me. They are bringing my curricle round, but this is more important."

She stood without a word and took his arm. It was absurd to feel comforted by his touch, but the solidity and latent power in the muscles beneath her fingertips spoke to something primitive in her soul. He led her out the front door of the inn and, skirting the edge of the rutted and muddy yard, took her to a small flower garden planted between it and the Brighton road. The rows of straggling plants had a neglected look and few blooms in October, but George was doubtless seeking privacy rather than beauty.

"What do you wish to discuss?" she asked stiffly, once the rickety gate had clicked shut behind them. "Marriage settlements? Terms? I am sorry if the news disappoints you, but there will be no dowry. I am already in possession of my inheritance and that, my friend, is all you are like to see. I doubt if we can even count upon Ralph to give us a handsome present."

George appeared unmoved. "I daresay we will manage to scrape by without his assistance."

"And another thing." She squared her shoulders, ready to do battle. "The bulk of my fortune is the legacy I received from my mother. It far outweighs the income I inherited from my father. But that money is irrevocably tied up in the Fairfax School. You will not be able to touch it."

"I don't want to touch it. Do you think I am the sort of chap who would take bread from the mouths of orphans?"

She felt a little ashamed—and relieved. "I don't know what sort of chap you are," she confessed. "You are obviously a charming rogue, and I have long suspected that there are hidden depths to your character. But—"

"But?" he prompted.

"I could be wrong." She peeped anxiously up at him, hoping he would reassure her.

"My poor Olivia." He shook his head in rueful amusement. "You are seeking comfort that I cannot give you. You know what my life has been. I can point to no virtuous act that would display for you the heart of gold beneath my rough exterior."

She was unsure whether to feel amused or annoyed. "There is nothing rough about your exterior," she said crossly. "If anything, you're too smooth! But you're an odd sort of fortune hunter. You have never even asked me what my income is."

"I already know what your income is." He tucked her bare fingers more securely into his elbow, protecting them from the cold. "Perhaps you will recall that I investigated you, to the extent I could, prior to meeting you. I bribed a bank clerk as part of that investigation."

She almost stumbled in her shock. His matter-of-fact delivery was nearly as upsetting as the news itself. He glanced down at her, his mouth twisting in an enigmatic smile. "You will be relieved to hear that the clerk in question is no longer employed where you bank. Apparently you were not the only client whose secrets he was willing to share. I was fortunate to tender my request before he lost his situation."

"You are generally fortunate," she said faintly.

George seemed not to hear the horror in her voice. He gazed at the horizon in an abstracted way. "You have already surmised, I daresay, that Beebe's eight hundred a year is all I have to live on."

Despite her distress, she almost laughed. "Frankly, I haven't given your income a moment's thought. Pray recall that it was none of my business until a few hours ago."

He glanced down at her briefly, his eyes glinting with amusement. "Ah, yes. How silly of me. I have lived in poverty for so long, I forgot what it was like to take one's wealth for granted. The truly rich never give money a thought."

"But you live in Mayfair." She swept a skeptical gaze over his highly polished boots, fashionable clothing, and immaculate linen. "You must have an income of some kind. What have you done? Bled your estate, I suppose."

She saw a muscle jump in his jaw, but his voice remained calm. "No, madam," he said dryly. "Every groat had been wrung from the estate before I inherited."

"Ah." She considered for a moment. Light dawned. "You did tell me that you wanted my money to pay debts that were not your own. Is that what you meant?"

He paused and bowed. "That is exactly what I meant." The abstracted look returned to his features. "I almost dread showing you Rye Vale," he said, as if thinking aloud. "But it will probably hurt my eyes more than it hurts yours. When I look at it, I see not what is, but what should be."

Olivia looked up at him and felt the ground shifting beneath her feet. Before her stood a man who loved his home. It was in every line of his sorrowing face, his tense shoulders, the stern set of his jaw. She would never have guessed this about him. She knew immediately, instinctively, that this was a side he normally hid from the world.

So. He had inherited a wasted property. A property that held immense meaning for him. An estate he had watched dwindle and decay, powerless to reverse the destruction. How it must have gnawed at him, she thought. Pity stabbed her and, in that moment, her heart went out to him.

It was not such an ignoble motive, after all, for marrying money. Had it been any other woman's money he planned to use, she might have felt even more sympathetic than she did. But it was her money, and no amount of sympathy would put that money back in her pocket after he had spent it. A corner of her mind stayed angry even as the rest of her burned with compassion.

"Why did you leave your home? It must have needed your stewardship."

"Oh, it did." He shrugged. "But there was nothing I could do. I was a boy, you understand, when I left home and moved to London. After my father died, I stayed there—partly because Rye Vale had deteriorated to the point where it was nearly uninhabitable, and partly because the metropolis offers more scope for a man of my talents. One cannot make a living, or even the pretense of a living, playing cards in the wilds of Sussex."

"I see." So the rumors were correct. He relied on the gaming tables to maintain his idle existence. She tried to keep the condemnation she felt out of her voice, but he must have heard it.

"I'm not doing much to calm your fears, am I?" he remarked, with a return to his usual self-mocking humor.

"No." She cleared her throat. "In fact, I—I must tell you, George, that I am having second thoughts about the wisdom of . . . that is, I am seriously considering ending our engagement. I sympathize with your situation, and I sincerely wish you well, but I have no desire to leave my home and devote my life to restoring yours."

If she was expecting a dramatic reaction to her statement, she was disappointed. He merely patted her hand again and bestowed a kindly smile upon her. "Yes. I know. One always regrets bargains struck in the dead of night. They look quite different in the clear light of morning."

Nettled, she opened her mouth to ask him what he proposed to do about it, and whether he would allow her to cry off—but she snapped her mouth shut with the words unsaid. It was extremely annoying to discover that his lackadaisical attitude toward their be-

trothal perversely rekindled her desire to wed him!
What was the matter with her? She walked silently
beside him, struggling to understand the wild swings
of her emotions.

He halted in his tracks and turned her to face him.
"I ask for one boon. Come with me," he urged, emotion vibrating in his voice. "Let me show you Rye
Vale. Let me show you why I need you. For I do need
you, Olivia, and not just your wretched wealth. I need
your vision and your managerial skills. I need your
advice. I need your help. I need you."

Riveted by his sudden intensity, Olivia stared wordlessly at him. Blast the man! He had just said the
magic words. She had never been able to resist an
honest appeal for help, especially one couched in
terms that flattered all the qualities she most prized
in herself. She nodded, not trusting her voice.

"Thank you," he said simply, and kissed her hand.
His mouth was warm against her cold skin, reminding
her with startling suddenness of the reasons why she
had said yes last night.

He was marrying her for her money. Very well. He
could have it.

A tiny smile played across Olivia's face as she
watched the wind catch a lock of his dark hair, ruffling
and playing with it as if the breeze had fallen for him,
too. It wasn't such a bad bargain after all, she told
herself bracingly. He didn't love her, but he valued
her. Perhaps she was better off, really, without his
love. Respect and friendship were solid, worthwhile
bonds, and often longer-lived than mere romantic
love.

But then he bent to kiss her lips—in broad daylight,
just as he had once told her he would. And the sweet
thrill of kissing him in the sunshine showed her, as
nothing else could do, that respect and friendship were
a poor and pale shadow of what she really wanted
from this man.

When he grinned and offered his arm to escort her to his curricle, she returned his smile gaily enough. But the hollow ache of sorrow remained, and when they drove smartly off down the Brighton Road it stayed—an invisible stowaway that clung to Olivia like a burr, no matter how determinedly she tried to ignore it.

23

*H*e supposed his body must be weary after two days of driving, but he could not feel it. No weariness could touch him. The closer they got to Rye Vale the more alive he felt, rigid with anticipation like a spaniel sensing the approach of home. The contours of the land grew more and more familiar, the sweep of grass and sky stirring a thousand half-remembered associations.

George had always been a closemouthed man, not one to confide easily in others, but today he was seized with a strange compulsion to tell Olivia everything. Words welled up from some forgotten corner of his soul and poured out of him. He wanted her to see Rye Vale through his eyes and understand the dream—before the reality had a chance to muscle in and prejudice her. So, on the way, he beguiled the tedium of the journey and distracted his humming nerves by sketching for her the outlines of his family history.

She was silent for the most part, but attentive, asking questions that indicated she was following the tale closely. He confirmed that his title, Rival, was a corruption of Rye Vale, and that Rye Vale itself was a corruption of an earlier place name, deriving not from the grasses that surrounded his property but from the meandering stream, the "rythe," that ran through it. He spoke of the ancient origins of the estate, of the waxing and waning fortunes of the barony, and how a branch of the Carstairs family had come into the inheritance several generations ago. And then he told her Rye Vale's more recent history—the excesses of the eighteenth century. He could not keep the rancor from his voice as he told her how, beginning with his great-grandfather, the unentailed portions of the property had been sold off, bit by bit, until there was little left besides the manor house and the park immediately surrounding it. The tenants that remained to him could ill afford to pay their rent, and what little income they provided was swallowed up in taxes. An elderly couple who had spent their lives in his family's service were kept on as retainers, but their presence was mainly useful in keeping the criminal element at bay. As far as he knew, the house had never been looted. But, he admitted with wry humor, it was well known in the neighborhood that there was nothing valuable there to steal. When his father died a swarm of creditors had immediately descended. Everything that could be sold, had been sold.

"Was there enough, then, to pay the debts?"

"Not all of them." He hated telling her this. "There was one sizeable parcel of land that my father had managed to mortgage. I have made sporadic payments to keep the mortgage holder from calling in the note. He would be well within his rights to do so but, fortunately, he's a city dweller and hasn't the foggiest notion what to do with the land." He gave her an ironic glance. "You will understand that the gentleman is a bit of a slowtop. No one with half a brain would have lent my father money, secured by land or not. At any rate, this creditor is satisfied to make threatening noises from time to time. When the dibs are in tune, I pay him. When they are not"—he shrugged—"you can't get blood from a turnip."

She questioned him closely about the details of the estate, displaying a quick mind and a grasp of land management that surprised him. But, as Olivia reminded him, she was not a Londoner. She had grown up on her father's estate, and those years had not been wasted. She had soaked up knowledge like a sponge, showing interest in everything, and had, she said, learned far more than was good for her. He caught the twinkle in her eye that belied her pious look.

He assumed an austere expression. "Did you usurp your father's authority and manage his estate for him? I hope you were severely punished."

"I was," she assured him. "The bailiff took my advice without a blink, but he also accepted praise for the results without a blink. It was painful for me to hold my tongue while my father marveled at Hinson's industry and excellent management."

George chuckled. "Most galling," he said sympathetically.

"Yes, but no more than I deserved. My family has always said it was a great pity that I was born a girl."

"I hesitate to contradict them," said George politely, "but I am deeply grateful that you were born a girl."

She laughed, but something flickered in the back of her eyes and he felt her withdraw from him a little. He understood her reserve. She was still toying with the idea of jilting him. There was no question of that, however. He had no intention of returning her to Chelsea until she was well and truly his. By that time, the announcement would be in all the papers—which was his whole purpose in sending Miss Fairfax and that silly little countess back to London. Olivia had said yes to him under the shakiest of circumstances, but the betrothal announcement would add the weight of a *fait accompli* to the scales.

He had to have her. He desired her, now, almost as much as her money. He stole a glance at her and felt his blood heat. It wasn't that she was conventionally pretty, although no fault could be found in her delicate features. She was better than pretty. A man could never tire of looking at that extraordinary, expressive face: the fine bones and clear eyes, the wonderful mix of strength and softness, intelligence and innocence, fire and laughter. And a man could certainly never tire of touching that soft skin of hers. But he wouldn't think of that—not now.

They left the main road and started down a track that wound through peaceful fields, meadows dotted with sheep, and vast expanses of nothing. George soon fell silent under the weight of memories. He felt as if he knew every blade of grass, every stone and stile. They were alone now, with only the whisper of tall grasses bending in the wind and the cry of birds to keep them company. The road dipped and rose, and he knew that when it reached the crest of the low hill, Rye Vale itself, the manor house, would be visible. Overcome with emotion, he pulled the horses to a halt. He must master himself before he could go on.

"What is it?" asked Olivia.

For a moment he could not answer her. With the curricle stopped, the wild silence, fresh with sea wind, surrounded them. "Listen," he whispered, closing his eyes. "Do the gulls sound like that anywhere else in England?"

Her low chuckle warmed him. "Gulls sound the same everywhere. Are we close to your home now?"

"Very close." He opened his eyes and turned to look at her. She sat beside him, straight and graceful, her smooth, pale cheeks spanked pink by the breeze. Amusement twinkled in her clear gray eyes—and understanding, too. He smiled. "I love this land," he said simply.

"It's beautiful."

"I am glad you think so. It's not to everyone's taste." He gazed out over the ocean of grass and tried to imagine how it might strike someone seeing it for the first time. "There are those who enjoy London and crave the excitement of town. They soon grow restless here. And then there are those who are accustomed to forests. This portion of England appears naked to them, strange and empty. They see no beauty in it."

"Then I feel sorry for them," said Olivia roundly. "I think it indicates a poverty of the soul, to perceive beauty only in the familiar." She sniffed the sea wind appreciatively. "My! It's lovely to breathe clean air, isn't it?"

"Yes, it is."

She held her hat on with one hand as a gust of wind rocked the carriage. "Invigorating," she remarked.

He chuckled. "Are you putting a brave face on it?"

"No!" she assured him. Pleasure sparkled in her eyes. "I truly enjoy it."

She really did seem to be enjoying it. His heart swelled with gratitude. What a dear she was. "I suppose you are wondering why we stopped," he said apologetically.

The look of understanding in her eyes deepened. "I can guess," she said softly. "There is something over the top of that rise. Something you are afraid to see. Is that it?"

He was a little startled by how near the mark she had come. "Not quite. Something I am eager to see— but afraid to show you, I suppose." He tried to smile. "Once we crest the hill, the manor house will be visible. I'm afraid we will find it in a sad state of disrepair."

"Never mind," she said cheerfully. "We're here to assess the damage, are we not? Let us begin."

She was right, of course. There was no point in delaying the inevitable. He urged the horses forward again and they crested the hill.

It was worse than he had pictured. He gazed at his boyhood home, his expressionless face hiding his distress. The wild grass had completely taken over,

obliterating what used to be lawn and garden and
graveled drive and neat rows of flowering hedges. The
stand of yews, no longer neatly clipped, still marched
beside what used to be the main approach to the
house. Otherwise, there was nothing to mark it. The
house rose out of the sea of grass like a drowning
man bobbing to the surface for a last gasp of air. And
the roof of the south wing had fallen in. Why hadn't
the Rugglesfords written to tell him of that?

Olivia uttered a soft exclamation when she saw it
and placed her hand lightly on his leg. It seemed an
unconscious gesture of sympathy and support, and he
was dimly grateful for it even through his pain. He
said nothing, but drove down to the house. They had
to approach it on a rough cart track leading to the
back of the buildings, where the kitchen was. Here, a
small yard had been cleared.

George drew the curricle to a halt before the low
stone steps to the kitchen door. He barely recognized
the place. Chickens flapped and cackled underfoot,
making his horses dance nervously. Rows of beans and
turnips were visible opposite the chicken coop ahead.

The ancient manor of Rye Vale had dwindled into
a farm.

Impotent rage held George silent. The Rugglesfords
were not to blame. How else were they to live? He
was grateful for their industry. They had done their
best to keep the place in repair; he could scarcely
expect poor old Rugglesford to mend the roof with
no funds and no help. Planting their own vegetables
and raising chickens had doubtless helped them make
ends meet. He could not blame them. No, he could
not blame them. He knew where the blame lay. He
sat like a statue as Mrs. Rugglesford, blessing herself
and beaming, appeared in the kitchen doorway.

George thought his face would crack if he tried to
speak or smile. He was profoundly thankful when
Olivia immediately stepped into the breach, smoothing

the moment over with her instinctive tact. She smiled and offered her hand to Mrs. Rugglesford, complimenting her on the smells wafting from her kitchen. The good woman blushed with pleasure and launched into a monologue that related, in no particular order, her surprise at seeing the master, her delight at welcoming him home, her fears that he would find it much altered, an anxious enumeration of the ways in which she and her husband had tried to keep the place from falling into ruin, and an incomprehensible recipe for quickbread. Olivia bore it all very well, and her kind intervention gave George sufficient time to recover his aplomb.

George Carstairs had always been a lucky man. This day he learned, beyond all doubt, that meeting Lady Olivia Fairfax was the most spectacular stroke of good fortune that had ever yet befallen him. He was in a fair way to thinking it was the most spectacular stroke of good fortune that had ever befallen any man, anywhere. He actually felt humbled by it. Amazed. Nearly unmanned.

It wasn't just that he did not deserve her, although he was keenly aware of that. No man deserved her. She was a wonder. A walking, talking, breathing miracle. She swept into the Rugglesfords' humble home—which had once been Rye Vale's kitchen, scullery, and butler's quarters—and thoroughly won the hearts of George's remaining staff. She knew exactly how to charm them. Ten minutes of her warm approval and expressions of appreciation for various tiny touches—which George would never have noticed had she not remarked upon them—and the job was done. The Rugglesfords were fairly tripping over themselves with eagerness to please her.

He was flabbergasted when Mrs. Rugglesford actually offered to show them through the major portions of the house. Olivia's smile swept everything aside; opposition and timidity alike withered in its sunshine.

So off they went, Mrs. Rugglesford's keys jingling at her waist, to tramp through the great hall and the central wing.

The manor's scanty furnishings were shrouded beneath holland covers and the place had the unmistakable smell of an uninhabited home: damp air and dust. He found it depressing, but such mundane hindrances as stale air and invisible furniture could not foil Olivia's imagination. Her eyes sparkled, her foot tapped, and the concentration in her face plainly showed that the house was catching her interest. She exclaimed over beauties that he himself could barely make out beneath the film of neglect. Nothing could be hidden from her penetrating vision. It sought out everything good, transforming Rye Vale in her mind's eye from a ruin to a showplace.

At the end of their tour, he waved the Rugglesfords off to their own quarters and drew Olivia aside into a window embrasure. "My dear Olivia," he exclaimed, "I am ready to fall at your feet and worship you."

She chuckled, briskly rubbing a smut of dust off her glove. "That won't be necessary, my lord," she told him demurely. "In fact, it would be a fatal mistake! Those who know me well would beg you not to encourage me. You haven't encountered me in one of my enthusiastic fits—I can become quite unbearable, I assure you."

"Do your worst," he said, smiling. "You will find me a difficult man to frighten."

She looked appraisingly at him. "I believe you are right. I can't imagine riding roughshod over you."

"You won't," he promised her. He linked his hands behind her waist and drew her close to him. "In fact, I pulled you aside to speak to you on that head. Before you calculate the cost of curtains and carpets and wallpapers and start firing off orders to the London warehouses, I need to make something clear to you."

"Indeed?" She looked affronted.

"This is important, Ivy," he said, as gently as he could. It was her money, after all. "I am delighted that you are able to see beauty in this ruin of a house. And I appreciate your willingness to transform it into what it could be. But if you mean to pour all your resources into the manor house, I must put my foot down."

Her eyes flashed. "How dare you! How dare you dictate to me? I have not even made up my mind whether I will truly marry you."

He winced. "I expressed myself badly. What I meant was, there are more important uses for your income than mere adornment."

"I don't know what you mean." She looked hurt as well as angry.

"Once the roof is repaired and the house made habitable, I hope to persuade you that we can be comfortable together without surrounding ourselves with luxuries. We shall have everything you want, in time. It hurts my heart to deny you. But even your income is not large enough to do everything at once, and we must not, cannot, shirk our responsibilities to the community."

She stared at him, apparently flummoxed. Whatever she had been expecting him to say, he had evidently said something else. He pressed his point, speaking low and urgently. "Ivy, there are people who depend on me. It is my sacred duty to help them, and until now I have been utterly unable to do so. Can you not see, sweetheart, that it would be indecent—dishonorable—to fill my house with expensive ornaments while my tenants still suffer?"

For a second or two she did not move. Emotions chased themselves across her face, too quickly for him to decipher what they were. She eventually seemed to arrive at a decision. Then she reached up, took his face in her hands, and went up on her toes to kiss him. Surprised, but pleased, he returned her kiss. Fi-

nally she dropped back onto her heels and smiled
blindingly at him.

"When can we meet with your bailiff?" she asked.
George thought he had never heard sweeter words.

24

*O*h, she was right to love him. It did not matter whether she had picked up clues about his character from his actions and discourse or whether she had simply known it instinctively. She had judged him aright. Lord Rival may have lived the life of a rake, but he had the soul of a hero. All her giddy happiness returned, growing stronger as she received more and more evidence to confirm this view.

The tenants welcomed him with relief. There was no hint that they resented Lord Rival or blamed him personally for their plight. The Rugglesfords obviously held him in respect and affection, and when he located his father's old bailiff—now stricken in years, but full of excellent advice—the old man choked with visible emotion at the end of their meeting and declared that it would be a blessing to have his lordship back at Ryo Vale. Surely the esteem in which a man was held by those dependent upon him, especially when he had been able to do so little for them as yet, was excellent evidence that there was a side to George that the *ton* had never seen.

Fears and doubts still niggled at the back of her mind, but she defied them. She was in love and she was going to marry the man she loved, and the devil take the hindmost! More difficult to ignore was the sorrowful ache that worried like a sore tooth at the edges of her consciousness. It was crazy to marry a fortune hunter with her eyes wide open. It was worse to marry a man who did not love her. But she wanted him so badly that she deliberately turned her back on her wiser self.

Life with him might make her miserable; life without him surely would.

This portion of Sussex, very near the border of Kent, seemed to her a land of wind and sky. She had lived near London for so long, she had forgotten what it was like away from the smoke and noise of town. The sky was enormous. Beautiful. Her second day there, George rode over to the inn where, for propriety's sake, she was staying. A horse was saddled for her and George took her out for a gallop. She laughed from pure joy as the wind snatched at her hair and flapped her clothing like a flag, loving the feeling of the horse's muscles bunching and stretching beneath her. It had been a long time since she had ridden a horse, and longer still since she had galloped one. She had nearly forgotten what it felt like, how close it came to flying. To rediscover that joy with George at her side was heavenly.

She loved it here. Even the tumbledown house seemed beautiful to her, steeped in history, proud and ancient. George's ideas marched with her own in every way. They put plans together to reclaim the lost fortunes of his family by paying down the debts and putting heart back into the land. After an initial infusion of cash, there was no reason why the estate could not become self-sufficient again. And the project would be exciting—restoring the land, restoring the house. Building a family. All of it thrilled her. She felt fired with enthusiasm and eager to begin her new life. It didn't matter that it was George's project; she could not have been happier had she chosen it herself.

The future looked, in a word, bright.

It was a busy three days. With the help of the Rugglesfords they interviewed and hired a skeleton staff to begin setting the house to rights. It was obvious that George had given all this a great deal of thought; he had a dozen plans already in place, and all they had to do was decide which things needed to be done first. Laborers were found to clear the park, resurface the gravel drives, and repair the roof. The central portion of the house would be thoroughly cleaned and the holland covers taken off the furniture. New mattresses and linens and other household necessities would be purchased, all under the supervision of Mrs. Rugglesford—a sharp-eyed, honest, and thrifty woman. And George and Olivia would return to London, where George would procure a special license. They would be married within a fortnight, arrange for the smooth operation of the Fairfax School during Olivia's temporary absence, and return at once to Rye Vale to direct and supervise.

Olivia felt as if she had been caught in a whirlwind, but her feverish happiness saw her through it. The happiness remained as she returned to Chelsea, buoyed by George's whispers of heartfelt gratitude and tender promises of future bliss, and drugged by his kisses. He would follow her tomorrow. Today, she rode in solitary state back to her home, dreaming, as the carriage rocked and swayed, of all the wonders in store for her.

She had almost convinced herself that she might win George's love one day. Stranger things had happened. And even if he never loved her the way she loved him, she could bear it. They would be partners and companions, come what may. That would be enough to make her happy, she told herself. And by the time she reached Chelsea, she almost believed it.

The mud-splattered coach pulled up before her town house as the autumn afternoon was drawing to a close. She climbed out, humming to herself, and was directing the driver regarding the disposition of her meager baggage when the door of her house flew open. Bessie and Edith rushed out to greet her as if she had been away for a year, and Mrs. Pratt waited, smiling, in the lamplit doorway. Olivia hugged her enthusiastic relatives fiercely. Her emotions seemed oddly close to the surface; a lump formed in her throat as she hugged Bessie.

She laughed and hugged her again. "Heavens! Don't mind me, pray; I don't know why I should choke up at the mere sight of home. I had a marvelous time."

"It's good to have you back, Ivy dear." Bessie looked her over critically. "Your pelisse is crushed."

"Yes. Dreadful, isn't it? I have worn it for three days in a row; I look like the ragpicker's child. Edith, pray do not pull on that sleeve—I very much fear it will come off! Have you spoken to Culpepper yet?"

An odd little silence fell. Bessie and Edith exchanged glances. Mrs. Pratt said, in her comfortable way, "Lady Olivia, you mustn't let them keep you standing in the street. Pray step inside. I shall have tea brought to you directly."

Olivia hid her curiosity and smiled at the housekeeper. "Thank you, Mrs. Pratt, I shall take your excellent advice. In the library, please." She calmly mounted the steps, stripping off her gloves, and walked into the library. Bessie and Edith trailed in her wake. Once the door was closed she turned to them, one brow raised. "Out with it! What was the meaning of that pregnant silence just now? Don't tell me you have let three days go by without speaking to Culpepper."

"We won't tell you that, for it isn't true," said Bessie bluntly. "We saw Culpepper the afternoon we arrived home. But—"

Edith rushed into speech. "Bessie was wonderful!" she said earnestly. "Culpepper fussed a bit, but she handled him beautifully. She was absolutely—I don't know how she dared! My marriage is in a fair way to be settled now. We shall have my pin money and a little besides, and Bessie and I shall live in a house—oh, the sweetest house you ever saw!"

"My word! That was fast work."

"It's Rose Cottage, Ivy. You'll remember it."

"I do indeed." It was a property that belonged to the family, not far from Ralph's estate. Her grandmother had lived in it last. "Will the two of you be safe there, do you think?"

Bessie gave a grim little chuckle. "We are hiring a very *large* butler."

Olivia laughed. "I see."

"And I do think we will be safe. Did Lord Rival say anything to you, Ivy, about that private conversation he had with Ralph? No? Well, whatever threats he made, he must've been convincing." Bessie shook her head as if mystified. "I never saw Ralph so cowed."

Edith looked anxious. "I do feel rather guilty when I think that Ralph shan't have an heir."

"Do you, my dear?" Olivia patted her fondly. "You needn't. Bessie's brother is next in line, you know. He's a kind fellow; you will like him. And he has a very large family, so the succession is assured."

"Then you don't—you don't mind? That your father's line will not continue?"

"Not in the least," said Olivia promptly. "Why should I?"

Edith laughed with relief and flew to kiss her sister-in-law's cheek. "Thank you! For although he could divorce me and remarry, I would excessively dislike being divorced—"

"Oh, pooh. No need to disgrace the family with a divorce. And besides, Ralph should not be allowed to remarry. It would be shocking to inflict him on some other unsuspecting female."

"So I told her," said Bessie approvingly. "But I'm

glad to hear you say it, since I can't be impartial on this score. Not with John as the heir, and wee Johnny after him."

Mrs. Pratt entered noiselessly with the tea and, as quietly, removed herself, bearing away Olivia's hat and gloves. Olivia sank blissfully into a wing chair, accepting a cup from Bessie. "This smells wonderful. It's good to be home." Her eyes twinkled mischievously. "Is my betrothal the talk of the town yet?"

Bessie and Edith exchanged another glance. "No," said Bessie gruffly. "For no one knows about it."

Olivia was startled. "But, surely . . . the notice in the papers—"

"Hasn't been placed." Bessie frowned. "Culpepper refused. Said he wanted to speak with you privately first. I'm sorry, Ivy, but he wouldn't budge. And he made me promise that I would not place the notice for you, either. The old rascal made it a condition of his recommending to Ralph that he give Rose Cottage to Edith."

Olivia set her teacup down very carefully. Edith hurried into speech. "You are angry, Olivia, but pray do not blame Bessie. We thought that a delay of only a day or two would make no difference, after all."

"Well," said Olivia slowly, "it does not, of course. Printing a notice is customary, but hardly a prerequisite for obtaining a marriage license. What disturbs me is that Culpepper set himself in opposition to my expressed wishes. Again." Her voice became more and more clipped as her anger grew. "My patience with Mr. Culpepper is wearing extremely thin. I make every allowance for his age and for the years he has spent in our service, but—*Really!* What could he possibly have to say to me?" She rose and tugged briskly on the bell rope. "If he wishes to speak with me, let him do so without delay. I only hope I interrupt his dinner!"

She knew that her peremptory summons was unreasonable, and expected a polite, regretful response informing her that Culpepper would wait upon her at her convenience in the morning. She decided that as long as the response was apologetic—in tone, if not in substance—she was prepared to let the matter slide. She was not expecting Culpepper to hasten to her the instant he received word from her. When he was announced, therefore, some three quarters of an hour after she had sent her message, she looked in surprise at the library clock. It had grown quite late. "Oh, dear," she murmured, feeling a little ashamed of her pettishness. "Send him in, please." She cast a rueful glance at Bessie. "He will be stiff-rumped and punctilious now, to punish me for displaying my ill temper. God grant me patience!"

Culpepper appeared in the doorway and bowed. He looked pale and slightly disheveled, as if he had dropped everything in his haste to reach her. She rose, an apology on her lips, but he spoke before she could say the words. "Thank you for sending me word of your arrival, Lady Olivia," he said, in a low, quick tone. "I did wish to speak to you immediately. I hope the hour is not too late?"

"Why—of course not," stammered Olivia, nonplussed. He was obviously not angry at all. Something was wrong, but that was not it. "Pray come in."

He did so, bowing again to acknowledge Bessie. Trouble was in every line of his face and in the tense set of his shoulders. He looked older, somehow, than when Olivia had seen him last. "Miss Fairfax, I hope you will excuse us," he said, with uncharacteristic humility. "I have something very particular I wish to say to your cousin."

Bessie looked as if she would like to stay, but she rose obediently and took herself off. Culpepper's manner indicated a gravity that brooked no argument. Olivia, feeling very much perplexed, waited for whatever it was Culpepper had to say. He said nothing, however, for several seconds after the door had closed behind Bessie. Instead, he wandered vaguely around the library, fidgeting first with his cuffs, then with the skirts of his coat, and finally with the inkstand on the writing desk, all the while refusing to meet her eyes.

"Well?" prompted Olivia, challenging him. "I notice that you have not wished me happy."

He looked, if possible, even more distressed, but he did stop pacing and fidgeting. "I beg your pardon, my lady. I—I cannot. I cannot, in good conscience, presume to wish you happy when I know . . . Bless me, what a terrible task is mine!" These last words were uttered in an explosion of feeling that was obviously genuine. Olivia felt her stomach turn over. She placed one hand on the back of a chair to steady herself.

"Why have you refused to place the notice of my engagement in the London papers as I requested?" she asked him. Her voice remained steady enough.

Culpepper removed his spectacles and began methodically wiping them with his handkerchief. "It must seem strange to you."

"It does."

"I thought it . . . unwise. I think you should not enter into this engagement." He cleared his throat. "Under the circumstances."

She began to feel exasperated as well as anxious. "Under what circumstances? I warn you, Mr. Culpepper, that if you utter one word of slander against Lord Rival—"

"Lady Olivia, you mistake. What I must say to you is not about Lord Rival. It is about you."

She stared at him in bewilderment. "About *me?*"

"Yes." He sighed. It was an old man's sigh, unutterably weary. He finally looked at her, and she was both astonished and dismayed to see that his pale eyes were red-rimmed and suspiciously watery. He looked, for all the world, as if he were on the verge of tears. And when he spoke, his voice was gentler than she had ever heard it.

"Sit down, Lady Olivia," he said sadly. "What I am about to tell you will come, I fear, as a severe shock."

25

The clock on the mantelpiece was just chiming ten when she heard George's voice downstairs. Olivia looked dully at the clock. It wasn't possible for George to be here this early. Perhaps she was hearing things. She was tired enough to be dreaming. But then she distinctly heard his laugh, followed by the words, "I'll announce myself, thank you." His light tread sounded on the landing outside her door well before she was ready for it. But, of course, she would never be ready for this interview. It hardly mattered that she must endure it several hours before she expected it.

There was no time to brace herself. There was no time to don a cheerful mask. The door opened and he was there, all the dear, massive, breathtaking bulk of him. As always, he seemed to fill the doorway, making her comfortable morning room seem small and overly fussy.

"Why, here's a welcome," he said teasingly. "Waiting for me in the dark, sweetheart?"

She realized, belatedly, that she had not bothered to draw the curtains this morning. Before she could gather her strength to move he had crossed the room and done it for her, talking to her as if nothing was wrong. It was hard, somehow, to remember that he did not know yet.

"Rye Vale was dull without you, Ivy. I finished my business and rode down to London last night."

Light flooded the room. She turned her face away, blinking painfully. She still did not stand or speak to him. She had a vague notion that if she left the anchor of her desk she would shatter and fall to pieces.

He came up behind her, his voice vibrant with warmth. "I couldn't wait to see you." She felt his hands on her shoulders and tensed, trembling. It was too much; her heart would crack if he touched her again.

"George," she blurted, her voice raw from weeping. "Don't." She had meant to say a complete sentence, but those were the only two words that made it past the constriction in her throat.

The hands at her shoulders paused, then pulled her bodily from the chair and turned her so he could see her face. Whatever he saw there wiped the teasing smile from his face. His brows knitted in a swift frown. "Good God. What has happened?"

She managed a wavering smile. "Bad news, I am afraid."

He immediately moved to take her in his arms. It took every ounce of willpower she had to rebuff him, but she did. He felt her rejection and murmured, "Let me hold you." His voice was rough with concern.

She pushed him away with the palms of her hands and managed to say, in a strangled voice, "Please. No. I think you should sit down."

He did not take her advice, but he did let go of her and walk around to the front of her desk. She sank back into her chair, trying to still the quivering of her limbs. His look of concentrated concern did not abate, but a note of anger thrummed in his voice as he said, "Tell me this news that is so bad I can't hold you while you tell me. There can't be any news bad enough to change your mind. Not now."

"Not my mind. Yours."

He looked thunderstruck. "What?"

She had to look away; it was too dreadful. She fastened her gaze on the neat stack of pens on her desk. "I'm afraid there has been a misunderstanding." She swallowed. "No. Not a misunderstanding. I mean . . . I mean that I have misled you. I didn't mean to mislead you, George. I didn't know . . . I didn't know until last night."

"What didn't you know?" he said roughly. "Tell me quickly, Ivy. I can't bear to watch you suffer like this."

She took a deep, shaky breath. "I'm not a rich woman."

There. She had said it.

She stole a glance at him; he was rigid with surprise and disbelief. "Is this a joke?"

"I only wish it were."

He sat, then, in the wing chair across from her. "Of course it's not a joke," he said slowly. "I can see that you believe it. But surely it's nonsense."

"I know it sounds impossible. Pray recall the—the peculiar methods my father employed to keep me . . ." She could not keep the bitterness from her voice. "To keep me in my place."

He cocked his head as if trying to hear her more clearly. "You mean that business about never letting you know the source of your income?"

Olivia nodded. Helpless anger flooded her. It was so beastly. So unfair. "Had I been privy to this information—had I any power whatsoever to manage my own money, or at least to influence the trustees—" She broke off abruptly. No sense in losing control. "Well. There is little point in wringing my hands over it. I had no information, and I had no power. And now, I have no wealth." An ironic smile twisted her features. "It seems that poor Culpepper has been depleting his own funds in an effort to continue my quarterly income payments. Postponing the day of reckoning, you know, hoping that matters would improve, or that one or another of the trust's investments would turn a profit. But that deception is no longer possible."

She stared blindly down at her hands, folded tensely on the desktop. "The last profitable investment—I suppose you would call it an investment—was the textile mill my father was kind enough to purchase for me. In Massachusetts, if you can believe that." Her voice was trembling with anger. "It seems that *all* the holdings my father placed in trust for me were foreign. To make it more difficult for me to control or sell them, should I somehow discover what they were."

"Did Culpepper know your father's motives?" asked George. There was an edge to his voice that boded ill for Culpepper.

She gave a short, mirthless laugh. "I doubt it. But they were instantly plain to me. I know exactly how my father's mind worked. At any rate, this mill, on which the trust held no policy of assurance, burned to the ground last year. The trustees had been using the slender profits from this mill to cover the losses of the other holdings. And now . . ." She looked up, forcing herself to meet George's eyes as she said the terrible words. "I am bankrupt."

He was completely expressionless, his face as blank and unreadable as a portrait in a gallery. She thought, detachedly, that this must be the face he showed over a hand of cards. But he could not hide such a huge wave of emotion. Not entirely. Not from her. She saw, in that blank and shuttered look, a man who had suffered a catastrophe. He was casting about in his mind for some way to defeat this disaster, some way to undo it. He had not yet grasped that there was nothing to be done.

He rose jerkily and strode to the fireplace, staring down into the ashes as if an answer could be read there. "You can't go from wealth to poverty over-night," he said. His voice sounded harsh and strained. "It's not possible."

"I said I was bankrupt. I am not a pauper," she told him quietly. "There are assets I can sell—this house, for one. And much of its contents. But I will never be rich again."

She must make it easier for him. Seeing him so stunned strengthened her. She had had all night to think about it, but he was still shocked and uncomprehending. He had not understood what it all meant. She must spell it out for him, as gently as she could.

"I will be unable to meet the obligations we have just spent three days incurring," she said, her voice soft with regret. "I am terribly sorry, but it can't be helped. There will be no money for Rye Vale. I will have enough to continue living in Chelsea, in a small way. But by no stretch of the imagination will I have enough to restore your estate." She straightened in her chair and managed to speak calmly. "Knowing my plight, Culpepper kept our betrothal a secret. He knew that we would need to—to reconsider. In light of these developments."

For his sake, she must put a brave face on this. For his sake, she must say what he was unwilling, at this moment, to hear. He would rail against their fate today, perhaps. He would go through the motions of trying to argue with her. But later, he would feel relief and gratitude that she had held firm.

"George, do you understand me? There is no betrothal. Our engagement was contracted under false pretenses. I release you."

He stared at her, still with that blank, stunned expression. It seemed an infinite distance from the desk to the fireplace; their eyes met as if across an unbridgeable void. "You release me," he repeated tonelessly.

"Yes."

Something like anguish flickered in his eyes. He reached up dazedly and scrubbed his face with his hands, as if trying to shake the grip of a nightmare. "No money," he muttered, and then his head came up like a beast scenting danger. He straightened and turned to her, white-lipped. "They've begun clearing the weeds. They'll be starting on the roof tomorrow. I must go back and stop them."

And in a few quick strides, without another word to her, he was gone. The sound of the door slamming downstairs as he left seemed a death knell to her every hope of happiness. Olivia's last ounce of strength left with him. She put her head down on her desk and wept.

She must have cried herself to sleep. Shadows slanted across the carpeting and the room was cold. The window behind her was rattling in the wind; a storm was blowing in from the west. The rattling must have awakened her. She sat up, stiff from the awkward position she had held, and reached automatically for the bell. Then she let her hand drop with the bell unrung. No sense in wasting coal—or lamp oil, for that matter. She had to consider such things now.

Culpepper had advised her to economize, but by taking only tiny steps that would not excite comment. Her house would fetch a better price, he said, if no one knew she was desperate. This had seemed like good advice and she had agreed to it, but it was hard to keep such a terrible secret. Mrs. Pratt would stare, for example, if she suddenly asked for tallow candles instead of wax. They had always burned wax candles, everywhere in the house. Even the servants used them in their own quarters. This now seemed extravagant to the point of profligacy, but what could she do? A sudden fit of thrift would doubtless alarm her household and the rumor of her bankruptcy would erupt like wildfire.

Too tired to think, Olivia dragged herself wearily up to her room and lay down on her bed, trying to recapture the sleep that had unexpectedly seized her in the morning room. Lying on her bed, of course, it would not come. She stared, unseeing, at the dark canopy of bedcurtains above her. It would be too much to say that she thought, or pondered. She simply lay and suffered, like a wounded animal, while her mind raced in circles, uselessly going over and over the same territory.

She would be alone. Now that she no longer wished to live alone, she would have to live alone. Bessie and Edith would move to Rose Cottage. They would probably welcome her, but she could not go with them; the only meaningful thing left to her was the Fairfax School and she could not leave it.

Why, oh why, could this calamity not have struck six months ago? She would have been able to bear it then. The loss of wealth and position meant nothing to her. It would be embarrassing, perhaps, to find herself an object of pity for a time. It might be uncomfortable as well, to dramatically reduce her household and live in straitened circumstances. But all that was nothing compared to losing George.

Tears burned her eyes as her jumbled thoughts returned to that miserable point again and again, forcing her to face the unfaceable. Now that she had had a taste of what life with George could be, life without him would be insupportable.

She even regretted losing Rye Vale. As part and parcel of the man she loved, Rye Vale had captured her heart, too. She moved restlessly against her pillow as she thought of all the promises she had made that must now be broken, all the people to whom she had given hopes—hopes that must now be dashed. As her present pain starkly illustrated, it was easier to live with no expectations at all than to watch a joyous future slip through your fingers.

If only . . . if only . . . there were so many if onlys.

It did no good whatsoever to torment herself with them, but her mind kept returning to them regardless.

If only she had known the investments that comprised her trust, she might have realized how risky they were and known that something like this could happen. For that, she could rail impotently against her father and Culpepper, but she had only herself to blame for her complete lack of savings. If only she had set aside portions of her income while she had it! Instead, she had spent whatever it occurred to her to spend and had given the rest away. There was always a worthy cause or a needy soul to give her money to. It had simply never occurred to her that her father's legacy might dry up and disappear. Her lingering resentment toward her father and the way he had left his money had caused her to fling away whatever he gave her that she did not need. With breathtaking conceit, she saw now, she had congratulated herself on her benevolence and told herself that setting money aside for a rainy day would be miserly and greedy. Too late, she realized that her true motives had been childish and petty. What a shortsighted, prideful ninny she had been. She deserved to lose George.

But this conclusion wrenched a sob out of her. No one deserved a catastrophe like losing George. She pressed her hands against her swollen eyes and struggled to compose herself, scolding herself for her wretched self-pity. She would still see George from time to time. Their friendship could continue.

Friendship. Friendship with George would be the torment of the damned. To see him and never touch him might, she feared, prove impossible—and she did not want adultery on her soul. Why, he would doubtless marry within the year. Whoever he next approached would be no more able to resist him than she had been. He would succeed. He would marry his fortune.

Then it occurred to her that once he had married a fortune he would no longer need Beebe's annuity. So she would not, after all, see him from time to time. And now she could not decide which fate was worse: to see him and never touch him, or to not see him at all.

How she survived the next twenty-four hours she could never afterward recall. She was plunged into a grief deeper than any she had experienced—deeper than she had believed possible. Life seemed to hold nothing further for her. She could neither eat nor sleep. It was worse, even, than the twenty-four hours she had endured after her mother's untimely death. And she could seek no comfort, since Bessie and Edith had left for a few days to ready Rose Cottage for their habitation. She told Mrs. Pratt she was ill and stayed in her room, spending the interminable hours alternately pacing the floor and tossing fitfully on her bed.

She finally fell into an exhausted sleep but, in the way of grief, woke after only an hour or two. Gray daylight dimly illuminated the room and rain pattered monotonously against the window. It seemed fitting. She dragged herself out of bed, washed her face, and dressed. She told herself she had indulged her emotions far too long. She could not hide in her room like a coward. She could not cry forever. She was a woman, not a child, and it was time to get up and get on with life.

She would distract herself with work. There were always letters to write and ledgers to balance. She walked down to her morning room and, this time, remembered to open the curtains. She rang for coal, lit a lamp—since the pouring rain let little light or cheer into the room—and sat down to sharpen a pen.

She heard the knocker downstairs and shrank back

in her chair. Visitors! Oh, dear God, no. She could not face visitors today. Unfortunately, ringing for coal had alerted the household to the fact that she was up and about. She would have to rely on Mrs. Pratt's good sense to deny her—after all, she had been pleading illness for the past two days. The murmur of voices floated up to her and then, to her alarm, she heard booted feet swiftly mounting the stairs.

She knew that tread. Disbelief held her frozen as the door flew open. He took two steps into the room and halted, staring at her.

He looked like a madman. His greatcoat was covered with raindrops and his boots were splashed with mud. His hair, wet and disheveled, was plastered to his neck and forehead. Rivulets of water streamed down his person and dripped onto her carpet. He had obviously not shaved, and his face was pale and haggard above the dark line of stubble.

She spoke without thinking. "You look terrible."

"So do you." His voice was hoarse.

Neither of them moved. A strong sense of unreality gripped her. "I thought you went back to Rye Vale."

"I did."

"What are you doing here?"

"I came back." He cleared his throat. "I canceled the work orders and sent everyone home. And then I came back." His voice dropped almost to a whisper. "I haven't slept."

She rose unsteadily to her feet. "Would you—would you care for some tea?" It was a perfectly natural thing to say to a just-arrived guest, but somehow it sounded idiotic.

"No. Thank you."

She gestured feebly to the sofa, inviting him to sit. He glanced at it, then back at her. "I'm wet. I'd spoil it."

She managed a crooked smile. "I'd like to say that

it doesn't matter, but I suppose it does." The thought was still strange to her. "I can't afford new upholstery."

A muscle jumped in his jaw, making him look fierce. "That's what I've come here to ask you. Or part of it."

"I don't understand."

He crossed toward her, his dark eyes burning. "Have you given any thought to what you will have? After all is said and done. The house sold, the staff pensioned off and all that."

His nearness was overwhelming. She reached behind her and clutched the edge of her desk for support. "Certainly. A little."

"Well?" He suddenly seemed to realize the invasiveness of his blunt question. Some of the heat left his gaze and he gave her a rather strained smile. "Sorry, Ivy. But it's important."

Tears stung her eyes again at the sound of her nickname on his lips. She laughed a little, shaking her head. "If you are hoping that it will be enough to justify marrying me, George, I'm afraid I must disappoint you. I think I might realize three to five thousand. No more than that." She added softly, "But I thank you for the thought."

It did heal something, in a bittersweet way, to know that he had hoped. To see him so drawn and pale, and discover that giving her up had cost him a sleepless night.

His powerful hands gripped her arms. "Olivia, hear me out." His voice was thick with emotion. "If I stay in town and continue working with you, I can continue receiving the annuity. That's eight hundred a year. Many couples make do with far less."

That sense of unreality returned. Was he still speaking of marriage? She stared at him, bewildered. "But . . . what about Rye Vale? There would not be enough for Rye Vale."

"No. Restoring Rye Vale must wait." Pain flickered

briefly in his eyes, but his smile was tender. "Our children will have to marry money, my sweet. For, by heaven, I can't do it. I love you."

If he hadn't been holding her up, she might have fallen. She stared at him, eyes wide with shock. "What?" she said faintly.

"I love you. I've been an idiot, a complete and utter jackass, thinking what I wanted was your blasted money. Damn the money. It's you that I need."

Incredibly, he went down on his knees before her. "Forgive me," he said hoarsely. "I've been shallow and blind and selfish. I've lived in darkness for so many years, my dear, that when the sun finally shone on me I hadn't the wit to recognize it." His dark head bent over her hand, gripped tightly in his. "Marry me, Olivia. I beg you. Marry me and save me from ruin."

"But—but—I *can't* save you from ruin," she stammered.

In a flash, he was back on his feet, emotion she had never seen blazing in his eyes. "You're wrong. Financial ruin is nothing, less than nothing. What is misspent money compared to a misspent life? You can save me from the only sort of ruin that matters." He stripped off his wet gloves and threw them impatiently to one side, then took her face in his hands. The intensity in his voice and features contrasted oddly, movingly, with the gentle reverence in his touch. "Don't you know, my darling girl, that you are the only breath of air my sorry, stale heart has ever breathed? I was a dead thing until I met you." His fingers moved achingly, caressingly, to cup her cheeks. "For God's sake, Ivy, don't send me back there," he whispered. "Don't condemn me to a wasted life."

A strangled sob escaped her. She flung her arms around his neck and he hugged her tightly. His coat was wet and cold against her face. "You do love me," he breathed. "Thank God."

"Of course I love you," she sobbed. "I've loved you for ages. Oh, George, what shall I do?"

"Do?"

"I love you too much to not marry you," she moaned, "and I love you too much to marry you." She pulled back and determinedly dashed the tears from her eyes, the better to see him. "Our marriage would prevent you from obtaining your heart's desire. Loving you, how can I allow that?" She took a shaky breath. "Abandoning your plans for Rye Vale is no small thing."

He smiled, but strain showed at the edges of his mouth. "I may go back and repair the roof, even if I have to do it with my bare hands. But as for the rest of it—" He shrugged. "I can't marry an heiress. If some other way presents itself, I'll take it, but marrying for money is no longer possible."

"Well, it's *possible*," she began, but he placed a warning finger against her lips.

"Olivia," he said gently, but with great finality, "I will marry you or no one."

She spent a last few seconds struggling with her conscience, then gave up. If George said it wasn't possible, it wasn't possible. Relief and joy flooded her and she melted against him, savoring the miracle. "Then marry me, please," she whispered. "Oh, George. Marry me."

Their lips met. For the first time, they kissed with nothing to hide. For the first time, there were no barriers between their souls and no game to win or lose. For the first time, both knew that they loved, and each knew that that love was returned.

It was a fairly shattering kiss.

26

Culpepper burst agitatedly into the breakfast room. He was waving a newspaper before him at arm's length, as if fearing it carried the plague. "Lady Olivia, it is an outrage," he began, but stopped in midsentence, goggling in astonishment.

She smiled at him over the rim of her cup. "Good morning, Mr. Culpepper," she said calmly. "Pray sit down. Would you care for coffee?"

He opened and closed his mouth a time or two, like a landed fish. "No," he said at last. "No, I thank you. I beg your pardon, my lady. I had thought you were alone." He seemed to recall his manners suddenly, and sketched a stiff bow. "Lord Rival."

"Sir." Lord Rival inclined his head graciously, but mischief twinkled in his eyes. "I hope you will reconsider the coffee, Culpepper. You look as if you could use it."

Culpepper seemed at a loss for words. He glanced uncertainly at the newspaper, still clutched in his hand. "I never drink coffee," he said absently. "Have you— I beg your pardon—but have either of you seen today's *Gazette*?"

Lord Rival nodded kindly at Culpepper's newspaper. "There it is," he said helpfully. "In your hand."

"No, no, I do not mean that I have lost my copy. I mean . . . that is . . ." He blinked confusedly. "Lady

Olivia, perhaps I will take just a spot of tea, if you don't mind." He sank bemusedly onto one of the spindle-legged chairs at the breakfast table. "Forgive me, but it gives me quite a start to see you here. Together."

Olivia raised an eyebrow. "My word," she said mildly. "You must be easily startled." She poured out a cup and handed it to him with a smile. "Come now, Mr. Culpepper. You knew of my friendship with Lord Rival."

"I did not know it had continued, madam," said Culpepper austerely. "I had thought all was at an end."

"Really?" Lord Rival looked mildly interested. "You can't have read this morning's *Gazette*."

Culpepper jumped like a frightened fawn, spilling a few drops of tea into his saucer. "Good heavens! You knew?"

"Of course I knew. I placed the notice."

"Oh, did they print it already?" asked Olivia, pleased. She took the newspaper from Culpepper's slackened grasp and began perusing it, a little smile playing across her features.

Culpepper stared from one to the other, looking more and more disturbed. "But this cannot be," he said at last.

"Why not?" asked Lord Rival.

Culpepper hemmed and hawed for a few moments and finally said, "My lord, I fear that Lady Olivia has not been frank with you."

Olivia looked up, frowning. "Well, if that is what you fear, Mr. Culpepper, you may set your mind at rest. I have no secrets from George."

Culpepper set his untasted tea carefully down on the table. He appeared genuinely upset. "Oh, dear. I do hope this is not my fault. But it could very well be my fault. Perhaps I did not make matters sufficiently clear to you, my lady. Perhaps you misunderstood me, the other evening." He took a deep breath and addressed Lord Rival earnestly. "My lord, if you have been misled, I heartily beg your pardon. It was not my intent and, I feel sure, it was not Lady Olivia's intent, to mislead you. I'm afraid that what I have to tell you now may come as quite a shock—quite an unpleasant shock—but I must, I really must, disabuse your mind of any false ideas you may have regarding Lady Olivia's circumstances."

Lord Rival closed his eyes as if in pain. "Not again, I beg you. It was painful enough to hear the first time."

Olivia's eyes flashed daggers at her solicitor. "Culpepper, really, I find this insulting. I am neither too stupid to understand you nor too dishonest to inform Lord Rival. I told him that I am no longer a rich woman."

Culpepper leaned forward impressively, still addressing Lord Rival. "Lady Olivia is *bankrupt,* my lord. Quite bankrupt."

Lord Rival shivered dramatically. "There, now!" he said, in a complaining tone. "I asked him not to repeat it, and he did so anyway. Shabby, I call it."

Olivia gave George her hand, her eyes alight with laughter. "Horrid," she agreed.

Culpepper's consternation increased as he watched this interplay. He plainly heard the undercurrent of affection in Lady Olivia's voice, and there was something in Lord Rival's eyes when he smiled at her that suggested . . . good God. He felt himself turning pale.

"Then—then you mean to marry despite it?" faltered Culpepper.

"We do indeed," said Lord Rival. He looked completely content.

"How will you live?" exclaimed the unhappy solicitor.

"Well, they do say two can live more cheaply than one," offered Olivia.

"Actually, I expect to be of great assistance to her ladyship," said Lord Rival. "I have a positive genius for economizing. I have lived on so little for so long that I venture to state, with perfect confidence, that if Lady Olivia must spend the remainder of her life in genteel poverty, she could hardly place herself in better hands."

"That, my lord, I am sure of," murmured Lady Olivia. She looked utterly besotted.

"Let me be sure I understand this," said Culpepper faintly. "Is this a—is this a *love* match?"

"Of course it is, you gudgeon," said Lord Rival, with some asperity.

Culpepper was too distraught to notice or take offense at Lord Rival's characterization. He rose from the table, trembling, and made an announcement. "My lord," he said awfully, "I have wronged you."

Lord Rival sighed. "Yes, well, never mind," he said kindly. "And don't fancy yourself unique. Everyone seems to misjudge me lately."

"No, no, you do not take my meaning," said Culpepper in a low, quavering voice. "But then—how should you, indeed?" He clasped his hands before him as if pleading for mercy. "I have made a monstrous error in judgment. Monstrous. Lady Olivia, I think you will accept my resignation, will you not? Do not, I beg of you, turn me off without a character."

Olivia was seriously alarmed by the draining of color from Culpepper's features. She half rose, reaching her hand toward the elderly solicitor. "Mr. Culpepper, pray—! You are talking nonsense. You will make yourself ill. Whatever error you have made, I am confident you acted in good faith."

He turned pitiful eyes upon her. "Aye, that I did. I meant well." He stood before them like a prisoner in the dock, took a deep breath, and made a clean breast of it. "I have lied to you, madam. I told you a deliberate falsehood. Indeed, I meant it for the best—but I fear I have acted very wrongly."

"What on earth! What falsehood did you tell me? And why?"

Culpepper's neckcloth appeared to have suddenly grown too tight. He ran a nervous finger round the edge of his cravat and cleared his throat. "You may recall, perhaps, a discussion that we had some time ago wherein I expressed my, ah, reservations about Lord Rival's character."

"Yes, I recall it. Well?"

"It seemed to me, at the time, that you had not taken my words to heart. I left our interview feeling extremely alarmed, my lady. I was deeply concerned for your future welfare." He cast an anxious glance at Lord Rival. "I do hope you will understand that I cherish the highest regard and affection for Lady Olivia, my lord. My actions may strike you as inexcusable and, of course, I see now that I overreached myself. But—"

"Yes, yes, you may skip over that part," interrupted his lordship. "We understand that whatever misguided meddling you next indulged in, your motives were of the purest."

"Yes, my lord," said Culpepper gratefully. "I am afraid I set a few inquiries afoot. Just to make certain in my own mind, you know, before I took any further steps to intervene. After all, I thought, perhaps I was wrong. But alas, all my inquiries seemed to confirm my fears."

"What fears?" asked Olivia. She was sitting very straight in her chair and two spots of angry color were beginning to heat her cheeks.

Culpepper coughed. "I feared, my lady, that Lord Rival was nothing but a common fortune hunter. It sounds dreadful, I know, but a single lady of means is at risk of being taken in by such a fellow. And those of us who care for you, my lady, must be forever vigilant on your behalf. Your brother has shown himself sadly lacking in this area, in my humble opinion, and it has fallen to my lot to look after you—to whatever extent I am allowed. And I have done my level best. Hence, the inquiry. Through my sources, I discovered that his lordship was not, perhaps, as plump in the pocket as his lifestyle might lead one to believe. In fact, it appeared to me that Lord Rival's life could rightly be described as hand-to-mouth."

"That's about the size of it," agreed Lord Rival. "You interest me extremely. I'd give a good deal to discover how you learned this."

Culpepper looked at Lord Rival sideways. "Perhaps, my lord, at a later time."

"Yes, George, do let him tell his story. I still do not understand where the falsehood comes in."

Culpepper sighed. "I will try to be brief." He looked miserable. "I had planned to meet with you, Lady Olivia, and share with you what I had learned. I hoped that my information might serve to dissolve what I deemed a dangerous and unhealthy friendship with his lordship or, at the very least, put you on your guard. Imagine my distress, then, when, prior to my securing an appointment with you to go over the information I had gathered, Miss Fairfax desired me to place a notice of your engagement in the papers." He spread his hands apologetically. "I thought you had been duped, Lady Olivia. I believed that marriage to Lord Rival would be a disaster of no small magnitude. I was sure he would make you prodigiously unhappy."

Olivia began to see where Culpepper's oration might be leading. She leaned forward in her chair, feeling almost faint with suspense. "Go on, Culpepper, for pity's sake. What did you do then?"

Culpepper began turning slowly pink. "It seemed to me, madam, that if it was your fortune that had prompted Lord Rival's offer of marriage, the disappearance of that fortune would result in the disappearance of the betrothal. And, therefore—"

"Oh, no!" Olivia was white with shock.

"Yes, madam." Tears started in Culpepper's eyes. "I am terribly sorry, but I'm afraid I—misrepresented your financial picture the last time we met." He looked in trepidation from one shocked face to the other. His audience seemed paralyzed. "I had thought, you know, that once your engagement was at an end you might be feeling a trifle low, and that I could cheer you up a bit by confessing my little deception. In the meantime, your eyes would have been opened to Lord Rival's true nature, so I felt sure you would forgive me at once. I was confident that you would actually be *grateful* to me, once you were out of danger." He waited, but still no one spoke. "I see, now, that I was quite wrong," he finished lamely.

The painful silence that followed was broken by a choke of smothered mirth from Lord Rival. The choking almost immediately gave way to out-loud laughter. He leaned his head on his hands and whooped helplessly. Olivia stared at him, furious. "I can't imagine what you find so awfully funny!" Her fiancé merely waved a limp hand, apparently unable to reply while in the throes of his laughing fit.

Olivia turned her wrathful gaze upon Culpepper. "Are you telling me that you inflicted all this misery on me for nothing? Speak! Am I still a wealthy woman, or am I not?"

"You are, my lady, an extremely wealthy woman."

Olivia fell back in her chair, speechless. Culpepper looked a little aggrieved. "Had you thought about it more carefully, my lady, you might have guessed that I would not betray my solemn promise to your father."

"What solemn promise?"

"That I should never divulge to you the source of your income."

He looked so prim and self-righteous that Olivia

uttered a little scream of vexation. George, still laughing, placed a soothing hand on hers. "Never mind, my love. We'll soon get to the bottom of this." He wiped his streaming eyes and turned, grinning, to Culpepper. "Very well, you exasperating old bounder. You kept your infernal promise to the late Lord Badesworth. Am I right in supposing that Lady Olivia's betrothal releases you from it?"

"In a manner of speaking, my lord." Culpepper placed his fingertips precisely together. "I may not discuss her holdings with Lady Olivia, but I may do so with you."

"Of all the *intolerable*—"

"Yes, yes, my pet. It is anything you like, but let us, by all means, end the suspense. Tell me, Culpepper— here and now—whether she does, indeed, own nothing but a stack of risky foreign properties. If you require it, you have my consent to discuss the matter freely in Lady Olivia's presence."

Culpepper shot a dubious look at Olivia and struggled with himself for a moment. It plainly went against the grain with him to speak in her presence, but he finally did so—albeit grudgingly. "Very good, my lord. I cannot think it wise, but I will tell you. Lady Olivia's holdings could hardly be more safely invested. Her inheritance is entirely in the Funds, which is why her income is able to be delivered to her in such good order and in such precise amounts."

"Thank you, Culpepper," said Olivia silkily. "You may leave now."

He took one more look at her face. Whatever he saw there caused him to pick up his hat and bow immediately. "Good day, my lady. Good day, my lord. I wish you both very happy." He exited, with more haste than dignity.

Olivia dove into George's arms and collapsed there, completely unnerved. "Well! That is the last straw. I shall give Culpepper the boot. Ralph has enough to keep him busy in his old age; let him go to Ralph."

George chuckled. "As you wish, but I must say, I'm profoundly grateful to the old codger."

"Grateful?" She pulled back against the circle of his arms, staring indignantly up at his laughing face. "Why, he *insulted* you! And put us both through the darkest days—"

"Very true. But if he had not done so, we both would have believed that I was marrying you for your money." His arms tightened around her waist. "It's worth a great deal to me," he murmured, "to know that I am making a love match."

An unwilling smile tugged at Olivia's mouth. "We would have discovered that eventually."

"I would have discovered it," he told her softly. "But you, my dear, would never have been sure."

Olivia grew thoughtful. "I wonder," she said slowly. "Good heavens. You may be right." She continued to ponder the question as George pulled her tightly to him and, humming under his breath, began to dance with her around the breakfast room.

"So we shall have a happy ending after all," he said exultantly.

"There was never any doubt." She smiled and looked up at him. He was obviously thinking of Rye Vale. His eyes were alight with plans and excitement thrummed through his body. He looked almost boyish.

She sighed and rolled her eyes. "Just—no more shocks, please. No more reversals. I vow, I can feel my hair turning gray. I cannot sustain one more shock."

He halted and held her off, his eyes suddenly focusing on her face again. "I forgot to tell you something. Sorry, Ivy! You've one more shock to bear." She looked up at him with misgiving. He grinned, and amended his statement somewhat. "At least, it came as a shock to me. It may strike you differently. It's about poor Tom."

"Tom?" she asked anxiously. "I hope he hasn't run off?"

"Oh, no. No such luck. You'll remember my frequent complaints that the old fellow was growing fatter every day."

"Yes?"

"Well, while we were in Sussex he gave birth to a litter of kittens. I would have mentioned it earlier, but in all the excitement—oh, yes, it's like you to laugh at my misfortune." He shook his head glumly. "One cat was bad enough, but a houseful of them—"

"Oh, dear! You know, we should have realized that Tom is female. Only look at the way he immediately attached himself to you."

"Yes," said George broodingly. "It struck me as unnatural at the time. I must say, however, he's a very good mother. Watches over the little blighters day and night, and works himself into a frightful state every time I come near them."

"You seem to have that effect on mothers."

"Had," said George firmly. "I'm a reformed character." An idea suddenly gleamed in his eye. "If you want to take Culpepper down a peg, I know how to do it. We'll give him one of Tom's kittens. Believe me, dear girl, I speak from experience. Nothing like a cat to humble a man."

"Really?" she murmured teasingly. "It had no discernible effect on you."

Up went one eyebrow. Down went the corner of his mouth. "Minx," he growled, and kissed her thoroughly.

"Brimming over with Passion and Excitement."
—Romantic Times

LAUREN ROYAL

AMETHYST   199510

A talented jeweler who's engaged to a man she does not love, Amethyst Goldsmith loses everything when the devastating fire of 1666 sweeps through London. But in the aftermath of disaster, she lands in the arms of the dashing, unattainable Earl of Graystone.

EMERALD   201426

Second in the dazzling *Jewel* trilogy, Royal presents the passionate adventure of Jason Chase, the Marquess of Cainewood...

AMBER   203917

The final novel in the acclaimed *Jewel* trilogy. When Kendra's brothers catch her with a mysterious highwayman, they demand that she marry him. But this dangerous, complex man may not be at all who he seems...

To order call: 1-800-788-6262

PENGUIN PUTNAM INC.
Online

Your Internet gateway to a virtual environment with
hundreds of entertaining and enlightening books
from Penguin Putnam Inc.

*While you're there, get the latest buzz on
the best authors and books around—*

Tom Clancy, Patricia Cornwell, W.E.B. Griffin,
Nora Roberts, William Gibson, Robin Cook,
Brian Jacques, Catherine Coulter, Stephen King,
Ken Follett, Terry McMillan, and many more!

**Penguin Putnam Online is located at
http://www.penguinputnam.com**

PENGUIN PUTNAM NEWS

Every month you'll get an inside look at our upcom-
ing books and new features on our site. This is an
ongoing effort to provide you with the most
up-to-date information about
our books and authors.

Subscribe to Penguin Putnam News at
http://www.penguinputnam.com/newsletters